THE GLASS COFFIN SOCIETY

ALSO BY SHIROMI ARSERIO

THE TALES OF MÄRCHEN

The Rogues of Märchen (short story collection)

The Order of Grimm

The Glass Coffin Society

THE GLASS COFFIN SOCIETY

THE TALES OF MÄRCHEN
BOOK TWO

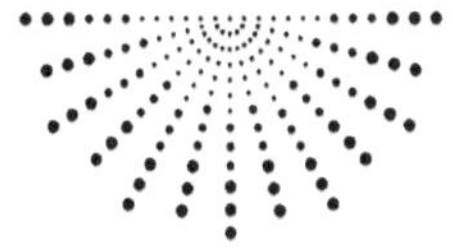

SHIROMI ARSERIO

GOBBOLINA PRESS

The Glass Coffin Society

To Robert. Two heads are always better than one.

CHAPTER ONE

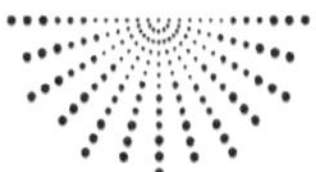

THE DARK HORSE OF HOLLOWHORN

WHO IS TORMOD LYONS, THE NEW LEADER OF THE THIEVES GUILD? HE WAS A LOYAL LIEUTENANT OF JACK FINNERTY, THE GUILD'S PREVIOUS LEADER. HE OUSTED HIS BOSS WITH THE PROMISE OF LESS BLOOD ON THE STREETS OF MÄRCHEN, AND SOMEHOW, IT SEEMS HE HAS MANAGED TO ACHIEVE JUST THAT. SINCE HE TOOK OVER AND RE-BRANDED THE THIEVES GUILD, THE MANY INCIDENTS OF GANG VIOLENCE HAVE DECREASED SIGNIFI-CANTLY, SOURCES AT THE CITY WATCH TELL ME. BUT ARE WE TRULY IN A NEW ERA OF PEACE?

— THE MÄRCHEN CHRONICLE

"*V*erdammt!" Samara inwardly cursed as hands closed around her throat, causing her vision to cloud. She recognised the imp. Of course she did. The same messenger Callista sent to Gewässer, which had started this whole mess. Even while struggling for breath, Samara noted the girl's improvement over the past few weeks. Determined to win her fight against the famed Hisada, no doubt. Well, today would not be that day.

The girl was speaking, but Samara couldn't focus on her words. Just that one thought: *Not today.*

The imp had her up against a brick wall which dug into her back. She'd ambushed Samara while she was on her way to her new home. She hadn't expected to be jumped while travelling across rooftops.

Samara's arm still throbbed from when the younger assassin grappled with her and the two bounced onto the roof of an outhouse and then down to the ground. She'd landed badly and hadn't had time to react when the girl grabbed her by the throat and pushed her into an alleyway.

The girl was saying something about Callista.

Well, of course she was. Samara tried to focus. What was the imp saying?

Then realisation dawned: the imp wasn't trying to kill her. She just wanted to make sure Samara received the message.

Samara stopped scrabbling with the hands around her neck. Instead, she took two straightened fingers and shoved them hard behind the imp's clavicle. The girl released her hold and stepped back. This time, it was her turn to cough and splutter. Air rushed into Samara's lungs. She shook away her own feeling of disorientation long enough to follow up with a hard front kick to the chest, and, once the girl was on the ground, a couple of punches to the face. For good measure.

She knelt over the imp. "You might want to remind your boss," she rasped out, "she has her money back, and I still don't know where the girl is. As far as I'm concerned, we're square."

Face bloody, the younger assassin tried to scramble up again, but Samara punched her again.

"Stay down," she ordered.

With a slight limp, Samara resumed her journey to her new

home. She didn't have the energy to climb up to the roof. Her left arm still throbbed from where she'd landed on it. So she took a long circuitous route, looking over her shoulder the entire way.

Eventually, she arrived at The Wishing-Table, a ramshackle pub at the smelliest end of the Hollow. But it was under the protection of the Lions, and the owner owed her a favour, so it was good enough. She entered through the back and climbed the rickety steps to the top floor. She tapped on the door. Two slow taps, followed by three, in quick succession, waiting a moment before opening the door.

Gerde and Hans sat at a table, playing a game of Tablut. Taking in Samara's dishevelled appearance, they both rose to their feet.

"What happened to you?" Gerde asked at the same time that Hans said, "Are you okay?"

Samara flopped down by the fire. Big mistake. She wasn't sure she would be able to get back up again.

She waved away the concerned faces.

"I was jumped. By one of Callista's people."

"She still thinks you're hiding Eloise?" Hans asked, taking a kettle off the fire to prepare tea.

Samara shrugged and winced. Who knew what was going on in Callista's head these days? Samara had collected up the money they had earned for the auction job and returned it weeks ago. Yet they were still forced to hide out from the daughters of House de Mörde, the assassin's house where Samara was raised.

Samara's skin tingled at Gerde's gentle touch as she busily rolled up Samara's sleeve to take a look at her arm. Leave it to Gerde to notice her injured arm. Samara glanced down and noted the swollen appearance. It was certain to leave a bruise.

"You should see the other girl," Samara smirked.

Gerde frowned at her joke and hurried away. Samara's eyes drifted shut, as the scent of saffron and other spices permeated the room.

Moments later, she felt a cool rag on her arm as Gerde returned.

"I hope Eloise really was able to get out. The talk in the Aurora is that Humphreys' men are still crawling all over the docks and the crossroads," Gerde was saying.

Gerde had taken on more hours at the Aurora, the tavern in Old Town where she worked the door. Samara gratefully accepted a cup of saffron chai from Hans.

"I put extra honey in it for your-" The old man gestured at her throat.

"Thanks, Hans," she croaked, taking a sip of the sweetened tea. She turned her attention back to Gerde. "I don't like you going there."

Gerde sat back on her haunches. "Yes, well, someone around here has to make some coin to keep us in this place."

Her work at the Aurora was always a source of tension. But it was a fight Samara was always going to lose because she knew Gerde was right.

Guilt flooded Samara once again. If she hadn't been so verdammt noble, and just handed Eloise over to the Matron of House de Mörde as planned, none of them would be in this mess. But Eloise had made clear she did not want to return to the house of assassins, and upon finding out that Callista, her former sister-at-arms, had lied to her once again, Samara made the decision to send Eloise away. And despite the fact they returned every damn crown they had earned on the auction job, Callista was still out for blood.

To make matters worse, Chetwin Humphreys, the auction host, had not been financially ruined as they hoped, but was now hunting them down.

But no, that wasn't the worst of it. The worst of it was that their crew had parted ways. She didn't even know how Ana and Art were faring these days. They both had some choice words for her the night of the auction when she told them what she'd done. Seb, she'd spotted working at the Zephyr as a card dealer. He was safe enough, given it was run by the Lions, the local thieves guild and Samara's former employer. Hans had been forced to shut down his print shop for the time being, while Gerde felt it wasn't safe to return to her family's coaching inn. That part really hurt Samara. Unlike the rest of her crew, Gerde was close to her family. It didn't sit well with her that Gerde was forced to be away from them. And yet here they were, in a shabby room in the worst part of Hollowhorn. Which was already in the worst part of Märchen.

Samara found herself at loose ends. She had told Tormod Lyons that she was out. Aside from the House de Mörde, being Tormod Lyons' enforcer was the only other job she'd ever held. She didn't know what to do with herself.

She could have gone back to her old job. Of course, by now, Tormod was probably the proud owner of an island somewhere in the Erythraen Sea. She had reluctantly cut Tormod in on the auction job, and now he was the only one of them to have benefited from that night. His number two, Lukas, took over the Lions. Lukas was trustworthy, and she was sure he would happily offer her her old job back, but it just didn't sit well with her.

For a brief moment, while they were planning the auction job, she had had a taste of something different. And verdammt if she was going to go back to the way things were. She wanted to be free of the Lions.

She could start over somewhere else. She had money hidden around Märchen, but leaving town was impossible at the moment.

Samara guiltily looked up at Hans and Gerde, who were still hovering nearby, and then glanced over at the Tablut board set up on the table.

She forced a smile. "So who's winning?" she asked.

~

THE COLLAR of the rough hewn wool coat irritated the skin on Art Templeton's neck. At least, he hoped it was the wool and not fleas. He had bought the coat and newsboy cap second hand.

After everything that had gone down with the auction two weeks ago, Art thought it wiser to walk around Märchen incognito. At least until things settled down. Which he hoped would be sometime soon.

He stopped at a local newsstand and picked up a newspaper. Holding it open, he surreptitiously glanced toward the building he lived in. When he'd left earlier that day, he had taken a leaf out of Samara's book and gone out the window. He had been suspicious of two rather heavily built men who had taken up residence on the street below. They might have been mistaken for beggars, but Art wasn't convinced. They both looked a little too well-fed. Not to mention he thought he recognised one of them as being in the employ of Chetwin Humphreys.

Sure enough, the men were still seated there, every now and again glancing towards the front entrance of the building, as though they were waiting for him to appear.

"You want to read that, you got to pay for it. Quarter crown," the ornery woman who ran the stand demanded.

"Oh, er, sorry," Art replied, hastily laying the paper aside and walking as calmly, and swiftly, as he could away from his apartment.

"Tosser," he heard the woman curse at him.

Art winced, fearing the loud, foulmouthed woman might

have alerted Humphreys' men to his presence. He walked hurriedly, not paying attention to where he was going, as he continued to glance behind him.

No doubt he was making himself more conspicuous instead of less, but still he kept walking as fast as he could, still glancing behind, and right into a wall of muscle. Turning his head to face his attacker, he tensed his own muscles, ready to make a run for it, when he recognised the light brown skin and warm dark eyes of the man standing in front of him.

"Seb!" he exclaimed, his voice an higher than he would have preferred.

"Art, I was trying to get your attention but—" Seb stopped, studying him. "Are you okay? Are you being followed?"

Art glanced back, studying the cobbled streets, but saw no sign of pursuers.

"No. I think everything's okay." He swallowed. "You can never be too careful."

Seb nodded his head in agreement. He wore his uniform as a card dealer at the Royal Zephyr.

"Still dealing at the Zephyr, I see," Art commented.

"Yeah. Samara thinks it's safer there for me, with the Lions and all."

Art's mouth twisted into a grimace at the mention of Samara, but he said nothing.

"I'm actually just taking my lunch break. Do you want to join me?" Seb gestured to the paper bag he held. The smell of warm pies wafted from it.

Art frowned even as his stomach growled.

"Should you really be out here having lunch, with the House de Mörde and Humphreys' people searching for us?"

Seb shifted. "I was just at the Four and Twenty, looking for Ana. But she wasn't around."

Art noted the tone of disappointment in his companion's

voice, but before he could ask what was wrong, his stomach growled again.

They took the hot pies to an alleyway next door to the Royal Zephyr, and amidst the pungent scent of meat, gravy and refuse, Seb filled Art in on what he'd been up to over the past couple of weeks.

"So, how *are* things with you and our lovely kinetic energy user?" Art asked around a mouthful of pastry.

When Seb seemed uncertain how to respond, Art added, "I couldn't help but noticing how cosy the two of you were at the party."

The celebration party after they had completed the auction job. Right before everything went to shit.

"We kissed," Seb admitted after a moment.

Art thumped him on the arm. "Congratulations! Ana's a lovely girl. So long as you don't get on the wrong side of her temper."

"I really like her." Seb started to say something, and then stopped. He grinned sheepishly. "You know she was the one to … initiate the kiss."

"Even better!" But he noticed Seb was frowning now. "Not better?"

Seb picked at the crimped edges of his pie. "I like her. I really do. I thought, maybe, after all this has blown over, she and I could go back to my village."

Art raised his eyebrows. He freely admitted he wasn't the best person to have relationship conversations with, but even he thought Seb might be moving too fast.

"So how does she feel about that?" he asked, wishing he had some ale to wash down the pie.

Seb sighed and balled up the paper bag with the remains of his pie.

"I don't know. She hasn't been around much. I keep going to

the bakery to see her, but she's hardly ever there."

Art didn't think that seemed like a good sign, but what did he know? His longest relationship had lasted three weeks.

"Why do you even want to go back home, Seb?" Art asked.

Frankly, life in a tiny village sounded like torture. And not the kinky kind one could find at a good brothel, either.

Seb huffed a laugh. "It's not like I've exactly done well for myself here. It took me exactly two days in Märchen to wind up indentured to the Lions. I'm not sure I'm cut out for the city. Now that I don't owe the Lions anymore—"

Thanks to Samara, Art knew, though Seb didn't say it aloud.

"Going home seems like the smart thing to do."

Art didn't argue with Seb. If anything, when put that way, he could understand where Seb was coming from. Still. The thought of going home to become a miner... The sound of shouting cut through Art's thoughts. At the opening of the alley, a young man was being accosted by two men.

"I know him," Seb murmured, his body tensing.

The man was a Lion. It was obvious from the outfit. The Lions didn't exactly wear uniforms, but their short coats, silk neck cloths and steel-capped boots all denoted them as members of Tormod Lyons' gang.

Two enormous men shoved the young Lion up against the wall. One of them had an arm pressed to his windpipe. They barely looked in Art and Seb's direction.

One of the men, a bearded man, was wielding a knife and speaking in a low voice.

"Oi," Seb called out. "What's going on?"

"Never you mind. This don't concern you," called out the one who had been speaking.

"Seb!" the young Lion cried, before receiving a punch to the nose.

"Seb, is it?" The bearded man turned to Seb and took in his

card-dealer uniform. "Work at the Zephyr, do you? Perhaps you'd be kind enough to help deliver a message to your boss." He then turned his attention to Art, who stood straighter, trying to make his wiry figure more menacing.

Bearded man frowned. "Don't I know you?"

"Schiesse," Art cursed, as he recognised Bearded man from the auction. He was one of Chetwin Humphreys' men.

"Get down," Seb yelled suddenly, grabbing something from his pocket and flinging it at the mouth of the alley.

Knowing what was coming, Art plugged his ears just as an explosion shook the ground.

CHAPTER TWO

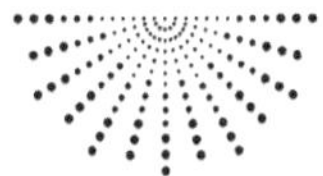

The world around them exploded, and even having been prepared for it, Art was knocked off his feet. It was only a mini explosion, but it was big enough. The kinetic force kicked up dust along the alleyway and caused the three men at the mouth of the alley to fall to the ground.

Time to move. If they stuck around, the City Watch was certain to be along soon.

Seb was on his feet again first, helping Art up, and together they ran towards the other men. The smoke was already clearing, and Bearded man and his friend were stirring. Seb grabbed the arm of the young Lion and placed it around his shoulder, heaving them both up. Art was about to grab the Lion's other arm, but Bearded man wrapped a hand around his leg. Art managed to give two swift kicks to Bearded man's stomach with his other leg before quickly glancing at the other goon who was still shaking his head as though to clear the ringing noise.

Art caught up to Seb at the doorway of the Royal Zephyr, where two entertainers dressed as faeries retreated in horror at the sight of the blood pouring down the young Lions' face and onto Seb.

Thankfully, other Lions were already milling about, ready to help.

Art held the door for them, as two Lions came running up to assist. Behind them a taller, lankier Lion with shaggy brown hair came striding up. Art clocked him as the new boss: Lukas Bernhardt. He had been Tormod's number two before the great auction heist when Tormod had absconded with close to three hundred thousand crowns. Since Art had pretended to be the auctioneer on that job, he was pretty sure on the numbers. A tall, blonde woman, who Art recognised but couldn't quite place, followed closely behind. At a snap of Lukas's fingers, two faeries descended on her, handing her a drink and keeping her from approaching the hubbub.

"What happened?" Lukas asked in a low voice, his attention on Seb.

"Two men jumped Arnaud in the alley," Seb replied.

"They were Chetwin Humphreys' men," Art supplied.

"They said they had a message for the boss," Seb began. "I had to use one of my explosives to get away."

"So, that's what that noise was," Lukas remarked. He studied Seb. "Did they get you as well?"

"No," Seb replied. "That's Arnaud's blood."

"All right, well, we'll get him taken care of." Lukas started to turn away, but then seemed to think better of it. "You should know, this is the third attack on Lions this week. You might want to be careful."

Seb smiled faintly. "That's why I've been walking around with explosive balls in my pockets."

Art wondered if perhaps Seb could spare a few of those explosive balls for him. He did not like the way Bearded man had looked at him with recognition.

"Still, you probably shouldn't be going outside wearing your Zephyr uniform, either. Humphreys is targeting anyone connected to Tormod."

Seb nodded. Lukas then seemed to really notice Art for the first time.

"You're one of Samara's crew."

"Was. Past tense," Art replied curtly.

"You won't be seeing her anytime soon, will you?" Lukas asked, not seeming to have heard Art. "I need to send her a message and she's no longer at her old digs."

Seb, apparently sensing Art's own darkening mood, piped up, "I can deliver a message. What do you need me to tell her?"

Lukas exhaled loudly and ran a hand through his thick hair. "Honestly, I could really use the Hisada right now. I know she quit Tormod's employ, but I've got Humphreys' men breathing down our necks. I've got the Magistrate here..." He gestured at the tall blonde woman.

It was then that Art realised where he had seen her before. Of course. She was the Magistrate of Märchen. Art had met her once, at one of his father's insufferable dinner parties, many years ago when his father had been trying to join Märchen's Stadtrat. Not that he'd succeeded. As far as Art could tell, she was the straight and narrow kind. She had her hands full managing the chaos that Tormod and Humphreys' gangs threw at her, as well as keeping the peace in the city. So, what was she doing here? At the base of operations for the Lions?

"She's not on your payroll, is she?" Art asked Lukas.

Lukas sighed and scrubbed a hand over his face. "No. I wish.

But with everything going on in the city, she's been talking about instituting a curfew."

"A curfew!" Seb exclaimed, a little too loudly. Art saw the blonde woman look up, trying to extricate herself from the dancing faeries.

"And after that little explosion…"

"I'm sorry!" Seb exclaimed again, his voice low and his face tight.

Lukas shook his head. Sighed. "You did what you had to do. I'm sure Arnaud's not sorry."

Just then, the Magistrate, Sylvain Duvall, Art recalled, came striding up to them.

"Somebody said that was an explosion. This is exactly what I'm talking about. If your boss and Chetwin Humphreys can't put your differences aside, then I have to do what I can in order to protect the citizens. I will not have a turf war—"

"Just let her know I could use her help," Lukas said to Seb before turning back to the irate Magistrate. "Perhaps we can discuss this further in my office…" he was saying as he led her away.

"Wouldn't like to be in his position," Art remarked.

"Me neither," Seb agreed.

"I'm betting this is not how he imagined things would go down when he took over the Lions."

"I don't think any of us could have," Seb mumbled. "Listen, are you okay going back to your rooms? It's just, I thought maybe that bearded man recognised you."

"Oh, he did." Art's eye darted to Seb's pocket. "I don't suppose you can spare some of those magic balls?"

"Yeah, course," Seb replied. "As many as you need."

Seb dug into his trouser pocket and extracted three balls.

"Just be careful where you set these off," he said, gesturing in the direction the Magistrate and Lukas had gone in.

Art gave Seb one of his winning smiles. "Oh, I'm always careful."

~

CHETWIN HUMPHREYS SAT in his office. He was attempting to go through some reports for his "legitimate business interests", as his number two, Alfred Vogel, preferred to call them. It was Alfred who had insisted that Humphreys take some time to go over the reports.

Chetwin had been neglecting his other duties, it was true. Ever since the night of the auction, when the Hisada and her crew had come in, pretending to be part of a fictional society trying to reinstate the line of Queen White. Ever since they had used Chetwin's own money to purchase the girl from him. Ever since the Hisada's boss robbed the auction.

It had been a minor miracle when the Order of Grimm told him they were considering holding their semi-annual event in Märchen, of all places, and wanted him to host. It was an opportunity. And a test. A test whether he and his organisation could operate at the level of the Order. He didn't know the names of the people behind the Order. No one did. But he knew they were powerful. They were the true power on the continent of Alsatia. To get in with them would be to gain access to the continent itself.

True, he already had businesses which spanned the continent. He had a healthy trade in humans, from all over Alsatia and beyond. It was a useful trade. Everyone needed labour. But there were those who looked down on him for it. The sale of people was legal in Alsatia. The only place it wasn't legal was Märchen. But even in Märchen, the buying of people was more of a grey area. As far as he was concerned, what he did was perfectly legal. Yet they still turned their noses up at him.

One could buy and sell weapons of war, and people wouldn't bat an eye. But to make your money from human labour. Well, that had created a societal barrier he could not break through. No one even cared that he imported Nepenthe, but he had seen first-hand the raised eyebrows when the toffs of society found out he imported people.

This had been an opportunity. And then fate had led him to the girl. He didn't really believe magic existed nowadays. Not Big Magic. The girl changed that. And the auction was supposed to change his fortunes.

Then that hündin, the Matron of House de Mörde, came along and had to drag the Hisada into things. And now the Lions.

When he discovered the news that the auction had been robbed and the people who bought the girl had duped him, he was ready to tear the city apart to find them. Make them pay. His biggest concern was keeping word from getting back to the Order. He figured if he acted swiftly, he could do just that. None of the attendees knew the auction had been robbed. Everyone who had paid had left with their items. Which was problematic, but Chetwin was swift in fixing things.

The first thing he did was disperse his most trusted men to the docks and the coaching inns. The second thing he did was contact the head of the Royal Bank of White to stop anyone from cashing those bank notes. Which was all very well for those who had paid from a Royal Bank of White account. But guests at the auction had travelled from all over Alsatia, which meant he would need to send messengers out to Richilde, Pentemarone and Perceforest hoping to stop Tormod Lyons from cashing those payments as well. Messengers left that very night.

Three days later, as he anxiously awaited confirmation that those payments had been stopped, his butler had entered with a package that had just been delivered. It was a box. His butler frowned when he pulled the strange-looking contraption from the box, but Chetwin recognised it. It was a speaking telegraph. He'd seen them on occasion but could never justify the cost when the postal service worked just as well. The enclosed letter explained how to use the speaking telegraph—turn the handle in order to speak to the operator, where he would simply announce himself and be immediately connected to the Order of Grimm. The note also stated that workmen would be there later that morning to connect the telegraph to the exchange.

It was with the arrival of the box that Chetwin knew he wouldn't be able to keep things secret. He also felt unreasonably angry at the speaking telegraph. If he had thought to ask the Royal Bank of White to use a speaking telegraph to ring the other banks, he might've been quicker with fixing things. But he had sent messengers, and that delay had alerted the Order that something was amiss.

He was even more resentful when he was forced to ring the Order and tell them exactly what had happened. Another man might have thought to run. But Chetwin knew there was nowhere he could go that the Order couldn't find him. And besides, running and hiding wasn't his way. Cretins like Tormod Lyons might run and hide, but Chetwin Humphreys wasn't about to be run out of the home he had built for himself.

The Order was surprisingly understanding. It turned out the Royal Bank of White owner had been the one to inform them, much to Chetwin's chagrin. None of the bank notes were cashed, and they had taken measures to keep it that way. But they agreed with Chetwin that face needed to be saved. One couldn't let a low life thief get away with stealing from the most powerful people on the continent. They emphasised that Chetwin's sole concern from now on was to hunt down

Tormod Lyons and see that he was appropriately punished for his impudence.

It was a relief for Chetwin until he realised he was expected to give daily reports to the Order to let them know his progress on the matter. He checked his pocket watch. Unfortunately, it was getting past that time now. And still, Vogel hadn't returned with an update.

Just as he had that thought, there was a tap at the door and Alfred Vogel let himself in. Chetwin looked at him, his blue eyes narrowed, but judging by the expression on his number two's face, there was nothing new to report.

Still, he gestured for Vogel to take a seat, which he did, his back rigid.

"Still no sign of the Hisada nor the Matron of House de Mörde. As for Tormod Lyons, no word on where he ended up. All we know for sure is that he fled the city, but nobody knows where to. Our men have stepped up the harassment of the Lions. During that time, one of my men spotted Templeton, but lost him in the confusion."

"Lost him?" Humphreys responded, barely controlling his own frustration. What he'd do to get his hands on the so-called auctioneer that had made a fool of him.

"There was an incident outside the Royal Zephyr."

Humphreys rested his hands on the pommel of his walking stick and leaned back in his chair.

"What kind of incident?"

"One of Lyons' men let loose an explosive. Not too long afterwards, the place was crawling with City Watch."

Humphreys breathed in deeply. His breath felt tight in his chest.

"I have one suggestion."

"Suggestion?" Chetwin muttered.

"It would seem that targeting the Lions gang isn't working.

But there is the Royal Zephyr. As the home base of the Lions gang, and a legitimate gambling institution, there may be some options there for added … pressure."

"Pressure?" Chetwin repeated.

"Financial pressure. Legal pressure even," Vogel replied, running a hand over his bald head. "As far as we know, Tormod Lyons still owns the Zephyr, even if he no longer runs the Lions."

Chetwin unclenched his hands on the pommel as he thought about Vogel's suggestion. It might be a way to draw Lyons back to Märchen. It was certainly worth a try.

"Do what needs to be done."

Vogel nodded and rose to his feet.

"Still no word from your men regarding the girl?"

Vogel's lips pinched together. Humphreys knew Vogel would prefer he give up his hunt for the girl, but he was too much of a professional to say so.

"No word as yet, but I have eyes everywhere. She will turn up soon."

Chetwin took a sip of the tea his butler had left for him, along with the paperwork. It was tepid. "Send more men out. You can take men off the next Nepenthe delivery if you need to."

"Is that wise?" Vogel asked, though he seemed to regret saying even this much.

Chetwin glared at Vogel. "That girl is worth more than three Nepenthe deliveries. I want her back."

Vogel straightened his waistcoat and nodded his head once, sharply. He strode out of the room, letting the door gently close behind him and leaving Chetwin to his ruminations.

CHAPTER THREE

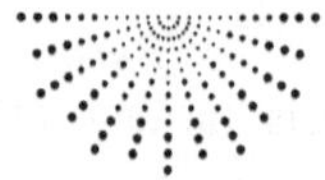

"It is with the greatest honour that I take up this role as the leader of the Stadtrat. As your Magistrate, I know full-well the responsibilities the citizens of Märchen have placed upon me. I take my vows to you seriously. I will use the full force of the City Watch to put an end to the gang violence and the growing Nepenthe problems and return our City-State to the glory it once was."

— ACCEPTANCE SPEECH, MAGISTRATE SYLVAIN

*I*t was dusk, but the streets of Hollowhorn were still full of workers, shoppers and people getting ready to go out for the evening. The city-state's homeless were now flooding the street corners as well, having been run off by City Watch during the day.

Seb kept his head low as he traversed the streets. He hoped his disguise worked, though he wasn't sure how well. Someone of his skin tone tended to stand out in Märchen, but in the Hollow, this close to the docks, he hoped it would be enough.

He wore rough wool trousers and suspenders, and a shirt that had seen better days. They certainly stank of the dockyards. The Lions gang had a good supply of spare clothes, which Lukas was happy to loan him if it meant getting a message to the Hisada.

He arrived at the dilapidated pub where he knew Samara, Gerde, and Hans were staying. Gerde gave him the address the last time he'd visited the Aurora. She wanted him to be able to get in touch if he was ever in trouble. Like oh, say, when both the assassin's guild and Chetwin Humphreys' gang were hunting them.

He stepped into the pub, and his gaze fell on the proprietor, an old man with a feral look in his eyes, who looked back at Seb suspiciously.

"I have friends upstairs," Seb said, unsure if the man would let him through.

His concerns were confirmed when the man replied with, "Got no one upstairs at the moment. Room's empty. You in need of a room?"

This was the place Gerde had told him about. The Wishing-Table. Samara had probably paid the owner well to keep their location a secret. Then again, judging by the look on the man's face, perhaps he could just as easily be persuaded to let him through.

"I'm with the Lions. Or used to be," Seb said, pulling a half crown from his pocket and pushing it across the bar.

The old man picked up the coin with knobbly fingers and bit into it. He grinned a gap-toothed smile and replied, "Upstairs, on the left."

Seb nodded, grateful that the proprietor had let him through, but also feeling a sense of disquiet at being allowed through so easily.

He walked up the rickety steps. At the top stood two doors,

side-by-side. Turning to the one on the left, he knocked uncertainly on the door.

There was no response.

He knocked again, beginning to wonder if this was to be a wasted trip.

Moments later, he heard the creak of the door on the right, and felt the sharp pointy tip of a blade at his neck.

"You need to be more careful," said a harsh female voice.

Seb let out a gasp, and relief flooded through him as he turned to the speaker and found himself face to face with the Hisada herself.

"Samara. I, uh…"

"We'll talk inside," she replied, and reached over to the door on the left giving it a rap with her knuckles. Two slow taps, and three quick ones.

The door was opened by Gerde, who burst into a grin upon seeing Seb. "It's so good to see you!" she exclaimed, giving him a hug and leading him into their cramped apartment.

Inside, he was settled into a worn armchair, where Hans handed him a cup of tea while the others settled on the floor beside him.

"How did you sneak up on me?" Seb asked.

"Old Yanni was kind enough to let me rent both rooms. There's an adjoining door, so I can sneak up on any unwanted visitors," Samara explained as she settled herself on the floor beside the fire. "He charges enough for that access, but it lets me get the jump on someone if I need to, so it's worth the cost."

Seb frowned and sipped his tea. "Yeah. I don't know how safe this place is. He gave you up pretty easily, for just a half crown bribe."

Gerde grimaced. "That little sneak took money from you? I told him to let anyone through matching either yours, Art's or Ana's description!"

She folded her arms across her broad chest, her face holding a scowl that could almost match Samara's. "When I speak to him next, I'm going to give him a piece of my mind."

Samara merely chuckled, placing a hand on Gerde's arm.

"What brings you here?" Hans asked. "Is everything all right with you and Ana?"

Seb clattered his teacup on the saucer. He hadn't realised just how many people seemed to know about his relationship with Ana.

"Y-yes. Everything's fine with me." Seb set his teacup aside for the moment. "Actually, it was Lukas Bernhardt who sent me."

Samara leaned back on the threadbare rug. "Really? And what does Lukas want?"

"Humphreys' men are all over the place. They're attacking Lions—" Seb stopped, noticing Samara's impassive expression. "Art and I had to stop one of the Lions getting pummelled just yesterday."

"How is Art?" Gerde asked.

"He's good, I think. As well as can be given … the situation."

He didn't want to meet Samara's eyes just then. They didn't need to rehash the fact that they wouldn't all be in hiding if Samara had just stuck to the plan.

"Anyway, Lukas says he could really use the Hisada's help."

Samara stretched out on the rug now and pursed her lips. "I don't know what kind of help I can be. I warned Tormod this would happen if he robbed that auction. He did it anyway. I'm done with the Lions."

"And yet it's not Tormod Lyons who appears to be paying the price," Hans said with a shake of his head.

Seb grimaced. "It's pretty rough out there. Lukas fears it will turn into a full-up turf war. The Magistrate's even talking about instituting a curfew."

Samara sat up. She seemed a little … lost in Seb's eyes. Of course, he didn't know her very well, but she had always seemed to have a sense of purpose, even after the first job turned out to be a trap and they had all been captured. After being beaten, knocked out and betrayed by her sister-at-arms, she had still been the leader they needed. It was disquieting to see her look as lost as the rest of them.

"I'm not going back to the Lions," she said, emphatically. "But I'll consider speaking to Lukas. Maybe we can exchange some information."

Seb ducked his head. It was all he could ask for, really. He took another sip of his tea. The room was painfully, awkwardly silent.

Gerde cleared her throat. "How is Ana? You didn't say."

What could he say? That after the night they had kissed, he had spoken to her a scant couple of times, and both times only briefly. That every time he went to the bakery, she was never around. The owner assured him she was out on break, and was still working at the bakery, but it worried him to no end that she kept going out when both Humphreys men and assassins from House de Mörde were looking for them.

But he said none of those things. Instead, he said, "She's fine. She's working at the bakery again."

"As long as she's staying safe," Samara muttered. She cleared her own throat and shifted uneasily. "Just so we're clear—I don't have any regrets sending Eloise away—it was the right thing to do. But … I am sorry things turned out the way they did."

Her body was rigid, and she stared hard at the coals in the fireplace, not meeting anyone's eyes. Seb doubted an apology like that was easy coming from someone like Samara. He wished Art was around to hear it. He thought it would go a long way to repairing their friendship.

Hans and Gerde looked like they wanted to go over to

Samara and draw her into a hug. But Seb knew Samara would never allow that. Maybe in private, but not in front of him. He suddenly felt like he was intruding on them, so he hurriedly rose to his feet and said his goodbyes, promising them he'd be careful, and that the next time he came around, he would bring Ana.

CALLISTA MEIER SAT in the receiving room at House de Mörde, a smile plastered on her face, as she listened to Lutz Kaiser, a Restorationist Party member plotting to restore the Royal House of White, as he lectured her on her failures. For the past two years Callista had suspected there was more to Eloise than they were telling her. And then Lutz Kaiser had arrived and confirmed every one of her suspicions. Eloise had Magic and was indeed the last descendant of Queen White.

It had been some years since someone dared speak to her this way. Well, besides Samara. And then there was the way Chetwin Humphreys had mocked her when he failed to keep up his end of the bargain and give back Eloise. Okay, so perhaps it wasn't as uncommon an occurrence as she'd thought.

The only reason she allowed this man to speak to her in such a way was because he had her over a barrel.

She was such a fool, agreeing to take in Eloise for a future-queenly sum of money. But money was tight now that she no longer bought a steady supply of girls from Humphreys to train as assassins. Where it really went wrong was when she'd lost Eloise. The girl had snuck onto a job where she, as well as her Magic, caught the eye of Humphreys. And what Chetwin Humphreys wanted, Chetwin Humphreys got. Even if it meant stealing from the House de Mörde.

She had made valiant efforts to get the girl back, both

through her own assassins, and then through Samara and her crew. But in the end, Sam had gone back on the deal, and Callista was left to handle the fallout.

She knew the people who put Eloise under her protection were growing suspicious. Eloise, who sent weekly letters to them via Callista, had suddenly gone silent. And Callista could only make so many excuses before they finally sent someone to Märchen to find out what was going on.

To say that Lutz Kaiser was unhappy with Callista was an understatement. The man was single-minded in his focus. He wanted the girl, at all costs, and as far as he was concerned, Callista was not doing enough to get the girl back.

She had already sent her own girls after Samara. But Samara had returned the money that Callista had paid her crew. And apparently, under Samara's thick-headed code, they were square.

"It seems to me," Lutz was saying, "that your love for your former sister-at-arms is clouding your judgement here."

Callista glanced up at the man. He was a sprite of a man. Small, lithe, with dark hair tied back in a ponytail, he looked half-fae.

"I sent another of my girls just a couple of days ago, as you well know, but she was incapacitated. We have yet to discover where the Hisada is holed up," Callista replied, trying to muster all the patience she had remaining to her.

"You see, this is what I speak of," replied the self-important man. "The entire job of the House de Mörde is to track people down and kill their targets."

"Often the clients provide us with that information," Callista responded, and then shut her mouth. It was useless arguing with him.

"Which tells me," Lutz went on, ignoring her, "that your *bond* is keeping you from doing the job you have been tasked with."

Her bond. She was fairly sure whatever bond she believed she and Samara shared no longer existed. She still couldn't believe how much it stung learning that Sam had gone and decided to let Eloise go without discussing it with her.

Callista recalled staying up all evening, waiting for Samara to show up. She had eventually arrived in the pre-dawn hours with the money Callista had paid them for the auction job. Told Callista the deal was off. That Eloise was now free to make her own choices. They had fought. Both with words and blades. But eventually Callista let her go. What use would it do to kill her former sister? It wouldn't bring Eloise back.

"May I remind you," Lutz continued, "that with a few words from my colleagues, I could make contract murders illegal."

Callista pressed her lips firmly together and breathed in through her nose.

No. She did not need reminding. He had made his point quite clear that the unique status of House de Mörde, in which the law allowed the fulfilment of such contracts, while also making the actual hiring of assassins illegal, left her in quite the precarious state. A word from Lutz's people to the right ears, a councilman on Märchen's Stadtrat perhaps, and the House de Mörde would be shut down. The daughters of the House deemed murderers.

Callista had killed enough people in her life. The only way she had got through her time as an active assassin was knowing that she was doing a job. And if she didn't do the job, someone else would do it instead.

She licked her lips and thought through her words carefully. "It still might be possible that Eloise has left Märchen already, before I could send my girls to the coaching inns and dockyard."

Lutz shook his head sharply in disagreement. "There has been no word from any of my people of a girl matching her description."

"Forgive me, but that does not mean—"

"I tire of being here in Märchen. I need you to step up your search, Matron. This Samara Dawa has friends, yes? Surely they know something. Track them down. Threaten them. For if I have to look elsewhere for assistance, there will be consequences for House de Mörde."

Callista opened her mouth to speak. And then shut it. She nodded at him. He was right.

~

HE WAS NOT RIGHT, of course. But Callista saw no use in arguing with Lutz Kaiser.

It was true; she hadn't gone after any of Sam's crew. Sam may have got them to go along with her decision to set Eloise free, but Callista knew Sam well enough to know she most likely didn't bother to consult with them. Sam made her own decisions and Callista saw no use in dragging others into their feud.

There were certain things she could do. Some trees she could shake without causing harm. But no. She would not do that. Her girls were trained assassins. Not thugs.

Callista walked to her office. It was late, so she lit a lamp before sitting down at her writing desk. She took out a sheet of paper and began scratching a note.

Sam. You had your reasons for releasing Eloise. I still don't agree with them, but I feel I should warn you. The people who brought Eloise to me are here in Märchen. They are using the House de Mörde to hunt you down. They believe you know where Eloise is. I don't know if you do, but I'm concerned for the safety of your crew. I may not have much choice but to—

She stopped. Balled up the paper and tossed it in the bin beside the desk.

She could write this note. She could put it in the hands of her most trusted assassin, but it was still unlikely Samara would read it.

Samara wouldn't leave her crew to fend for themselves. She was loyal. To everyone but Callista, apparently. Although Callista would be the first to admit that she hadn't really helped in that department. Even if she managed to get this message to Samara, she doubted it would do much good.

Samara didn't trust Callista. She would think there was some other reason for her sending the warning. Or worse. Samara would do something to rile Lutz Kaiser's anger.

No. She needed to bide her time. Continue making her own inquiries. She wasn't sure if Eloise was still in Märchen. But she would continue her efforts. Anyway, it would be best if she found Eloise herself.

Once again, she cursed herself for putting her faith in Samara. Apparently, they were both fools for trusting each other.

ANA CLUTCHED her paper bag of bread rolls and hurried out of the Four and Twenty Blackbirds. As was now usual, she was taking a proper lunch break. She had made it a condition when returning to work there. The owner, Helga, still fuming about Ana's sudden disappearance during the day's leading up to the auction job, argued with her but eventually agreed.

Ana had never cared for the woman, though she worked in her bakery and lived in a small bedsit above the shop. She felt taken advantage of, which made her resentful. It surprised her to learn that the old lady and her husband had actually been worried about Ana.

She took in her surroundings. There was an alleyway next to

the bakery. A heavyset man was heaving enormous bags of flour off a cart. A delivery for the bakery, no doubt. She reached out with her senses, feeling the energy he expended as he carried the sacks to the shop's back entrance. She pocketed just a dab of that energy for herself.

Ana continued on her way. She no longer needed to worry about Tormod Lyons trying to capture her. He had left the city. And though she had been heavily involved in the auction job, she had been in disguise, virtually unrecognisable even to herself. But still, she kept her eyes open for signs of any assassins from House de Mörde.

Hurrying along the cobbled streets of Old Town, she passed an errand boy on a bicycle peddling vigorously down the street so fast she had to jump out of the way to avoid being hit. She glanced his way as he vanished up the road, stole a dab of kinetic energy from him as well, pocketing it deep inside herself.

She continued on her way down a narrow street and found herself in a market. She cut straight through the market, keeping an eye out, as always, for danger. A few weeks ago, she would never have attempted to be around so many people. But she was much more confident in her abilities these days.

Some fish mongers were energetically tossing fish. One man would hoist up the order and call it out to another man, who would shout the order back, catch the fish and wrap it in paper and twine for the customer. Their work was part performance, trying to draw people to their stall and away from their competitors. They did a mighty fine job of it, and Ana paused to watch them, despite the whiff of dead fish that caused her nose to wrinkle. She noticed a girl dressed in a long blue skirt and pinstripe high collar blouse who had stopped to watch the show as well. Only, was it her imagination, or was the girl watching Ana more than the men tossing fish? Feeling the kinetic energy of the fishmongers, she stole a dab from each of them and pocketed that too. One fishmonger dropped the fish, which startled Ana.

She continued through the market. There was a stand selling exotic fruit, oranges and others that Ana didn't recognise. The girl from the fishmongers was behind her. As Ana passed the fruit stand, she flicked her fingers, releasing the stored up kinetic energy and effectively upsetting the fruit stand. Fruit rolled in all directions and came clattering down ahead of the girl in the blue skirt.

Ana took that opportunity to zig right, cutting through a small alleyway and down some steps. After several seconds, she glanced backwards, but saw no one following her. Breathing heavily, she took in her location. She was in a residential area of Hollowhorn. Besides a few pubs and inns, it mostly consisted of boarding houses.

She continued on her way, taking a circuitous route before arriving at a quiet square. Looking over her shoulder and still seeing no one about, she went to the corner, picked up a small pebble, and threw it at a tiny sash window on the side of a house, using kinetic energy so the stone would meet its mark.

A few seconds later, the window opened, and a face appeared. A girl with ebony hair, pale skin and rose-coloured lips popped her head out.

Spotting Ana standing on the corner, the girl, Eloise, broke into a wide grin.

"I'll be right down," she said.

A few minutes later, the younger girl opened the ramshackle door to greet her. Ana was glad to see the girl no longer had bags beneath her eyes. Eloise never mentioned having trouble sleeping, but the evidence was there, and Ana knew from experience the toll being held captive took on a person even after you were freed.

"I brought lunch," Ana said, holding up a paper bag of pastries she had brought from the bakery.

Eloise's eyes lit up, her smile extra bright. "I'm starving!" she said. "Let's eat outside."

Ana bit her lip and frowned. She glanced back the way she had come. "Are you sure that's a good idea?" she asked, thinking of the girl in the blue skirt.

Eloise gave her a look that said she thought she was being silly. "You wouldn't have come here if you thought you were being followed. Plus, I hate being cooped up inside all day," she said, as she led the way to the gate to the garden.

Ana's brows knit together, but she followed Eloise all the same. Sometimes it felt to Ana that Eloise was enjoying her newfound freedom a little too much. Perhaps it was natural, given all the girl had been through, Besides, the garden *was* fenced in, and given the girl was only here because she wanted to stay close to Ana, a fellow magic user, she wasn't about to deny her.

They settled on a bench next to a spindly apple tree.

"I thought I was being followed. Thought it might be someone from House de Mörde, but I used the techniques you taught me to lose her."

She handed Eloise a bun.

Eloise's blue eyes flashed with delight. "You pocketed energy?" she asked around a mouthful of pastry.

"Mmhmm," Ana replied, chewing slowly. "Just a little here and there. Then I used it to upset a cart."

Eloise flung a celebratory hand into the air. "I *knew* that would work. I knew it!"

Ana found herself sitting taller and smiling, feeling chuffed about the breakthrough with her powers. It was good having Eloise here. Ana had been furious when Samara had told them she had put Eloise on a coach out of Märchen. She and Eloise had bonded at the party and then Samara had sent her away before she could say goodbye. Upset, Ana had fled the party, returning to her room above the Four and Twenty Blackbirds, because where else could she go? She didn't have the money from the job. Samara insisted they return it. And so, she couldn't go home to Richilde.

When she went down to work the next morning, Helga hadn't said a word, just handed her an apron. Seb had come in to see her, but she hadn't felt up for company. She was back at square one—trying to save enough money to go home. But, later that afternoon, just as the shop was closing up, she had a surprise visit from Eloise. The girl had used her innate Magical abilities to track Ana down. She had stayed in Märchen and had taken rooms of her own, just so she could spend more time with the only other magic wielder she had ever met. Even with Chetwin Humphreys and the House both looking for her, Eloise had stayed—for Ana's sake. She made Ana promise not to tell anyone that she was still in Märchen as she was terrified of getting sent away again. So, Ana kept her secret.

"Show me," Eloise said around another bite of pastry.

Ana laughed. "There's nothing really to show."

"How did it feel, having the energy inside you?"

Ana considered the question. "I thought it would feel strange. Having someone else's energy inside me. But it was no different from any other time I've collected energy. Easier, in fact, because I was only taking small amounts."

Eloise scrunched up the paper napkin she had been using and leaned towards Ana. "I bet you could take more than just small amounts."

Ana blinked, uncertain what Eloise was getting at. "What do you mean?"

"I mean, if you wanted to, I bet you could take all of it."

"All of it?" Ana repeated uncertainly.

"Yes," Eloise continued in a rush. "Think about it. Rather than using your powers to steal a bit of energy and knock over a cart, you could steal enough energy to make someone limp. Perhaps even knock them out."

Ana blinked again, her breath caught in her chest. Could she? She didn't know. This wasn't the type of thing her family had practiced, but if she could, then she wouldn't have to be afraid of anybody ever again.

CHAPTER FOUR

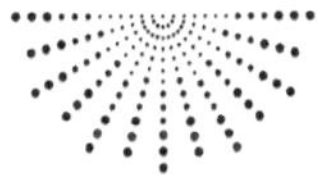

In need of new adventures? Consider a Grand Tour of Alsatia. See the Magic spindle inside Queen Zellandine's castle in Perceforest. See Queen Cenerentola's golden slipper with your own eyes in Pentemarone. Or visit Queen White's many castles in Richilde. For all your Grand Tour needs our agents at Tomas & Sons can help you with your travel arrangements.

Samara carefully adjusted the newsboy cap on her head as she stepped out of The Wishing-Table onto the muddy streets of Hollowhorn. It was mid-afternoon and Lukas Bernhardt would most likely be in his office at the Zephyr by now. She still wasn't crazy about working with the Lions, but if it helped them get Humphreys off their back, she'd do it. She glanced down at her short coat. She hated its lack of pockets, but she knew being seen in her signature frock coat would be like painting a giant target on her back. Unfortunately, there was little she could do about her caramel skin, so she still stood out on the streets of the Hollow. Gerde suggested she wear a cloak, but that seemed even more like the wearer was trying to conceal their identity. No. As naked as she felt without her frock coat, this would just have to do. Besides, it wasn't as though she were without weapons, she just had fewer places to conceal them. Gerde had offered to accompany her to the Royal Zephyr, actually she had insisted, but Samara felt it too risky if they were spotted together. Better she go see what was happening with the Lions on her own.

She meandered through the streets of the Hollow, casting her eyes about for any sign of an assassin from House de Mörde, when she caught sight of a pair of large thugs wearing bowlers and great coats. She couldn't quite get a glimpse of their faces, but judging by their size, the bruises on their knuckles and the poorly concealed weapons that not even their coats could hide, they were gang members. And the only gang member bold enough to step onto the Lions' turf was Humphreys'.

They apparently weren't after her, though. Instead, they were circling a man she couldn't quite make out. It was in her best interest to keep away from Humphreys' men. Still, these thugs outnumbered their prey, something which offended her sense of justice.

Shaking her head and muttering *schiesse* under her breath, she stepped closer. She sucked in a harsh breath when the person she thought was a Lion was shoved to the ground and one thug reared back. It wasn't one of Tormod's gang on the ground. It was Hans. The old man lay in the dirt, crouched amongst the scattered ingredients for cabbage rolls. The lifts she insisted he wear whenever he had to leave their hideout had caused her to nearly dismiss him entirely.

One man, a giant, bald man, reared back to launch a kick at Hans, who lay curled up, trying to protect his head. Her vision momentarily tunnelled as rage flooded her and, in a flash, Samara gripped a blade in her hands. She would slit this scum's throat for attacking her people. But before she could raise the blade, the large bald man landed heavily on his back.

Samara blinked, glancing about. Ahead of them on the street, she spotted Ana. The girl was standing in the middle of the street, glaring fiercely in Samara's direction. Just then, Samara heard another thud. She spun to find Hans' other assailant on the ground too. Dead? Or unconscious? She noticed the gentle rise and fall of their chests.

With Hans' assailants momentarily incapacitated, Samara replaced her blade and rushed to the old man, Ana arriving seconds later. Gently, Samara clasped him under his armpits and helped haul him into a seated position.

"Are you okay?" she asked, feeling him for any signs of fractures.

Hans sucked in a breath.

"Are you having trouble breathing?" she asked. If he had broken ribs, they would have to take him to the Lions' doctor at the Zephyr.

Hans shook his head. "No, no. I am fine," he replied, a sheepish smile touching his lips. "Thanks to you."

"Not me," Samara replied archly, glancing towards Ana.

Hans seemed to notice Ana for the first time, and his smile widened. "Ana, it's good to see you."

Samara's attention was still focused on her former landlord. Blood poured from a minor cut above Hans's left eyebrow, but aside from a few bruises, he seemed to be in one piece.

"Let's get off the streets," she said, putting his arm over her shoulder to haul him up. Ana took Hans' other arm and together they walked into a nearby alleyway between two smoke shops.

When they were well enough concealed from passers-by, Samara took out a handkerchief and wiped the blood from Hans' head wound.

"What were you thinking going to the local Pentemarone grocers?"

Hans' face flushed and he withdrew a handkerchief to mop his face. "I was thinking we could all use a hearty meal instead of the slop Yanni provides."

Samara swallowed, a shudder running through her. She honestly didn't know what she would do if anything ever happened to Hans.

She placed her hands about his shoulders, holding him at arm's length to reassure herself that he really was all right.

"Hans, your life is worth so much more than a hearty meal," she said sternly. At Hans' grimace she softened and added, "especially more than cabbage rolls. The place smells bad enough being so close to the Klara without adding in the aroma of cabbage."

Hans chuckled and shook his head. Samara could tell he was embarrassed to have taken such a risk.

"I should probably leave," Ana said, her voice tight. Clearly uncomfortable with the display of affection emanating from the Hisada.

Samara finally turned and gave Ana her full attention. She looked good. Still far too skinny, though. There was something different about her that Samara couldn't put her finger on. A new found confidence.

"Thank you," she said. "I don't know what I would've done if anything had happened to Hans."

Ana shrugged, still uncomfortable. "It's okay. Who were they, anyway?"

"Humphreys' men," Hans supplied. "They wanted to know where Eloise was."

Ana flinched and Samara felt her stomach tighten. She may have taken her crew by surprise with her decision, but she still wasn't entirely convinced she had done the wrong thing. Eloise deserved to choose her own path.

Ana looked ready to bolt when Samara suddenly remembered something. When Ana took down those men using her kinetic powers, she hadn't been waving her hands around like she usually did.

"How'd you do that back there?" Samara asked. "You took them down without grasping their energy."

"I've been practicing my technique," Ana replied curtly. Though she steadily returned Samara's gaze, Samara couldn't help feeling Ana was hiding something. "I should probably go. I was just on my way to see Seb."

Judging by her evasiveness, Ana was definitely still holding a grudge against Samara for letting Eloise leave.

"You really shouldn't be hanging about the Hollow these days. It's too dangerous."

Ana bowed her head. "You're probably right." She turned to Hans. "I'm glad you're okay," she said, offering him a small smile. With that, she turned and hurried back out of the alley.

Samara sighed, turning to her landlord. "We should leave before those two,"—she jutted her head toward the unconscious thugs—"wake up."

Hans nodded, but he winced as they walked to the mouth of the alley. "I think I might've twisted my ankle with these damn lifts."

Samara cursed. She'd hoped the lifts would help him blend in, since Humphreys and Callista would be looking for a Little Person. She hadn't even thought about how much they'd hinder him if he was actually in a fight. "Next time you decide to go out, lose the lifts," she said, putting his arm about her shoulder once again to support him.

"I don't want to keep you from your meeting," Hans protested.

"It can wait," Samara replied as the pair slowly made their way back down the streets of the Hollow, Samara on her guard the entire way.

⌇

ART RAN a hand inside the itchy collar of his jacket. He really needed to find more comfortable clothes for these excursions. Not that he exactly had the money for it these days. Certainly not helped by his run of bad luck tonight. He had visited one of the smaller taverns in Old Town, hoping to meet a mark he might make some coin from, but no such luck. Apparently, his disguise meant people were less likely to pay for his drink, much less invite him up to their room. All he wanted to do right now was order up some hot water and take a nice, long bath.

Reaching the crossroads where his building stood, practically beckoning him inside, he warily glanced about for any sign of the thugs that had been there the other day. No sign of anyone about besides the usual homeless faces he knew. Art wished he had some coin to offer, but that had not been in the cards tonight. He spied two large burlap sacks on the front steps of his building and felt bad for the poor sap. It looked like Mrs Tremblay in 3b had finally found out her husband was cheating on her and thrown his sorry arsch out. It was a gloomy evening and the heavy clouds suggested rain was on the way. He wouldn't want to be that chap, trying to find a room while hauling his belongings in this weather.

It wasn't until he actually reached the top of the steps that he realised it was his belongings which lay on the front steps. He recognised his maroon dressing gown sticking out of one sack. Just to be sure, he rummaged through the silk shirts and other odds and ends, confirming these were indeed his own belongings.

He narrowed his eyes, glaring at the front door. Then he heaved both bags back into the front lobby of the boarding house. He had just managed to drag both bags inside, and was about to drag them back up the stairs to his room where they belonged, when Emmett, the proprietor, stepped forward to block his path.

"Can't let you do that, Art," Emmett said. The man was a giant, with a wall of a chest and massive legs, easily blocking Art's way. Art, still panting from the exertion of moving his belongings, straightened up and gave Emmett a winning smile.

"Come on Emmett. I'm not *that* far behind on rent. Why don't we discuss this over a drink?"

Emmett scowled. "You're three months in arrears," he pointed out. "You promised you would pay in full two weeks ago. I'm not running a bloody charity here."

Art grimaced, blowing a lock of blonde hair out of his eyes. He rubbed his brow wearily, recalling once again how he should have had the money to pay Emmett two weeks ago if Samara hadn't decided to arbitrarily send Eloise on her way, thus making an enemy of the Matron of House de Mörde.

Art held his palms out wide. "I can explain. There was a job, but it fell through. But," he said, before Emmett could respond to his previous sentence, "there is money on the way. I promise you."

Emmett ran a hand through his salt and pepper hair. "It's too late for that. The room's been sold to a *paying* customer."

Art took a step back, his body going weak. "You sold my room?!" He forced himself to breathe. "Okay. We can work this out. Just give me another room for now. I don't care how abysmal it is. When my old rooms are free, I'll pay everything you're owed, and one month in advance." Desperation laced his words.

Emmett shook his head and glanced back to his office as though he really didn't want to be having this conversation.

"Emmett. Please," Art said, lowering his voice. "Come on. You can't send me out there. It's going to rain. I don't have anywhere else to go."

He didn't understand it. He'd always had a decent relationship with the proprietor. True, he was frequently late with his rent, but this was his home.

Emmett's jaw hardened. "It's out of my hands."

"What do you mean, it's out of your hands? You're the proprietor. I very much believe it is entirely *in* your hands."

Again, Emmett swiped a hand through his hair. "I mean, a gentleman came here today and paid me a lot of money to stop renting rooms to you. And considering how much you owe me, I was glad to do so."

Art's already dry throat tightened. "Who was this gentleman?"

Emmett sighed, ready to be done with this ugly conversation. "Don't know. Didn't ask." He started to walk away, but turned back again, a look of undisguised disgust on his face. "You brought this on yourself, Templeton. You could have just gone to your toff father and got the money from him. The godmothers' know he has sent you enough letters these past few days. But no. You'd rather play at being a scoundrel. Well, this is how scoundrels end up: living in the gutter."

With that, Emmett walked back to his office, leaving Art stunned, with more questions than answers. Who was this person who had paid Emmett to kick him out on the streets? It didn't seem the style of House de Mörde or Humphreys' people. But it sounded a lot like his father. His father, who had apparently been sending him letters recently.

Art hunched down next to his bags, paying no attention to his ground floor neighbours, who were peering out to see what the commotion was about. He began digging through his belongings until he found a pile of letters. Amongst the bills, he recognised three featuring the seal of Lord Templeton.

The *arschloch.*

~

THE SUN HAD BARELY RISEN and the air still held a chill behind The Wishing-Table. The tavern shared a courtyard with three other buildings: a smoke shop, another tavern, and a lodging house. At this hour of the day, the courtyard was normally empty.

Samara had been awake all night. She hadn't been able to sleep. Not since the attack on Hans. The longer she lay in bed, the more her anger consumed her.

Hans was all right. She and Gerde had cleaned up his cuts, and he otherwise seemed fine. But still, she couldn't control the fear running through her. What would have happened if she and Ana hadn't come along when they did? She didn't know what she would have done. The idea of losing Hans terrified her, especially if it was because of her mistakes.

Hans was right. She should never have gone up against Chetwin Humphreys.

When Gerde left to go to work that evening, Samara had followed her via the rooftops. She felt compelled to make sure Gerde got there okay. She spent the night watching the Aurora her body on high alert, searching for signs of danger. It helped her feel more in control...

Later, when Gerde was finishing up her shift, she called out Samara's name and Samara had sheepishly revealed herself. Gerde had known all along that the Hisada had been following her. Samara appreciated that Gerde never made a fuss about being followed. She'd known that Samara needed to do this. The pair walked home together.

Sleep remained elusive for Samara. Eventually Gerde roused her, and the pair did some early morning sparring in the courtyard. It had been her one outlet while they were holed up at The Wishing-Table.

Over the previous weeks, Samara had looked into all the people who worked in the neighbouring buildings. None appeared to have a connection to Humphreys. Still, it wouldn't take much for word to get back to him that the Hisada had been beating someone up in this little corner of the Hollow.

A part of her welcomed the confrontation. Even though it had been her decision, lying low just didn't feel right.

Neither did lying flat on her back. Gerde held a hand out to help her up and Samara accepted it, noting the callouses on Gerde's fingers from mucking stables and cleaning tack.

"You're still too tense. You're telegraphing every move," Gerde said, taking a swig of water.

"Of course I'm tense," Samara snarled back, wiping sweat from her brow.

Gerde nodded to her, and the pair returned to their fighting stances, fists raised.

"It's not working Gerde," Samara huffed as she blocked a jab Gerde threw her way. "I can't just sit here doing nothing while Humphreys goes after the people I care about."

With her left hand, she caught a jab Gerde attempted, and countered with her own punch. Gerde easily blocked it.

"I know hiding isn't something you're used to, but you can't let this get to you. Hans is fine." Gerde panted, dancing just out of Samara's reach. "If you go after Humphreys now, you'll be playing right into his hands."

Samara could tell Gerde was waiting for her to grow impatient and move in for an attack. With her longer reach, Gerde would easily catch her. Instead, she shifted to the side, preparing a feint. "I'm not built for sitting around, waiting for things to happen."

Gerde stopped, just for a moment, a smile touching her full lips. Samara wasn't sure what prompted her to stop so suddenly, but she took advantage of it by coming in with a one-two jab that Gerde only barely blocked. Gerde scowled at her and then did something that took Samara by surprise. Instead of dancing away, she hit Samara squarely in the chest with a front kick that landed her on the floor again, knocking the breath out of her.

Samara raised herself up on her elbows, her eyes widening in surprise, before leaping to her feet again. She'd never seen Gerde do more than bare-knuckle boxing. Apparently, she had a few moves she was still keeping to herself. They danced around the courtyard again.

"You could always go see Lukas."

Samara made a face at the reminder she still needed to visit the new leader of the Lions.

"We just need to wait things out. When they can't recover the stolen money, the Order will go after Humphreys."

Samara wiped the sweat from her eyes. "But what happens in the meantime? Who else gets hurt?"

She threw a couple of punches out, just to keep Gerde talking. Searching for an opening.

"What're you going to do? Kill him? The hangman's coming for him. Just give it more time."

"I thought that. I really did," Samara replied, evading another kick from Gerde. "But that's just not how things work, is it? The hangman never comes for people like him." When she thought about how long Humphreys had been in power, the wealth he had accumulated built on the backs of so many people, herself included, a wave of adrenaline washed over her. She leaned into her attack, pummelling Gerde with quick jabs, no longer caring about staying out of Gerde's longer reach.

Gerde was quick to defend herself. Blocking each of the punches and once again sending Samara to the ground with a well-placed frontal kick. Gerde stood above her, eyes studying Samara with concern.

"Had enough?" Gerde asked.

Samara nodded and accepted Gerde's outstretched hand.

"You're feeling better aren't you?" Gerde asked.

Samara had to admit that she was. She hadn't wanted to go down and spar this morning. She was exhausted from her sleepless night, but Gerde had known. Somehow Gerde always knew.

"Thanks for forcing me up this morning. Even when I resisted."

Gerde grinned. "It's what I do. Come on. I'm starving."

As Samara followed the taller woman back into the dreary tavern, she still couldn't quite shake the feeling that sitting around was the wrong move.

CHAPTER FIVE

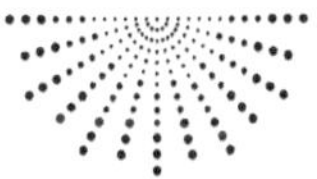

*I*t was mid-afternoon as Seb made his way into Old Town. He had switched shifts just so he could come out at lunchtime and surprise Ana at work. The wiser option would be to stay at the Zephyr. It was unsafe to be out on the streets these days, between the Humphreys-Lions rivalry heating up, and everything that had gone down at the auction. Ana would probably be dismayed to find he had taken the risk just to have lunch with her. It was obviously why she hadn't been to visit him. He hadn't seen her since the night after the auction.

He was dressed in a thick woollen coat to protect against the cooler weather, as well as corduroy trousers and a plain shirt.

His head was covered with a chequered newsboy cap. It wasn't dissimilar to what many working-class people in Old Town wore, yet he still felt he stuck out too much.

When he arrived at the Four and Twenty Blackbirds he peered through the glass pane in the door, but saw only the bakery's proprietress. No sign of Ana. Still, he pushed the door open and asked after her. Perhaps he'd get lucky and find she was in the back, taking things out of the oven or something.

The owner, Helga, scowled at him as he sheepishly walked to the counter.

"She's out for lunch," the woman said before he could even say a word.

"Do you know when she'll be back?" he asked.

"Can't say."

Seb frowned, unsure whether she couldn't say, or wouldn't say. Helga eyed him with distrust. Ana had often complained about the owner of the bakery, but maybe Helga was just being protective of her, in which case she was to be commended.

"Could I leave a message for her?"

The woman stepped back from the counter, crossed her arms and looked pointedly at the display holding her baked goods. Despite her clear hostility, the smell of fresh baked bread reminded Seb that he had eaten little this morning, so he ordered a Geflügelrolle before asking for a pencil so he could write Ana a note.

It was a disappointment that Ana hadn't been at the bakery. This was the fourth time Seb had attempted to go see her. Still, he tried not to let the frustration get to him as he climbed the steps into a distinctly sketchy doss house back in the Hollow. He'd visited the place himself, his very first day in Hollowhorn, but hadn't made it through the doorway. He knew there was no way he could stay in a place like that, no matter how cheap the rent.

The doss house was rundown, even by Hollowhorn standards. He swore he saw a woman on the stairs swaying as though her body were still in the throes of Nepenthe fever. Not that he had much experience with Nepenthe addicts, but he'd heard the stories from the other Lions.

That was another thing Humphreys was responsible for. Besides the trafficking of people, he was Märchen's number one supplier of Nepenthe. Seb wanted to ask the woman if she was okay, but when he turned to her, she gave a cry and ran off deeper into the boarding house. Seb made his way up to the first floor to the address he'd been given. He raised his fist to knock on the door when a couple arguing on the landing caused him to pause. They had been whispering with emphatic jabbing of fingers, but that had now changed to loud retorts. He wondered if he ought to intervene.

"I wouldn't if I were you. It's pointless. They'll just be at it again," drawled Art, who now stood in the doorway.

Seb turned to see his friend, who looked surprisingly none the worse for wear for having been kicked out of his home.

"How'd you know I was at the door?"

Art touched a hand to his head. "Clairvoyance. But also coincidence. I was just about to escape this pit hole and get a drink. Care to join me?"

Seb readily agreed, eager to be gone from the clawing confines of the doss house. They walked to a nearby tavern. It wasn't a whole lot better than the boarding house, but at least it was clean.

"I wish you'd let me know about your situation," Seb said, taking a sip of warm ale and wincing at the taste.

"I didn't exactly have much fore-warning," Art replied testily, grimacing at the bad ale.

"At least your old landlord gave me your new address," Seb responded mildly.

Art scowled. "Probably thought you were one of my creditors."

Seb doubted he looked much like a creditor to Art's old landlord, but he said nothing.

"I just can't believe he did that. It's the same story over and over though," Art continued. "Lord Templeton says jump, and everyone says 'how high?'"

"Lord Templeton? As in your father?" Seb interrupted, rubbing his forehead. "What does he have to do with anything?"

"He's the reason Emmett kicked me out," Art said, draining his ale. "He paid off the man."

"Paid him off? Your landlord told you that?"

"Yes. He said a *gentleman* had paid him a lot of money to stop renting rooms to me."

Seb blew air out of his cheeks as he took in the room they were sitting in.

"So, your landlord said a gentleman? Did he actually say it was your father?"

Art indicated to the barkeep that he wanted a refill before replying. "Well, no, but it's obviously him."

Seb rolled his hand, gesturing for Art to explain himself.

"For one thing, why on earth would Humphreys or the Matron kick me out? Kill or maim me, certainly. But make me homeless?"

Seb squinted. While he certainly couldn't figure out why the people hunting them might wish to do that, it made even less sense that Art's father was behind this. Certainly, he'd heard enough from Art to know that he and his father didn't exactly get along, but still, he was his father. In the end, fathers wanted what was best for their sons. Didn't they?

"But even more damning," Art continued, "is the handful of letters he's sent me over the past few weeks."

"What did they say?"

Art waved a hand. "Oh, just letters demanding my presence back at the manor. Apparently, he's been wanting to have a word with me for weeks."

"Did he say why he wanted to speak to you?"

"Oh no, that's not how Lord Templeton operates. He demands your presence, and if you ignore him, which I was decidedly doing considering we haven't spoken in over two years, he makes life difficult for you."

Seb frowned. "Still, making you homeless seems a little extreme."

"Not if he wants me to come home."

"Do you think that's what he wants?"

Art shrugged. "I don't know."

A barmaid came over to deliver more drinks even though Seb wasn't finished with his first one.

"So, are you going to see him?"

"I'll have to. With things the way they are with Humphreys' and Callista's people, I can't exactly access any lines of credit. Honestly, he must love knowing that I have to come grovelling back to him. You know, he and I haven't spoken since the day of my mother's funeral."

Seb blinked. He hadn't realised Art had lost his mother. Having also lost a parent, he felt like he suddenly understood Art a bit more.

"The man actually blamed me for her death."

Seb looked up, startled. "Blamed you? Why?"

"Said my lifestyle had put a strain on her heart." Art took a long swig of his ale. "He also blamed me for never seeing my mother, even though he's the one who banished me from the manor."

"Schiesse." Then, after a moment's hesitation, he added, "You know, if you're looking for a place to stay, Samara, Gerde and Hans have two rooms at The Wishing-Table. It might be tight, but it's a lot better than the place you're in now. I'm sure they wouldn't mind-"

Art waved a hand to cut him off. "Go back to the Hisada with my tail between my legs? I don't think so. You know she's the reason we're in this mess."

Seb opened his mouth. Then closed it again. Art had made his feelings clear. No sense arguing about it.

"You should know that the reason I came looking for you was to let you know Lukas has extended a line of credit for you. For helping during the fight the other day."

Art's eyes lit up. "He did?"

Seb nodded. He'd been surprised himself. He figured this was some way of trying to butter Samara up, since she still hadn't gone to see him, and he knew Art was part of her crew.

Art's mouth twisted into a grin as he lifted his glass of ale.

"Well, why are we drinking this swill? We should be at the Zephyr!"

GERDE WAS MAKING breakfast when Samara walked back into their flat. The smell of porridge wafted through the small room. It was one of the few things they could successfully cook over the small fireplace, and she was tiring of greasy tavern breakfasts.

"Did you run Magda off?" Gerde asked, as she continued to stir the oats.

Gerde had told Yanni the previous night that she planned to

cook and wouldn't need his wife to drop off breakfast. Despite that, they still received a knock on the door in the morning. An increasingly agitated Samara had snuck through the room next door, just in case it wasn't Yanni's wife, Magda.

Samara closed the door and strode to the small table they used as a dining table, dropping an envelope onto it. "You have a letter," she announced.

"Me? But who would? Oh," Gerde said, realising just who the note must be from.

Hans got up from his seat by the fireplace. "I'll stir the oats," he offered.

She nodded gratefully at the old man. He looked a lot better today. The bruises weren't nearly as bad as Gerde had feared when Samara had brought him home the previous day. Of course, it didn't seem to stop Samara from continuing to fuss over him. She still hadn't gone to see Lukas. Samara seemed terrified of leaving them all alone. It worried her. She admired Sam's strength. She even admired her recklessness. But Sam was used to working alone. Now that she had people she cared for that were in danger, she seemed paralysed. Gerde had never seen her like this.

Walking over to the table, Gerde instantly recognised her mother's handwriting.

Gerde hadn't told her mother exactly what she was mixed up in when she stopped working at the coaching inn. She didn't want her to worry. She hated leaving her mother in the lurch like that, but it was safer if she stayed away from the family stables. At least until things blew over.

Samara, she knew, would prefer she stop working at the Aurora as well, but in truth, it was less about the money and more about being able to keep an ear to the ground. And what she was hearing was not good. As Seb had reported, rumours of a turf war between Chetwin Humphreys' thugs and the Lions were fast spreading. There was also talk of a new group in town. There wasn't much information about this new group, but if there really was another group trying to carve out some territory in Märchen, the already tense environment in the city would prove to be a powder keg.

Not that any of this was foremost on Gerde's mind. She worried why her mother would feel the need to reach out. Her mother knew not to contact her unless it was an emergency. Heart racing, she tore open the envelope and read its contents.

My dear Gerderl,

I hope you are safe and well. I know you told me not to contact you unless it was the direst of emergencies. However, you should know that a gentleman visited the inn yesterday asking questions about you and your friends. He asked if I knew where you were staying. I told him I did not. He didn't believe me. Said that I could get into a lot of trouble if I was lying. I insisted I didn't know where you had gone. I told him you had left in a coach, but he said he knew that wasn't true. Honestly, he wouldn't stop asking questions, even after I asked him to leave. It wasn't until your brother threatened to report him to the City Watch that he finally left.

I was careful about sending this letter. Just as you told me to be. I had little Corinne take it with her to post while she was picking up my grocery order. We worry for you. Ahren is upset because I won't tell him where you're staying. I will keep your secret. But you must promise to stay safe, little Gerderl.

Your Mutter.

With clenched jaw and shaking hand, Gerde silently showed the note to Samara. Samara quickly scanned the letter, her own expression tightening with each word she read.

"What is it?" asked Hans from beside the pot, sensing the sudden tension in the room.

"They're going after my family," Gerde replied quietly, walking back to the stove to take over the stirring.

Hans read the letter while Samara stalked to the adjacent room, pulling out her roll of weapons.

"Wait, Samara. Wait!" Hans said. "You can't go running off like this."

"Just try to stop me," Samara muttered, returning to the room with a handful of blades that she began concealing about her person.

Gerde, for her part, silently but furiously stirred the pot. "He's right," she agreed through clenched teeth. "This is just what they want."

"I can't keep sitting here hoping it'll go away," Samara replied.

"Just listen," Hans said, raising a placating hand. "This doesn't make any sense. If they were really looking for Gerde, it would be easy. She still works at the Aurora. They could easily go after her if they wanted to. Which means they're just trying to draw *you* out."

"So, what do you suggest we do?" Samara asked, throwing out her hands in frustration and stalking around the small confines of the room.

Gerde could tell the former assassin needed to strike out at something. She caught Sam's eye and silently pleaded with her. She couldn't do this. She couldn't worry about her mother and Samara at the same time. Surely, Sam knew Hans was right.

Samara didn't move. Her hands gripped the weapons roll, still not willing to relinquish it.

Gerde left the pot and strode to Samara. She held Samara's gaze as she gently took the weapons roll out of Samara's hands. Samara's arms wrapped her in a hug and Gerde could feel some of her own tension releasing.

"I don't want to sit here waiting for them to come for us either," Gerde said, quietly. "But we need a plan first."

CHAPTER SIX

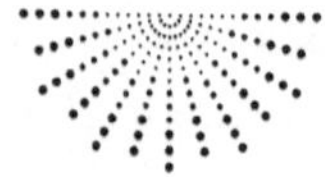

Henry Templeton, LORD. *b*. 16th Mai 1824 8th Lord of Witanhurst. ed. Shule königlich and Breitofen University. Landowner with mines in Richilde, Märchen and Alkebu. *m*. Mary Langford.

SONS LIVING

Hon. James Templeton, *b*. 14 th März 1845

Hon. Arthur Templeton, *b*. 5 th Juli 1847

— GOTTARD'S GUIDE TO PEERAGE

*I*t was a chilly day and just starting to drizzle by the time Ana arrived at the boarding house where Eloise was staying. She was ready to get inside and warm up, but even she was surprised by Eloise's enthusiasm when the door opened. Her blue eyes sparkled, and she practically dragged Ana up the stairs. The teenage girl bounced up and down with excitement.

Ana was always glad to see her this way. The girl spent so much of her time alone, cooped up in her room, it couldn't be good for her. Especially after what she went through being Humphreys' prisoner, which Eloise still never spoke about.

When Eloise let Ana into her shabby little room and shut the door, she spun around, a wide grin on her face. "I've finally figured it out," she announced.

Ana frowned. "Figured what out?"

"How to make us some money," Eloise said, as though Ana was wilfully being dense.

Ana pursed her lips. "Oh?" she asked, taking a seat in the cramped space and opening up the bag of pastries she had brought with her.

Eloise picked up a coin purse and showed it to Ana. "What do you make of these?"

Ana opened the coin purse to find it full of gold crowns. There must have been twenty in there, at least.

"You made these?" she asked, while chewing on a pastry.

Eloise nodded eagerly with a gleam in her eye.

Ana pulled one out and held it towards the window. It was an extremely well-done copy of a Märchen crown. Right down to the little letter "M", which delineated the mint mark for the city-state.

"It's very impressive," Ana replied, her mind already thinking about everything she could do with the money. She could afford the postage to Richilde to let her family know she's all right.

"Thank you," said Eloise. She had yet to take a bite from her own food. "But the trouble is, I can't maintain their form for very long. I could go into a shop and pay with it. But with me not nearby to maintain the magic's hold, they will just disappear. That won't do. I can't exactly start paying my landlady with coins that will disappear. She'll eventually catch on and report me to the City Watch."

Ana's shoulders drooped. That wouldn't do, verdammt. "So,

what have you figured out?" she asked again, taking another bite of pastry and trying to hide her disappointment.

Eloise responded by reaching out and holding Ana's hand. "This is the part where I need your help."

Ana's head reared back in surprise. "My help?"

"Yes. We can't go around the city spending fake coins. So, what we need to do is take real money, and make it so people don't notice."

Ana blew out a puff of air. "What do you mean?"

"You use your powers to make someone's purse fall to the ground. I'll create a duplicate which we will give back to them. As far as that person is concerned, they have their money back. They won't even know the purse is missing, and when they eventually notice, they'll just assume they misplaced their purse. We spend real money, and nobody is the wiser." Eloise grinned at Ana and triumphantly tore off a piece of bun, popping it into her mouth. "Fool proof."

Ana's lips twisted in distaste. "You're talking about stealing from people?"

Eloise pinched her lips together. "You stole from that lady to get the invitation."

It was true. She, Samara, and Seb had stolen some cash and jewels to make it look like an ordinary robbery. But that woman could obviously afford it. And all of it was done to help rescue Eloise herself, who was the headlining item at the auction.

"Besides," Eloise continued, "we'll make sure to only steal from rich people who will hardly notice a few crowns going missing."

Ana shook her head. She had to remind herself that Eloise had led a sheltered life, moving countries and households every few years. She had very little concept of the outside world, not least of which was just how much *a few crowns* could buy. But at least she was talking about only stealing from the rich. Even though if Ana's experience working at the Four and Twenty was anything to go by, it was the well-off people who were the most penny-pinching, and, she'd wager, more likely to report it to the City Watch.

Ana pursed her lips. "What if they somehow put two and two together and report us?" The last thing either of them needed was to attract the attention of the authorities.

"They won't," Eloise assured her with the confidence only the young could possess, Ana thought, even though she was only a few years older than her.

"But—"

"I'll disguise us. I know I can keep up a disguise for at least a short time."

The girl sounded so certain Ana relented. "That would be for the best. Chetwin Humphreys' men are still trying to hunt you down. They actually attacked Hans in the street. You remember him? The old man who owns the print shop?"

Eloise stilled. "Is he okay?"

Ana nodded, and gave a shy smile. "I used my powers to intervene."

Eloise tensed. "Did they see you use your powers?"

"No."

"Well, that's all right then," Eloise replied, brightening. "And you used your powers to help people."

She had. Samara didn't necessarily need her help, but it had felt good to protect someone instead of being the victim. She wouldn't have gotten to this point without Eloise's guidance. She felt a warmth in her breast. To think it took her being kidnapped and brought to Märchen to meet someone outside her family with magic. Big Magic, no less.

"It will be good to finally have some money," said Eloise. "We can get a place together and practice our magic all the time."

"You'd really want to stay in Märchen?" Ana asked, surprised.

"If you wanted to," Eloise replied. She hesitated. "Unless you preferred going home to Richilde?"

Did she? Ana wasn't so sure. It would be a safe place for them both. Eloise didn't have family of her own. But Ana knew she wasn't ready. Her mother would never allow them to experiment with magic the way they'd been doing.

"Here's good for now," Ana replied.

They'd figure out where to go eventually. Until then, they had to be careful and not take too many risks.

They would be two girls with magic, against the world.

It was with trepidation and a great deal of resentment that Arthur Templeton paid the brougham driver and stepped towards Witanhurst, the great Templeton manor house. It had been two years since he had last visited, and it all looked much the same. Not that it had changed much while growing up. Witanhurst never changed. It was a place stuck in time. And so was his father.

Four enormous pillars graced the front entrance. It was a style typical of the era it was built, some two hundred years ago, and yet, both as a child and now, as an adult, he imagined the columns to be like the bars of a prison cell.

As he walked up the cream-coloured steps with a heavy heart, the enormous black front door yawned open like a mouth before he could even reach for the bellpull and Art was greeted by Philippe, his father's butler, immaculately turned out as always. Not a hair out of place. He looked Art over with stern eyes that softened just a fraction as he met Art's tremulous gaze.

"Master Templeton. I shall let your father know you are here."

From Philippe, that was as good as a hug. The man, like much of the staff at Witanhurst, was ever the professional. Never were they allowed to openly show favour to him or his elder brother. His father felt that in order to build a strong son love wasn't needed. Neither was attention. Or even a kind word.

Art merely nodded his head and allowed himself to be shown into the waiting room. In any normal family, he would surely go directly to the family drawing room. But the Templeton's were not a normal family. And some minutes later, Art was led to a formal drawing room where he was served tea in delicate china whilst his father finished up whatever it was he was doing.

He sat for several minutes, examining the room, which also had changed little from what he recalled growing up. Cream-coloured marble columns decorated a large fireplace, where a fire crackled. The ceilings and walls were decorated with bas relief designs. Art perched himself on a parlour chair, awkwardly sipping his tea. He munched on a biscuit because, verdammt, he may hate having to come here, but it had been a long carriage ride and he was hungry.

When it became clear his father was planning on keeping him waiting, Art removed a pipe, matches, and a small packet of hash. He sprinkled the hash into the pipe, tamped down on it and lit it with a match. As the pungent smell of hash-smoke filled the room, he could feel the consternation of the footman who stood quietly in the corner, though to his credit, the man said nothing.

When, a few minutes later, his father strode into the room wearing a three-piece suit, he stopped in the doorway, sniffed the air, his eyes zeroing in on Art and his pipe and said, "Put that out Arthur. Disgusting habit," and took a seat in the adjacent parlour chair.

While Art put out the pipe, gleeful to have annoyed his father so early in their meeting, the house maid poured tea for his father, which he accepted, and then indicated her dismissal with a finger.

Deciding he needed *something* to hold in his hands to offer him a small measure of strength, Art took up his own teacup and studied the elder Lord Templeton whilst taking a sip.

His father looked much like he remembered, although his hair was a little greyer, he looked much the same. However, Art noticed with some dismay that his father's hairline had continued to recede. *Please don't let me inherit that.*

Though his father had clearly been working from home that day, he still wore a dove grey frock coat and matching trousers, and a dark waistcoat. It was not a particularly inspiring outfit, but the cut and quality of the fabric could not be denied, and Art felt a tiny pang of loss for the luxuries his old life had afforded him.

"My goodness, what are you wearing, Arthur?" his father asked, dismay twisting his mouth down into a frown.

Art glanced self-consciously down at himself. His own frock coat and waistcoat attire had certainly seen better days, but that was hardly his fault, given the circumstances his father had placed him in.

Jaw hardening, he ignored his father's question. "You wanted to see me?"

"Ah, yes. Frankly, I had hoped you would come a lot sooner, but you've always been stubborn like your mother."

Art inhaled sharply, but again said nothing. Not yet, at least. First, find out what Lord Templeton wants, then he could give his father a piece of his mind.

"To be honest, it's something I've been wanting to discuss for some time," his father continued amiably, taking another sip of tea. "Your brother James has taken a wife."

"He's getting married?" Art asked. *I wonder what the future Mrs James Templeton must be like? With a bit of luck, she'll have enough of a sense of humour for the both of them.*

"He *got* married," his father said, taking a sip of tea. "Six months ago."

Art's mouth fell open. He wasn't sure how to feel. His only brother had gotten married and nobody had bothered to tell him?

"That must've been a quick wedding. He didn't get her knocked up, did he?" Art replied. Sarcasm was always a good defence in the Templeton household.

His father scowled, which gave him some small satisfaction.

"Don't be vulgar," his father replied, his eyes briefly flashing with anger. He placed his teacup down on the table. "If you must know, their engagement was announced over a year ago. And yes. She is now with child."

This news, too, caused Art to jerk his head back. He was going to be an uncle.

"Which is why I have been wanting to meet with you. As you know, you were formally removed from the will some time ago."

"Yes, your solicitor went to great lengths to explain to me precisely why I was no longer in the will," Art replied testily.

If his father wanted him to come back into the family fold, he certainly wasn't going about it the right way.

"I had thought that would be enough," his father continued, ignoring Art's comment. "But it appears your antics have left Julia, your sister-in-law, somewhat concerned about the family name."

Art jerked back in the chair. "What?"

"Julia and James, as am I, are concerned about you dragging

the family name through the mud and what that might do to the chances of James' son finding a place for himself in society."

"She hasn't even met me," Art replied stupidly. Of course, perhaps that was the problem. All she was hearing about him was a clearly biased account from his father.

He was disappointed to learn that James hadn't felt the need to defend him.

"Just this very week, we had visitors come to the house, concerned about your whereabouts and your involvement in illegal activities."

Art straightened in his chair. "What people?"

"So, I am here to make you an offer."

"An offer?"

"You relinquish ties to the family name. Choose another name. I don't much care what. And I will pay you a one-time fee that will set you up, ideally some place *outside* of Märchen."

"You're banishing me?" Art said, feeling suddenly light-headed.

"It will be a very good deal. I can have my solicitor draw up the documents this afternoon."

"I'm sure you can." Art leaned in. "So let me get this straight. All your efforts to get me here, having me kicked out of my home, were just so you could get me out of your hair once and for all?"

The elder Lord Templeton raised his eyes to the ceiling as though asking the godmothers for strength.

"What are you carrying on about? Nobody kicked you out of your home. You left of your own accord, swearing never to return, if I recall correctly. You were welcome to come home at any time, so long as you behaved like a Templeton."

Art gritted his teeth. "I didn't mean this house. I meant—"

"Here we go again. You were always so argumentative. Just like your mother."

Art rose to his feet. "Mother wasn't argumentative. She was just tired of not being listened to," Art said, raising his voice.

Utterly unfazed by Art's outburst, his father said, "I don't believe there's a single quality you inherited from me."

"Well, thank the godmothers for that!" Art replied, glaring down at his father. "I may not represent the Templeton name the way you would like, but it is part of *my* identity. You don't get to take that away from me."

Breathing hard, Art realised there really was nothing more to be said. His father was still the same arrogant, condescending arschloch he had always been.

Glancing down at the plate of biscuits, he grabbed a handful and stuffed them in his pocket. When Philippe made to escort him out, he said, "Thank you, but I'll see myself out!"

CALLISTA WIPED the sweat from her brow and re-tied her ponytail, still panting from her exertion. She had spent the morning sparring with Elsa, the weapons master, and she felt happy for having done so. Her body was the good kind of tired, and she knew her muscles would be sore tonight. Maybe it would be enough to get a good night's sleep, which was rare for her these days, ever since Lutz Kaiser showed up on her doorstep.

The real answer to her sleep problems was simple. Find Eloise and thus get Kaiser out of her hair. But tracking down Samara was proving tricky. It turned out the Hisada had friends in Hollowhorn who were not ready to give her up.

"Good workout, Matron," Elsa called back over her shoulder as she left the training room. Callista waved to her. She was still busy gathering up her belongings when the door to the training room opened again and Lissa stepped through.

"Matron," she murmured. "A word?"

Callista frowned. "Lissa, what are you doing here? You're supposed to be monitoring Kaiser."

The young assassin bit her lip. "That's what I wanted to talk to you about. I followed him this morning to Old Town."

"Okay." Callista bade her continue.

"He was meeting with Franz Hoffner."

Callista drew in a sharp breath. Why would Kaiser be meeting the head of the City Watch? Despite his position, Hoffner was as crooked as they came. Both Humphreys and Tormod Lyons paid him to turn a blind eye to their illegal activities. Frankly, she was surprised nobody had ever hired the House to take him out.

A furrow grew between her brows. "Lissa, where did Kaiser meet Hoffner? At City Watch headquarters?"

She shook her head. "At a tavern."

Callista's stomach plummeted. If Lutz Kaiser wanted to formally bring in the City Watch to search for Eloise, he would have gone to City Watch headquarters. A clandestine meeting at a tavern meant only one thing: he was bringing in crooked City Watch to ferret out Samara and her crew.

She took a moment to collect herself, then put a hand on the younger assassin's shoulder.

"Where is Kaiser right now?"

"In the office you gave him, writing letters."

"You did well letting me know. But you best get back to watching him. I want to know who else he meets with."

Lissa bowed her head and left without another word.

Callista let out a long exhalation. So, Lutz Kaiser had grown tired of waiting for her to find Samara. It's not like she was protecting Sam. Her girls had been hunting for Sam's crew for weeks, but ever since that one encounter Lissa had with Samara, the trail had gone cold. The explosives expert, Seb, was still indentured at the Royal Zephyr apparently, but there had been no sign of Sam there. Word on the street was that Tormod Lyons had fled Märchen and his number two was in charge, but she didn't know what that meant for the Hisada's status.

What could the City Watch do that her own girls couldn't? That was the question that concerned her the most. It was well known that the City Watch was riddled with corruption. But how would it benefit Kaiser?

She rubbed her forehead and shook her head. Of course. He was going after friends and family. Anybody they could threaten to lock up in order to draw Sam out. Samara didn't have any family nearby, and her only friends, as far as Callista knew, were her crew. But her crew had family.

The thought of going after family made Callista's skin crawl. She hated thugs like Hoffner, who used their position to threaten other people. As Matron, she would never allow one of her girls to ferret out a target by going after family members. That was not how she ran the House. Not even her mother, the previous Matron, would have done something so despicable.

She considered warning Samara. But, as usual, besides sending a message to the Lions, she had no way of reaching her former sister. And Samara was so verdammt distrustful she probably wouldn't believe her, anyway. Which meant she needed to talk to Kaiser. A man she had been doing her very best to avoid. As she strode off to seek him out, she reminded herself that this was not for Samara. She was doing this because Hoffner was bad news.

Breathless, she stormed into his office without knocking. "You can't use Hoffner," she said, without thinking.

"You've been having me followed," remarked Kaiser mildly, raising his head from his letter-writing.

"For your own protection," Callista replied, the lie easily slipping from her lips. Quickly gathering her thoughts, she continued, "You're not from here. You don't know Märchen. The City Watch are not to be trusted."

Lutz Kaiser finally put down his pen, swivelling in his seat to face her, a hint of a smile on his lips. "And you are?"

Before Callista could reply, he rose to his feet and strode to face her.

"Miss Meier, I have spent several weeks now waiting for your people to either find Eloise Adelman or bring to me the one they call the Hisada. You have done neither. Which is, frankly, disappointing. I cannot simply sit here in Märchen for weeks on end. Neither money nor the threat of outlawing your assassin's guild has proven to be enough motivation for you. Thanks to your incompetence, the princess could be halfway to Alkebu. So, I ask you what choice I have?"

Callista smarted at the accusation of incompetence but ignored it. Instead, she took a deep breath and once more gathered her thoughts. She knew she couldn't appeal to Kaiser's sense of decency. He was too much of a royalist fanatic to care who got hurt so long as he got back his lost princess. So, she tried a different tack.

"The man who stole Eloise away, Chetwin Humphreys, is the prime importer of Nepenthe into Märchen. And that is all down to Franz Hoffner. That is the kind of man you're dealing with."

Kaiser might talk a good talk, but he was no criminal—aside from wanting to overthrow the Richildan government so he could install Eloise. He didn't know the underworld like she did.

In response, Lutz smiled at her. "I understand what you're saying, Miss Meier."

Callista's jaw twitched at his repeated lack of acknowledgement of her title.

"But it really is too late. Events are already in motion," he continued. "Might I make a suggestion? If you'd rather I keep Hoffner out of things, then perhaps you should use all the tools at your disposal to discover Eloise Adelman's whereabouts instead."

He held her gaze, but she refused to be the first to look away. Then Lutz simply turned back to his writing table and took a seat—a dismissal.

Both stunned and furious with this treatment in her own House, she stormed out of the room, letting the door slam shut behind her. Leaning against the door, she rubbed her temples and took a deep breath to calm herself, while envisioning all the painful methods she wished she could employ to murder Kaiser.

CHAPTER SEVEN

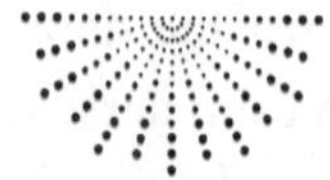

The basic difference between Big Magic and so-called small magic is, put simply, the creation of something from nothing.

— BASIC PHYSIMANCY

Samara danced out of her attacker's way as he threw a punch at her. She caught his arm, spinning and twisting it behind his back. But he just. Would. Not. Stay. Down. The man jabbed an elbow into her gut and she staggered back, coughing. To her left she spied Gerde still holding her own against his companion. *Schiesse.* She needed to put this one down quickly and go help her.

In her momentary distraction, she caught a glancing blow to her side. She responded by rushing her target, dragging him down with her. Soon she was on his back with an arm wrapped about his throat. She pressed against his throat as she had been taught at the House.

The House taught many non-lethal techniques to take out pesky guards, since they could legally only kill those named in their contracts. Samara felt it was all semantics. Contract or no, murder was murder. But she would gladly use a sleeping death hold in this instance. He dropped to the ground, unconscious.

She fished into her frock coat, digging around in one of her hidden pockets. She was glad to have it now. Since they knew they were walking into an ambush, she'd forgone a disguise in favour of wearing her most useful item of clothing. Eventually her fingers grasped what she was looking for: a bottle of trichloromethane. She fished out a rag and opened the bottle.

"Gerde!" she shouted.

Gerde looked up from her own fight, nodded her head, and in a beautiful piece of performance that even Art would be impressed by, she delivered a feint which the man fell for, pretending to fall to the ground before flipping him over so she had him pinned.

Samara raced down the wide road to the man Gerde had pinned and shoved the rag in his face. After a few seconds of struggling, he was out. Gerde staggered to her feet and dusted herself off. She glanced at the rag Samara was stuffing into her pocket.

"Tricholoromethane?" she asked.

Samara nodded, too winded to speak. She knelt over the sleeping form and checked his pockets until she found what she was looking for. A badge denoting the man a sworn member of Märchen's constabulary.

"So, they really *were* City Watch!" exclaimed Gerde.

Samara stood back up, her jaw tight. Although Chetwin Humphreys regularly paid off the City Watch to turn a blind eye, he would never employ them for this. He had his own men.

"Something doesn't add up," Samara murmured, looking ahead on the road to the Kreuzang Coaching House.

Gerde gazed at Samara, her expression grave. "Well, we knew this was going to be a trap."

Samara had finally gone to see Lukas the day before, after they'd received the letter from Gerde's mother. But he had been unavailable. He was still unavailable when she had returned later that afternoon. She didn't know what the Lions could even do for them, but it was the only plan she had.

Then, Gerde received an urgent message from her mother while she was working at the Aurora last night. The man had come back, this time accompanied by officials. They shut the place down, claiming horses from the inn had been used to commit a crime. Which was true. They had used horses for both their initial break-in to Humphreys' home and for the auction job. Gerde's family was accused of aiding and abetting the escape of criminals.

Humphreys hadn't reported the initial break -in. And it was doubtful he would've reported the auction job, making this the most obvious of traps.

They had debated whether it was the Order who had brought in the City Watch as they walked the final distance to the coaching inn. But why go after them? It was the Lions who robbed the auction.

As they approached, Samara couldn't help noticing how oddly quiet the coaching inn looked. No sign of the usual hubbub one would expect first thing in the morning at this type of establishment. Samara scouted around, checking the attached stables and anywhere else the City Watch could be lying in wait. Nothing. Either the City Watch were waiting for them inside the inn, or they had already dealt with the trap.

There was only one way to find out.

Gerde strode to the door and tried it. It was locked. She rapped on the door while Samara hid nearby, just in case. A few moments later, they spotted a face peeking through the curtains. It was Gerde's mother, who opened the door and beckoned them in. Samara drew in a nervous breath and followed Gerde inside. While mother and daughter hugged, she carefully went about checking the other rooms for any surprises. Not that she thought Gerde's family would purposefully lead them into a trap, but old habits die hard.

In the backroom, she discovered a tall, broad-shouldered, blonde-haired man. She reached for one of her khanjar blades but paused when he stood up, struggling to his feet due to what could only be an old injury.

She released a tense breath. "You must be Ahren."

"You must be the Hisada," was his stony reply.

"Is anyone else here?"

"No. They ran off the guests yesterday and my father is still away on business."

"So, it's just you and your mother?" She studied his face for any sign of deception, but there was none. The only thing she spotted was naked dislike. It wasn't the impression she wanted to make on Gerde's family, but it certainly wouldn't be the first time someone disliked her.

She allowed Ahren to lead the way back into the main tavern where Gerde's mother was pulling up pints for them. She started to pass one to Samara, but Gerde placed a hand on her mother's arm.

"Sam doesn't drink, Mutti."

Gerde's mother passed the drink to Ahren instead.

"Can I get you something else?" she asked, but Samara shook her head.

"So, you're the infamous Samara," Gerde's mother said, as she sat on a stool at the bar.

Samara inhaled sharply. She hadn't realised Gerde had told her mother her name. Most people in Märchen knew her only as the Hisada.

Although Samara had seen her in passing, she had never been properly introduced to Gerde's mutter. Glancing about at the people in the room, it was easy to see the resemblance. They were all tall and muscular. They shared the same nose, and all had the same dirty blonde hair. Gerde's mutter wore hers in two braids that reached just below her shoulders.

Samara took a deep breath to calm her nerves. She knew she should have been worried about the City Watch, but she couldn't help wanting to make a good impression on Gerde's family.

"I'm sorry to be meeting you in such dire circumstances," Samara said. "I never meant for your daughter to be wrapped up in all this."

"You mean robbery and being hunted by gangs?" Ahren retorted.

"Ahren, be nice. You know they were trying to save a girl!" Gerde's mother admonished. "You can call me Christa." She gave Samara a warm smile and reached out a hand for her to shake. Samara took her hand, noting the firm grip.

"Mutti, can you tell us exactly what happened?" Gerde asked, taking a sip of her own ale.

"They came yesterday evening during the dinnertime rush," Christa began. "It was mortifying. They forced everyone out and searched the place, including the guest rooms."

"Tore the place down looking for evidence you were staying here," Ahren added.

Samara could see Gerde's hands grip the edge of the bar, her knuckles white. She tentatively placed a hand on top of Gerde's.

Samara gnawed on the inside of her lip. Why would they search the place? They'd already been round to question Gerde's mother. Even if her crew had been staying there, they'd never stick around after that.

"They didn't have to do that, you know," Ahren continued. "What they did, it wasn't protocol."

"Did you know them?" Gerde asked her brother.

That's right, Samara realised, *Ahren worked for the City Watch before he injured his leg.*

"No. I think they purposely sent people I wouldn't know." His eyes hardened. "They weren't looking for you. They were just trying to send a message."

"Message received," Gerde murmured, looking pale.

"And then what happened?" Samara pressed on.

"They cleared everybody out. Sent everyone home. I even had to send the staff away," replied Christa. As she spoke she busied herself wiping the bar top. An unnecessary task.

"We had to give refunds to people who had already paid to stay the night," Ahren added, with another glare in Samara's direction.

Gerde noticed the glare and turned to her brother. "Don't blame Sam. It was my choice to join her crew."

"Crew!" Ahren exclaimed. "Since when are you a criminal?"

"Enough!" said Christa, raising her voice and holding out a hand. "What's done is done."

She walked to the till and pulled out a paper, sliding it across to Gerde and Samara. "They served us this notice."

Samara skimmed it. Apparently, they were shutting down the Kreuzang Coaching House for the time being.

"This isn't remotely proper procedure," Ahren spat. "They confiscated the horses, for godmothers' sake."

"The horses?" Gerde jerked back in surprise.

"They wanted you to message us, so they could ambush us," Samara murmured.

"Ambush you?" Christa's face had gone ashen.

"It was just a couple of them. We took care of it," Gerde assured her mother. "Knocked them out," she added for her brother's benefit.

"They were probably just meant to watch the place. Send word when we arrived," Samara surmised.

Gerde and Samara shared a wary glance. "Which means more could be on the way."

"We need to leave." Samara glanced up at the ceiling. "Is there a loft? A way up to the roof from here?"

To his credit, Ahren immediately got to his feet. "I can show you."

Samara turned to Gerde. "Stay here. I'm just going to do a quick scout."

She followed Gerde's older brother up the stairs, his long legs taking the steps two at a time, even with his limp. He seemed like he could manage well in most everyday activities, yet he'd been sidelined by the City Watch, which told her his injury wasn't the only reason for this.

"The loft is just that way," he said, pointing to another rickety wooden staircase leading up to a scuttle hole in the ceiling.

"One thing my mother forgot to mention."

"Oh?"

"There was a man accompanying the City Watch. Wore fine clothes. Walked with a cane."

"Was the pommel shaped like a bear head?" she asked, thinking of Chetwin Humphreys. But even as she asked the question, she dismissed the idea. Ahren used to work for the City Watch. He would know what Humphreys looked like.

"No. It wasn't Humphreys. This man was from Richilde."

Samara sagged. If the man was Richildan, then he definitely wasn't one of Humphreys' people. Maybe the Order was finally here to hunt them down. Though she still couldn't figure out why it was so important to hunt for her crew when it was Tormod who so brazenly robbed the auction. She groaned. Much as she was loathe to return to the Lions' headquarters again, she really needed to have a conversation with Lukas.

She made her way up the rickety steps and pushed open the

hatch that led to the small attic. It was dim. The only light came from a small rooftop window, but the space was otherwise clean. There was even a small bed and wardrobe in the corner. She imagined it was used for guests only when the rest of the inn was full. She opened the window and peeked her head out. It was chilly, and the sky was grey as she heaved herself out through the window and climbed slowly along the edge of the slate roof.

Below her stood the courtyard where carriages would arrive and guests could alight for the night. Staying low, so she wasn't an obvious target, she crawled across the rooftops to get a view of the road. When she was sure there was no sign of City Watch approaching, she squeezed back through the window and climbed down the ladder.

"Looks like the way's clear," she announced when she returned to the common area.

Gerde, who had been quietly murmuring to her mother, physically sagged with relief.

"I should never have sent that letter," her mother whispered.

"You did the right thing. We needed to know what was happening," Gerde assured her.

"We will fix this," Samara promised.

"How?" Ahren asked with a raised eyebrow.

Samara clenched her jaw. "I don't know exactly, but we will."

She glanced at Gerde, who was giving her mother a hug.

"I'll send word as soon as I can," Gerde promised as the pair hurried out of the coaching inn.

THEY TOOK A MEANDERING path back into Märchen, avoiding any open stretches of road and sticking to brush. What started as mild nausea had developed into a tightness in Samara's chest as they made their way back into town. She was quiet as they returned, and she could sense Gerde's unease.

Was Gerde upset at her? She had every right to be. Samara had been the one to drag them into this mess, after all. All for her own vengeance. She had been so caught up in trying to bring Chetwin Humphreys down, she'd deluded herself into thinking the only thing she needed to do was steal the girl to destroy Chetwin.

She should've realised one thing: Chetwin Humphreys always comes out on top. It was a fact. Callista had stopped buying girls from him and did it hurt his human trafficking business? No. They and the Lions robbed his auction and now the Order were after *them* instead of punishing Humphreys for his incompetence.

She had already lost two members of her crew. And now she was probably going to lose Gerde as well.

When they eventually got back to The Wishing-Table, it was late afternoon. Samara wondered if Hans had made anything for lunch. He was another person she had let down. Because of her, he'd had to abandon his beloved print shop and they no longer had a home.

She was almost shaking by the time they climbed up to their room. When they reached the top of the stairs, Gerde touched her on the arm.

"Are you okay?" she asked. Samara noticed a furrow between her brows, which only seemed to enhance her green eyes.

Something softened in Samara. She found herself wanting to brush a finger across Gerde's brows to wipe that furrow away. "I will be," she promised. She would make this right. Somehow.

As she pushed open the door, the first thing Samara noticed was the brown frock coat tossed casually across a chair. It didn't belong to Hans; she knew that much. They had a visitor.

She placed a protective hand on Gerde's arm and indicated with her eyes towards the strange coat.

Gerde stiffened, her body already getting low, preparing for a fight. Samara pulled out a slim blade and peered around the doorway. She sucked in a breath at the sight of the lanky blonde-haired fellow seated next to Hans at the small table. Art looked up at her, his eyes widening, but otherwise his expression was unreadable. Then again, she never could get a good read on her friends. Targets, enemies, those she could predict.

What did it say about her that she could never tell what her friends were thinking?

Gerde, however, visibly relaxed beside her. The next thing she noticed was the smell of saffron chai permeating the room. Hans gave her a welcoming smile and bade her join them.

"Look who came to visit!" Hans said, as he hurried to find more seating for the cramped space.

In three quick strides, Gerde crossed the room and enveloped Art in a hug.

"It's good to see you." She grinned.

Samara shucked off her frock coat and hung it on the back of a chair. When Gerde and Art pulled apart, everyone seemed to turn to Samara expectantly.

"What are you doing here?" she asked cautiously, her breath tight in her chest.

A look. Disappointment? Crossed Art's face.

"I came to see you," he replied, his voice small and not at all like the confident, charming man she knew.

Samara didn't need more of this today. She didn't need to be reminded yet again of how she had let her friends down. Clearly, that's why Art was here. He looked terrible. As though he were sleeping poorly. And though his shabby dress could easily be put down to a disguise, there was something genuine about his dishevelled appearance that told her things were not going well for him. Samara had never backed down from a fight before. And yet she felt the urge to run away.

A discreet clearing of the throat came from Hans, who signalled with his eyes towards Art. Gerde too was gesturing for her to do something.

Maybe, just maybe, Art wasn't here to rip her a new one.

Samara swallowed nervously. "It's good to see you," she said, taking a step closer.

Art broke into a wide grin and closed the distance between them, drawing her into a tight hug. The tension in her shoulders melted and the knot in her stomach loosened. Samara blinked away tears. The Hisada didn't cry. Thankfully, only Hans and Gerde could see her face right now, and she knew they wouldn't spill her secrets.

It was only when Art pulled away that she really noticed the mild unwashed stench emanating from him. What had happened to him these past few weeks?

"You could use a bath, Art," she said with a smirk, hoping her tears weren't still showing. She refused to wipe her eyes.

Art sighed. "You don't know the half of it."

HANS BREWED MORE of his precious saffron chai, and for once, Art welcomed the sweet, comforting warmth. Why had he been so quick to pooh-pooh this drink? They sat around the table. That is, he, Hans and Gerde sat at the table. Samara leaned against the wall, close by, cradling her own cup. There weren't enough chairs in the shabby rooms they occupied.

He hadn't quite known what he was doing when he made his way to The Wishing-Table. Seb's words had seemed like a beacon to him. While his father had cut him off and insisted he renounce his family ties, he somehow knew that even after everything he had said to Samara the night of the auction, he would be welcomed back. It wasn't as though Samara had made any outward entreaties to him. It was just the deep knowledge that Samara, as well as Gerde, Hans, Seb and maybe even Ana, accepted him just as he was.

He related the encounter he had with his father. How his father had had him kicked out of his apartment, just to force his hand and make him comply with renouncing his name.

He didn't know why exactly he resisted agreeing to his father's request. It cut deeply that his brother had married, and his wife was with child, and he didn't even know about it. In some ways, he would be happy to be done with the Templeton name and all the baggage that came with it. He could take his mother's maiden name and become a Langford.

But no. Verdammt. His father and brother had no right to ask this of him. He may not like being a Templeton, but it was his family name, and that meant more to him than a few coin. And besides, even if he gave up the family name, he wasn't about to leave his hometown just to appease that man.

Gerde was looking at him with a furrow between her brows. She started to speak and then stopped.

"What?" Art asked cautiously.

"How certain are you it was your father that had you kicked out?" she asked.

He stretched his arms above his head to loosen the knots in his shoulders.

"As sure as I can be. Who else would it have been? That's not exactly Chetwin Humphreys' style, is it?"

"Not Humphreys' no," Samara said thoughtfully. She and Gerde exchanged a worried glance.

Gerde got up and stepped away.

"What are you saying?" Art asked.

Gerde returned and dropped a note on the table in front of him. He glanced at it.

Gerderl,

City officials came here looking for you. They've forced us to shut down the coaching inn. We're all right for the time being, but it's not safe here.

Be safe.

Your Mutti

Art dropped the letter on the table and chewed his lower lip.

Art's brows knitted together. "Somebody went after your family?"

Gerde grunted in the affirmative.

"Humphreys has the City Watch in his pocket," Art remarked. "But he knew where I lived. I saw his thugs hanging about…"

Surely it was his father behind it. It had to be. He'd made it clear he wanted Art to leave Märchen.

Hans was looking at Samara. "Who do *you* think is behind it? Not Callista, surely?"

"No." Samara's response was emphatic. Art wasn't so sure. Even now, Samara seemed to have a blind spot when it came to her former sister-at-arms. "Gerde's brother said a Richildan man came to see them when they shut down the coaching inn. Which makes me suspect it was the Order."

Art blinked. It was a possibility he hadn't even considered. He'd been so convinced it was his father who'd had him kicked out. But hadn't his father said he didn't know what he was talking about? He gave a low whistle. "You think the Order came all the way to Märchen to punish little old us?"

Samara pushed off the wall and set her cup down. She folded

her arms. "You know that world better than any of us, Art. How likely is it?"

Art didn't take long to think about it. All he had to do was consider his own father's actions to know it was certainly possible. "I'd say there's a pretty good likelihood they're behind it. Punish us and anyone connected to us." His mind briefly went to his own family before he shut down that line of thinking. "Just to make sure nobody ever considers crossing them again."

"But we didn't cross them," Gerde insisted. "It was Humphreys' money we stole, not theirs."

"It might not matter to them," Samara muttered. She looked over at Art. "You're welcome to stay here. But, I'll be honest, if it is the Order after us, you'll be safer at the doss house."

Art practically shivered at the thought of returning to that place. "I'm not so sure about that. If what you say is true, they're already after me."

"I'll make this right," Samara vowed, looking around the table.

For the first time, he could see the tension on her face. He sighed. "Listen. I'm sorry about my part in what happened after you let the girl go. I was, perhaps, a little too strong with my words. You did the right thing. It still would've been better if you'd told us what you were going to do. But letting her make her own decisions was the right thing."

Samara stiffened, and then seemed to let out a little sigh of relief.

"If you're ready to get everyone back together to go toe-to-toe with this Order, I'm all in. Those arschlochs had me kicked out of my home."

Samara smirked. "All in? Really?"

He chuckled. "Really. So, what's your plan?"

"We're not the only ones Humphreys has been harassing. And my guess is, if the Order is going after us, they're definitely going after the Lions as well. I need to talk to Lukas. Find out just what he knows."

~

THAT AFTERNOON, Samara made her way past the gossamer-clad faeries who knew better than to court the Hisada's attention. Realising Art was no longer by her side, she turned to see him accept a drink ticket from one faery. He gave her an unrepentant grin.

"You go on to your meeting. I'll find some way to occupy myself."

Shaking her head, she made her way deeper into the Royal Zephyr. Art had only come along so she could help him move his things to The Wishing-Table. Gerde had initially volunteered to help, but his place wasn't very far from the Zephyr. Moreover, Samara didn't want Art and Gerde out on the streets by themselves. Not until she knew what they were dealing with.

As she made her way past the casino floor and deeper into the bowels of the Zephyr, the noise of the casino faded to a murmur, and she spotted more faces she recognised. Some of the Lions merely stared at her as she passed them. Others, who knew the Hisada from jobs, nodded to her. What struck her though was the tension in the air. All the Lions were openly armed, which was unusual. Sure, everybody had their favoured weapons, but most kept them concealed unless they were gearing up for a job. There were also considerably more Lions milling around than usual. If she had to guess, they were under strict orders to stick to the Zephyr unless they were on a job.

She wondered who had been promoted to Lukas' number two. All these thoughts came to a halt when she was stopped as she tried to turn down the corridor that led to Tormod's old office, where she figured she could find Lukas.

"I can't let you down there, Hisada," said a Lion with red hair whose name she couldn't recall.

"I'm here to see Lukas."

"I gathered that, but I still can't let you down there."

She scowled but agreed to wait while he sent a runner to message Lukas. A few minutes later, Lukas strode down the corridor. His clothes were rumpled. He looked harried. Tense.

"It's good to see you, Hisada. We can talk in the manager's office."

He kept on walking, leaving Samara to catch up as he led her back towards the casino floor.

"I'd have thought you'd be all moved into Tormod's office by now," she remarked as they walked through the maze-like corridors of the Zephyr.

He grimaced. "Been a bit busy," was all he said.

"Too busy to see me," Samara remarked. "I came by twice yesterday."

"I've been dealing with… a lot," Lukas said with a grimace.

Which was probably true given both Humphreys, and the Order were after them, but it felt like there was something she was missing. When they reached the casino manager's door, Lukas knocked once and strode inside. Devan, the casino manager, had been hunched over his desk. He startled when he saw Lukas enter and jumped to his feet. His eyes widened when he registered the Hisada's presence before quickly exiting.

Samara took in the small office. Every inch of the desk was covered in paperwork, which Lukas carefully moved aside before seating himself. Samara remained standing.

"He looks like he could use a holiday," she remarked by way of conversation.

"Believe me, we could all use a holiday," Lukas muttered, leaning forward and resting his elbows on the hard surface. "Truth is, I'm up to my neck in paperwork."

"Being the boss not all it's cracked up to be?" she asked with a wicked grin. She just couldn't help herself.

Lukas glared at her.

"I hear you've been having some trouble," she continued.

Lukas ran a hand through his shaggy hair. "Yeah. It seems Chetwin Humphreys doesn't take being robbed very well."

"Well, none of us do, really." Samara smirked.

Lukas gave her an annoyed look.

"I warned Tormod he was bringing a whole lot of trouble down on the Lions." She stopped. Considered, and then continued, "in fact, I distinctly recall you were there and all. Remember? It was right after you had me kidnapped and held in the cellar."

Lukas leaned back in his chair. "Now you know that wasn't my idea."

"Yeah, but you still went along with it."

Lukas spread his hands out wide. "I'm sorry."

Samara's lips twitched. He did seem genuinely sorry. Not that she was exactly in the forgiving mood. It turned out, when you were stolen as a child and sold as a slave, you kinda hold a grudge when people you considered, friends wasn't the right word, *colleagues*, went and kidnapped you. But she was here for information, so the least she could do was hear him out.

"What's been happening?" she asked, finally taking a seat at the desk.

Lukas's expression turned sombre. "Humphreys is looking at starting a turf war."

"Understandable, considering Tormod broke the peace. What do you need me for?"

"It's hairy out there, Hisada. His men are jumping any Lion they find outside. He's on the warpath."

"He wants the money you stole back."

"He wants Tormod," Lukas corrected her.

"So, give him Tormod," she said with a shrug.

Lukas shook his head. "I'm not going to do that, Hisada. Come on. He may be an arschloch sometimes, but he was my mentor. Besides, I don't know where he is."

"He said he might buy an island. Any islands go up for sale recently?" she asked. It was possible she was still holding a grudge after the whole kidnapping thing.

Lukas ignored her comment. "It's gotten to where the Magistrate wants to institute a curfew."

"Yeah. Seb said as much." She leaned forward so her own elbows rested on the desk. "You ought to watch out for her. She's looking for any excuse to bring down the Lions and Humphreys' organisation. She only allows you to operate while everyone is keeping the peace, but if this turns into all-out war, it makes Märchen unsafe and makes her look bad."

Although given the sheer number of corrupt men in the City Watch, Samara wasn't certain just who the Magistrate would use to enforce the law.

Having said her piece, she glanced down at the stacks of papers on the desk. She picked up one of the papers. It was an overdue notice. She raised her eyebrows at Lukas, who let out a heavy sigh.

"Yeah. That's the other issue. It seems Humphreys isn't satisfied with going after the Lions—"

"He's going after Tormod's properties?"

"Yep. Suddenly, shipments that were supposed to come through from our regular vendors are delayed. Payments that aren't yet due are now overdue."

"Well, that's just vindictive," Samara replied, although she was beginning to doubt that Humphreys was behind it. "Let me ask you something. Are you sure it's Humphreys that's going after the business?"

Lukas narrowed his eyes. "Why? What do you know?"

"I warned Tormod about making enemies of the Order."

"The Order of Grimm?"

"Yeah. That one. From what I can tell, they've been coming after me and mine in a big way. In a *legal* way."

Lukas leaned back in his chair and ran his hands down his face. "Verdammt! Humphreys we can just about handle, but some mysterious Richildan organisation with deep pockets and a huge grudge…"

He looked up at her, his eyes full of hope. "There's still a place for you here, Hisada. We could really use you."

Samara shook her head and pinched the bridge of her nose. "What could I possibly do?"

Lukas leaned in. "The Lions is a thieves guild. We know Märchen. We know who to rob and who to bribe, but we don't know nothing about the rest of Alsatia, much less about dealing with members of the aristocracy. You came from House de Mörde, you've dealt with outsiders. Probably rich outsiders, I'm guessing."

That wasn't exactly true. Although she had, occasionally, left Märchen for jobs, it was Ursula, not her, who handled the clients. Still, she understood why Lukas would look to her for help with the Order.

"Yeah. I'm not really interested in re-joining the Lions," Samara replied, and verdammt if she didn't feel empowered by saying that.

"Freelance then."

She scowled at him. She had technically been freelance before and had still been subject to the whims of Tormod. Which wound up with her getting kidnapped by the Lions. Samara wasn't going back to that again.

"*Properly freelance.* Just this one job. You don't work for us. We just … exchange information," Lukas amended.

She considered the offer. It wasn't like they didn't need the money. Though she had money stashed about town, it was difficult to get to when Callista, Humphreys and now the Order were breathing down her neck.

"An exchange of information. That's all you get from me. And it'll cost you."

They came to an agreement, after which she made her way back to the casino floor and spotted Art at the Spindle, Apple, Slipper table where Seb was dealing cards.

She nodded to Seb during a break in the round. "They treating you all right?

"Yeah," Seb replied, rubbing the back of his neck. "I mean. It's not a whole lot different than when I was indentured. But at least I get to keep my tips."

"How'd it go?" Art asked, taking a swig from a frothy concoction.

"Looks like we have a common enemy," was all she said.

SEB WAS EXHAUSTED when he finally got off his shift. Despite his tiredness, he still considered visiting Ana. But it was getting late. The shop would be closed, and he doubted the owner would welcome his after-hours visit.

It was nice seeing Art and Samara together again. The Hisada still scared him, but she seemed more relaxed now that she had patched things up with Art. Art, too, looked a lot happier. He seemed more well-rested than the last time he saw his friend. During a lull at the table, Art had filled him in on what happened with his father, which Seb had no words for. But the upshot was that Art and Samara were friends again. Apparently, Samara was going to help him bring his things from the boarding house back to The Wishing-Table.

Seb was grateful to stay at the Zephyr, but he found he was

itching to do another job. If the Order was after them, which Art suggested was the case, Seb preferred the idea of going on the offensive instead of trying to lie low and hope it all went away. He just hoped the Hisada would hurry up and bring him and Ana back into the fold sooner rather than later. Assuming Ana wanted to come back to the crew. He preferred not to dwell on that.

Deciding that he wanted to be ready to help when the time came, Seb decided to go down to the lower levels of the Zephyr to experiment with explosives.

He made his way down to where the armoury was located. There were guards everywhere, but nobody bothered him. Though he wasn't technically part of the Lions anymore, Lukas had already given Seb access to the catacombs.

Seb made his way down the stone steps to where the more volatile weapons were kept. It was chilly down there but also blissfully quiet after the cacophony of the casino floor. Seb had been tinkering with the magic balls, trying to figure out if he could use them to release smoke for concealment, but without the explosive component. He also needed to figure out a name for them. Some of the Lions had nicknamed them Seb's Magic Balls, which, while funny, was completely inaccurate. Black powder balls, perhaps? Black powder spheres?

Lost in thought, he hardly noticed his surroundings as he made his way directly to where the black powder was kept.

"What are you doing down here?" asked a panicked voice.

Seb stopped mid-stride and stumbled, almost sending a box of nitro skittering. He turned to face the speaker. He knew that voice. And it wasn't one he thought he'd ever hear again.

Seeking the speaker, he finally spotted him in a corner of the cavernous room, under a pile of blankets. The man studied Seb and cautiously rose from the blankets to reveal himself. In the dim light, Seb saw a man in rumpled pinstripe trousers. A leather jacket lay discarded on the ground next to a bottle of wine and a pile of playing cards.

The man himself was none other than Tormod Lyons, the former leader of the Lions.

"Wha— what are you still doing here?" Seb stammered, his heart racing.

Who else knew that Tormod Lyons was down here? Did Lukas know?

The two stared at each other warily.

"I could ask the same of you," said Tormod, rising to his feet. "Eze, right?"

"Yeah," Seb replied, surprised Tormod even knew his name. "I just came down here to experiment with some explosives."

"Not stealing some for another job for the Hisada, I hope," said Tormod, though he didn't seem nearly so menacing hiding in a cot in the bowels of the Zephyr.

"No. No job." Seb paused, then tried again. "We thought you left Märchen. Humphreys has been after you."

"Tell me about it," Tormod replied, taking a swig from his wine bottle. "The plan was to cash the banker's notes the next morning and leave the city. But Chetwin Humphreys was already ahead of me. The banks refused to cash the bank notes, the arschlochs, and Humphreys' people were crawling all over the port."

"So, you've been here the entire time?"

"Unfortunately." Tormod grimaced, removing his neck scarf and flinging it on the ground. "And don't you tell no one. You got me? Nobody except Lukas and a few other Lions know I'm still here. I'm only hanging about long enough for things to die down and then I'll make those bankers pay up."

Seb doubted things would die down but didn't argue with him. "But why are you hiding from the Lions?"

"Chetwin Humphreys will do anything to get to me. Pay

anything. It's not that I don't trust my own people, but it don't take much to make a man squeal." He took a step towards Seb, his gaze locking onto Seb's own. "Except you. You won't squeal, will you, Eze?"

"N-no. Who would I even talk to? I spend all my time here."

"Yeah, about that," Tormod began, taking another swig of wine. "What you still doing here? Didn't I release you from your contract?"

"Things have been a little hot for us too."

Tormod grimaced. "I'm sure. Chetwin Humphreys isn't the forgiving type."

Seb didn't know what to say to that, and so they lapsed into an awkward silence. It was weird. Tormod Lyons had terrified Seb for so long. The man had once controlled his life. And now, looking at where he was hiding out, it just seemed rather pathetic.

"I should probably just get those ingredients now."

"Yeah, you do that," said Tormod. He sat down and picked up his cards again. "Oh, and Eze?"

Seb turned back to face his old boss.

"Don't mention this to the Hisada. I really don't want her coming back here to gloat."

"I won't tell her," Seb promised.

And he wouldn't. Seb wasn't stupid. He knew better than to cross the former Lions leader, no matter how weakened he might appear right now. And especially not when they still might need the Lions' help to get out of their current mess.

CHAPTER EIGHT

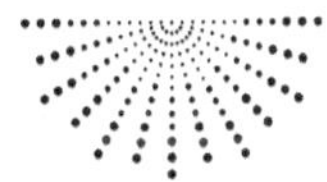

Chetwin Humphreys had summoned him. Vogel wasn't sure why, but, as usual lately, he could only hope that it meant Humphreys was ready to return his focus to business interests and let all this Order and auction business go.

Vogel knocked sharply on the door and waited respectfully for the gravelly voice of his boss, telling him to "enter" before striding into the office. He came to a stop at the large roll-top desk and straightened his waistcoat.

"You wanted to see me, Mr Humphreys."

Humphreys, who had been busy staring out the window, swivelled his leather chair to face Vogel. The man looked like he had lost weight over the past few weeks. His complexion was dull. Even his smile didn't seem to dazzle with the usual white brilliance. Stress did all kinds of things to a human being, Vogel knew. And stress was clearly taking its toll on Humphreys.

As Chetwin Humphreys' number two, it was his responsibility to deal with that stress. Take care of the things that were distracting his boss from his actual business, which he knew, eventually, he could do. If only Humphreys would let him do his thing. For too long, Humphreys had been consumed by the auction. And now, if Vogel didn't act soon, this botched auction would bring down the whole organisation.

"Any word on the Hisada?" Humphreys asked.

"Nothing yet. But I have my men camped out at her usual haunts." Vogel managed to hide his disappointment at his employer's continued obsession with the auction.

Vogel didn't mention that his men had missed a chance at getting the Hisada and two other members of her crew just a few days ago. Humphreys didn't need to know that. What he needed was results.

"And Tormod?" Chetwin shook his head. "I don't understand how the man could just disappear."

"We're sure he's hiding out here in Märchen. Just leave it to me to ferret him out," Vogel promised.

"I know exactly where he's hiding," Humphreys murmured. "The Royal Zephyr."

"Most likely yes, but—"

"I want you to torch the Zephyr."

Vogel blinked back his surprise. "Excuse me, sir?" he said mildly, hoping he had misheard.

"You heard me. If Tormod Lyons wants to use the Zephyr as his little stronghold. Then we need to operate using siege tactics. We'll burn him out. Force him into the open."

Vogel knew his boss wasn't getting enough rest, but he still couldn't help feeling shocked at his words. Tormod and Chetwin had kept a tentative peace for over a decade now. Sure, things had heated up lately. It was spilling out into the streets now that Humphreys was after Tormod for showing up the Order. But this? Burning down the headquarters of the Lions? There would be no coming back from an event like that. Not to mention this could break any tentative arrangements they had with the City Watch. The Royal Zephyr was a popular hotspot. Burning it down, the potential lives lost ... it would do irreparable damage to their organisation and future business dealings. It wouldn't matter how much they paid the City Watch to look the other way, the Watch would have no choice but to go after their organisation.

"Fire is the only way to truly deal with vermin," Chetwin was saying.

Vogel needed to put a stop to this. "There are other ways to lay siege," Vogel said, ignoring the comparison to vermin.

"Oh? Like what?"

Vogel smiled thinly. "Like taking away their resources. Something I've already taken the liberty to do."

Chetwin's eyes lit up, and he leaned back in his chair to let Vogel know he had his attention.

"Let's just say I've been cutting off the Zephyr's suppliers. Making it extremely difficult for Tormod Lyons to keep operating."

To Vogel's surprise, Chetwin shook his head. "And this would bring me Tormod Lyons' head? How exactly?" He slammed a fist on the desk. "That little cockroach won't give up easily."

Shaken, Vogel took a deep breath and then smoothly replied, "No. But word is Tormod Lyons isn't in charge there anymore. It's Lukas Bernhardt. And pretty soon Bernhardt will tire of protecting Lyons."

Vogel could feel Chetwin's eyes boring deeply into him, and he genuinely didn't know what his boss was going to say. His body sagged with relief when Chetwin finally agreed, "All right. We'll do it your way for now. But no more delays!"

ANA MADE her way through Hollowhorn, careful as always. She was brimming with energy that she had pocketed from people, just the way Eloise suggested. They hadn't yet tried out their plan to steal money, but Eloise was convinced it would work. Her Magic wasn't just an illusion; it was a genuine replica. Until it disappeared.

Ana was slowly coming around to Eloise's plan. Her friend had promised that they would only operate in Elphame Park, where the potential marks were rich and could afford to lose some coin. They had even talked about getting a little flat together. Something in Old Town.

Ana didn't know how practical it was for either of them to stay in Märchen given all the people after them, but Eloise reminded her that all the ways in and out of the city-state were monitored. Ana didn't understand why Eloise couldn't just use her powers to disguise them so they could flee. Or they could have Art's contact at the theatre give them disguises. Every time she brought it up, Eloise changed the subject. She got the feeling that since Eloise had been forced to move around so much growing up, the girl was reluctant to leave yet another place she called home.

In truth, Ana was in no hurry to go home herself. Her old life felt far away now. She couldn't return to a life of hiding her powers. And after she had been kidnapped from her village, her mother would surely keep her under lock and key. But she would love to disappear into the city. Or perhaps visit Pentemarone. She adored Hans, Samara's landlord, and the little delights from his home country he had offered them the night of the auction.

With that thought, she decided to visit the little shop that sold Pentemaronian goods. She had a little money from her job at the bakery. And if she was going to be going along with Eloise's plan, money wouldn't be a problem much longer. She could afford to buy a few things to nibble on. She remembered it had been just a few doors down from the print shop.

Ana navigated her way through Hollowhorn to where she remembered the print shop was located, and spotted the little deli with its red, white and green awning. She stopped in front of the shop window, studying the display, when she felt a hand on her shoulder. She reacted instantly, gathering up the fizzing energy inside her and mentally shoving it towards her attacker. Her attacker landed on the ground behind her and made an "oof" sound.

Ana spun, getting ready to tear off in the other direction when she realised it was Gerde, on her back, on the dusty ground.

"I'm so sorry," Ana gasped, bending down and hoping she hadn't called too much attention to themselves.

"It's okay," Gerde panted, rising to her feet and dusting herself off. She eyed Ana with some surprise. "That was something else. I didn't even see you move."

Ana gave her a small smile in response.

"What are you doing in Hollowhorn?"

"I was going to visit Seb at the Zephyr," Ana replied, the lie forming on her lips in an instant.

Gerde's brows furrowed. "I don't think that's a good idea," she said, gently taking Ana by the arm.

Ana felt the familiar urge to resist as Gerde pulled her into an alley away from prying eyes. She had to remind herself that Gerde was her first friend here in Märchen and was only trying to protect her. Not that Ana felt like she needed protecting. The fact Gerde thought she needed to be protected annoyed her further.

"Things are getting heated at the Zephyr. Even the Lions aren't safe to go out alone these days. Humphreys wants to punish everybody involved in the auction."

Ana's mouth went dry. She knew from Helga's complaints that Seb had been to visit her several times over the past week. The thought that he had been risking his life to see her left her shaken. Yes, she had been trying to avoid him. She didn't want to have to lie to him about Eloise's whereabouts. But if something ever happened to him because he had been trying to visit her… She let that thought trail off as she continued to listen to Gerde relate everything that had been happening to the rest of the group. The coaching inn getting shut down. Art being kicked out of his home—well, that she cared less about. Knowing Art, it was just as likely he got kicked out for owing rent.

Still, it didn't sit well knowing this was happening while Eloise was happily here in Märchen, planning to rob people just so they could make themselves a little more comfortable.

Ana's stomach churned. Had she been wrong about keeping Eloise's secret? She decided right then to come clean to Gerde. She didn't know what the others would say, but Gerde would know what to do. Ana opened her mouth to speak but stopped when she heard a ruckus in the streets.

"Hans," Gerde gasped, pushing past Ana and rushing back to the high street.

But it was too late. Hans was being arrested by City Watch. Two men guarded the old man while another plastered a poster to the front door of the print shop.

"I can take care of them," Ana said, already her mind going into the hyper focus she needed to siphon energy. But Gerde placed an arm on her and gestured. A City Watch wagon pulled up and more constabulary poured out.

"There's too many of them," Gerde said, though she couldn't take her eyes off Hans as he was forced into the wagon.

Ana vehemently disagreed with Gerde's assessment, but knew even if she subdued them all, she'd draw a lot of unwanted attention. She wished Eloise was here. She'd be able to help them get away. Instead, Ana allowed Gerde to guide her back into the mouth of the alleyway.

When the City Watch eventually cleared off, they slowly crept out of the alley. Most of the passers-by on the street had moved on, now that the wagon was gone.

Ana saw that Gerde was shaking. Her skin ashen. She looked as though she were going to be sick.

"I shouldn't have left him alone. I was supposed to be keeping an eye on him while he picked up some belongings," she whispered.

Ana wanted to reassure Gerde, but what could she say? What use was false hope? The City Watch were after them, perhaps at Chetwin Humphreys' behest, and now Hans was under arrest.

Her eyes travelled to the little print shop where she first met Hans and the others. She found her gaze drawn to the poster the Watch had put up. Grabbing Gerde by the hand, she made her way to the shop door.

Closed by order of the City Watch due to the printing of banned and malicious materials.

CHAPTER NINE

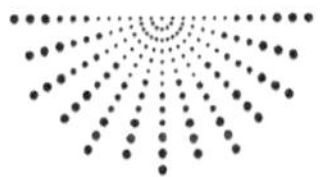

Despite all the House de Mörde has gone through to gain legitimacy, Märchen's assassin's guild exists in a unique grey legal area. The hiring of assassins continues to be illegal in Märchen and the rest of the continent of Alsatia, while the fulfilling of such contracts remain legal. Given the House de Mörde's long history though, it is unlikely the House's legal status shall ever change.

—A HISTORY OF THE MÄRCHEN GUILDS

Samara's face was a mask of fury as she stalked about the room. Gerde sat on the edge of the bed, watching helplessly, as Samara pulled out her roll of weapons and began stuffing blades into pockets. She'd said nothing when Gerde told her what happened. Which was somehow so much worse. Gerde wanted Samara to yell at her. Blame her for not keeping an eye on Hans. It had been her one job: to accompany Hans while he picked up some belongings from the flat.

They shouldn't have done it during the day. They shouldn't

have gone at all. Samara hadn't even known they were going out. She'd been busy talking to her ties in the underworld, trying to uncover information on the Order.

While Samara was out, Hans came up with the idea of bringing some of his forgery tools back to their rooms, figuring they might be useful for trying to get closer to the Order. It seemed like a good plan, despite knowing Samara wouldn't go for it.

Samara had become edgy about any of them leaving the flat. Not that that stopped Art from going out to play cards at the Zephyr. So Gerde decided to take the risk and accompany Hans.

They'd been careful. She was sure of it. She had seen nobody suspicious lying in wait. But then she'd gotten distracted by Ana. She'd left Hans to pack up, knowing she would only be a couple of minutes, but in that time, the City Watch had arrived.

She wondered if one of Hans' neighbours had tipped off the Watch.

After saying goodbye to Ana, Gerde sent a note to her brother to see if he could be of help, though she doubted it. She then went back to the inn to wait for Samara. It was dark outside by the time Samara finally returned. Her expression tightened the moment she walked in the door, as though she already sensed something was wrong. Maybe it was because the air lacked the aroma of chai that usually permeated the room.

"What happened?" Samara had asked in a voice laced with dread.

And now, having explained the situation, Gerde helplessly watched Samara get ready to start a war with the City Watch. She'd tried to stop her twice already. Tried to hold Samara, but the former assassin was having none of it. She was focused on equipping herself for a fight. Gerde wished Sam would get angry with her. Let it out. Punch her, even. The godmothers know she deserved it for letting this happen. But Samara was singularly focused on vengeance.

Gerde lowered her head to her hands and rubbed her face as she watched Samara stalk back and forth, adding items to her belt.

"Sam. Sam! For the last time, listen to me. At least wait and see if Ahren has any suggestions."

"You said yourself he hasn't worked there for years."

"What are you going to do? Mount an assault on City Watch headquarters?"

"If it comes to that," Samara replied tightly, finally stopping, if only for a moment.

Gerde shook her head. "You know that won't work."

"I just need some more of Seb's balls."

"It's a fortress. You'll get yourself killed," her voice hitched at the last word. If anything happened to Sam because of this, she would never forgive herself.

When Samara didn't immediately reply Gerde stood up and took a step towards her.

Samara remained rigid, her jaw clenched. "Then I'll go after Humphreys. Force him to order Hans's release."

Gerde swallowed. "I'm going with you."

Samara glared at her. "No, you're not. You'll slow me down."

"We spar together all the time. You know I can back you up," Gerde insisted.

Samara crossed her arms, looking up at Gerde defiantly. "I'm not letting you put yourself in danger. I won't lose you as well."

"Oh, but it's okay for me to lose you?!" Gerde exclaimed, throwing her arms up in frustration. "You get to have a death wish and I just have to quietly wait here?"

Samara's eyes widened. "I don't have a death wish."

"Don't you? You know it's suicide." Now it was Gerde's turn to stalk around the small bedroom, fuelled by frustration and fear. "This is exactly what they want. They're waiting for you to try something stupid like this."

Samara slammed her palm against the wall, which, although it made Gerde jump, also made her feel better. At least Samara was finally showing her feelings instead of keeping them bottled up. She hated when Sam did that, though given Samara was raised in a house of assassins, she understood why she kept her feelings bottled up.

"Well, what do you expect me to do?"

"I expect you to think things through. Bring me and Art, if it comes to it. Hans wouldn't want you to go racing into trouble all by yourself."

"I can handle myself! I'm a former assassin, for Manāt's sake," Samara retorted.

"Maybe, but I don't want to lose you."

"You're not going to—" Samara began, but stopped. "What are you talking about?"

"You know what I mean. I'm talking about *you*," Gerde replied as she helplessly gazed down at Samara. "Your vow."

Samara blew a strand of hair out of her face. "You're holding me to a vow after everything that's happened?"

Gerde stepped away from Samara. "You made that vow for a reason," she said in a quiet voice, sitting down on the bed. "Because you wanted to be a better person. But if you do this ... If you go in there planning on a bloodbath, it will change you. And I don't want to lose the woman I love."

She mumbled the last sentence, dropping her head into her hands. She didn't know what else she could say. Samara knew how she felt. They had never properly talked about it. Not really. There was always some new emergency, but she knew.

Gerde felt Samara kneel in front of her. Felt her warm hands as she gently lifted Gerde's face up to meet her gaze. Her chocolate eyes bore into Gerde's own. Samara started to speak, stopped, and then started again.

"You love me?" Samara said, a tiny smile playing on her lips.

Gerde couldn't help the blush creeping into her cheeks. Godmothers, she felt so exposed.

"You're really going to make me say it again?" Gerde replied, brushing a lock of hair out of her face.

Samara took a deep breath. "You know I feel the same way, don't you? About us?" Samara spoke joltingly, stumbling over her words.

Gerde nodded, her gaze never leaving Samara.

"You might have noticed I have a difficult time trusting people, so it's hard for me to be open."

Now a small smile was playing on Gerde's lips.

"But I do feel the same way," Samara said.

Even as she spoke, Samara looked amazed. Like she couldn't believe she was actually opening up in this way. She swallowed, and then collapsed into Gerde's arms, hugging her fiercely. After a moment, Samara pulled back and looked deeply into Gerde's green eyes. She bit her lip. Paused a moment, and then leaned in. Gerde felt Samara's warm lips brush her own, and she reached up and pulled Samara closer.

When they finally broke off their kiss, Gerde pulled away and met Samara's eyes. "Tell me you're not still going to rescue Hans until we have a proper plan."

Samara stiffened and then sagged in her arms. "I won't," she mumbled into Gerde's shoulder.

Gerde smoothed back the loose strands of Samara's dark hair as she held her.

"We'll figure out a plan," Gerde promised, though how, she didn't know. Samara was the one who usually came up with the plans.

They sat there just hugging each other, Gerde appreciating

Samara's nearness, when the door to the flat opened and they heard Art's voice call out, "I'm home! There better be something to drink besides chai! Oh…" Taking in Gerde and Samara in the bedroom, a roguish glint reached his eyes.

"Am I, er, interrupting?"

~

"HE DID *WHAT*?!" Callista almost dropped her hairbrush at the news, turning away from the mirror to face Lissa.

"He had the old man arrested," Lissa repeated.

"You're sure he was behind it?" Callista asked, although she needn't have. Of course, Lutz Kaiser was behind it. He had made it very clear to her that events were already in motion.

Before Lissa could respond, Callista added, "Tell me exactly what happened."

"I had girls watching all the usual haunts, just as you told me to," Lissa replied. She frowned down at Callista, who realised she had been gripping her hairbrush so hard her knuckles were turning white. "Anyway, Ida noticed a lot of activity at the print shop. City Watch. Only they weren't in uniform. I don't know how long they've been there watching the place. Ida suspected nothing. She wasn't even sure they were staking out the print shop. The old man and the one named Gerde showed up. Ida was about to intercept them, but a blonde woman showed up, who Gerde went to speak with. Right after that, the City Watch intercepted the old man."

"But not Gerde or the blonde woman?"

Lissa shook her head. "The watch didn't seem to notice them. Ida wasn't even entirely sure it was related to the Hisada, but then the wagon arrived and Hoffner showed up."

"Hoffner," Callista muttered.

She slowly exhaled through her nose. No, she supposed

Franz Hoffner might not be interested in Gerde if she would be of more use acting as a messenger. Lutz needed to draw Samara out. He *wanted* her to find out the City Watch had arrested Hans.

"Did they say what they were charging him with?" Callista asked. Not that it mattered. They were bound to make up something.

"Reproducing malicious and banned materials."

So yes, it was made up charges. What did that even mean? Callista laid the hairbrush down on her dresser. Things were about to get bad. Really bad. She just hoped Samara wouldn't be stupid enough to try to break Hans out of gaol.

Samara. If she found out about the Restorationists. That Lutz Kaiser had been responsible for the print shop owner's arrest. If she found out that he was staying here...

Callista had already begun sleeping with weapons, ever since the night Samara had almost tried to kill her. But if Samara really believed Callista had betrayed her again, this time Samara wouldn't hold back. And it didn't matter that Sam had betrayed Callista by not returning Eloise. Sam would want revenge. And Callista couldn't blame her.

Callista got to her feet. "Lissa. I need you to find the Hisada."

"We're working on it," Lissa began.

"No. Not the other girls. Just you. Don't worry about Kaiser anymore. I want your priority to be finding Samara."

Lissa's lips twisted and Callista could tell she was obviously looking forward to going another round with the Hisada. "What do you want me to do when I find her?"

"I need to send her a message."

ONCE SHE'D RELAYED to Lissa the message she wanted to pass to Samara, Callista went to her wardrobe and pulled on a gown she usually only wore on formal occasions when she was greeting a client. The lines were harsher than she normally favoured. The fabric was stiff and gave her the feeling of wearing armour. She scraped her hair into a bun. She then placed a couple of choice poison-tipped items of jewellery on her person, looped a belt around her waist with a holster for a dagger and strode to Lutz Kaiser's room.

Callista could see the glow of the candle as she reached the doorway, so she knew he was still up. Probably awake, writing letters to his compatriots back in Richilde, reporting on the progress he had made in recovering Eloise. Or lack of progress.

She paused at the door, her stomach suddenly clenching. She shook her head and almost chuckled to herself. Could it really be that Samara was right in letting Eloise go? Not in the way she went about it. That was clearly underhanded. She was still mad at Sam for the trouble that little stunt had brought down on her. But perhaps Eloise was better off away from the Restorationists. They didn't care about her well-being. They only wanted to use her so they could claw back the power they lost when the last descendant of Queen White passed away. What did it say about the organisation that they would lock up an old man, just in the hope they could get Eloise back?

Something settled inside her. Yes. This was the right thing to do. It would not do her any favours around the House. Between dropping the contract to purchase girls from Humphreys and now having this man stay here, the second time in a month she'd allowed a strange man into the House, her position as Matron was tenuous.

Of course, who knew if there would still be a House after this? Kaiser might still come through on his threat to have the laws changed regarding contract killing. *Did he really have the power to do that?* She might be remembered as the Matron who brought about the end of the House de Mörde. That thought left her uneasy.

Taking a deep breath, she strode into his room without knocking. Kaiser sat with his back to the door. He looked the most relaxed she'd seen him, with rolled-up shirt sleeves and bare feet. He abruptly rose to his feet, spinning to face her. Taking in her stern gaze, he gave her a thin smile.

"Matron! I wasn't aware you were in the habit of entering men's rooms so late at night."

"I'm not. Nor am I in the habit of allowing men to stay at House de Mörde. I made an exception for you so that we may work together in recovering Eloise."

An exception only so she could keep a close eye on him. But all it did was bring more trouble to her doorstep, because now Samara would hold her personally responsible for anything that happened to her landlord. She had seen how Samara interacted with the old man. She knew he meant a lot to her.

Kaiser continued to smile at her, his eyes dancing. "Ah, yes. So, am I to presume that since you have entered my room without knocking, you have some urgent news to relay? Perhaps you have discovered the location of the princess?"

She winced every time he referred to Eloise as a princess. It felt to Callista less like a title and more like he was referring to Eloise as an object.

She took a deep breath. "It's come to my attention that your dealings with Franz Hoffner, which I advised against—"

"Yes, I recall."

"Has led to the capture of an innocent man."

Kaiser leaned back against his desk, picking up the silver cane he favoured and studying it intently, not in a threatening manner, but more as though Callista were not worth his time.

"If you mean the landlord of your former sister-at-arms,

then yes. Though he is hardly innocent. You yourself said he was involved in the forging of documents—"

"To rescue Eloise!"

"Which means," he continued, raising his voice, "that he was heavily involved in Samara Dawa's crew. Personally, I think Hoffner outdid himself. The print shop owner will either break down and reveal the whereabouts of the princess, or he will provide the perfect bait to lure Samara Dawa out."

He placed the cane down and held Callista's gaze.

"Don't worry yourself, Matron. Hoffner has placed extra guards at the City Watch headquarters, in case Miss Dawa is foolish enough to break her landlord out."

"There is a third thing that might happen," Callista replied, holding his gaze and pushing a strand of hair out of her face. "Samara Dawa might be pushed over the edge and attempt an assault on the House de Mörde. Of course, if she does, I can always just tell her you were behind it and point out your room. I'm sure she would love to meet you, Mr Kaiser."

"And I would enjoy meeting her."

Callista sighed, frustrated at Kaiser's lack of response and his single-mindedness when it came to Eloise.

"As interesting as that would be to watch, I am going to have to ask you to leave, Mr Kaiser. Through your actions, you have endangered the girls here—"

"Endangered a house full of assassins? I think not."

Callista fought the urge to slap the bureaucrat. "You have placed them in danger and for that, you must leave. I will arrange to have what funds the Restorationists paid me for the care of Eloise returned in the morning, but I must insist that you, Mr Kaiser, leave tonight. This very moment."

His jaw clenched, and for a second, she thought he was going to be a problem. But then his body seemed to relax.

"Well, if you insist. But you should know, Matron, severing

ties with the Restorationists does not wipe the debt. Your actions have endangered the princess and there will be consequences."

Having said her piece, Callista decided now was the best time to leave. She would have one of the girls make sure he packed up his things and arranged a carriage. Without another word, she turned and left, shutting the door behind her. She then leaned back against the wall and exhaled.

Oh, she *knew* there would be consequences. There always were.

CHAPTER TEN

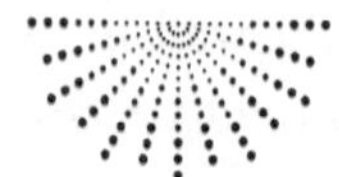

ANTI-PAIN!

Banish pain forever!! Using new technology in the form of trichloromethane, use it for relief of toothache, earache, rheumatism etc. You can even give a drop to your child to help it sleep at night!

It was a clear night in Elphame Park. The air had a bite to it. Samara sat huddled in her frock coat, crouched on the roof of a nearby townhouse, looking across the way to the townhouse opposite. Gerde and Art were down below, acting as lookout.

It almost felt like old times.

The street itself wasn't nearly as ritzy as most of the properties she'd scouted in Elphame Park. Which honestly, she was glad of. When she found out that Sylvain Duvall, the Magistrate of Märchen, lived in Elphame Park, she feared the woman was yet another corrupt official taking money to look the other way. This townhouse was modest. Expensive, but not ostentatious.

It had been Art's idea to speak with the Magistrate. He

remembered seeing her at the Zephyr and thought she could be of help. Ordinarily, it would've taken some convincing. Samara had a distrust of those in power. But Gerde helped her see the rightness of the plan. Gerde. Gerde, who always supported her and had her back. Who *left* her family coaching inn to go on the run with Samara and Hans.

She'd told herself Gerde was just trying to keep her family safe. Which was true. But there was more than one type of truth.

A romantic relationship was uncharted territory for Samara. It scared her.

Samara forced her thoughts back to the mission. She had a lot of things to make right before she could allow herself to think on their relationship. Her priority being getting Hans out of prison. And, according to Art, the woman who could help with that, slept just across the street from where she was crouched.

Satisfied she had noted all the security measures at the Magistrate's home, a rooftop patrol as well as two guards who patrolled the inside of the house, she swiftly climbed down to meet up with the others.

Making her way to a large cypress tree, she let out a whip-poor-will call to let the others know she was done with her surveilling. A few moments later, Gerde arrived, followed closely by Art.

"I make one on the rooftop and two inside the house. You agree?" she asked the others.

"I spotted the one in the kitchen having a hot drink. There was another servant there, housekeeper maybe, but it looks like she went to bed," Art added.

"It looks to me like the three of them trade off every half hour. That sound about right to you?"

Gerde and Art both nodded in agreement. It wasn't easy for

Samara to ask for their help. Or to even ask their opinion. Normally she would spend several days scouting out a property, but she needed to get in to see the Magistrate tonight.

"Okay. Art, you think you can lure the one in the kitchen away?"

Art shrugged. "Not a problem. A quick rap on the kitchen window. The wheel of my carriage is stuck. Come help!"

Both Gerde and Samara grimaced.

"Don't do that one!" Gerde exclaimed.

"What's wrong with it?"

"For one, you don't have a carriage," Gerde replied with a raised eyebrow.

"I'll take out the guard while I'm leading him to my carriage," Art replied, raising his own brow.

Gerde made a face and looked at Samara, who winced.

"Oh, come on! You think I can't handle one guard?"

"No," said Samara, a little louder than intended, but she really wanted to stop the arguing. "But you're a lordling—"Art opened his mouth to protest, and she put up a hand to stop him —"They *think* you're a lordling. So, pretend you just came from the gambling dens and are having trouble finding your way home. The guard will help you find a coach stand. The nearest one is a good five minutes' walk away, which will give us ten minutes to take out the other two guards."

"What do you want me to do?" Gerde asked.

Samara sighed. She knew Gerde wanted to be included more. She was certainly more than capable of handling herself. But, especially after their most recent conversation, how could Samara endanger her? The only thing keeping her from leaving Gerde at the inn was that she knew Gerde would follow them anyway.

"I'll take out the one on the roof, and then we can both handle the one on patrol," Samara replied.

"There's no time," Gerde protested. "You take care of the one on the roof. I'll take out the guard patrolling inside, while you find the Magistrate."

Samara pursed her lips but said nothing. It was a plan. She didn't like it, but it was still a plan.

~

TEN MINUTES LATER, Samara and Gerde watched from the safety of the Cypress tree while Art went around the side of the building to the kitchen window and rapped on the glass. They heard voices speaking and a few minutes later a giggling, swaying Art could be seen accompanied by one guard walking quickly down the darkened street.

Samara turned to Gerde and put a hand on her shoulder. "You're sure you're okay taking out the guard inside?"

Gerde covered Samara's hand with her own and smiled softly. "I'll be fine, Sam. Besides, it's not like we could trade places."

Samara smirked. No. That wouldn't work. Not when Gerde was terrified of heights.

"Wait five minutes before going into the house."

Gerde nodded and knelt back down while Samara hurried across the road, keeping an eye on the roof for any signs of movement.

It was a tight schedule to keep. She needed to free climb to the roof and take out the guard while Art kept the other guard busy.

Samara found the drainpipe she had chosen as a good route to the roof, and, after ascertaining that the rooftop guard wasn't anywhere nearby, she quickly scaled the iron pipe as silently as possible.

At the top, she crouched behind a chimney, listening for the sound of footsteps. Instead, she smelled pipe hash. Apparently, the guard was busy smoking when he was supposed to be patrolling the roof. It looked like this would be easier than she thought.

She followed the smoke up the slope of the roof until she spotted her mark. He was sitting on the rooftop facing the street, pipe in hand.

Carefully, Samara pulled out a rag and her bottle of trichloromethane. It wasn't a substance she made a habit of using, but more and more, it seemed the better option. Especially in this case, since she figured offing one of the guards wasn't the best way to ingratiate herself with the Magistrate.

She poured a little liquid into the rag, pocketed both items, and snuck around to come up behind the guard. She almost made it too, before he turned around, a puzzled look on his face. *Schiesse!* She pulled the rag from her pocket and lunged for him. He grappled with her and she winced at the noise they were making. She *really* hoped the guard patrolling inside was downstairs. Eventually, she was able to pin the struggling guard and clamp a hand down on his mouth, fixing the rag to it until he finally went still.

Grumbling to herself, she dragged him back up to the apex of the roof so he didn't fall off and hurt himself while he was unconscious. She lost precious time searching for and recovering the pipe, putting it out and laying it on his chest. She also didn't think the Magistrate would be especially happy with her if she was responsible for accidentally burning the house down.

With that all taken care of, she shimmied down the pipe to the top-floor window, which appeared to be a child's bedroom. Of course it was. The window was open. She hated the thought of the child waking up to her sneaking in, but she had to take what she could get. She eased the sash window open a little higher and slipped inside.

The child, boy or girl she couldn't tell, stirred in their sleep but didn't awaken. *Please just stay asleep,* she begged as she took great care to silently cross the room.

When she reached the door, she turned the doorknob ever-so-gently and cracked the door, listening for the sound of the other guard. Nothing. Thanking Manāt, she crept out of the child's bedroom, pausing a moment to get herself orientated. She thought she heard the guard walking around downstairs. Samara fought the urge to help Gerde. There wasn't enough time, and Gerde wouldn't appreciate her butting in. She had to trust that Gerde could handle the guard while she went and spoke with the Magistrate.

From across the street, she had seen the Magistrate, sitting in a room adjoining her bedchambers, reading a book. Samara located the room and quickly made her way there. She stopped at the door she believed was the Magistrate's bed chamber and took a moment to listen in. She thought she heard the sound of paper rustling. The gentle tap of fine china being set down on a wooden surface. She listened for other sounds coming from within the house. All was quiet.

There was nothing more to it. She lightly tapped on the bedroom door and slipped inside. The Magistrate glanced up, her body stiffening as she took in the intruder. She was curled up on a chaise lounge with a hot drink. She quickly set her book aside and drew her dressing gown about her.

"You," she said, recognition filling her eyes, and something else Samara couldn't identify.

"What are you doing inside my home? Are my guards...?" She trailed off and her eyes widened. "My daughter—"

"Is fine. So are your guards." *Although they are going to have a massive headache when they wake up.*

"How did you get past my guards?" the Magistrate demanded. She didn't seem afraid of the Hisada. More annoyed than anything. "And what are you doing here? I was made to understand you no longer worked for the Lions, so I know you aren't here on Lions' business."

"I needed to speak with you."

"So you broke into my home?" she asked incredulously.

Samara forced a calm, neutral expression onto her face. This was not exactly off to a good start.

"The City Watch arrested my landlord. His name is Hans Manfredo. He owns a print shop in Hollowhorn."

"What does that have to do with me?"

"He was arrested on made up charges in order to get to me."

"Well, why would someone be after you..." For a second time the Magistrate's words trailed off. "You think it was on the orders of Chetwin Humphreys?"

Samara found herself caught off guard. She hadn't been expecting the Magistrate to make the connection so quickly. "Yes."

"Because you robbed his auction."

"Yes," Samara repeated, and this time, she was really caught off guard. "How do you know about the auction?"

She'd seen the invitation list. The Magistrate wasn't on that list. Her mouth went dry. Was the Magistrate part of the Order of Grimm?

"I make it my business to know this city," the Magistrate coolly replied, taking a sip of her drink. "Especially when you and Tormod Lyons decide to break a decades long peace and rob Chetwin Humphreys."

"Technically, he broke the peace first," Samara couldn't keep from saying.

The Magistrate's eyes narrowed. "It doesn't matter. Your little stunt has turned this city into a tinderbox. Do you know there were actual explosions outside of the Royal Zephyr just the other week? And now you people are dragging the City Watch into all this."

Samara pulled herself up to her full, albeit petite, height.

"We didn't drag the City Watch into this. Your guards have been taking bribes from Lyons and Humphreys."

"Oh, of course I know about that," the Magistrate scoffed. "I've been trying to stamp it out for years. But there is a vast difference between paying people to look the other way and all-out war in the streets."

"An innocent man was arrested—"

Gerde took that moment to step inside, causing the Magistrate to pull back into her seat. "I took care of the last guard." Gerde glanced back and forth between Samara and the Magistrate. "Madame Magistrate," she said with a nod of her head.

"What does that mean? You took care of my guard?" the Magistrate demanded.

"He's just unconscious," Gerde reassured her.

"You both took out all three of my guards?" the Magistrate asked, glancing between Samara and Gerde.

Samara nodded her head.

"Are you also a former assassin?" she asked, addressing Gerde.

"No. I'm just a hostler," Gerde replied with a grin at Samara.

"My associate's family owns the Kreuzang coaching inn. They've also been forced to shut down owing to corrupt City Watch officials harassing them," Samara said.

The Magistrate sat up. "So, what do you want me to do about it?"

"Your job. Release Hans Manfredo and go after those corrupt City Watch."

"As much as I would love to remove those guards, that's no simple matter. The constabulary is stretched thin as it is."

"Well, of course they're stretched thin," Gerde remarked. "When the Watch only recruits from half the population."

The Magistrate ignored her. "I tell you what, I'll look into your friend Hans and find out why he's been arrested. If it is as you say, and my guards are being coerced by Chetwin, then I will make sure he is released. But I need you to do something for me."

Samara felt some of the tension leave her body. Hans will be going home soon. That's all she wanted to hear. As for doing something for the Magistrate, she didn't expect any less.

"What can we do for you?"

The Magistrate sighed and got to her feet. "You can end this. You and your people helped start this mess. I need you to fix things between Chetwin and Tormod."

Almost immediately the tension was back in her neck and shoulders. Samara almost barked out a laugh, the request was so absurd. Who was she to broker a peace treaty? The last treaty had occurred before she or even Lukas joined the Lions.

"Tormod's not even in Märchen," Samara protested.

"Then you and Bernhardt will need to find another way to make peace with Chetwin."

"I'm not with the Lions anymore."

"I'm sure you'll come up with a plan," replied the Magistrate.

"Just so we're clear," began Gerde. "Are you saying that you won't even consider releasing our friend, even though we've told you he's innocent, unless we do this for you?"

"I don't know he's innocent. I only have your word. But to answer your question: you're correct. I won't be releasing your friend until Chetwin and Tormod make peace."

"But that's an impossible task!" Gerde exclaimed.

Cold fury roiled around inside Samara, but she knew the Magistrate had her over a barrel. If she wanted Hans back, then she would need to put aside her own feelings about the Lions and Humphreys and broker a peace.

"We'll do it," Samara replied through gritted teeth, exchanging a weary look with Gerde. "For Hans."

Just then, a man barged into the bedchamber without knocking. It was the guard Art had lured away. Breathless, he took in the Magistrate and the two strangers.

"Madame Magistrate, are you all right?"

"I'm fine, Anton," the Magistrate replied coolly. "I'm just having a chat with our visitors."

"I found Ernst unconscious," said Anton.

"Was he injured?"

"Not that I can tell—"

"Why don't you make sure Ernst doesn't need anything while I finish up my conversation," the Magistrate suggested.

"There's another guard taking a nap on the roof. You might want to check on him too," Samara supplied.

Anton scowled at her but said nothing, obeying his boss and retreating from the bedchamber.

"So, there you have it," the Magistrate continued once the door clicked closed. "You end this madness between the Lions and Humphreys men, and I'll make sure your man, Hans, is released."

Samara reluctantly nodded her head. She didn't know how they were supposed to pull this off, but if this was the deal they had, then they would come through. For Hans.

ANA WOUND her way through Hollowhorn after another visit with Eloise. The girl wasn't eating enough at that boarding house, so Ana made a point of stopping by every day with a batch of stale or otherwise unsellable baked goods. She worried about the girl spending so much time cooped up on her own. Ana counted herself lucky that she had met Gerde soon after her arrival in Märchen. Gerde had helped her get the job at the bakery. It wasn't much, but it gave Ana something to focus her mind on instead of dwelling on what had happened to her. Even then, it wasn't until she had met Samara and her crew that she was able to feel a tiny sense of security. She wished she could give that to Eloise. The girl was all bravado, but Ana saw through the façade.

The muddy roads and the encroaching smell of the Klara River were familiar as ever, but lately Ana sensed a tension in this part of the city. People looked wary as they shopped, their heads bowed, their shoulders hunched. Some shops were shuttering earlier than usual, she noticed.

She was as careful as ever, holding onto the energy she had pocketed along the way in case she needed to access some on short notice, but she was thinking Eloise was right. They needed to make some money any way they could and get out of Hollowhorn. It wasn't safe here. Of course, nowhere in Märchen was safe for them.

Seb, with his warm Alkebu features, was easy to spot on the streets of the Hollow. He was wearing a newsboy cap pulled low over his face and wearing drab brown trousers and an oversized coat, but she recognised him instantly. She was just debating whether to hide from him when he turned her way, immediately spotted her, and raised his hand in a wave.

Schiesse.

She smiled and wove through the crowd to greet him.

"What are you doing out here in the Hollow?" were the first words out of Seb's mouth. "It's dangerous."

Ana pressed her lips tightly together, breathing in through her nose. Even with all her power, even after everything they had been through, he still thought of her as someone who needed to be saved. Her eyes flashed in warning.

"I can take care of myself."

Seb's brown eyes widened, and he seemed momentarily at a loss for words. *Good*, Ana thought to herself.

"I know you can take care of yourself. It's just you live in Old Town and things are really hairy in the Hollow at the moment. Chetwin Humphreys is waging war with the Lions. I'm not even supposed to be out at the moment."

Ana felt a familiar knot in her stomach. She knew things had felt off in Hollowhorn lately but knowing that she was somehow responsible for it was another thing entirely. That, added to what happened the other day with Hans getting arrested, didn't sit well with her.

"So why are *you* out here, then?"

Seb looked instantly uncomfortable. He rubbed the back of his neck and couldn't seem to make eye contact with her. "I was actually coming to see you."

Ana frowned. If things were really that bad here, and she knew deep down they were, why would he risk coming to see her...?

Oh.

She felt a different sort of knot in her stomach. Guilt mixed with frustration.

Seb was warily eyeing the people passing them on the street. "I feel like we haven't spoken properly since the night of the auction."

Since we kissed, Ana mentally filled in the part he wasn't saying. "No. I don't suppose we have," Ana softly agreed.

Seb tentatively took her wrist. "Could we just..." He gestured with his head to duck into a nearby alleyway.

Ana looked warily at the alley. She didn't think it was the brightest idea to go where they could be cornered, but she was confident she could handle things if someone tried to jump them. She acquiesced, allowing him to lead her away from the main high street.

"I've visited the Four and Twenty, but you're never there," Seb said once they were away from prying eyes.

"I know. I've been very busy," Ana said. Her words came out stilted.

She flinched when she saw the hurt in Seb's eyes.

"Busy doing what?"

She sighed and chewed the corner of her lip, trying not to be annoyed at him. Why did he care what she did in her own time?

"Does it matter?" was all she said in response.

"I just thought maybe you were avoiding me," Seb said, rubbing the back of his neck again.

"I'm not avoiding you, Seb. I've just been busy," she replied, hating having to lie to him. But it wasn't entirely untrue, she reasoned. She was very busy with Eloise these days.

Ana gave him a tiny smile.

"Oh. Well, that's good then," he said, smiling back at her. "Ever since that night we kissed, things have just been nonstop. We haven't had a moment to ourselves."

He closed the distance between her and started reaching towards her with outstretched arms.

Is he going to hug me?! No, no, no, no, no. Without thinking, she used a tiny bit of the energy that was bubbling inside her, bursting to get out, and sent it Seb's way. It wasn't a lot of energy. Just enough to cause him to stumble back a couple of steps and maintain distance between them.

Seb's eyes widened and then narrowed.

"How did you—"

"I've been practicing," she snapped back at him. "Look, Seb. I know we kissed that night, but I am just not ready for a relationship right now."

Seb frowned. "But *you* kissed *me.*"

"I did?"

She did?! It was weird. Until just now, she hadn't remembered that it had been her who had initiated their kiss. It came back to her in a rush. They were celebrating. She was so excited, having successfully completed their job, and gotten to befriend a *real* Magic user. Big Magic. Someone who could teach her. Ana remembered drinking two glasses of honey liqueur. She felt powerful. She had gone into a den of people who would sooner lock her away, and she had rescued Eloise. Then, when Eloise had gone out to speak with Samara, Seb had come over to talk to her. She had been buzzing with energy. Unlike the kinetic energy she could hold within herself, this one needed an outlet. Impulsively, she hugged him, and when she felt his warm arms wrap around her and saw the beaming smile on his face, she couldn't help herself. She had indeed kissed him. *Schiesse.*

"Look, you're right. I kissed you. It was an exciting night. And there was honey wine..."

Even to her ears, it sounded lame. Her heart twinged at the hurt look that fell across Seb's face.

"So, you didn't mean to kiss me. I was just … convenient?"

Seb took a step away from her, and Ana tried to close the distance. *Was* it just that he was convenient at the time? She didn't think so. Surely she wasn't that heartless. She liked Seb. He was cute. And besides Gerde, he was her first real friend in this city.

"No. I like you. I do."

Seb's features tightened. "Then I don't get it. You know I like you. You must know this, Ana." He broke off. Shook his head. "Godmothers! I built this all up in my head. I actually thought I was going to introduce you to my ma."

Ana didn't know if that was supposed to endear him to her, but all it made her feel was cross. She didn't want to meet anyone's ma. Did Seb think that just because they shared one kiss that they were now somehow fated to live happily ever after?

"This is just what I mean, Seb," she said. "I'm not ready to meet your mother. I'm not interested in a relationship. Godmothers! I was literally kidnapped just a few months ago. Before that, I was forced to keep my powers hidden. Maybe I just want to be by myself for a while. Maybe I don't need yet another person trying to take care of me."

"I wasn't trying to take care of you!" Seb shouted in frustration.

"Yes. You were!" She shouted right back at him.

Godmothers, she didn't want to be in a relationship, and she *really* didn't want someone following her around like a puppy.

"Then why couldn't you have been honest with me?" Seb yelled. "Why all the subterfuge?"

Ana didn't know what to say about that. She couldn't exactly tell him the truth. That Eloise was still in Märchen and had used her Magic to track down Ana. She'd promised to keep Eloise's secret.

"All those times I visited the bakery," Seb continued. "Did you just get your boss to lie and say you weren't there?"

"No, of course not," Ana protested. She really had been out all those other times. Visiting Eloise.

"You knew I wanted to talk to you, though, and you still couldn't leave a message for me." It was obvious to Ana that Seb was just warming up.

"I'm not your mother. It's not my responsibility to tend to your wounded feelings!" Ana snapped back, and now she was finding it increasingly difficult to control the kinetic energy buzzing inside her.

"What?" Seb replied, startled.

"I said—"

"No. Not that," Seb responded with a wave of his hand. "Is that smoke?"

Ana sniffed the air. He was right. There was smoke billowing from the street. They both rushed to the mouth of the alleyway and peered out.

"It's the Zephyr," whispered Seb.

CHAPTER ELEVEN

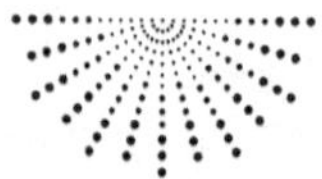

Samara sat in the manager's office at the Royal Zephyr. Lukas Bernhardt was seated in front of her, fingers steepled as he listened to her relay what happened with Hans and her subsequent conversation with the Magistrate.

"My question is," she continued. "Can she be trusted?"

She got the sense the woman was trustworthy, but she also

knew that nobody came to power without stomping on those in their path. Maybe the Magistrate was telling her what she wanted to hear in order to get her out of her home. Samara didn't blame her. She would've done the same.

"She's reliable," said Lukas thoughtfully. "If she says she doesn't know why your landlord was arrested, then she's not behind it. I am curious, though, how she thinks you can possibly restore the peace."

Samara scowled. "You and me both."

She crossed her arms in front of her and leaned forward, resting her elbows on the table. "Thoughts?"

A smile played on Lukas' lips. "So just to be clear, Hisada, we're teaming up, yes?"

"For now," she reluctantly confirmed, reminding herself yet again, that she had no choice. "But as I said before, I'm not a Lion. This is temporary."

Lukas looked relieved, and his smile widened. But then his expression sobered. "If I'm honest, Hisada, I don't think we have a way to restore the peace with Humphreys."

"Surely there's something you can give him to make amends."

"Sure. It might clean us out, but it's not impossible." He rubbed his brow thoughtfully. "But you know it's not just about the money."

"It's face," she agreed.

"Yep. Tormod embarrassed him in front of his allies. How do you make amends for that?"

"Especially when Tormod isn't even here," Samara muttered with a shake of her head.

"Exactly," Lukas quickly responded.

He leaned back in his chair, stretching his long legs out, and Samara copied him, each of them in thought. In the silence, it suddenly became apparent to the both of them that the usual cheers and ruckus of the gambling den had stopped. Instead, there were people speaking loudly and urgently.

They both got to their feet just as Devan came racing in, coughing and rubbing at his eyes. "Fire. There's a fire," he wheezed.

Running out onto the main floor, they discovered the casino in chaos. Smoke rose from somewhere further inside the back hallway, pouring into the main floor. Lions, patrons and Zephyr employees were hurrying towards the exit.

Lukas caught a nearby Lion by the shoulder.

"There's a fire in the wine cellar," said the Lion without being asked.

"In the wine cellar?" Lukas asked in disbelief. "What caused it?"

The Lion shrugged.

"You should consider the possibility Humphreys is behind this," Samara began.

"Agreed," said Lukas, turning back to the young Lion. "Get everybody out but be careful. Humphreys' men could be waiting for us out there."

The young Lion's eyes widened at the implication, and he hurried on his way.

"Devan," Lukas called out to the manager, who was helping guide patrons to the exit. "Make sure all the customers and employees get out but stay close to the Lions in case there's more to this."

"What are you going to do?" Devan asked, still coughing.

"We've got to put out this fire before the whole place goes up," Lukas replied. He turned to Samara. "I could use your help, Hisada."

"Thought you'd never ask."

〜

THEY MADE their way into the heart of the Royal Zephyr, smoke stinging their throats and clouding their vision, Lukas muttered, "There's no way this is an accident."

"You thinking someone on the inside did it?"

"Not one of the Lions. Maybe one of the casino employees."

As the smoke overwhelmed them, Lukas pulled off his kerchief and placed it over his mouth. Samara did the same with the corner of her frock coat. Through the smoke, she spotted Seb and, much to her surprise, Ana.

"I'll catch up with you," she said to Lukas, jerking her head in their direction.

Lukas nodded and continued on his way.

"What are you two doing here?" she asked when she caught up with them.

Although Ana and Seb were helping people leave, it was clear they themselves were moving deeper into the casino.

Seb coughed once and lowered the kerchief he was holding to his own mouth. "Ana and I are heading to the catacombs. If the fire sets off the explosives, the entire building could be destroyed."

"I might be able to release the kinetic energy slowly so it doesn't bring everything down," added Ana.

Schiesse. She had forgotten all about the multitudes of explosive materials the Lions stored at the very bottom of the building. Supposedly, the area was protected by Magic, but if so, the spell hadn't been reinforced in nearly a hundred years. She wouldn't like to test that theory now. Could Ana manage the energy before it brought the building down around them?

"There's something else you should know," Seb added. "Tormod Lyons is living down there."

Samara felt her blood boil. Oh, she was going to have words with Lukas when this was all over.

Well, that settled it then. They needed to make sure the fire didn't spread to the catacombs. It would be a whole lot easier to end this turf war if Tormod was actually alive to make amends. A corpse *might* work, but not if his body was burned beyond recognition.

"Let's go," she responded, but just before following them out, she grabbed another Lion by the collar who was making his way through the casino floor. "Lukas is in the wine cellar trying to put the fire out. Get to the kitchens, start a water line and go get him some help."

The Lion immediately turned and fled towards the kitchen, leaving Samara to follow Seb and Ana into the bowels of the Zephyr.

THEIR FIRST STOP was the armoury. Nobody tried to stop Samara this time. They were all too preoccupied elsewhere. So many explosives and, in the chaos, nobody had thought to secure it.

"I can feel the energy in them," Ana gasped. "It's not stable at all. Why do they keep them here?"

"Not the time, Ana," Seb replied with a cough. "Can you make them inert?"

"I can try," she murmured, already closing her eyes. With the smoke, it was difficult for Samara to see what she was doing. Unlike when Ana had effortlessly used her powers on the street, she now appeared to be struggling with the volatile energy.

"The building may shake," Ana warned them.

"We'll be ready," Seb replied.

Samara grasped Seb's elbow. "How dangerous are those ingredients in the catacombs?"

"Extremely."

"We need to get down there."

"But Ana's not finished yet."

"She could be some time. We need to get Tormod out."

Seb was clearly not ready to leave Ana behind.

"Fine. I'll do it myself," Samara said, cursing under her breath.

She rushed away, sending any Lions she met off to the kitchen to help with the water line. They couldn't lose the Zephyr. If the Zephyr fell, it wouldn't matter if Tormod were alive or not. There would be no peace. What would be the plan, then? At best, it would mean taking herself and the people she cared for and getting them out of Märchen before the Lions and Humphreys tore the entire city apart.

Smoke stung Samara's eyes and she could hardly see as she made her way down the rickety steps to where the explosive materials were kept. The catacombs were located just below the wine cellar in the deepest part of the Zephyr. It was said the Royal Zephyr had once been the home of a mad eccentric, who fell in love with a beautiful girl. The man, a wealthy toff, was afraid the girl would meet someone else and leave him. He built the catacombs and used his magical connections to make it virtually impenetrable. No ordinary weapon could break through. Not fire. What's worse, no one could hear the girl. She could shout or cry and nobody would know she was down there.

That part was true. There was, indeed, a spell on the catacombs that meant no one could hear you down there. The story always made Samara feel very murderous. In the stories, the girl had a fairy godmother who lured a young duke down to the catacombs. The duke was a guest of the eccentric. The story got a little fuzzy after that. Supposedly, the duke discovered her and killed the eccentric, stealing the keys and freeing her. But how would he have known she was there if she couldn't be heard, even if she screamed? Callista always said it was because of true love. Samara didn't buy that for a second. True love made his hearing better? Really? Besides, how could you fall in love with someone you'd never even met before?

She shook off those thoughts as one of the steps gave way beneath her. Someone caught her by the arm before she could fall and twist an ankle. Thank Manāt. Otherwise, she would be the one needing saving.

She looked up to see Seb. "What are you doing here?"

Even through the smoke, she could make out Seb's expression. He wasn't happy. "Ana had me follow you. Said any dummkopf could see she had things under control."

Samara smiled grimly. That Ana always told it like it was.

Carefully, they continued their way down the stairs. Thankfully, the fire hadn't spread here yet. Who knows? Maybe the Magic really was holding up.

The space was rapidly filling with smoke. Surely, if Tormod, the little arschloch, really was hiding out at the Zephyr, he wasn't still down here. Only a real idiot would stay here with all that smoke.

She hoped Ana could handle the explosives. For that matter, she *really* hoped Lukas and the other Lions could handle the fire in the wine cellar.

"Tormod!" She called out, only to get a lungful of smoke. She doubled over, hacking, before feeling Seb tugging on her arm. He pointed to a corner of the darkened cellar, but she couldn't make out what had his attention.

Together, they made their way deeper, and again she hoped the verdammt cellar would hold. Being a daughter of House de Mörde, she had long considered how she might die. But she never figured she'd end up dying in an explosion, caught in the middle of a gang war between two arschlochs.

The smoke was so dense now she almost didn't spot the small cot and pile of blankets. She was about to search the pile when nearby liquor bottles started to tumble, her first sign that the building was rumbling. That was either a good sign, that Ana was handling the explosives, or it was bad. Very bad. She grabbed Seb and crouched on the ground until the rumbling subsided. As she was slowly getting to her feet, her hand connected with flesh. Tormod.

She gestured to Seb and then slapped Tormod's face. He was out cold. Either from smoke inhalation or from the many empty bottles of liquor littering the place.

Schiesse. Of course, this wasn't going to be easy.

The first thing she did was pull a clean rag out of her pocket and wrap it around her nose and mouth. Awkwardly, she grasped hold of Tormod's upper body while Seb grabbed his legs. They could barely see their way, and who knew if the stairs would hold.

Cursing Tormod, and all the petty decisions he'd made that led them to this point, she awkwardly attempted to make her way to the stairs. It didn't help that they were heading deeper into the smoke. She cursed Lukas, and her own poor decisions, as they attempted to ever-so-slowly mount the stairs. She had to keep checking each step to make sure it still held. When she found the broken step, she tried to indicate to Seb, but had no way to communicate with him between the smoke and her hands being full.

Muscles straining, she hefted Tormod's dead weight higher and awkwardly moved past the broken step. Thankfully, Seb seemed tuned into her movements and copied her. Which was good. She didn't want anything to happen to Seb, especially not while trying to save the head of the Lion's life. Former head of the Lions? What you called him, he was just about the only person who could maybe end this turf war.

When they reached the level with the cellar, it was difficult to tell how things were going. Through the smoke, she could make out a group of Lions passing buckets down the line. One Lion, seeing her and Seb struggle with a body, tried to step out of line, but she vigorously shook her head.

Godmothers, what had caused this fire? Was the Order responsible? Maybe they had in their possession some sort of magic fire. Something that used alcohol to burn hotter.

Smoke continued to pour out from the wine cellar. In this part of the Zephyr, she could really feel the heat of the flames. The only sounds she heard were coughing and the shouting of orders. She was grateful for Seb beside her. They couldn't communicate, but it was reassuring having him here, knowing he was okay. She hoped Ana had gotten out of the building and hadn't thought to follow them.

They were almost back to the Lions barracks. From there, they could leave via the back way. She really hoped there wouldn't be a bunch of Humphreys' men out there waiting for them. Tormod hadn't stirred once. She tried not to think about that as well.

Samara was so fixated on trying to get to their exit, she didn't notice when a beam of wood came crashing down towards her. She didn't have time to react. She thought she heard Seb call out her name.

But the wooden beam didn't connect with her head. She watched as it flew harmlessly away. Through the smoke, she saw Ana's tiny figure emerge. She breathed a sigh of relief. But rather than leading the way to the exit, Ana continued past them.

"Ana, where are you going?" Seb shouted, though his shouts were muffled by his kerchief.

"I can put out the fire," Ana yelled over her shoulder.

Schiesse. How had she not thought of that? Ana's magic was based on transferring kinetic energy. Fire had kinetic energy.

Seb, for his part, looked as though he were about to drop Tormod right there and follow her back.

"Seb. Seb!" Samara snapped at him. "We need Tormod alive or we're all gefickt."

~

ANA STUMBLED THROUGH THE SMOKE, blindly following the line of men passing buckets. Not that she needed them to guide her. She could feel the fire's energy. It was a raw, intense energy. Hungry and needy and desperately looking for an outlet.

The water line wasn't working, she could tell. The building would come down before they could get the fire under control. She had to make a choice. She could take care of the explosive materials. Or she could go to the root of all their troubles. In truth, she'd much rather choose the former. The latter meant using her abilities in front of the Lions.

She tried to conceal herself within the smoke. She could do this. All she had to do was make it seem like the water line was working. She needed to do this. Saving Samara from that falling beam made her feel powerful. She *was* powerful. And, verdammt, she was tired of hiding.

She reached out with her powers, feeling the shape of the fire's energy. It didn't buzz like normal kinetic energy. It wasn't like a normal fire at all. Instead, it burned with a ferocity. It felt like it could overpower her.

Was this fire created using magic? she wondered.

Ana pulled the energy into her. Not all at once, like she might normally have done. There was too much intensity. Unlike normal kinetic energy, it fought her. She had to physically grapple with it. She really hoped she was concealed within the smoke.

Piece by piece, she pulled apart the energy and released it

into the ground. Even then, she had to be careful, lest the energy be too much for the building, which was already under intense pressure. The building rumbled, and she could hear the cries of fearful Lions. Above that, she heard the shout of one Lion, telling them to keep at it.

She knew when the fire was finally under control. She could sense that the energy changed. As it grew weaker, it no longer fought her. It allowed her to resettle the energy into the building's walls. She had managed to leach out the magical elements of the fire. Now it was a small fire. One she knew the Lions could handle.

When her job was done, Ana slipped back the way she had come, through the main floor of the gambling den. There was probably a better way out, but she didn't know this place.

When she got out into the open air again, she almost doubled over with relief, her lungs desperately trying to take in the clean outside air. She'd done it. She'd stopped the fire. Ana chuckled, even as she coughed out black soot. Then she felt a hand resting on the middle of her back and she straightened to find Seb there, wordlessly watching her.

Eventually, when it was clear the fire was out, she allowed Seb and Samara to guide her back to Samara's place at the other end of the Hollow. Samara remained on guard the entire time, but nobody jumped them. Which was good, because honestly, Ana was all out of energy. She supposed she could borrow a bit of energy to get through. But even that thought tired her.

Eventually, she was led into a rough-looking tavern. It was the kind of place she would have avoided a few weeks ago. Too close to the Klara. Too many sailors. But she allowed herself to be led up the stairs, where Samara knocked on the door and then let them all in.

She did a double take when she spotted Art. She knew Gerde

and Hans were staying with Samara, but after the fight the night of the auction, she was surprised to see Art there as well.

They all got to their feet, taking in the sorry state of herself, Seb, and Samara.

"What happened to you three?" Art asked, looking them up and down.

"There was a fire at the Zephyr," Seb hoarsely explained.

Gerde hurried to Samara's side, Ana noticed, while Art went to the makeshift stove to make hot drinks.

Samara tugged off her coat and flung it on a chair. "I don't know if I'm ever getting the smoke smell out of that," she grumbled before, to Ana's shock, hugging Gerde.

"*Schiesse.* Was anybody hurt?" asked Gerde.

Exhausted, Ana took the seat Art had vacated. Now that they were well away from the Zephyr, she knew she too reeked of smoke.

"Nobody was seriously injured," Samara said as she sat down.Nobody, including Tormod Lyons. Ana still didn't know how to feel about the fact she had been involved in saving his life. But Seb and Samara seemed to think it was important.

"Thanks to Ana, the Zephyr survived," Seb added.

She could feel Art and Gerde's eyes on her. "It was nothing," she mumbled. Even though it really wasn't nothing, she knew. She had kept a building from burning down using her powers!

"It was amazing," Seb continued. "She used her powers to put out the fire."

"You did?" She could hear the amazement in Gerde's voice.

They would want an explanation, Ana thought to herself. Surely nobody could get that powerful in just a few weeks, on their own.

She was grateful when Art passed around mugs of saffron chai. "I wish I had more honey," he grumbled.

Gerde was kneeling down beside Samara's chair. She

supposed things had changed a bit here in the past few weeks, and not just her and her powers.

"Was it an accident, you think?" Gerde asked after letting them enjoy their tea for a few minutes.

Samara shook her head. "No. It was some kind of magically accelerated fire. Started in the wine cellar too, which makes no sense."

"Humphreys," Art muttered.

Samara gave a half shrug. "I think so. Either acting on his own, or on behalf of the Order."

"The Magistrate will not like this fresh development," Gerde murmured, though Ana did not know what she was referring to.

She let herself enjoy the sweet taste of the tea. The conversation settled over her like a blanket as she sat there. She was surprised how happy she felt, having them all back together again. Except for Hans, who was still conspicuously missing.

She found herself going back over the events at the Zephyr. She hadn't even realised it was possible to control fire.

After a moment, she noticed the conversation had stopped, and the others were looking at her. "What was the question?" she asked with widened eyes.

"What were you doing in Hollowhorn?" Gerde repeated.

"She was just coming to see me," Seb replied without looking her way.

She turned toward him. He knew. He knew she was keeping something from them and, rather than call her out for it, he was going to let her keep her secrets. She felt a warmth settle in her chest, which did not come from the saffron chai. She was going to have to tell the truth, wasn't she? This fire, all the recent events, had happened because people were after Eloise.

She opened her mouth. Paused. Closed it. Opened it again and cleared her throat, which was still sore from all the smoke. "I wasn't there to see Seb."

Seb turned toward her in surprise. She hated how small her voice sounded at that moment. She took a sip of tea and tried again. "The truth is, I was in Hollowhorn because Eloise is hiding in a boarding house here."

Seb's mouth dropped open in shock, as did Art's. Gerde looked disappointed in her.

Samara's dark eyes flashed. "What?!"

CHAPTER TWELVE

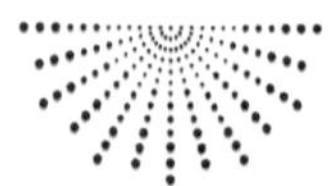

LAST NIGHT A FIRE BROKE OUT AT POPULAR GAMBLING ESTABLISH-MENT, THE ROYAL ZEPHYR IN HOLLOWHORN. IT IS UNKNOWN WHAT CAUSED THE FIRE. THOUGH THE FIRE WAS EVENTUALLY PUT OUT AND NO LIVES WERE LOST, IT IS UNCLEAR HOW SOON THE ZEPHYR WILL RE-OPEN, OR IF IT IN FACT SHOULD RE-OPEN AS MANY BELIEVE THIS FIRE IS JUST THE LATEST INCIDENT OF MANY IN AN OUT-OF-CONTROL GANG WAR.

—THE MÄRCHEN CHRONICLE

Samara was back in the Royal Zephyr, being led by a contrite Lukas to see Tormod. It was freezing cold inside the gambling hell, due to all the windows and doors being wide open. Not that it helped much in reducing the stench of smoke, which clung to the walls and upholstery.

The place was closed for business and, according to Lukas, would be shut down for quite some time. Lions and Zephyr employees alike worked to clean the space, removing draperies and smoke-damaged furniture. The hope was to open in some capacity over the next few days, but the fire had destroyed the gambling den's entire alcohol supply. They were trying for a new shipment, but it would require an extra protection detail since they were sure Humphreys would go after that next.

It was amazing how extensive the smoke damage was, even though the fire itself remained in the cellar. Thank Manāt Ana had been there to help quell the fire. Samara's lips twisted at the thought. Not that she was particularly thrilled with Ana at the moment. They had spent the past few weeks hiding from the House de Mörde when Eloise had been in the city all along...

But now was not the time to think about Eloise. She'd deal with her later. First, it was time to deal with Tormod. Who had, apparently, been in hiding, in the Zephyr no less, the whole time.

Lukas led her into Tormod's office, which looked no worse for wear, although it too had the stench of smoke clinging to it. Lukas knocked once on the door and then wordlessly let Samara in. He at least seemed sorry for having lied to her.

Samara studied Tormod as she walked in. He looked healthy enough, if a little pale. Apparently, he had drunkenly passed out in the catacombs and not been aware of the fire at all. He wore his usual brown leather jacket and worn-looking pinstripe trousers. He had his head bent over his desk. When she entered, he looked up and gave her a cocky smile, though even Samara could tell that it lacked his usual enthusiasm and charm.

"Hisada, it's good to see you." This, at least, seemed genuine. "Have a seat."

Normally she'd get bent out of shape with him for calling her Hisada, which meant "reaper" in her native country of Akadd, but she'd recently learnt it had a more nuanced meaning as "gatherer", so she let it slide. She sat down obediently without putting up a fuss.

It was strange. Now that she no longer worked for him, she didn't feel the need to fight his every order.

"You're looking well," she remarked.

"Wish the same could be said about this place," he muttered.

"I did warn you," she said, keeping her voice light.

"Don't start, Hisada. I appreciate you saving my life and all, but I'm in no mood for I-told-you-so's."

Samara leaned back in her seat. She could feel Lukas hovering behind her.

"I'm not here for I-told-you-so's. You have a Humphreys problem. Turns out, we both do."

Tormod rubbed his forehead and knocked back a drink from a mug on his desk. It smelled of liquor. Apparently his private liquor supply had been untouched by the fire.

"I shouldn't even be here," Tormod muttered. "He had the bank notes cancelled, you know that, Hisada?"

"I figured that's what happened."

"His men were crawling all over the docks. Couldn't even go back to my own verdammt house because that arschloch was hunting me."

"So, you stayed here. Makes sense." She was still kicking herself that she hadn't realised Tormod was in Märchen all along. Perhaps if she had remained part of the Lions Lukas would have cared to mention it.

Tormod poured more liquor from a silver flask into his mug, making Samara wonder why he bothered to even use a mug.

"You realise, of course, that if I never got any of the money, then the money was technically never stolen. None of those toffs lost money, but he still burned down my place."

Lukas cleared his throat at the door. "It's been my opinion that Chetwin Humphreys is very concerned with saving face."

"Oh, he wants to save face all right," Tormod replied, banging his fist on the desk. "He's more interested in crawling up the arses of the toffs in this city than in keeping the peace. Well, I'm not having it."

Samara pressed her lips together and breathed through her nose. Suppressed the urge to lunge across the table at her old boss. "Meaning?"

"Meaning, I know you've made some arrangement with the Magistrate to keep the peace, but I have face of my own to save. I can't let this go."

This time, he was looking at Lukas.

She didn't think much of Tormod Lyons, but in this instance, she couldn't blame him. Going after the Zephyr was an act of aggression above and beyond what was necessary. It made Samara wonder again whether it was Humphreys behind it, or the Order. They would certainly care nothing about maintaining the peace in Märchen.

Still, her agreement with the Magistrate was very clear. She would ensure Hans' release, *if* Samara fixed things.

"The way I see it, we have a common enemy," she said slowly. "Chetwin Humphreys won't stop coming after me and mine, either. I don't want to broker peace with him. I think you know exactly how I feel about that man. So, the question is, where do we go from here?"

Tormod leaned forward, a grin forming on his lips.

"This city ain't big enough for myself and Humphreys. Not now. What would you think about backing me in a little hostile takeover?"

Samara pressed her lips together and grimaced. Of course it would come to this. *Schiesse.*

Alfred Vogel was a man of routine. He worked with his boss every night until eight in the evening before taking supper at

Gatti's, one of the few restaurants in Old Town that stayed open so late, and then went home to his modest flat. Vogel was a saver. A money man through and through. He was frugal, and it was that very frugality that Chetwin Humphreys valued. Not that the crime lord always listened to him. The crystal bannister in Chetwin's Elphame Park home was proof of that.

Vogel had met Chetwin early in Humphreys' career. He lacked a formal education, but he'd always had a mind for numbers, and he recognised Chetwin's potential the first time he met him. He'd started as just another member of Chetwin's crew, but as the business grew, he soon made himself indispensable to Chetwin. In a few short years, Vogel had officially gone from thug to partner in Humphreys' enterprises. They made a good team. Chetwin was good at the big picture—making contacts and deals. And Vogel quietly took care of the day-to-day running of the business. He made sure that should a government official look into Humphreys affairs, things were all in order. Chetwin wasn't a generous employer, but Vogel enjoyed the work. Nobody else in Märchen could do what Vogel did so efficiently, taking businesses of questionable legality and making them appear legal.

But lately, Chetwin had been swept up with the auction and the Order. He was obsessed with saving face. It was infuriating. A problem with no solution. No matter how much Vogel tried to keep his boss focused on the business, Chetwin just couldn't be swayed. It made Vogel think. Perhaps it was time to part ways? Vogel had money. Quite a bit of it saved up by now. Perhaps it was time to retire before things went too far and the Magistrate took action. He didn't feel ready to retire just yet, and he wouldn't know what he would do with himself, but things were getting dangerous. Too dangerous.

All these thoughts swirled through his mind as he shifted his briefcase in one hand, unlocked his door, and entered his flat.

Closing the door behind him, he dropped his briefcase and reached up to turn up the gas lamp but stopped. He noticed the small fire in the grate that his maid had lit for him was guttering. Strange. He looked to the window and realised it was open.

Someone was here.

His eyes glanced to his practice sabre. The blade was stored in a bag by his umbrella stand. Would he be able to get to it?

"Is it all right if I turn on a light?" he asked into the darkness.

"Sure. Just no sudden movements," came a female voice.

He turned the knob, and the gas lamp flared to life. Seated at his dining room table was the Hisada. To his dismay, he spotted his practice sabre on the table in front of her.

Noticing him eyeing the blade, she remarked, "Nice blade. You take good care of it, I see."

He sucked in a breath. Should he run? No. She would catch him, surely.

"What brings you here?" he asked, trying to quiet his fear.

"I have a message"

"For Mr Humphreys?"

"No," she replied. "For you. From Tormod Lyons."

He briefly wondered whether "message" was a euphemism. Was the Hisada about to kill him and use his mangled corpse as a message for Chetwin? But no, she said the message was for him.

He nodded and slowly approached the table.

"What's the message?"

"Tormod would like to meet with you."

"Why me?"

"Because he thinks you're the only one working for Humphreys with a lick of sense. You know Humphreys is going too far. Tormod wants your help."

"Mr Humphreys doesn't listen to me much these days," Vogel replied. An admission he hated to make, but it was true.

The Hisada stood up and Vogel took a step back. "Not my problem. My job was to connect the two of you. Job done."

She strode to the open window and climbed out. Vogel waited. When it was clear she wouldn't return, he drew a shaky breath, walked to the window, and closed it.

SAMARA STALKED home from her meeting with Vogel. There. She had done what Tormod requested. She had connected him to Vogel. Beyond that, she refused to promise him anything. She didn't even know why he thought he needed her help. He had the entire Lions gang, for Manāt's sake. If Tormod thought she was going to go back to killing people, even Humphreys, as a favour to him, then that smoke must've truly addled his brains.

Of course, if it meant saving Hans, she was willing to do just about anything. And she *had* made a promise to the Magistrate. She found herself cursing the bureaucrat for forcing her to team up with the Lions again.

She travelled via the rooftops. It was slow going, but necessary with everything going on. She still hadn't had a chance to digest the news that the last descendant of Queen White, Eloise, was still in the city. The thought really burned inside her that Ana hadn't trusted them enough to come clean. No wonder she had gotten so good with her powers since they had last seen each other. She was receiving training from Eloise.

Upon learning the news, she briefly contemplated just telling Callista the girl was still in Märchen and washing her hands of the whole affair. She still hadn't come up with a good reason not to do so.

Samara was getting ready to leap across a small gap between buildings when she noticed a figure across the street, bathed in shadows, also making their way across the rooftops, following her. She let out a loud exhalation, narrowing her eyes, but didn't stop. She wasn't about to let on that she knew she was being followed. Samara didn't fancy another rooftop fight. She wanted to control her environment.

She continued on with her jump. As she made her way across the next rooftop, she assessed her surroundings. Ahead of her was a café. Although it was evening, the café was still open. It was a gentleman's only establishment, where the businessmen of Hollowhorn came to conduct their affairs. She'd visited it a time or two back when she was still working for Tormod. Yes. This would do nicely.

She slipped down a drainpipe and made her way into the café. A man at the door tried to bar her way, but then he recognised who he was dealing with and let her pass. Thankfully, not everyone was aware she had parted ways with the Lions. Those who weren't otherwise occupied with smoking, drinking and making under-the-counter deals observed her with wariness. She ignored them and approached the sole female occupant. A buxom woman who worked behind the counter. She'd had dealings with her before.

"I need to use a room upstairs."

The woman turned to retrieve a key. "Room 12," was all she said.

Samara accepted the key and made her way up the stairs where a businessman and a scantily dressed woman were slowly exchanging money. If the House de Mörde hadn't bought her, that could've been her life. Bile rose in her throat as she watched the man, still tucking his shirt back into his trousers. She reached out to take hold of his arm.

"You know who I am?"

The man's eyes widened. She hated the looks people got when she addressed them as the Hisada. But in this case, a bit of intimidation seemed the right course of action. He nodded, not quite making eye contact with her.

She tightened her grip. "Come with me."

Locating room 12, she unlocked the door and pushed him inside. She turned up the tap on the gas lamp to brighten the interior. The room was sparse. A bed took up most of the space. It was an end room with a corner window, that in any other place might've brought brightness and energy to the space, but here, the peeling paint on the window ledge only added to the squalidness.

She sat down on the bed, keeping the window to her back, indicating the man should do the same.

"Just look like we're in a meeting."

"W-what?" the man stuttered.

She motioned impatiently with her head.

He obeyed, sitting beside her at the very edge of the bed.

"So, what's your line of business?"

"I swear, I don't owe Mr Lyons any money."

She rolled her eyes. "How's your day been?"

"I'm sorry. Why am I—"

"Nevermind," she curtly responded, finally hearing what she had been waiting for. The soft click as someone from outside opened the window. She breathed in deeply. Exhaled. Waiting for her assailant.

The man started to turn his head, but Samara poked him with a finger. "Keep your eyes on me."

Again, he obeyed, although she thought she heard a whimper. She wasn't in the mood to coddle some drunken businessmen who paid desperate women for their company.

She heard the window slide open.

The man whimpered again.

But still, Samara waited patiently. Took another deep breath in, then out. Calmly, she twisted behind her, and was on her assailant in a moment.

At first, she couldn't tell who it was, only that it was a young, lithe girl, who clearly had had previous fight training, which meant she was from House de Mörde.

"Get out!" she snapped at the man.

He didn't need to be told twice. He bolted from the room, leaving the door wide open behind him.

The girl took advantage of Samara's momentary lapse in attention and thrust upward, flipping Samara off the bed, and the pair landed on the worn wooden floorboards. Samara reached for a khanjar blade. She hadn't wanted to do it earlier with the businessman in the room, but now she was prepared to use everything at her disposal. If Callista had sent someone to kill her, then she wasn't about to oblige them.

She spun on the ground to face her opponent, finally noticing the short dark hair and cocky smirk of *her*. The imp.

"*You*," she snarled.

"Me," the imp replied, again with the cocky smirk.

"How'd you pick up my trail, anyway?" Samara growled.

The imp's grin widened. "You smell of smoke," was all she said.

Again, Samara considered telling Callie all about Eloise and how she was still in Märchen, but for some reason, she found herself so enraged at seeing the imp, she decided against it. Samara knew the imp's type. She had seen many of them at House de Mörde. Hungry to prove themselves. This little brat needed a lesson in humility.

Samara flipped the knife in her hand and darted forward. The girl followed with a block, only to realise at the last second it was a feint as Samara kicked her legs out from under her. The girl grunted loudly but, with a flip of her legs, was on her feet again. Samara followed suit, although her body protested. She was still sore and achy from carrying Tormod. The pair grappled with each other, banging loudly into walls, though nobody came up to see what was going on. That was one thing about being the Hisada, nobody tried to interfere in her business.

With a flashy spinning kick, the younger girl knocked the blade out of Samara's hand. Samara responded by reaching for another, but the girl followed up with a punch to the stomach, sending Samara into a wall. Just as Samara got her wits about her, she felt a woollen scarf cinch about her throat.

What was with this girl trying to strangle her all the time?

Samara snarled. Rather than try to pull away, she grabbed the imp's wrists with both her hands and dragged her forward, the tension in her throat immediately loosening. *Stupid girl!*

Seeing that she was losing her advantage, the imp spoke. "I have a message from Callista."

She could guess what kind of message that would be. Once again, Samara pondered handing Eloise over. Maybe it wasn't the right thing to do for the girl, but the silly fool had made the choice to stay in Märchen, and Samara had her team's safety to consider.

Panting, the imp continued. "There was a man staying at House de Mörde. A member of some group called the Restorationists. He's hunting you and your people. Using the Watch."

"Restorationists? Who is this man? What does he want?"

"He's here to take Eloise back."

"What do you mean take her back? To do what?"

"Something about making her queen."

Samara remembered back to the auction. Hans had had to do some fast talking. He claimed he was a member of an association trying to put the last living descendant of Queen White back on the throne. He'd called the group the Glass Coffin Society. But apparently there really was a group trying to do just that.

And Callie was working with them.

Samara studied the imp's face. It was clear the girl knew nothing more about this group. And since she was only supposed to pass on a message, it was also clear this girl was not worth her time.

"Thanks for the information," Samara muttered before punching the girl in the side of the head and leaping for the window.

ANA STOOD NERVOUSLY on the doorstep. She didn't want to be there. She fought the old urge to flee. After the fire, after she told the others the truth about Eloise, she had quickly made herself scarce. She just couldn't face their ire. She knew that by keeping Eloise a secret, she had broken their trust. But then Gerde came by the bakery and left a message for her. Said they should all talk. In the message, she told Ana she could even bring "her friend". But Ana decided it would be better to go alone. Ana knew Samara wouldn't arbitrarily hand Eloise to the House de Mörde, but she didn't truly know how the Hisada would react when backed into a corner.

She rapped her knuckles on the door. Three quick taps and two long ones.

A moment later, the neighbouring door opened, and Samara revealed herself. She stared stonily at Ana. "You'd better come inside," she said.

As the Hisada closed the door behind her, Ana couldn't help noticing the bruised knuckles. They seemed to match the purple bruises beneath her dark eyes.

When Ana entered the room, she wasn't at all surprised to see everyone there. Well, everyone minus Hans, who she assumed was still under arrest. She hoped the old man was well.

She took a shaky breath and gave a tiny wave. Seb's eyes were downcast. He couldn't or wouldn't make eye contact with her. She turned back to Gerde, who gave her an encouraging smile and offered her a seat at a worn wooden table.

"I'm glad you came," said Gerde.

Ana looked to Art, who sat with his long legs stretched out in front of him. He had his arms crossed over his chest and he gave her an amused look. "Ana," was all he said.

"Have some chai," Samara said, pouring from a metal pot on the table.

Again, Ana noted the bruises and cuts on her knuckles.

"What happened to you?" she asked, wanting to fill the awkward silence.

It was Gerde who responded. "Someone was fighting again." There was a warmth in the way she spoke those words, but also something like worry.

Ana sipped the pinkish-brown chai. It was good, but too sweet. "I just came to apologise. About Eloise. I wasn't sure if you would change your mind and send her back to the House. I should have told you she was still in Märchen."

The weight seemed to lift from her shoulders. It felt good having everything in the open. After everything they went through together to rescue Eloise, she owed them this much.

"Yes, you should have," replied Art, but there was no admonishment in his tone.

Samara didn't sit down. Instead, she leaned against the wall nearby, one leg propped up behind her. "Is she safe?"

Ana bit her lip. "For now."

"We asked you here to warn her. She shouldn't stay here," Samara said. "It's not just Humphreys and Callista what's after her. There's a new group calling themselves the Restorationists."

Ana took in that news. "Who are they?" she finally asked.

"Eloise never mentioned them to you?" Gerde asked.

Ana thought about it and then shook her head. "No, not by name, at least."

"They are people who very much want to go back to the age of the Three Queens. Or at least, One queen," Art said, pulling out his pipe.

It was strange for her to think that Eloise might be a descendant of Queen White. Ana was more interested in Eloise's Magical abilities than any potential royal inheritance. She somehow couldn't imagine the young girl on a throne. Although Eloise looked like a young Queen White, she didn't act like a queen, or a princess, or whatever it was they were claiming she would become.

She licked her lips and finally forced herself to meet Samara's hard gaze. "What will you do now that you know Eloise is still here?"

Samara shrugged. "I don't much know. That girl's caused me a world of trouble, but I have other things to worry about."

"Hans is still being held by the Watch," Gerde supplied before Ana could ask any further questions.

"Do you have a plan to get him out?" Ana asked.

Art took a puff from his pipe. "Turns out the Magistrate will gladly help, so long as Samara here can stop a turf war."

"Can you do that?" Ana asked.

If she was being entirely honest with herself, she wasn't so sure Samara could accomplish something like that. Nearly every job they had gone on, things had gone wrong in some unforeseen way. Stopping a turf war sounded like a tall order.

"As a matter of fact, yes," Samara replied with a grim smile. "Now that Tormod has crawled out from his hiding hole, he's asked me to help him take down Humphreys once and for all."

Ana swallowed. "Take down how, exactly?"

Samara ran a hand through her hair. "He wants to take over Humphreys' organisation."

Ana felt her body grow cold and still.

"Knock out the competition. Two arschloch gang leaders enter. One arschloch leader survives," Art muttered, blowing out a puff of smoke, the stench of which irritated Ana's nostrils.

"He doesn't want you to—" Gerde said in a halting voice.

Samara shook her head. "He knows I won't kill for him."

Ana glanced at the others around the room. Seb was still not looking at her. She opened her mouth. Closed it and opened it again. "Please tell me you're not actually thinking about helping him."

Samara shrugged. "I think he's a bit of a dummkopf, but he's a lot less dangerous than Humphreys. I'm not saying he's good for the city, but he'd much rather see people spending money at his tables than blowing it on Nepenthe. That's got to be something."

"He supports human trafficking. I thought you were against that." It was a low blow, Ana knew, given Samara herself was kidnapped by slavers.

Samara gave her a withering look. "You know I am."

Gerde stood up. "Look, none of us like teaming up with him, but it's the only way to get Hans back. We're not asking you to help. We just wanted to warn you—"

"You *do* remember he wanted to buy me, don't you?" Ana interrupted, cutting Gerde off.

She gripped the table in front of her with white knuckles. Samara straightened and said in a cold voice: "You know I wouldn't support him if he was getting into trafficking. Which he isn't. Tormod may be King of the Hollow, but he doesn't have the contacts to maintain trade."

Ana abruptly rose to her feet, knocking the wooden chair back with a loud clatter.

"He wouldn't have to, he'd have Humphreys' network,

wouldn't he?" When Samara didn't immediately respond, she said, "Well, wouldn't he?"

No one answered.

She huffed out a breath. "I thought I could trust you," she muttered, glaring at the others one final time before turning to flee the room.

She was halfway down the stairs when Seb caught up with her.

"Ana," he said, grabbing her by the arm.

"Why didn't you say something back there?" she demanded.

Seb leaned in and spoke in a quieter voice. "Because I agree with Samara. I think Tormod would be better for Märchen than Humphreys."

"You were indentured to him for months!"

"Yeah, and I saw how he is with the Lions. He's a lot less ruthless than Chetwin Humphreys."

"You know he wanted to buy me," she whispered. "I can't go along with this."

She noticed a tick in Seb's jaw. "Yeah, well, it wouldn't be the first time."

She glared into his brown eyes. "What's that supposed to mean?"

"You know what I mean. You *hid* Eloise. Kept her a secret from us for weeks. Even though you knew the House de Mörde were hunting us because of her. And every time one of us saw you, you just lied to us."

"I did what I had to. She's my friend," she replied defiantly.

"Yeah, well, I thought we were your friends." He glared at her. "Nobody supported you back there because we can't trust you, Ana."

Shrugging out of Seb's grip, Ana fled down the stairs and out of the inn.

CHAPTER THIRTEEN

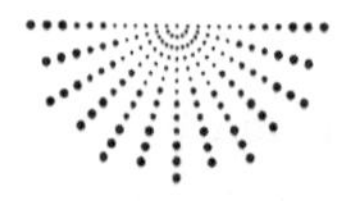

I found this sketch pad and pencil in a drawer. Since I don't actually enjoy drawing, I've decided to do some journalling. I've never kept a journal before, unless you count the letters I had to write to Richilde about my progress. They wanted to know what I was learning. But I never told the truth. Why should I? They didn't care about me. They just wanted to know that their future queen was safe. Not one of them asked if I wanted to become queen. All my life it's been like this. When I was kidnapped by Humphreys, it was just one more person who wanted me for my Magic... I used to wish I didn't have Magic. Until I met Ana.

—DIARY OF ELOISE ADELMAN

"*E*xcuse me, sir. I think you dropped your coin purse," said a fiery-headed girl with wide green eyes.

The man, a businessman in a suit, stopped and turned towards her. He glanced down at the purse she held in her outstretched hand, checked his pocket and then smiled gratefully.

"Thank you, my dear. Not everyone would be so honest as you," he said as he stuffed the coin purse into his coat pocket and doffed his hat to her.

The fiery-haired girl walked back the way she had come, down into a small alleyway between a cake shop and a shop selling lace. Upon seeing a girl with flowing blonde hair, she grinned widely at her. "It worked!"

"I told you it would work, Ana!" Eloise's voice came out of the blonde girl's mouth. "How much did he have?"

Ana, the fiery-haired girl, pulled the drawstring on the purse and poured the coins into her palm. She counted ten silver nobles.

"Not bad," said Eloise, a touch of smugness in her voice.

"Not enough to get our own rooms though. Or send a message to my family," Ana lamented.

"All in good time," Eloise replied. "In the meantime, I think we deserve a treat, don't you?"

"We should probably save it," Ana replied, doubtfully.

"We just successfully used our magic to get money, we should celebrate," Eloise insisted. Then, seeing Ana's serious expression she added, "A bag of fudge doesn't cost much. We'll save the rest."

Not wanting to disappoint the exuberant teenager, Ana allowed herself to be dragged into a nearby cake shop, where they ordered a paper bag full of creamy fudge. It cost two of their precious nobles, but the sweets practically melted in her mouth.

As they walked the cobblestones back to the Hollow, it was a relief to not have to keep looking over their shoulders. Eloise had really outdone herself with her illusions. Ana had heard of small magic users who could create illusions, but they would never pass any real tests. A man might create an illusion to appear a foot taller, but if a bird were to swoop by, the illusion would fail.

But Eloise's Magic created something that both looked *and* felt real.

This illusion would grant freedom, and the ability to make money. Yet her stomach was in knots and soon Eloise was giving her concerned glances.

"What's wrong?"

Ana forced a chuckle. "It's nothing."

"You're eating fudge from Pentemarone while walking openly down the street, and you still have a perpetual frown on your face. Not to mention you didn't come to visit me yesterday. What's happened?"

Eloise stopped in the street and turned to face her friend, causing some Old Town shoppers to scowl as they adjusted their course on the cobbled street.

"It's just…" Ana bit her lip. Where to even begin? "I saw Samara and the rest of the crew yesterday."

"Are they still mad at you about keeping me a secret?" Eloise asked, popping a piece of fudge in her mouth and hooking arms with Ana. They began to walk again.

"Yes. Seb said I can't be trusted, which is unbelievable. They're all criminals, but somehow *I'm* the one who can't be trusted."

"Seb doesn't understand," Eloise said with a mouthful of fudge. "He doesn't have magic"

"It gets worse, though. Now they plan to team up with

Tormod Lyons to take down Chetwin Humphreys. Tormod was the man who wanted to buy me for my powers."

"He's the head of the Lions, isn't he?"

Ana answered with a nod of her head. For a few minutes Eloise said nothing as they strolled the street. Finally, she responded with a "hmm."

"What?" Ana asked, feeling somewhat defensive.

"Well, I just think perhaps that wouldn't be a bad idea," Eloise said while savouring her fudge.

Ana frowned. "Really?"

Eloise shrugged and hugged Ana closer. "Humphreys is a dangerous person. And he's obsessed with Magic. We would be a lot safer if he were out of the picture. If that means the Lions take over, maybe that's not so bad."

"I don't trust Tormod Lyons," Ana mumbled.

She couldn't help sending a glare in Eloise's direction. Tormod was as bad as Humphreys. Why couldn't Eloise see that?

"Do you trust Samara?" Eloise asked.

Ana thought about it. In many ways, Samara was closed off and unknowable to her. But she saw how she shared her space with Art, Gerde and Hans, tight as it was. She didn't have to do that. She took care of her people.

"I suppose," Ana replied, reluctantly.

Eloise grinned. "Then trust that she knows what she's doing. And have some more fudge before I eat it all myself."

Ana slowly took a piece of the confection from the paper bag, rolling it between her fingers in contemplation. She still didn't appreciate what Seb had said to her. Although she begrudgingly could admit that she saw his point of view. She had lied to them and kept Eloise a secret. And one of the reasons they were being hunted was because Samara had gone out of her way to help Eloise.

"Something's still bothering you?" Eloise asked, giving her a sidelong glance.

"They also mentioned a group called the Restorationists."

Eloise stopped mid-chew. "What about them?"

"They're here in Märchen. They're looking for you. Is it true they want to make you Queen?"

"Yes," said Eloise, quietly, not meetings Ana's eyes.

"Maybe we should be saving our money to leave Märchen," Ana suggested.

"It wouldn't make a difference," Eloise mumbled.

Ana saw the fear in the girl at the mere mention of this other group. It frightened her that, even with their combined powers and their disguises, Eloise didn't think they could outrun these Restorationists.

"Maybe we should help Samara and the others," Ana mused. She let out a long breath. "If we help them with Humphreys, they can help us with the Restorationists."

Eloise seemed to consider it for a long time. "As long as she doesn't try to send me back to House de Mörde, I'll help."

Having had her efforts at connecting with Sam rebuffed, Callista finally took it upon herself to speak with Sylvain Duvall. They had a cordial relationship. Surely she would be willing to look into matters regarding the arrest of Samara's landlord. It was with that in mind that she was ushered into Duvall's office.

The older woman greeted her warmly. "Matron, it's always a pleasure to see you."

"It's good to see you as well," Callista replied as she seated herself.

"Tell me, what brings you here today?"

The Magistrate had never hired the House, but their paths crossed from time to time. Usually in social situations, and occasionally when Callista felt she needed to gain some political favour by warning the Magistrate of illegal activities her girls had learnt about.

"I recently heard about the arrest of a Hollowhorn print shop owner named Hans Manfredo."

The Magistrate's eyebrows scrunched together. "I'm familiar with the case," she replied in a neutral tone.

"I have some concerns regarding how the arrest was made."

The Magistrate raised a hand. "Let me stop you there. I looked into it, and I saw no connection with this arrest and Chetwin Humphreys."

"Humphreys?" Callista replied with surprise. "No. He isn't behind it."

The Magistrate studied her intently. "I was visited by the Hisada. She told me Humphreys had paid the City Watch to have her friend arrested."

"She was mistaken. The man who ordered Manfredo' arrest is a Richildan citizen named Lutz Kaiser. He is working directly with Hoffner in the City Watch."

The Magistrate leaned back in her seat and crossed her arms. "I viewed the evidence from the arrest. There *were* forged documents."

Callista touched her hair. "They must've been planted."

The corner of the Magistrate's lip twitched. "The House sometimes uses a forger when on jobs, don't they?"

Callista rubbed her brow. "That's beside the point. A foreign individual is paying off the Märchen City Watch to conduct illegal searches and arrests. Surely that must concern you," Callista insisted.

"How do you know they were illegal searches?"

"Oh, come on Sylvain. Was Manfredo named in a crime? By

who? At least look into it, because I guarantee you that when you pull that thread, you'll find there was no reason for the Watch to be in Manfredo' shop."

The Magistrate shrewdly studied Callista before eventually saying, "I'll do that," she said, reaching for the bell by her desk.

A moment later, the door opened and her secretary entered. "Yes, ma'am?"

"Lester, I need you to look into the activities of one Lutz Kaiser. Oh, and ask around and find out who constable Hoffner has been meeting with."

Callista exhaled. "Thank you. I had a question about something else. Kaiser made certain threats against the House de Mörde. I want to know if he has the power to go through with them."

SAMARA SAT in a darkened corner of The Wishing-Table with a large pint of ale, though she hadn't drunk of a drop of it. She was surprised to have received a message from Ana about arranging a meeting with Eloise. Though it certainly wasn't the first time Ana had stormed off only to come back later, so perhaps surprise wasn't the right word. *Grateful* was a better word, she decided. Though she was loath to use Ana solely for her gifts, it couldn't be denied her abilities, especially now she'd been practicing under Eloise's tutelage, would be invaluable.

When a pair of strange girls, wearing lace-edged dresses and wide-brimmed hats approached her table, she glared at them.

"Can't you see this table is taken?" she remarked, picking up the glass of ale as though she were about to take a sip.

One of the girls, the one with the fiery red hair, pinched her lips together and said, in Ana's voice, "I thought you don't drink."

Samara jerked back, her eyes widening at the two girls in front of her. She studied their faces closely. She'd heard of small magic users who could create illusions, but never had the opportunity to see it up close. This was incredible.

Schooling her features, she slowly settled back in her seat and kicked a chair out next to her, indicating they should sit down.

"Nice disguises," she remarked. "Although you look far too well-off to be wandering around the Hollow."

"I can take care of any thieves," Ana replied curtly.

"I know you can." Samara turned to the other strange face. Eloise, presumably, though the face she wore was that of a fair-haired girl with flowing locks, thus concealing her resemblance to Queen White. "I see you decided to stay and see the sights."

"Technically, I've lived in Märchen for a couple of years now," Eloise replied.

Samara shook her head. She didn't like Eloise. She had done nothing but bring trouble down on her and her crew. And although it was interesting to see Ana's abilities grow, she didn't like Eloise's influence on her.

Gerde would remind her that Eloise was only a teenager, and she had been through a lot. But it didn't change her opinion of the girl.

A muscle twitched in her jaw. "Remember when we agreed you were going to leave Märchen?"

"You know I'm being hunted all across Alsatia right? It wouldn't matter if I left. And besides, it sounds like you could use my help."

She had a point. But Samara couldn't help but bristle at the girl's arrogance. When Samara had last seen her, the girl had been afraid. Held captive by Chetwin Humphreys for weeks, about to be sold to some magic-obsessed toff, she was beaten down. But freedom, both from Humphreys and whoever this

Restorationist group was, now made her arrogant. Samara eyed the out of place outfits. She was sloppy, too.

Then Eloise did something that surprised Samara. She leaned forward and lowered her voice. "I'm sorry that all these things have been happening to you because of me. I'm grateful for all you did, rescuing me and not sending me back to the House. I'm here to help. Really."

Samara shook her head. It was amazing how the girl could switch from acting like an arrogant teenager to an earnest young woman who could maybe become a queen. She huffed out a breath. "What do you know of the Restorationists?"

The fair-haired girl's expression faltered slightly. She shrugged. "I've heard the name a few times. I don't know much about them, except that they want a descendant of Queen White on the throne."

"A descendant of Queen White," Samara repeated. She still couldn't believe Callie had been right all along. If her former best friend hadn't been intent on killing her, she would've apologised for laughing in her face when Callie first suggested the possibility. "As in, you?"

The girl merely shrugged.

"I take it you don't want to go back to them?" Samara asked, tapping her foot impatiently. She couldn't blame the girl. Not exactly. She knew what it was like to be forced into a life you didn't want.

"Not particularly," Eloise replied. "I've been shafted around my whole life. I never knew my parents, and my aunt and uncle sent me to the Restorationists as soon as I started exhibiting Magic."

"How old were you when you first got your Magic?" Ana asked suddenly.

"Eight," Eloise replied.

"Me too!"

Samara rapped the table with her knuckles to get their attention again. "Do you even want to be..." She lowered her voice. "Queen?"

The girl shrugged again.

"Use your words," Samara said.

Eloise sighed. "Do I want my whole life decided for me? Do I want to be forced to follow other people's wishes and be someone's puppet?" She gave Samara an indecipherable look. "Would you?"

"Fair." Inwardly, she cursed. Of course the girl wouldn't want to go back to the Restorationists. Because that would be too easy. "Look, according to information we received from Callista, it's the Restorationists what's been behind all our problems. Hans' arrest, Gerde's family's coaching inn—"

"What happened to the coaching inn?" Ana interrupted, concerned.

"The Watch shut it down. I need to put an end to this. Get the Restorationists out of Märchen and out of our lives for good. What can you tell me about them?"

"I don't know much," Eloise said, reaching for Samara's mug of ale. "If you're not going to drink that..."

Samara snatched the mug away from her. "First, you tell me everything you know. Names. Anything we might be able to use to fight them."

"HERE. LET ME GET THAT," Seb said, jumping to his feet and helping Gerde carry a platter of rouladen that had been delivered from the kitchens below. Gerde smiled gratefully, letting him take the platter from her while she grabbed the metal jug of ale and a glass of water for Sam. She kicked the door closed behind her and gazed around the room sadly.

Even with the rest of the crew there, the room felt so empty without Hans. Her stomach churned, thinking about how she'd failed him. Sam assured her she didn't blame her, but Gerde didn't quite believe her.

The room was cramped with Samara, Art, and Seb at the table. Samara hadn't thought it a good idea to invite Ana. She didn't entirely trust the girl anymore, which Gerde understood, even so, it didn't change how much smaller their little crew had become.

"Warm and edible. It's a triumph," Art announced, having already dug into his heaped serving of rolled beef. Gerde took a seat next to Samara and picked up her fork. The food looked greasy and not particularly appetising, but Gerde had eaten little all day. Taking a bite, she was surprised that it didn't taste altogether terrible. Not as good as what her mutter would make, but it was tolerable.

They ate in companionable silence, and when they were done, Seb, ever the agreeable guest, was the first to jump up and place the tray in front of their door again. Art stretched out languorously and took out his pipe while Samara heated water for chai.

"So don't keep us in suspense. Will Eloise help us fight the Restorationists?" he drawled while placing a fat pinch of pipe weed into the bowl of his pipe.

"I think so," Samara replied, her back turned while she prepared tea. "She's as eager as anyone to be free of the Restorationists."

Gerde walked over to assist her. Now that Art was staying with them, they hardly had any alone time anymore, and there was so much Samara was still keeping to herself. Gerde brushed a finger against the back of Sam's hand, and she glanced up with a raised eyebrow.

"Are we sure she can be trusted?" Seb asked.

Gerde helped Samara carry the mugs to the table.

"I don't know how reliable she is," Samara admitted. "She doesn't seem to like people telling her what to do."

"I was the same way when I was her age," Gerde replied.

Samara gave her a look as though to say she seriously doubted that. "But she listens to Ana, and Ana has her convinced she should try and help us."

"Are you sure about that?" Seb asked. "It seemed like Ana was the one following Eloise about to me."

Art released a puff of smoke. "Now, now. I know she broke your heart-"

"It's not that. And she didn't break my heart-"

"But Ana had her reasons for keeping her a secret. She already said she didn't know if we would turn around and hand her back to Callista," Art continued, talking over Seb.

"I suppose," Seb mumbled, his eyes downcast.

Gerde gave Seb a small, comforting smile. *Poor kid*, she thought. She knew he had been sweet on Ana, and she had seen Ana kiss him after the auction. Things were no doubt extremely confusing, but she agreed that Seb's judgement in this instance might be a little clouded by his hurt feelings.

"So, was she able to tell you anything about this Restorationist Party?" Gerde asked. "If it really is them that have been coming after us and not the Order."

"It could be both of them, certainly," replied Art. "But why would the Order use the City Watch when they already have Humphreys after us?"

"My thoughts exactly," said Samara, reaching behind into one of the pockets of her coat that she'd left carelessly slung on the back of a chair. She retrieved a folded piece of paper. "Here. She could only give me a handful of names."

She unfolded the paper and passed it to Art. "Do any of these names look familiar to you?"

Art held the note up. Four names were on there. Both Gerde and Seb leaned in to have a look.

Art exhaled a ring of smoke. "I think so. This name here, Johann Müller, looks familiar. I'm not sure if he's connected with my father or if it was just an aristocrat I met while I was touring in Richilde." He leaned back in his chair. "Let me think on it."

"Could you ask some of your old connections?" Gerde asked. They didn't have time for Art to maybe remember who this Johann person was.

Art raised an eyebrow. "You mean from the days before I was twice disowned?" He twisted his lips. "I'll see what I can do. What about Hans?"

Samara frowned, and her lips pinched together. "Tormod's meeting with Vogel right now. Once he does, I'll know what's actually involved with this hostile takeover he wants to do. And then the Magistrate will help us with Hans."

She let out a long exhalation.

Art spoke up. "Maybe I could visit Hans in gaol. At least make sure he's okay."

"It's not safe," Samara replied. "Even if you're in disguise, we have to assume they're watching any visitors." Samara turned to Seb. "I don't suppose you ever heard any chatter about this Restorationist Party being active in Märchen?"

Seb shook his head.

Gerde hesitated. Now that things were different between them, she wasn't altogether sure how to approach certain conversations with Sam. Which was frustrating. Despite their growing relationship, she'd always been honest with Sam. Supportive, but honest. She didn't know why things felt different. But ever since she had confessed her feelings to Sam, and found out that Sam truly reciprocated, she didn't want to do anything to mess it all up. But this was important and needed to be said.

"What about Callista?" When all eyes, including Samara's, turned to her, she continued. "Other than Eloise, she's the one person who might actually have information on them."

"Because she's working with them," Samara said. Her tone was mild, but there was still an edge to it.

"But she sent a messenger—" Samara snorted at the word. "She sent one of her girls to give you a message about them. Callista was warning you. She didn't have to do that."

Samara sat hunched forward in her chair. This time she fully turned to face Gerde, her brown eyes searching Gerde's face "You're suggesting we trust Callie? She lied about not using Eloise—"

"Yeah, I'm with Samara on this one," Art agreed. "I'm not sure the Matron of House de Mörde has our best interests at heart."

Gerde looked to Seb for support, but he merely shrugged his shoulders. "She betrayed us to Humphreys. I never understood why we trusted her again."

Samara pushed the list of names towards Art. "Go over this list. Talk to some of your former toff chums. There must be a way we can get to them."

Seb raised a hand. "Just so we're clear. We don't want to give Eloise back to them. Why?"

Gerde glared at him. "Because she doesn't want to go back. And even a gilded cage is still a cage, Seb."

Art clapped him on the back. "Plus, Ana would never forgive us, and from what you lot have said about how her magic has grown, we don't want to get on her bad side!"

～

TORMOD WAS glad to be back in his old office again, though the place still reeked of smoke. The casino was still closed. Oh, and they were bleeding money. Worse. The wine shipments were held up while they hired extra security, since Humphreys might go after that too.

All in all, things were not looking good. The Lions, the thieves guild, were now little more than security for his establishments, of which the Royal Zephyr was his most visible one. There were still smaller places. Taverns, coffee houses, music halls. The Zephyr was the only one in his name, but the others were his in every other way. Protection money and a piece of the profits. If you thought you were patronising a gambling den not connected with Tormod, you were most likely mistaken.

Vanity. That's what had caused him to buy the Zephyr and turn it into what it was. Before he came along, it was yet another tired old gambling hell with décor about fifty years out of date. Tormod had been more interested in its potential as a base for the Lions. The warren below made it ideal for those who came by their money in less than legal ways.

The truth was though, it was something of a dream of his to own the Royal Zephyr. He had practically been raised here. His mother had been an entertainer. An aerialist. He remembered being ten years old and watching her rehearse. The skill and physical prowess. The lightning-fast reflexes. He had inherited those skills from her, and they had served him well. She'd only worked at the Zephyr for a couple of years. The owners got rid of the stage to make way for more gaming tables. So, they moved on, but he never forgot the Zephyr and the endless warren where he used to play.

Now, the Zephyr had nearly become his tomb. Worse. Someone was trying to kill his business. Tormod wasn't afraid of death. Over the years, he had seen things far worse than death. What concerned Tormod was legacy. Chetwin

Humphreys was trying to destroy his legacy, and that he couldn't countenance.

Tormod was roused from his gloomy thoughts by the arrival of Lukas, who announced he had a visitor. Lukas frowned as he handed Tormod a business card. Tormod glanced down at the name and a slow grin spread across his face. The Hisada had done good. If she'd still worked for him, he would've given her a bonus.

"Where is he?"

"The Seven Ravens," Lukas replied. "I have men stationed all around. I checked the place out myself. He's alone."

Tormod was so excited that he actually whooped and slammed his hands down on his desk.

"Don't look so down, Lukas. We finally have some good news!" he said, rising to his feet and putting on his leather jacket and newsboy cap. Catching sight of Lukas's dour expression, he asked, "What?"

"Maybe you should go in disguise. Just in case."

"The Seven Ravens is a two-minute walk from here. It's one of our establishments, and I want him to see me as I am."

Lukas gave a look as though to say *fair enough*. Tormod grinned again. Lukas was a good number two. Just about the best kind you could get. Ambitious, yes. But he remembered where he came from. He was loyal to those who raised him up.

Unlike the person they were meeting.

Lukas and two other Lions accompanied Tormod out the back way. It was a slightly longer route. They had to go through another alleyway to reach the main high street again, but Lukas didn't want to take any more risks than necessary.

The Seven Ravens was one of the nicer taverns Tormod ran. Like a lot of the taverns in Hollowhorn, it had seen better days, but it had good bones. More importantly, the owner was always respectful. Always knew his place, which made things easier for everyone.

Case in point, the owner had cleared the place out just for Tormod and his guest, who he spied seated at a corner table, his back to a wall, facing the entrance. Alfred Vogel met Tormod's gaze and gave him a slight head nod. He sat, rigid, his hands clasped in front of him, though Tormod suspected it had less to do with fear and more to do with having a stick up his arsch.

"Mr Lyons," said Vogel as Tormod approached.

Tormod strolled forward and pulled out the chair to sit. Lukas and one of his men were standing close beside him, and it was getting on his nerves. He turned to Lukas.

"Has he been checked for weapons?"

"He has."

"Well then, give me some space, will you? You're sticking to me like fleas on a dog."

Lukas obeyed and motioned for the other Lion to take a step back.

"Mr Vogel," Tormod said as he sat down. "Good of you to come meet with me."

"Your message indicated it would be in everyone's best interest if I did."

Tormod smirked. "Yes, indeed."

"Before we begin, I want to say one thing," Vogel interrupted. "I am glad to see you are well. I had advised Mr Humphreys against the course of action he took, but he ... he hasn't been thinking clearly of late."

Tormod's smirk transformed into a grin. This was even better than he could've hoped for.

"Yes. It will take some time to return to business. As you can imagine, it would normally be in my interest to take action."

"I understand and appreciate that you have not done so already," Vogel replied.

Tormod chuckled and shook his head. "I apologise. I've given you the impression that there will be no retaliation. Chetwin broke the peace," he reminded Vogel.

"You robbed his auction."

Tormod rested his chin in his hands. "Yeah, but before that, you captured one of my people."

Vogel smiled curtly. "I'm sure we could go round and around trying to decide who started it."

Tormod placed his hands on the table and leaned forward. "I reached out to you, Mr Vogel, because your boss man has taken things too far. And perhaps you think that too. After all, you look like a businessman to me. You know what's good business and what isn't. So, tell me this. Why would burning your competitor's building down seem like a good strategy to you? You have the money. I was never able to cash a verdammt crown."

Vogel took a deep breath, and Tormod knew he had him. He could tell, from the moment he laid eyes on Alfred Vogel. Though the man wore the threads of a well-cut businessman, he looked harried. The smudges beneath his eyes suggested a few sleepless nights. Vogel surely knew that Chetwin Humphreys was acting irrationally and that no good could come of continuing down this path.

"There is the matter of the girl," Vogel said.

"The girl?" Tormod innocently asked, though he knew very well which girl Vogel referred to.

"The top item in the auction. While no money was stolen, the girl was taken. By an employee of yours."

"Ah. I assume you're referring to the Hisada, but unfortunately, you've been misinformed. The Hisada doesn't work for me anymore." He chuckled then and shook his head. "In fact, if you'd ask her, she'd say that she never worked for me."

"I understand. But the missing girl has been the cause of

some concern for Mr Humphreys. And while the money was recovered, there is a matter of saving face."

Tormod chuckled and leaned back in his chair. "Vogel, I understand saving face. Believe me, I do. But you and I both know that a war, a proper war between our gangs, will only result in lost revenue and lost assets. And I ask you, what is the point? For face? I'm the thieves guild. There was no malice in what I did. It was a job, like any other. But Humphreys tried to take me out. He tried to take out my gang *and* my business. So, I ask you, what possible way forward is there? Because currently I have the Magistrate breathing down my neck, and I imagine you do too. She won't tolerate a turf war. She will shut us both down. Chetwin must realise this is folly."

Vogel's eyes widened momentarily, as though seeing Tormod for the first time. With his rough speech and poor manners, Tormod was used to being underestimated. He met Vogel's eyes with a steady gaze. Vogel pinched his lips and took a slow breath through his nose.

"As I said, Mr Humphreys is under certain pressures. You've heard of the Order of Grimm, yes?"

"The one what organised the auction?"

Vogel nodded his head once. "That's them. They are … unused to how things work here. They have no concern about keeping the peace in Märchen."

"They have their money. What more do they want?"

"I feel confident they are satisfied with how things have been handled so far," Vogel replied. "But Mr Humphreys eggs them on. He is obsessed with impressing the Order."

Tormod cocked his head to the side. "What is your thinking on how things lie?"

"I fear vengeance fuels Mr Humphreys. He no longer has his business' best interests at heart," Vogel confessed.

Tormod crossed his arms and leaned forward. "So, where do we go from here?"

Vogel thought about it. "It would be helpful if the Order were no longer a concern. Then perhaps the peace could be resumed. Even … the possibility of a new business relationship."

Tormod leaned back and laced his hands behind his head. Yes. This would do.

SAMARA GRUNTED, attempting to dodge one of Gerde's spinning kicks. Gerde missed her target, but she was already adjusting her stance and preparing for her next attack. It was getting harder to dodge her attacks. She was glad Gerde urged her to come and spar with her. She preferred it to standing around waiting to hear what Tormod's next move would be.

Even Art was out this morning. He was going to pay a visit to one of his old school chums in the hope of getting more information about these Restorationists. They were a group looking to overthrow the Richildan government. Someone had to know something about them.

It was chilly and Samara's joints felt stiff. The mornings were starting to have a real bite to the air. She was already muddy after Gerde tackled her earlier. Gerde was good, and only getting better now that they sparred together most days.

She supposed the sparring helped take Gerde's mind off things too. She didn't talk about it, but Samara knew Gerde was concerned about her family. About the coaching inn, and what this was doing to the business.

It would be so easy to hand over Eloise. The girl wasn't enslaved. She was just another little rich girl, unhappy with what life had dealt her. But deep down, Samara knew she'd never do it. How could she? Just because she hadn't been given options in life, didn't mean she had the right to take them away from someone else.

They circled each other. Gerde had the longer reach, and staying on the defensive was tiring Samara out, so she decided the best option was to wait for her moment to rush Gerde. "Win the fight. Don't prolong it," as Ursula would've said. Rushing Gerde also meant she got to be close to her, and it amazed her how much she craved that closeness these days. Gerde was a comfort. There was no doubt about it.

Gerde swung out with her left arm. It was a probing manoeuvre. She assumed Samara would dance out of the way. But Samara grabbed the arm and lunged in close, causing them both to topple to the muddy ground, knocking the breath out of both of them. Gerde laughed, which released a knot in Samara she hadn't even realised was there.

"What?" Gerde asked, her face inches from Samara.

"I just thought you might be upset because I didn't listen to you. The other night. About talking to Callista," she admitted.

Gerde studied her face before her lips crooked into a smile. "You seriously thought I was upset about that?"

"So you're not?" Samara asked, uncertainly.

Gerde pressed her face closer to Samara, "I don't hold grudges," she said softly

"Could've fooled me," Samara replied, with a grin, gesturing to her position on the ground. She wrapped her arms about Gerde's neck and Gerde leaned more comfortably atop Samara. Suddenly it was like the rest of the world had disappeared. It was just the two of them. Samara gazed into Gerde's green eyes, wondering what she was thinking about right now.

They heard footsteps in the mud and quickly got to their feet. Gerde's face was flushed. Samara hid her own smile while bending over to wipe the mud from her trousers. Suddenly she heard Gerde exclaim, "Hans!"

Samara glanced up, stunned to see Hans standing there in the muddy courtyard. She inhaled sharply, noticing his arm in a sling. He also looked thinner than she remembered. His clothes were rumpled. His face wore a sheepish grin.

Samara ran to him and gave him a hug, trying not to jostle his injured arm. Gerde joined her, and thank goodness for that, because Samara was sure she had been shaking with relief as she held Hans, making sure he was real and not some kind of illusion.

"When did you get out?" Gerde asked when they finally released him.

Tears, Samara noticed, pricked at Hans' eyes. "The Magistrate let me go an hour ago."

"What happened to your arm?" Samara demanded.

A dark expression flashed across Hans' face. It was there, and then gone just as quick.

"I dislocated my shoulder. But it's okay. The Magistrate had her physician look at me when she had me released."

Gerde and Samara shared a baffled look. They had made a deal with the Magistrate but had yet to fulfil their part.

"I should add," said Hans, "that she only let me out after the Matron of House de Mörde visited her office."

"Wait. Callista got you out?" Samara stilled. She felt grateful, but also confused. She thought Callista was working with these Restorationists.

"We can talk about it upstairs," Gerde said, pulling away and giving Samara an I-told-you-so look. "Anyone for chai?"

They took their reunion back to their rooms. Hans entered the room first, eager to have a wash. Before Gerde could follow him in, Samara laid a hand on her shoulder.

"I guess it's time for me to have that chat with Callista."

CHAPTER FOURTEEN

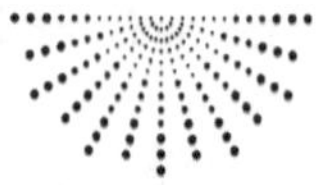

It was evening and the Matron of House de Mörde had ordered her usual saffron chai. This time with two cups. She inhaled the scent of saffron and honey and waited for her guest. Callista looked over some evaluations about some of the younger daughters-in-training while she waited, until she heard the sound of the sash window being eased up. She turned to Samara and gestured for her to take a seat. Callista suppressed a smile at the scowl on Sam's face. Sam didn't enjoy finding out that she was expected.

Samara stalked across the room and sat down on an extra stool Callista had brought in especially for this meeting. She scowled again but accepted the tea. She stared into the cup for a moment, gathering her thoughts, before she cleared her throat.

"I came to thank you. Hans was being held by the City Watch and, from what I understand, the only reason they released him was because of you." Callista opened her mouth to respond, but Samara interrupted her. "Although I have a feeling that the only reason he was captured was because of you."

Callista gave her own scowl in return. "I had nothing to do with his capture."

"No, but a man staying here did, from what I understand." Samara leaned forward, her dark eyes penetrating Callista.

Callista sighed heavily. "He's not staying here anymore. I kicked him out when I learnt what he had done."

"Yeah. The imp used the past tense when she mentioned him. I figured. So just who is he?"

Callista took a sip of her tea. "Remember the girl I hired you to rescue and bring back to me?" Callista said, not able to help herself. There had been betrayal on both sides as far as she was concerned. "Remember how you laughed when I said she had big Magic?"

Samara also took a sip of her tea. "Yeah. I'm aware she has Magic."

Callista's lips parted, and she wanted to hear more, but she knew now was not the time for it. "Anyway, the man's name is Lutz Kaiser, and he's part of the organisation that sent her to me. They want to see her placed on the throne of Richilde."

Samara smirked. "And what would happen if maybe the government of Richilde objected to that?"

"You know, I didn't actually get around to asking him about that," Callista remarked, and they shared a humourless chuckle.

"But they must have a plan in place. I can't imagine that whoever is currently in power over there would happily step aside if they produced the girl."

This was something Callista had been thinking about a lot lately. It was partly why she was so upset with Samara for letting Eloise go, so cavalierly. "No. I don't suppose they would. It's why they are keeping her in hiding. They're trying to keep her presence a secret until whenever they deem the time is right. I assume they must have people inside the government doing their part to pave the way."

"Hmmph," was all Samara said.

Callista sat with her back leaning against the dresser. "Tell me. Why did you really let her go? She would've been safer if you brought her back to me. Kaiser would never have been sent here."

Samara gave her an incredulous look. "I told you. She didn't want to go back. And besides, you lied to me."

Callista furrowed her brows. She honestly didn't know what Samara was talking about. She gestured for Samara to explain herself.

Samara set the teacup back down on the dresser. "You told me you never sent her on jobs. But the only reason Humphreys knew about her was because she was out on a job."

Callista sighed and ran a hand through her hair. "It's true. I didn't think you'd help me if I told you about that. You *had* just been trying to kill me right before then."

"Entirely warranted."

She couldn't deny that. "But, you have to believe me, Eloise was only out on that job because she wanted to be there."

From the way Samara narrowed her eyes and shook her head, it was clear she didn't believe Callista.

"I said I didn't train her. It's true. The whole circumstances of her getting sent to me were too mysterious. I wasn't about to put her in danger. I let her take part in some of the standard lessons: history, language, etiquette, that sort of thing." She let out a long exhalation. "But Eloise was getting, shall we say, restless? She didn't like being cooped up, and she started trying to sneak out. She was always caught, mind you, and that seemed to make her more determined. I slowly let her join a few more classes. I thought if she could pretend to be a daughter of House de Mörde by participating in some weapons training, she'd realise she had no skill and would tire of it."

Eloise had been a handful, Callista recalled. Far more wilful than any of the girls she had ever trained before. She'd supposed Eloise would hate training with the younger girls, and eventually quit. But she didn't.

"I don't know how she did it, but she began beating some of the younger girls in their sparring. I think she was probably cheating. Using her Magic. I couldn't prove it. I wasn't meant to know she had Magic, but there were things that happened that were unexplainable."

Samara took another sip of her tea. "Unexplainable?"

"Like her being able to sneak out. She got better at it. One time she went right out the front door and my girl on watch swore she never left her post. So, I suspected magic of some sort." She gave Samara a look. "But no. I never sought to use her magic on a job. I wasn't about to upset a bunch of monarchy fanatics. But Eloise, she has a way of making friends with the other girls. A way of persuading them to do things they might not agree to otherwise."

Samara snorted. "I've noticed."

Callista waited for Samara to elaborate. When she didn't, she continued. "I think she got wind of a job. The contract was to go after The Raven. He has top security, but he throws lavish parties. It was a very different job than usual. We had a handful of girls pretending to be serving girls. She went with them."

Samara didn't respond and Callista could feel her former sister scrutinising her.

"I only discovered this afterwards, but yes, I believe that's where Chetwin Humphreys found out about her."

"He caught her doing a spell to put everyone asleep because your spiked drink didn't do the trick," Samara replied.

"She told you the story?"

Samara's jaw tightened. "She may have led me to believe that you had sent her on the job."

Callista gazed steadily into her former sister's eyes. "I didn't. I swear."

Samara studied her for a moment, then said, "I believe you." She smirked. "You're not doing your tell."

Callista smiled and shook her head. Samara would swear up and down that whenever Callista was lying, she always touched her hair. Of course she didn't believe her, until Samara would point it out.

"I should've warned you about her," Callista said. "She is very good at manipulating people. She'd make a grand future queen."

"Yeah. I don't know that she wants that for herself," Samara said thoughtfully.

Callista cocked her head. "Okay, now *you're* not telling me something."

Samara leaned back, and to Callista's dismay, she could tell that Samara was still trying to decide whether she could trust Callista.

～

IN THE END, Samara kept whatever she knew to herself. Which, admittedly, hurt. But she invited Callista to attend a meeting with her crew. The meeting took place at The Seven Ravens. It was one of Tormod Lyons' strongholds. She found it curious that Sam chose to meet there given she had separated from Lyons.

Tormod wasn't around. No one had seen him in weeks. Apparently, he was lying low after his disastrous attempt to rob Humphreys' auction. She didn't know the details and didn't really care to. All Callista knew was that it was her fault the Restorationists were after Sam. Yes. Samara had made things a whole lot worse by letting Eloise go, but they wouldn't even know about Sam if Callista hadn't agreed to house Eloise.

The rest of Sam's crew were already there when she arrived. She sometimes wondered whether Samara purposely gave a different time for everyone else, just so Callista could be the last person to enter. She wouldn't put it past her.

She forced a smile onto her face and nodded at the wary faces that greeted her. They were in a back room upstairs. High stakes card games normally took place here, but now it was just Samara and her crew.

"It's good to see you all," Callista began. What did people say in such circumstances? They had been partners, then enemies so many times, at this point.

Samara jutted her chin in greeting and Art gave a half-hearted wave.

Studying them up close, she could see how the past few weeks had taken a toll. They appeared much more guarded. The driver, Gerde, was the only one who didn't look at her with distrust. Instead, she nodded her head in greeting and pushed a chair out for her. Upon doing so, she placed a hand briefly upon Samara's, which Callista couldn't help noticing. It always made her feel unsettled seeing Samara with her friends.

Samara, the loner who had escaped the House's clutches, had somehow found people she could count on, whereas Callista, surrounded by daughters of House de Mörde, felt lonelier than ever.

She noted Hans' absence. "Is Hans okay?" she asked as she took a seat.

"He's fine, thanks to you," Samara replied, and she pointedly eyed the others around the room when she said that. "But he needed the rest."

"I'm glad," Callista said softly. "It's good to see you're all doing well."

"Besides being kicked out of one's home, having their family business shut down and being hunted by the House de Mörde, yes. We're dandy," Art drawled.

Callista frowned. "Kicked out?"

"We suspect that in addition to having Hans arrested, your Restorationist friend has been harassing us and our family in other ways." This came from Gerde.

"He's no friend of mine. I can promise you that much."

"Why don't you tell us about him," Samara urged.

Callista drew in a breath. "As I told you, his name's Lutz Kaiser. I've had the unfortunate luck of having spent several weeks with him, so I think I have a good idea of the type of person he is. He's a bureaucrat. And a bit of a fanatic. Not the type to get his own hands dirty. He would much rather use someone else. Like the House de Mörde. Or, when I refused to help him, the City Watch."

"So, you had him brought here to recover Eloise. You gave him rooms in your home." Art turned to Samara. "Why are we agreeing to work with her again?"

Samara scowled back at him. "Because she wants to help. And in case you hadn't noticed, we need all the help we can get. Or did you happen to find anything about the Restorationists from your toff friends? Because I thought you said they knew nothing."

Art sat up straighter in his chair. "Well, yeah, but—"

"He's not my friend. And I *didn't* invite him to Märchen," Callista interrupted. "He knew something was wrong. Eloise was supposed to send weekly letters to an address in Richilde."

"Do you have that address?" Gerde asked.

"I can get it," Callista affirmed. "They were already suspicious and growing concerned. He arrived just after the auction occurred. I assume they became aware of the auction and knew I'd been lying about her well-being. I was forced to admit Eloise had been taken, and you were the people who bought her."

She shrugged. It wasn't *her* fault Samara had allowed Eloise to manipulate her into letting her go.

Callista noticed the thin blonde girl, Ana, shifting in her seat, but she said nothing.

"So, these Restorationists have bought the City Watch. What can we do about it?" Gerde asked.

Callista shook her head. "He won't stop looking for her. They have people tearing apart the entire continent right now, but since the last known sighting of her was here, and the ports and coaching inns are being monitored, he believes she's still here."

Callista looked to Samara, who turned her head away. So, she was still here. And Samara knew it. Sam wasn't the only one who could read tells, she thought smugly.

The blonde girl continued to shift in her seat uncomfortably. Seb, the supposed explosives expert, rested a hand on her and the girl practically jumped. "Why can't they just let her be? She obviously doesn't want to be found," he said.

Callista agreed with him. She knew better than most what it was like to be forced into a position just because of blood relations.

"As I've said, he's a fanatic. These Restorationists won't rest until there is a royal of fae blood on the throne of Richilde." She gazed about the room again. "But it's important to remember, Eloise isn't necessarily safer on her own."

"As we saw with the auction," Gerde muttered.

"That, yes. But also, consider what might happen if someone in the Richildan government discovered her existence. They might see her as a danger to their position. If so, they wouldn't stop until she was found and dealt with."

She glanced up at Samara, trying to meet her gaze, but Samara carefully avoided it.

"Okay, so he can't be stopped," Samara said instead. "What about the Magistrate? You told her that her people were being bought by this Kaiser. Surely she can intervene."

"To be fair though, isn't the City Watch always known for taking bribes?" asked Art.

"Some of them, yes," Gerde replied. "It's one reason my brother left."

"Still it's different, isn't it? Taking money from a few local gangs versus taking money from foreign nobles," Samara replied. "Surely that's something that will make her want to intervene."

"I didn't say he was a noble," Callista corrected. "And I don't think the Magistrate can do much. She's spread thin over there. She doesn't have the manpower to enforce the City Watch. The Magistrate only released Hans because I vouched for him."

She knew she was perhaps overstating her role in getting Samara's landlord released but felt justified in doing so.

"There must be something she can do. She offered to make a deal with you, Sam," said Gerde and Callista couldn't help but flinch a little at the diminutive that used to be something only she had the privilege of using.

"Yeah, and I suspect she's going to hold me to it," Samara muttered.

"I know that a brewing turf war isn't helping matters," Callista pointed out.

"Wonderful," groaned Art, leaning back and cradling the back of his head with his hands. "So, on the one hand, we have these Restorationists who are using the City Watch to go after us and hunt down the girl. And on the other hand, we have Humphreys, most likely with the Order, who pretty much want anybody who had anything to do with the auction dead."

"We don't exactly know what the Order wants. But I am working on the Humphreys thing," said Samara.

"Remember your history lessons," Callista responded. "Fighting a war on two fronts is never a good idea."

"History lessons," Samara repeated with a chuckle. "Okay. So, what do you suggest?"

Callista lifted one shoulder in a shrug. "Maybe we can figure out a way to use the City Watch to keep Humphreys occupied?"

"How?" asked Seb, leaning in.

"I might know how to go about it," said Gerde, hesitantly.

Art raised an eyebrow. "Well, now I'm intrigued."

"Use the City Watch, huh?" Samara smiled one of her trademark wolfish grins. "I'm up for anything that causes Humphreys problems. As for Kaiser, I think it's time to see the Magistrate again. Cut a new deal with her."

"It can't hurt," said Art.

Samara's gaze met Callista's. "Care to join me, Matron?"

SAMARA PEERED out the window of the Matron of House de Mörde's carriage. The carriage that would have been hers had she accepted the position eight years ago, she thought with some degree of chagrin. She didn't like the current plan. Going right up to the Magistrate's door. Announcing her presence for all to hear? That wasn't how she operated. But Gerde opined that taking out the Magistrate's guards again wasn't the best way to begin an alliance. And the Magistrate would not say no to a meeting with the Matron.

So, she, Gerde and Callista found themselves crammed together in the carriage. Crammed was probably not the right word for it, since the carriage was spacious but it felt appropriate. She and Gerde sat together their shoulders occasionally brushing up against each other, whilst Callista perched on the bench opposite. She glanced over at Gerde, who also looked uncomfortable. Most likely because she was used to being the one driving the carriage rather than riding in it.

Samara would have preferred Gerde not come at all. But Gerde had insisted on it. Samara got the sense that she didn't entirely trust Callista, even though it was her idea to patch things up.

"This feels weird," Samara muttered.

"It's fine. It's not the first time I've visited her at night. Stop worrying," Callista replied.

Samara wondered what cause the Matron of House de Mörde would have for visiting Märchen's Magistrate late at night. Was the Magistrate one of the House's clients? But of course she was. Nobody who got to be Magistrate got there without a few bodies in the Klara.

The thought actually made her relax a little. In the end, even a refined woman like Sylvain Duvall was no better than someone like Tormod. At least Tormod was honest about who he was. And even though he often used her and Lukas to do his dirty work, he wasn't afraid of getting his own hands dirty.

The carriage pulled up in front of the Magistrate's massive home and a footman came to open the door. He offered Samara his hand, but she glared at him before jumping down. She did, however, hold out her hand for Gerde, who laughingly accepted it.

They were led into a reception room with a marble fireplace and decorated in shades of cream. It left Samara feeling once again uncomfortable. She didn't know where to sit and was afraid of getting the upholstery dirty. Callista, for her part, sat down and pointedly indicated that Samara and Gerde should do the same. But Samara chose to stand, and Gerde stood with her.

Refreshments arrived soon after. Tea and a few small square cakes. Samara didn't touch it, and neither did the others. A few minutes later, the woman herself sashayed into the room. The Magistrate had clearly been heading to bed judging by the way her hair tumbled about her shoulders. She was enveloped in a beautifully embroidered wrapper. Loose enough to be comfortable, it cinched at the waist to still give her a look of elegance.

The Magistrate smiled warily as she greeted them. "I must say, this is a surprise," she said. "Please, have a seat. Will you have some tea?"

Callista politely declined, as did Samara.

"Oh. That's right. You daughters of the House don't drink something you haven't poured yourself. Correct?"

Samara noticed Callista's smile grow strained. "Something like that."

It had been a long time since Samara was part of the House, but even for her, it was difficult to shake that rule. Sure. She didn't adhere to it all the time, but in Callista's company, she felt compelled to follow her example.

There was a moment of uncomfortable silence.

"I'll have some tea," Gerde said, and inwardly Samara smiled. Gerde was always so much better than Samara at making people feel comfortable.

The Magistrate poured the tea herself. And with the opportunity to keep her hands busy, she seemed to relax a bit. "So, what brings you ladies here?" she asked.

Samara straightened. "I wanted to thank you for having my landlord released."

The Magistrate picked up a ceramic pot filled with sugar and glanced at Gerde.

"Yes, please. Two."

As the Magistrate spooned sugar into the cup, she replied, "It's really the Matron here you should thank. There was compelling evidence found in his shop. But as she kindly pointed out, it was an illegal search, instigated by a City Watchmen in the payroll of a foreign agent. I couldn't very well keep him in gaol under those circumstances. Although I haven't forgotten about our deal."

Samara kept her face neutral. The evidence was compelling because it was real, she knew. Hans was a master forger, and there was surely evidence of it all over the print shop. But, in her experience, two things could be true.

"I think you understand now the depth of the corruption problem you have," Callista pointed out.

The Magistrate glanced up from pouring milk. "I do," she said, grimly.

The Magistrate handed the cup and saucer to Gerde, then settled into a cushioned seat. "For years, practically half the City Watch have taken payments from the likes of Chetwin Humphreys and Tormod Lyons. I've let it go, as long as the balance of power was maintained, and the peace kept. But ever since Tormod and Chetwin went to war, things have been out of control. Now there's a Richildan gang operating in Märchen."

"Kaiser isn't part of a gang," Samara pointed out.

"He's a royalist. Part of a group called the Restorationists, plotting to overthrow the government of Richilde," Callista explained.

The Magistrate's eyes widened at that, and she muttered, "I may have to ring the bell for something stronger to drink."

"Do you know what you'll do about the City Watch, Sylvain?" Callista asked. Samara was startled to discover they were on a first name basis.

The Magistrate shook her head. "I'd like to believe they didn't know who Kaiser was, but Hoffner is too smart not to do his research," she muttered.

"Which means he knew, and took the money anyway," said Samara.

"He doesn't have any loyalty to Märchen, and neither do the men under his command," agreed Callista.

"So far," Gerde added, "besides locking up Hans, he was also behind shutting down my family's coaching inn, and we think he had another of our team kicked out of his home."

"We need your help to get the City Watch off our back," said Samara.

"Tell me why this Richildan group is targeting you?" the Magistrate demanded.

"Let's just say we've been a thorn in their side as far as them trying to get someone onto the Richildan throne."

The Magistrate pinched her lips together. "Does this have anything to do with why Tormod and Humphreys are going to war?"

"That wouldn't be inaccurate," Callista murmured.

The Magistrate sat back in her chair. "I would love to help you. But I don't see how I can possibly help without getting rid of a large portion of the Watch."

"You could open the Watch to women," Gerde replied mildly.

"Yes, well, I can't do anything like that now with a gang war brewing. Unless you've made some progress towards brokering a peace?"

"The good news is that Tormod is still in Märchen. If you

want to call that good news. And I've spoken with him about making nice," Samara replied. "But after the fire at the Zephyr, he's not feeling too olive branch-y at the moment."

"If Tormod's not willing to pursue peace, why not just remove Humphreys from the board?" Callista asked. "No Humphreys, no gang war."

Samara looked up sharply at Callista. She knew Callie had her own issues with Humphreys but was she actually suggesting assassinating him? As much as she would delight in spitting on Chetwin Humphreys' grave, what Callista was suggesting would be considered murder without a contract.

The Magistrate looked equally askance. "Even if that wasn't illegal, who would fill the power vacuum?"

"Tormod," Samara reluctantly replied. "He could even take out the contract."

Samara tried not to notice how Gerde stiffened at these words.

"This isn't something I feel comfortable discussing," the Magistrate replied. She breathed in deeply and slowly exhaled. "That said, Chetwin Humphreys has grown brazen of late with his Nepenthe dealings in Märchen. I wouldn't be sorry to see him go."

"I think I might have a way of keeping Humphreys busy until we can find a non-lethal way of getting rid of him. It will also help us find the Watch who are on Kaiser's payroll," said Gerde.

Callista nodded to show she would be amenable to a non-lethal path.

The Magistrate looked positively relieved. "I'd certainly like to hear what you have in mind."

"If we do this though, you need to help us as well," added Callista. "In order to deal with the Restorationists once and for all, we need a contact in the Richildan government. Someone you trust, who will hear us out. You went to university in Richilde, didn't you?"

"I did," the Magistrate confirmed. She bit her lip. "I might have an old school chum you could speak with. He's part of the Richildan opposition party. I could probably convince him to hear what you have to say, assuming this threat is real."

"Oh, it's real," Samara replied.

"Okay then. I'll send a message to him tomorrow." She turned to Samara. "But I need you to stop this gang war."

CHAPTER FIFTEEN

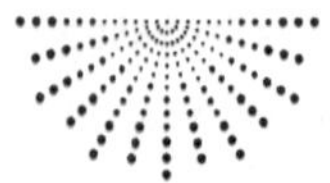

HE IS A FIXTURE OF THE ELPHAME PARK ELITE. A MAN WHO OWNS SEVERAL IMPORT-EXPORT BUSINESSES IN MÄRCHEN. IN ADDITION TO HIS LEGAL BUSINESSES, SUCH AS IMPORTING SLAVES AND LAUDANUM, IT IS SAID THAT HUMPHREYS IS NOW THE MAIN IMPORTER OF NEPENTHE INTO OUR FAIR CITY-STATE, AND ONE OF THE MOST VICIOUS GANG LEADERS MÄRCHEN HAS EVER SEEN. SO WHY ISN'T MORE BEING DONE TO LOCK HUMPHREYS AWAY? COULD IT BE DUE TO HIS CLOSE TIES TO THE STADRAT?

— THE MÄRCHEN CHRONICLE

The Aurora was full to bursting. Gerde was on break, but rather than take a tankard of ale outside to get a breath of fresh air, she slipped into the corner and kept her attention on the group of off-duty City Watch who were knocking back drinks at the bar. They were regulars. They always showed up when the music hall had a band playing. It was a wonder that Hoffner never realised she worked there, but then again, he was usually fairly drunk even before he got to the music hall.

She recognised Hoffner in the middle of the group. The others circled around him. You could tell, even from a distance, that he was the leader. If Hoffner wanted to stay for more drinks, they would stay for more drinks. She noticed he also seemed to get rather handsy with the barmaids. Not that the barmaids could complain given his position.

She wasn't sure how she felt about this plan, even though it was her own suggestion. Samara approved of it, though she clearly hated involving Gerde. But it's not like she would be implementing it. She was just here to make sure things went to plan.

She didn't see the Lions approach until they were already at the bar, placing themselves right next to the group of City Watch. Gerde studied both groups, wondering if she would spot the moment the information got passed on. To her, it was just two groups of venue goers, albeit ones that didn't normally interact. She thought she glimpsed one of the City Watch guards nudging Hoffner. She imagined she saw Hoffner straighten and lean in to hear what the other Watchman was saying. He traded places with the guard and now she could definitely tell he was on the alert.

Not long after, Hoffner and his group left. They always stayed for the entire show, but not this time. This time, something had caught their attention. And Gerde knew exactly what that something was.

After Hoffner and his team left, she then made her way to the front door and waited. A few minutes later, the group of Lions stepped out. One of the Lions stopped and turned to her, doffing his hat.

"You can tell the Hisada that it's done."

Gerde nodded her head, though she didn't need to tell

Samara anything. At this very moment, Sam was outside, most likely on the move now, following Hoffner and his men.

"Thank you," she said.

He sucked in a breath. "I just hope this works."

"Me too."

Sleep eluded Chetwin Humphreys. Lying awake in bed was becoming a regular occurrence for him these days. After the Zephyr burned down, he'd hoped he could finally feel some relief. But then came rumours Tormod Lyons was not only in the city but had survived the burning of the Zephyr. He didn't know what had happened. How had they put the fire out so quickly? The Order had assured him this would be no ordinary fire. It should have consumed the place entirely.

The fact it didn't served as proof, in his eyes, that Eloise was still here in Märchen.

But if Eloise was out there, he couldn't find her.

He lay in bed, stewing. He had let the Order know that Tormod was alive and in the city, but they simply thanked him for his efforts. When he had tried to engage with them about what else he could do to take care of Lyons they had disconnected the call. To add to his ire, at no point in his few conversations with the Order had they acknowledged the Hisada's part in events. Apparently, retrieving Eloise was his problem, not theirs.

Meanwhile, Alfred kept pestering him to focus on his other business dealings. There was a new Nepenthe shipment due soon. One of his traffickers wanted to renegotiate the contract, since he felt he was taking all the risk. Chetwin knew he should focus on these things, but he just couldn't.

Instead, he fantasised about having a team of men invade the

House de Mörde to retrieve his property. But he knew he couldn't fight a war on two fronts. He would destroy Tormod Lyons first, then go after the Matron.

Although reports that she was also hunting the Hisada and her crew suggested Eloise hadn't returned to the House.

And thus he kept going around in circles.

The speaking telegraph still sat in his office, taunting him. What did their silence mean? What was their end goal?

Lying awake in bed, he heard a commotion downstairs. First, there was the sound of a carriage drawing up. Then banging on the door. Puzzled, he peered outside, and his eyes widened to see two City Watch wagons parked in front of his home.

Deep down, he sensed this was Tormod's doing. The lowlife had somehow convinced the City Watch to go after him. Alfred had warned him about escalating things with Lyons.

Chetwin grabbed the silk dressing gown he had discarded on a chair earlier and threw it on. He then reached for his trademark walking stick.

When he opened the door, he could hear the sounds of voices arguing. He recognised the voice of his butler speaking to Hoffner, the City Watchman he had been sending monthly payments to for over a decade. His eyes narrowed as he listened in. Again, he cursed Tormod Lyons. Hoffner had no reason to go after him. He knew he had been distracted, but it's not like he was running behind on his payments. Hoffner got good work from him. Besides looking the other way on Nepenthe shipments, Chetwin often hired Hoffner and his men as extra security.

He strode across the corridor and peered over the crystal bannister. Just then, Hoffner looked up.

"Just the man I've been looking for," Hoffner sneered.

"What's the meaning of this?" Chetwin asked as he thundered down the two flights of stairs. He was met part way by two City Watch. More flooded up the stairs. One of the Watch, a young wet-behind-the-ears boy, attempted to restrain him but he sent a withering icy blue stare at the boy.

"Unhand me or so help me, you will hear from my lawyer and find yourself unable to so much as get a job as a rent boy at the local pleasure house."

The boy let go, but not without a glance at his superior, who nodded once.

"What's the meaning of this?" Chetwin snapped as he reached Hoffner.

"I have a warrant to search the premises," replied Hoffner.

Dread crept into Chetwin's veins. Hoffner acted as though they had never met before.

He drew a paper out of his pocket. Before handing it to Chetwin, he glanced down at the paper and said, "Actually, I have a warrant to search all of your premises."

Chetwin snatched the paper out of his hand and glanced at it. The Magistrate had signed it herself. He could feel his face go flush. His heart racing.

His first thought was, *how did Tormod Lyons get the Magistrate to issue this warrant?*

But then he read through the paper and grew even more confused. They weren't looking for proof of his Nepenthe dealings. This was about the girl, he realised.

He glared Hoffner down, picturing himself stabbing the little rat in the eye with a fork. Hoffner stared blandly back at him, while his men continued to search Chetwin's home.

"You know as well as I do that the purchase of human flesh is perfectly legal."

Hoffner didn't reply.

"Fine. Search all you like. You'll find nobody here besides myself and my staff."

Hoffner crossed his arms in front of his chest. "We got a tip that you are hiding a free citizen of Märchen here. If we don't find her, we'll have to bring you in for questioning."

"A tip?" Chetwin stared hard into Hoffner's own grey eyes. "Can one dog truly have two masters, I wonder?" he asked, looking Hoffner up and down.

Hoffner smirked. "What can I say? Someone wants that girl back something fierce-like. They gave me a better offer."

The pair glared at each other, but it was clear to Chetwin that Tormod Lyons had paid Hoffner quite a bit of money to cause this chaos because the City Watchman refused to back down. Instead, Hoffner nodded to two of his men.

"Escort Mr Humphreys to the wagon. We could be here some time."

The two men grasped Chetwin by the arms and led him out of his own home and into the wagon. Chetwin could feel the blood pounding in his ears now. He was in disbelief. He didn't even have a coat on. They sat him in the wagon and closed the door, leaving him to stare out of a tiny window.

Chetwin blinked several times. He needed to think. Chetwin knew, once he learnt that Tormod Lyons lived, the response would be devastating. He thought he'd have time. He never thought, never even imagined, that Tormod would use both the Magistrate *and* Hoffner to take him down.

But was it Lyons? Tormod wasn't interested in the girl. And besides, he *had* to know that Chetwin didn't have her. It was the Hisada's own people who had bought her. Unless there was another player involved? Perhaps the dwarf had been telling the truth? Maybe there really was a Glass Coffin Society trying to recover the girl.

He shoved these thoughts to the back of his mind and tried to think of the practical. First, he would send for his lawyer. If he didn't, he knew Alfred would. But where was Alfred? He said he was staying late to go over the accounts. Chetwin hadn't seen him amid the chaos. His butler had been the one shouting orders and trying to deal with the invading City Watchmen. Maybe it was better that Alfred wasn't around. Hoffner would've surely brought him in too, being Chetwin's number two. His butler would send for his lawyer. Gerard would have them out within an hour. And then…

And then… What would happen then? He'd have to take care of Tormod Lyons once and for all. But first, he would deal with that little rat, Hoffner. He would have his body cut up into so many little pieces that not even Hoffner's own mother could identify him.

The minutes seemed to crawl by as he sat in the cold, darkened wagon waiting to be hauled to City Watch headquarters. He didn't give a fig what his neighbours thought right now, but it certainly didn't help his ambitions. He strained to hear what was going on in his home but heard nothing. Surely they'd finished searching by now. But, if Tormod really was behind this, he suspected the City Watch had been instructed to tear the place apart.

A thump pulled him from his thoughts. It sounded like something heavy landing on the ground. He peered out the window only to find himself face to face with his number two. He let out an enormous sigh of relief.

"Alfred. It is good to see you!"

He could hear the jangle of keys as Alfred unlocked the door and then it was open and he was free.

"We have to leave now. I overheard them. They're not taking you in for questioning," said Vogel, in an urgent whisper.

Chetwin sucked in a breath. He shouldn't be surprised. He had helped perpetuate this war. Stumbling from the wagon, he glanced down at the body on the ground. In the streetlight's glow he saw a City Watchman with a dart sticking out of his neck. He glanced back up at Vogel to thank his number two, but as his eyes travelled upwards, he spotted the City Watch issued cutlass held in Vogel's hand.

Chetwin had always considered himself a smart man. He trusted almost nobody. Whatever happened, he was always three steps ahead. And yet, despite the cutlass, the notion still didn't cross his mind that Vogel was there to kill him until the blade was buried in his stomach.

He wanted to say something. Anything. Cry out for help. But the words wouldn't come. All he could think was that the one person he trusted with his business, with his life, had betrayed him.

CHAPTER SIXTEEN

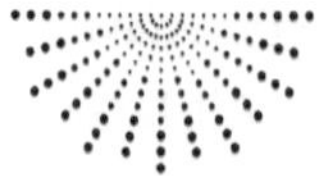

My colleagues will often report about the increasing crime rate in Märchen, making bold suggestions about the gang leaders of the city and their close relationships to the Magistrate and the City Watch. But any long-time resident of our fair city-state will know differently. Just a decade ago, residents feared walking the streets of Hollowhorn in the day or night for fear of being caught up in gang violence. A study of crime statistics as reported by the City Watch actually show the number of theft and murder trending downwards.

— TOMAS HERMAN DURING HIS CAMPAIGN FOR A
POSITION ON THE STADRAT

Samara watched as the blood seeped out of Chetwin Humphreys' lifeless body into the grass. She saw as Alfred Vogel, the man she had reached out to just a few days ago, dropped the cutlass he held and staggered back. He was shaking, but then he seemed to pull himself together. He bent down and removed something Samara couldn't see from the City Watchmen's neck and walked back to the house. It was only when Vogel was out of sight that she dragged her eyes back to Humphreys.

She had grinned wickedly at the sight of Chetwin Humphreys being marched to a wagon like the petty criminal he truly was. She knew it wouldn't last. But verdammt, it had felt good.

But this. The man who had sold her to the House, bleeding out on the grass after being fatally wounded by his own number two…

She watched him take his last, rattling gasps of air, and she felt … nothing. Empty. She thought she might feel triumphant, but her thoughts went to Gerde instead. How would Gerde feel knowing her idea had led to this?

She couldn't have saved Humphreys. Samara had dealt enough fatal wounds to know one when she saw one.

Would she have saved him if she could? That was the question. A man who made his fortune selling human beings didn't deserve life.

But to keep Gerde from having to bear that guilt, she might've been willing to try.

She watched on for a long time until eventually she saw the City Watch guards leave Humphreys' home. They'd find his dead body. And even though Vogel made it appear that Humphreys died in an escape attempt, they'd surely know they were being set up.

She deftly made her way across the roofs and away from Elphame Park.

Samara had the information she needed anyhow. She had seen each and every face of Hoffner's men.

In the morning, she'd go to see the Magistrate.

But for now, she just wanted to go home. She needed to be the one to tell Gerde what had happened.

She met Gerde at the Aurora after her shift, appearing from out of the shadows, as Gerde was leaving.

"What's wrong?" Gerde asked upon seeing Samara's expression.

"Humphreys is dead," Samara replied, forcing the words out.

Gerde sucked in a breath, and Samara noticed how her hands curled into fists, but she calmly followed Samara as they made their way to The Wishing-Table. Gerde kept asking Samara how she was feeling, and she didn't know how to answer. Elated that Humphreys had finally gotten what he deserved? Fury at Tormod for making her culpable for his death?

In truth, Samara was more interested in knowing how Gerde felt.

"Honestly? I just feel sick," Gerde confessed. "I think I need to sit with everything that's happened."

So that's what they did. They went to bed. Samara lay awake, knowing that Gerde was awake as well. She tossed and turned, but Samara just lay still, pretending to be asleep. Finally, Gerde slipped into a fitful sleep.

But Samara still lay awake. Not sleeping. Furious at Tormod for having used her like this. Because he had to have been behind Humphreys' stabbing. She blamed herself too. She should've known what Tormod intended. Or had she known deep down, and conveniently ignored it?

Eventually, she heard the first chirping of birds. Dawn was not long away.

She sat up in bed, startling Gerde awake.

"What is it?" Gerde mumbled.

"I'm going to go see Tormod," Samara said, trying to keep her voice light.

"Now?"

"Yes. I'll be back in a couple of hours."

"I should come with you," Gerde replied, struggling to sit up.

"Go back to sleep," Samara said. She was already out of bed now.

"You should at least go in disguise," Gerde said, apparently knowing it was useless to argue. "And be careful."

"Always," Samara said, forcing her trademark smirk as she got dressed.

IT WAS JARRING to see the Zephyr with no lights. Even in the early hours of the morning, the building would normally be lit up. As she hammered on the door, she wondered how long it would be before Tormod re-opened the joint.

Lukas greeted her with a look of consternation.

"Did Tormod put him up to it?" she demanded as soon as he opened the door.

Lukas, who appeared paler than usual, shrugged. "Tormod said Vogel acted on his own."

"Do you believe him?"

Again Lukas shrugged. "He's my boss."

Not a proper answer.

"Where is he? I want to see him."

Lukas beckoned to her, and she followed him through the unnervingly empty casino floor.

She entered Tormod's office to find him awake and celebrating.

"Hisada. Good to see you! Here to celebrate, I take it."

Tormod held out a glass of expensive wine, momentarily forgetting that she didn't drink.

Samara knocked the glass aside and grabbed Tormod by the collar, pushing him up against the wall.

"You had me put you in touch with Vogel just so you could have Humphreys murdered!"

Tormod's face held a surprised smirk, even as Lukas stepped between them.

"Back off, Hisada," Lukas said, his tone cool and detached. His eyes met hers. Urging her to back away but letting her know if it came down to it, he would protect his boss.

Breathing heavily, she let go of Tormod's collar and took a step away.

Tormod too seemed shaken, but he forced a grin. Took a swig of his wine. "I don't know why you're all worked up Hisada. Humphreys is the one what sold you to the House. You should be happy he's dead."

She should be. So why wasn't she? For so long, she had made it her mission to bring Humphreys down, and now he was dead. Murdered by one of his own; how pointless.

If Tormod really had planned this, that mean't she had more blood on her hands. Even after leaving the House de Mörde, she still couldn't get away from death.

Tormod always came across as happy-go-lucky. He's the man whose plans always somehow came together by luck and chance and, occasionally, a bit of brute force. After all these years, had she underestimated him?

"Killing Humphreys was never part of the plan. You used me." *You used Gerde,* she didn't say.

"I didn't put Vogel up to it," he said with a shrug. "And let's not forget, tonight, my people were helping you and the Magistrate."

"Yeah, well, the Magistrate's not gonna like this," she said, her hands clenching and unclenching. Samara could feel Lukas' wary eyes on her.

"The Magistrate can kiss my arsch," Tormod said, sitting down and leaning back in his seat. "She wanted an end to the war. That's what she's got. With far fewer lives lost, I might add."

"If you wanted to kill Humphreys, you should've taken a contract out with the House."

Tormod rolled his eyes at her. "Like I said, this was all Vogel's doing. I didn't even know the Watch would act so quickly. If she wants to arrest him, I'll be happy to hand him over."

"You say that, but you won't, will you?" she murmured. "You need him. For when you take over Chetwin's operations."

Tormod shrugged, as though he hadn't given it much thought. But she knew. He'd given it a *lot* of thought. Had she done this? Given him the help he needed to take out his arch-rival?

Humphreys was bad for Märchen. But was the city any better off with Tormod running things?

Tormod seemed to know what she was thinking, because then he said, "Let's say you're right. Let's say I take over the Nepenthe business. Vogel runs it. He gets a cut. Better for everybody, don't you think? Surely better than having some new arschloch to deal with?"

Samara wasn't so sure about that, but she zeroed in on something else that he'd said. "Just the Nepenthe business? Not the human trafficking?"

"Well, now—" Tormod began.

She straightened up, and her eyes turned hard. "You get the Nepenthe business, but that's it. I don't want you picking up the human trafficking."

Tormod chuckled, looking her up and down. "Look, Hisada, I don't know that you're really in a position to—"

"Because whoever takes over that business," she said, interrupting him, "is going to have to deal with me."

She glared at Lukas, to let him know that if she really meant to come after his boss, there wasn't anything he could do about it.

"If I don't take it over, someone else will. You *know* that."

She shrugged. "Like I said, whoever that someone else is, is going to have me coming after them."

Tormod smiled and shrugged. "Why not? I'm a generous man. Got enough businesses to deal with now, anyway."

Samara let out a breath. She was pretty sure Tormod hadn't been planning on taking the trafficking business. If he had really set his sights on it, he wouldn't have given in so easily.

She hesitated. "One more thing. I want Vogel to hand over all the records he has on the trafficking."

Tormod whistled. "Fine. But only because I value our long-standing relationship."

Her belly fluttered. She needed those records so she could go after traffickers. Take them down. But a part of her still wondered if those records might also hold the key to finding her family, and wasn't that why she went after Humphreys in the first place?

"Oh, Hisada, there's one last piece of business," Tormod said. "The Order. I sent them a message."

Samara's eyes narrowed. "How?"

"Well. When I say *I sent,* I meant I had Vogel send them a message. Turns out Humphreys has a speaking telegraph in his home. One line, going straight to the Order. Vogel told them Humphreys was dead and asked them if that made us square. They said yes."

Samara wrinkled her nose. That's it? Humphreys is dead and they're all square? That didn't add up. "The Order just let you off the hook?"

Tormod leaned back and flung his legs on his desk, crossing them. "Yeah. Why not? Turns out even rich toffs understand good business. All those bank notes, yet I never ended up getting a crown." He grimaced. "Humphreys was the one who failed them with the security. Turns out they're quite reasonable."

Samara studied him. "Really?" she asked sceptically.

"Well, I may have promised to cut them in on Humphreys' Nepenthe trade."

She blinked in surprise. "You're working with the Order now?"

"Yeah. Apparently, these auctions are expensive to run. But. Eh. Why not? It's a percentage of a business I didn't have yesterday."

"Don't suppose they mentioned me and my crew?"

Tormod shrugged. "Not that I'm aware of."

Well, that was something at least.

"Not worried about the Watch getting blamed for Humphreys death?" she asked.

Tormod grinned and rubbed his hands together. "There will always be someone else willing to look the other way for a few coin, believe me."

Samara didn't know what to say. So, she said nothing. Chetwin Humphreys was dead, and the Order was no longer a problem. She could use the win.

SAMARA'S MIND was still reeling as she left the Zephyr. Humphreys was dead. The Order would apparently no longer be a problem, and soon, their City Watch problems would go away too.

Which meant they could finally focus on their Restorationists problem.

She couldn't help wondering how things might change with Tormod taking over Humphreys' business. Would he run the Lions as well?

As Lukas walked her out, she turned to him and said, "Out of curiosity, what's he cutting you in for? You *were* supposed to take over the Lions."

"Still am," Lukas replied with a stoic smile. "I get the Lions. Tormod keeps the Zephyr and his new business interests."

Samara shook her head. "Just don't let him charge you rent for using the Zephyr as Lions headquarters."

The corner of Lukas' lip quirked up a little higher. "We're in negotiations," he replied as he let her out.

It was still early. Golden rays of sunlight made the streets of Hollowhorn glow. Workers already hurried along the streets. Stall owners were setting up their wares. Drunkards struggled to make their way home. It was that in-between time. Not quite morning, not quite night. She liked this time of day. There were so few people about. She could think.

And did she ever need time to think! Her head spun with so many tantalising possibilities she didn't notice the man tailing her. Not at first. She wore a disguise, just as Gerde had suggested: a long skirt with a bonnet pulled low over her head. It was a surprise that anyone had recognised her.

One man she could handle. She just needed to lead him into an alley with a dead end, then she could make quick work of him. She still had plenty of blades concealed on her. To her dismay, her tail got a friend. He popped up out of nowhere as though he had been waiting for her. Well, she couldn't go back to The Wishing-Table now.

Two on one wasn't as good a combination, but she still felt confident she could take them easily enough. It was when the third man appeared ahead of her that she began to re-evaluate her position. She hoped for a moment that he wasn't with the others. But then she noticed his hard stare, and curled lip, both directed at her. She thought she recognised him from the City Watch. But she couldn't be sure.

"Three on one's no fair," she murmured.

Since they were clearly trying to force her down an alleyway, she decided it would be in her better interests not to oblige. Without warning, she held her right hand in front of her and, with a flick of her wrist, released the blade, which buried itself in the thigh of the burly man. She then spun and aimed her left arm, again flicking her wrist and this time burying a blade in the shoulder of one of her other pursuers, who she definitely recognised as one of the City Watchmen she and Gerde had fought near the coaching inn.

She smiled wolfishly at her third pursuer. One on one was much more to her liking.

"She's over here," the guard called out.

Schiesse! Samara strained to see who he was speaking to but kept her focus on him. He lunged at her, but she dodged out of the way, whipping a blade concealed in the waistband of her skirt as she did so. Just then, she heard the clatter of horse's hooves and a large wagon rolled up, pulling to a stop beside them. The wagon had the seal of the City Watch. She tried to make a dash for it, but two men grasped her by the arms, wrenching the blade free. Kicking and punching out, she refused to make it easy for them, but there were too many. Quickly, Samara found herself bundled inside the darkened wagon.

～

SHE WAS TIED UP. Again. Funny how she always seemed to find herself in this position. She had a hood over her head. They had taken all of her blades. She cursed herself for wearing a disguise and not wearing her frock coat with all its hidden pockets. She cursed herself for not bringing Gerde along. But these days, she hated doing anything to endanger Gerde.

No sense crying over it now. She was where she was and there wasn't a verdammt thing she could do about it.

She did not know where she was being taken. It was obviously nowhere in the Hollow because the carriage would've stopped by now. If they were taking her to City Watch headquarters, she would have a bit of time. Although, she very much doubted that's where they were taking her. She was pretty sure hoods and ropes weren't usual for arrests. So much for thinking they were okay now the corrupt Watch had been identified.

She knew she needed to make her escape soon. Once they reached their destination, escaping could be much trickier. Her hands were bound behind her back. *As if that ever stopped her.* She shifted in her seat, contorting her body and shimmying her arms under her so that they were now in front. Breathing hard, she ripped the hood off, only to find four burly City Watchmen staring at her with amused looks on their faces.

"Schiesse!" she cursed.

"If you wanted to see out, you could've just asked," one of them commented, noting her surprised expression.

She ignored him and instead said, "Where are you taking me?"

"You'll find out soon enough."

They didn't replace the hood, but nor were there any windows for her to see out of.

Eventually, the carriage came to a stop, and she was marched down the steps. She noted her surroundings. It appeared to be a residential street in Elphame Park. Naturally, she tried to make a break for it. Elbowing one of her captors so hard in the face that she was pretty sure she broke his nose. She kneed another one in the groin, but three others came hurtling down the steps of a townhouse and soon she was overpowered again.

The guards practically carried her into the building. Samara made a show of struggling the entire time, but she was actually paying attention to her surroundings. She was led across a black and white parquet floor, past a library to her right. She was then dragged up a staircase to the left and led into a drawing room. Samara spied two windows, which she knew she could get open in a jiffy, given the opportunity.

The room itself was difficult to judge. Aside from one chair, the rest of the furniture was covered in sheets to keep the dust off. She was shoved into the one uncovered seat and told to wait there. But as soon as the guard was gone, she got to her feet and hurried over to the window. With her hands bound, it wouldn't be easy to climb down. She could jump, but there were no bushes to break her fall. There was a drainpipe she could swing her body over to. She didn't like not having the use of her hands, but she could lower herself down using her legs to brace the drainpipe.

She unlatched the lock on the window and slid it open. The ledge was small. All she would need to do was climb out and perch on the ledge, then reach out to her right and try to grasp the drainpipe. Leaning forward, she was getting ready to shimmy out the window when she spotted the City Watch down below. They waved at her. A moment later she felt a hand grasp her shoulder and roughly drag her away, shoving her back in the chair.

She cursed. She had to hand it to the City Watch. They were getting better. She hadn't even heard this one approach. In the doorway, she spied a man she didn't recognise. He wore a tailored grey suit. She knew little about clothing, but she imagined it was expensive. His face appeared unlined, and he wore his hair tied in a ponytail.

He clapped his hands as though amused.

"And so," he began, "I finally get to meet the one they call the Hisada. I've been wanting to meet you for some time."

"Can't say the feeling's mutual, Mister…?"

"Kaiser. Lutz Kaiser," he answered, strolling into the room. "I assume you've heard of me."

She nodded her head in confirmation.

"The Matron of House de Mörde claimed you and she were enemies. But I found it extremely suspicious the way she always seemed unable to capture you."

This was news to Samara. It warmed her to know Callie protected her even after Samara had gone back on their deal. She would have to thank her. Once she got out of this mess.

"If you're after Eloise, she's long gone."

"So everybody keeps telling me," Kaiser replied. "And yet I don't believe you."

Samara shrugged. "Well, I don't know what to do about that. I can only tell you what I know."

He tapped a finger on his chin. "I find it curious that you went to so much effort to send a message to me that Chetwin Humphreys was holding her prisoner."

Again, she shrugged. "He was."

"Yes. But not anymore. I knew that already. Unfortunately, these twits did not. They thought to gain my favour, not realising this was a trap. Quite clever, I must say. An efficient way to get rid of Chetwin Humphreys for good. Thus, taking one thorn out of your side. Interesting that you used the City Watch to do that. I suppose you didn't want to get your hands dirty. I've heard rumours you don't kill people anymore. You just let other people do it for you."

Her jaw clenched. "That's not what happened."

"Isn't it? Ah well, whatever happened, you certainly got the City Watch all hot and bothered. I figured since you were obviously still working for Tormod Lyons, you would eventually show up at that gambling hell, and I was right!" He smiled thinly. "I know you know where Eloise is. So why don't you just tell me the truth?"

"I haven't seen her since the night of the auction," she replied. It was, technically, the truth. Eloise had been in disguise the last time they'd met.

Kaiser leisurely strolled to her chair. He studied her face as though looking for any signs of deception. And then he backhanded her. The force took her by surprise, and she nearly toppled over, but wasn't about to let an opportunity escape her. It was because of this man that Hans had been locked in a cell for days.

She lunged at him, using her bound hands to hit him with an uppercut to his chin. He went sprawling, and she was on him again, her hands wrapped around his throat. His face was red, and he gasped. But seconds later, she was being hauled backwards and shoved back into the chair.

Kaiser scrambled up to his feet. His hair dishevelled, glaring at her.

"If she won't act civilly, tie her to the chair," he ordered. "I will get those answers out of you one way or another."

CHAPTER SEVENTEEN

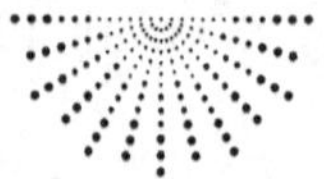

Notorious Gang Leader Slain Whilst Attempting to Flee City Watch Custody!

Chetwin Humphreys, gang leader and leading human trafficker was slain last night after a surprise raid of his Elphame Park home.

—THE MÄRCHEN CHRONICLE

Gerde bounced on her heels in their little living room at The Wishing-Table. She had been pacing but knew that it only made everyone else anxious. Still, she twiddled her fingers. Ana offered her a cup of tea, but she declined, so Ana offered it to Hans instead. She knew the girl was just trying to make up for all the deception earlier. Eloise also stood in the kitchen, no longer in disguise. She seemed unsure what to do with herself, plaiting and un-plaiting her dark tresses to keep her hands busy. Art stood at the window, smoking his pipe, looking down at the busy streets below.

"He's back," he announced, hurrying to put out his pipe.

Gerde's heart leapt. She rushed to the door, not caring about any secret knocks. She just wanted to know what Seb had to say.

When Samara hadn't returned in the morning, Gerde and Art had gone to the Royal Zephyr in search of her. If something had kept Samara away, she would've at least tried to send a message via one of the younger street kids who acted as messengers for the Lions. The fact that she hadn't left Gerde ill at ease.

It had taken them far too long to convince one of the Lions to get hold of Seb. Then Seb had gone and spoken with Lukas, who informed his boss, Tormod. And now they knew for sure. Samara had left hours ago. Tormod had been unconcerned. Chetwin Humphreys was dead. His organisation in shambles. And the City Watchmen who had been after them would soon be dealt with. He seemed to think Samara made a habit of disappearing, but Gerde knew better.

A sympathetic Lukas had agreed to ask around. They quickly learnt about a fight that occurred not long after Samara left the Zephyr. A group of men had attacked a foreign servant girl and forced her into a City Watch wagon.

Gerde pushed back her fears and convinced Tormod to send out his Lions in search of Samara. Seb stayed at the Zephyr to await news.

But Gerde wasn't just going to sit in their rooms waiting while the woman she loved was in trouble. She and Art went to see Ana at the bakery. If they needed to mount a rescue, they might need someone with Ana's powers. They then went to collect Eloise from her boarding house.

All of which led to the present moment, when she opened the door to greet Seb. To her dismay, his expression was grim.

"What did you find out?"

"Nothing," Seb said, with a shake of his head. "They lost the trail completely. She's not at City Watch headquarters. Nobody knows where they've taken her."

As they filed into their cramped rooms, Art said, "Perhaps it's time we spoke to the Matron."

Gerde had wondered about that. She had no issue contacting Callista, but from the way the Matron had described her relationship with Lutz Kaiser—and she had no doubt that was who was behind Samara's kidnapping—it was doubtful she knew where he was holed up.

Eloise paled at the mention of Callista. "We don't need the House. I can help find her," she said.

"How?" Gerde asked.

"I could scry for her."

"Have you done that before?" Ana asked, turning to her friend.

Eloise shook her head. "No. But I know the principles involved."

Hans laid a gentle hand on her shoulder. "What do you need from us, Eloise?"

The girl thought about it. "Since I don't have a crystal ball, perhaps a mirror would do."

Gerde and Hans shook their head. "Maybe Yanni has a polished silver tray we could use," suggested Hans.

But Art was already hurrying to his bags in the other room. He returned with a small handheld mirror with a silver handle, and despite the tremendous worry Gerde was feeling, she couldn't help a chuckle. Of course Art would have a mirror.

"Here," he said, handing it to Eloise.

Eloise accepted the mirror and held it up in front of her, taking several deep breaths and staring into the mirror. The others crammed in behind her, determined to see what was going on. At first, they saw nothing except Eloise's own reflection. But then the reflection grew misty, as though a bank of fog had rolled in, and Eloise's reflection disappeared entirely, to be replaced by Samara. Gerde flinched at the sight of Samara with a split lip. Immediately, she felt Seb's hand on her shoulder.

"Is there any way to see where she's located?" Art asked.

Eloise was staring hard into the mirror. "I can try," she muttered.

Her view of Samara seemed to pull away, and Gerde almost wanted her to stop. She wanted to hold on to that image of Sam, roughed up, but currently okay. It was as though someone were backing away from Samara. Except when they reached the wall of the building, the backing away continued until they were looking at a house.

"That's Elphame Park," Art suddenly exclaimed.

"Are you sure?" Seb asked.

Art nodded. "I know that street. I used to meet up with a married woman at a townhouse on that street."

"Do you think you can find it again?" Gerde asked.

Art shuddered. "Trust me. You never forget the first time you leave a woman's bedroom via drainpipe wearing only your underpants while her husband brandishes a sabre."

Gerde breathed out a small sigh of relief. "Okay. So we know where she is at least. Now we just need to come up with a plan."

"We could use some of Seb's explosive balls. Create a diversion," suggested Art.

"What about the Lions? Could they help?" Gerde asked. She didn't want to think what their chances were like attempting this on their own.

Seb looked hesitant. "I doubt it. Mr Lyons is busy consolidating his new empire."

Gerde bit her lip, then took a deep breath. "We need to bring Callista in."

Eloise, who by now had put down the scrying mirror, her attention fully in the present, immediately looked dismayed.

"I know I'd prefer a group of trained assassins coming to my rescue," muttered Art.

Ana looked uncertain. "Can she really be trusted?"

"Yes. Even when she turned us in to Humphreys, she did it knowing Sam could get away. I think she'd want to help us now." Gerde turned to Eloise. "I know your feelings about the House. If you want to leave us to it, that's okay. You already helped us find her. But we could really use your abilities right now."

Eloise glanced over to Ana, and there seemed to be some unspoken conversation happening before Eloise said, "Samara let me leave when she could've sent me back to the House. I'll stay and help. But I'm not going to House de Mörde."

Gerde agreed. "You don't have to. I'll see the Matron myself and tell her what's happened."

"Whatever you do, be quick," said Hans, his voice wavering, the worry lines deepening in his face.

CALLISTA PACED HER OFFICE, anxiously awaiting news of Samara. She had been shaken awake by Lissa, who gave her the news that someone resembling the Hisada had been taken by City Watch outside the Royal Zephyr. She sent a message to the Magistrate, but it was plainly obvious Samara hadn't been taken to Watch headquarters. Kaiser had her. She was sure of it. Now, she had several of her girls scouring the streets for updates.

A tap sounded on the door and Callista hurried to see what news they had for her. Lissa was at the door.

"You have a visitor. It's the hostler."

Callista stilled. She had been expecting to hear from someone on Sam's crew. The only reason she hadn't reached out herself was because she was still trying to get information on Sam's whereabouts.

She cleared her throat. "Have you shown her into the parlour?"

Lissa ducked her head in confirmation.

"I'll be there in a minute."

When Lissa left, Callista took a deep breath to calm her pounding heart. She then stood up and made her way to the parlour.

It was with surprise that she learnt Gerde already knew where Sam was held. It was as she'd feared. Kaiser had Samara.

Gerde's voice shook when she told her how Kaiser was torturing Sam. Callista wanted to reach out to her, but didn't. They didn't know each other very well, and her touch wouldn't be welcomed.

"Can I ask?" she began and licked her dry lips. "Where did you get your information?"

"I can't say." Gerde's voice was tight.

"I understand," Callie replied. It was Eloise. It had to have been.

"Mounting an assault on this place," Gerde was saying now, "it's not something we know how to do. We could use your expertise."

"Of course," Callista replied without hesitation.

There was no question she would help in the rescue. She only wondered how many of the daughters of House de Mörde would help. Samara had been well-liked. But she had also left the House before her required twenty years were up. By tradition, she should have been killed. Instead, Callista left her alone, which had drawn consternation amongst the daughters.

She would have a difficult time persuading them to help, and time was of the essence. She was surprised to learn Kaiser had it in him to torture a woman. But she shouldn't have been. If this job taught her one thing, it was that people were capable of anything. Seemingly harmless old ladies might order a contract on a daughter-in-law who was having an affair. A little girl could be shaped to be a weapon to fulfil that contract.

Callista agreed to meet Gerde near the Elphame Park address in two hours, with whoever she could scrounge up for this fight.

But if she had to go in there alone to rescue her sister-at-arms, so be it.

When Gerde left, Callista arranged for Lissa to bring all the daughters who weren't out on assignment to the great hall. It would take some time to gather them. There were currently sixty-five of the House who were under contract. The numbers had been dwindling over the past few years, ever since she dropped her supplier, Humphreys. Thirty-seven daughters were currently out on assignment. Which left just twenty-eight daughters, including herself.

While Lissa gathered the daughters, Callista went to her room. She changed into loose-fitting trousers, which she wore tucked into comfortable boots. She wore a blouse and, over that, a padded corset. It would help take the brunt of a blow, though it would do nothing in the event of a stabbing. She plaited her hair and retrieved her roll of weapons, placing a variety of blades into her belt.

She then retrieved the gun. It had belonged to her mother, the previous Matron. Callista remembered being shocked to discover it since guns were illegal in Märchen. Even the possession of one could result in a hefty charge. Occasionally, she took it out to the forests nearby to practice firing with it. Though she knew she could get into a lot of trouble if she was ever caught with it.

If she ended up using it, she just hoped the Magistrate would go easy on her.

She then proceeded downstairs and into the great hall where the other daughters were already assembled. Her hands shook as she gazed at their faces. She took a deep breath, wondering just who would stand with her, and who would object. There were many older daughters who saw Samara as a traitor. And many younger ones who were still children when Samara left, felt the same way. Others, however, were fascinated by the legend of Samara.

Truth be told, she didn't feel confident she could win their support. "Samara Dawa is in trouble," she said without preamble.

Already a murmur rose in the crowd.

"Some members of the City Watch are holding her prisoner for Lutz Kaiser."

"Kaiser!" shouted one daughter. "The *man* you allowed to stay here?"

"One of the men," another daughter loudly muttered.

Callista inwardly cursed. She was already losing them. She placed a hand out in front of her. "I know you question my judgement in that regard. As Matron, I had my reasons."

"Eloise," said a voice. One of the younger daughters who had befriended Eloise.

"Yes," Callista confirmed. "Kaiser is after Eloise, and right now, as we speak, he is torturing Samara to find out where she is. Now I know Samara left our family—"

"Traitor," someone murmured.

"But she is still a daughter of House de Mörde. She is still your sister-at-arms. She is still my friend. Samara made her choice to leave, because, like many of us, she wasn't given a choice when she joined. But she is one of us, and I won't leave a daughter of House de Mörde to be tortured. I know where she's being held. But her friends cannot do this on their own. I am going to help rescue her. And I am asking you now, which of you will come to Samara's aid?"

Camille, a daughter who had been in Callista and Samara's year stepped forward. "Samara and I started in the same class together. We trained together and lived together for years. She was my sister. But the day she left she broke my heart. She left us behind and chose a different path. I say she reap what she sows," Camille walked away. A dozen girls trailed after her.

Callista cursed. She had hoped that someone from their year might be compelled to join her cause. After all, they had grown up with Samara.

"I agree," said Emily, another of the older daughters. "And I question your judgement of late. Allowing all these strangers to stay here. And now this." Emily walked away, shaking her head in disgust.

Callista gazed hopefully over the crowd. Another girl, this time much younger, stepped forward. "I don't know this hündin. I'm not going to risk my skin to save hers."

Many of the younger girls muttered their agreement, leaving Callista deflated. She had hoped that even if they didn't want to do this for Samara, they'd do this for Callista, their Matron.

"If any of you feel the same way, you can leave. I am not ordering anyone to do this."

To Callista's dismay, the room began to empty out.

By the end, she had just seven other daughters of House de Mörde. Three were older daughters who knew and had sparred with Samara. Four were younger girls, eager for a fight. Callista was pleased to see that Lissa was amongst those younger girls. She met Callista's eyes and bowed her head.

That meant there would be just eight of them. Not exactly an army, but it would have to do.

~

IT WAS mid-afternoon when Callista and her small cadre of daughters from House de Mörde arrived by carriage, although she had the driver park at a carriage stand a couple of streets over so their presence wouldn't alert anyone. The cool air was bracing. It gave her energy for the coming fight. But her stomach churned. Her mind dwelt on all the things that might go wrong.

When she reached the street corner where she was to meet Gerde and the others, she was unprepared for the sight of the slim, dark-haired girl standing with them. Her mouth fell open. Eloise, for her part, glared defiantly at her. *She probably thinks I'm going to drag her back to the House,* Callista mused. She had no interest in bringing Eloise back. That girl had caused her enough trouble.

She nodded a greeting at Eloise. "I'm glad to see you're well," was all she said.

Art was studying her group of daughters with a wary eye. "Not exactly the rescue force I thought we were getting," he said to no one in particular. Then he laid eyes on one of the daughters. "Ah, Lydia. It's good to see you again."

Lydia muttered a greeting in return, trying to hide the blush creeping up her cheeks. Callista observed the exchange with raised eyebrows but decided to address it another time.

Gerde strode forward and shook hands with Callista. "Thank you again for agreeing to help."

"Sam would do the same for me. Do you know how many City Watch are in there?"

"We've caught glimpses of one or two guards, but nobody's come in or out, so we have no idea how many are actually inside," Art replied. "Which, you know, I could find out. All I'd need to do is sneak in, knock one of them out, put on the uniform and go see for myself."

"It's too dangerous. We don't want to alert them until we're ready to go in," Gerde replied in a tone that suggested this wasn't the first time they'd had this conversation.

Lissa, who stood by Callista's side, ready to follow any instructions the Matron might have, spoke up. "I can do a quick reconnaissance."

Callista would've preferred to do it herself, but Lissa was an excellent climber. Almost as good as Sam. She would have better luck spying on the house. So she agreed.

And they waited yet again.

It was … awkward.

While Lydia chatted with Art, the rest of Callista's sisters-at-arms kept their distance, mistrustful of Samara's crew. Eloise looked uncertain if she should go over and say hello to the faces she knew, eventually deciding against it. It was for the best. The girl might've been temporarily welcomed into House de Mörde, but as Callista had observed earlier in the great hall, the daughters of the House cared little for those who left their ranks. Even if Eloise was never technically part of their ranks.

Callista made awkward conversation with Gerde and the explosives expert, Seb. She breathed a sigh of relief when Lissa finally returned.

"What did you see?" asked Gerde.

"She's being kept in the back of the house, on the top floor. I only counted nine guards. All City Watch. And Kaiser himself."

"How did Samara look?" Gerde pressed.

Lissa's lips turned downward. "Okay, but he is not happy that she won't give Eloise up." Lissa cut a glance towards the girl in question.

Out of the corner of her eye, Callista observed Eloise listening in on the conversation. A guilty look on her face. *Good,* Callista thought. *If it wasn't for Eloise's foolish act of running away from the House, Samara wouldn't be in this mess.*

"Tell me exactly what you saw," Callista said.

It didn't take them long to come up with a plan. Hoffner and one of the other guards were upstairs with Kaiser. The rest were in the basement where the kitchen was located. Lissa had done her job well, breaking into the house and making sure there were no other City Watchmen lurking about.

Callista didn't like the idea of going down into the basement to fight them. If they got trapped down there, anything could go wrong. Better to draw them out. That was where Seb's explosive expertise came in. He and Ana would set off some explosions to draw them upstairs. Callista didn't know why they needed two people to do this, but Ana insisted on accompanying him. Gerde and most of the daughters would be downstairs.

Callista, Lissa, Hilda and Genevieve would sneak in through an upstairs window. When the explosions went off, they would use it as their signal to take out Kaiser and Hoffner.

The daughters hadn't been happy when Callista stressed the need to use non-lethal force. But they understood why. They were licensed assassins, not mercenaries. And they were dealing with men of the law.

Art and Eloise would be outside, keeping watch in case Kaiser somehow managed to escape. Art didn't seem happy about his role, but someone needed to be there to help Eloise in case Kaiser spotted her. Callista felt it was a mistake to have brought her along. Eloise claimed she could disguise herself, but Callista didn't want to leave anything to chance.

She let out a low exhale. The plan was as good as it was going to get.

CHAPTER EIGHTEEN

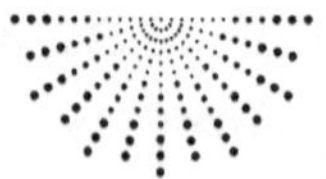

Ever since the House de Mörde became the official assassin's guild of Märchen, the organisation has only grown. Every year, the Matron of the House traditionally takes in 10 girls as young as six—typically girls sold by their family or brought in by slavers—to be trained to become daughters of the House. It is said the dropout rate can be as high as fifty percent. But what happens to the girls who do not make the cut and go on to become an elite assassin?

— THE DARK HISTORY OF THE HOUSE DE MÖRDE

Samara saw Hoffner's punch coming and reacted as she had been trained to do. She clenched her jaw, lodging her tongue firmly against the roof of her mouth. The result was that even though she still spat out blood, her jaw was intact and her head didn't whip around which would have caused the chair to topple.

Like the chair she was tied to, she wobbled, but refused to fall over.

Lutz, who stood in the corner, was growing irate. She figured she could call him Lutz now. Surely they ought to be on a first-name basis after all they'd been through together. He with the questioning and threats. She with the surly responses.

He mopped his brow with what looked to her like a silk handkerchief, his eyes narrowed, staring imperiously down at her. She liked it that she made him irate. She couldn't do anything tied up in this chair, but she could torment him in her own way.

It would be nothing to tell him that Eloise was still in Märchen. She didn't know where Eloise was staying, and he already suspected she was here. But he wouldn't believe she didn't know. And really, she hated the idea of giving this man, who had been responsible for locking up Hans and shutting down the coaching inn, anything.

Unfortunately, she couldn't properly get the measure of Hoffner. The only thing she really knew was that he was *furious*. Apparently, he hadn't appreciated being made a fool of with the Humphreys misdirection. And he really didn't appreciate being implicated in Humphreys' death.

Not that she'd had anything to do with that.

Hoffner ran a thumb across her lip and showed it to her. She supposed it was meant to be intimidating, but seeing the saliva mixed with blood oozing down onto his fingers was just gross. It was a good thing she hadn't eaten anything today.

She couldn't help herself. She spat a wad of blood-mixed saliva into his face. Which caused Hoffner to backhand her. But again, she was ready for it.

She didn't know what kind of training the City Watch underwent, but the daughters of House de Mörde's training was extremely thorough.

She looked up at him and smiled a presumably bloody smile.

A look came into Hoffner's eyes, and she knew that if he

wasn't being held on Kaiser's leash, he would try to kill her. And, to save her life and get back to her crew, she would have no qualms killing him.

Thankfully, it didn't come to that, because Lutz interrupted Hoffner. "That's enough. I need answers from her. Which means she needs to physically be able to talk."

"If that's the only requirement..." Hoffner said, turning back to his boss with a sick grin on his face.

"Leave," replied Lutz. "Now!" This time more forcefully.

Hoffner stalked out of the room, allowing the door to bang shut behind him. Lutz inhaled and then exhaled slowly. He strolled over to Samara and knelt down in front of her, careful not to touch her.

"You look tired. You must surely be hungry." His voice was soft. Friendly even. "I can get you something to eat. It doesn't have to be this way."

Samara rolled her eyes. *Oh, so we're doing that routine now*, she thought. *How pathetic.*

CALLISTA EASED into the bedroom behind Lissa, quickly unhooking her harness from the rope to allow her fellow sister-at-arms to climb up.

Her heart raced. She hadn't done something like this in over eight years. She trained and maintained her skills. But actually going into the field? No.

A tiny part of her worried she would hold everybody up. Was she risking the mission by coming along? But she needed to be here. She couldn't leave Sam like this.

It had been bad enough when she had handed Sam over to Humphreys. This was even worse. She had allowed Lutz Kaiser into their lives, and she needed to fix this.

She took in the room. It was an average bedroom. Floral wallpaper. Dense carpet. She could make out the shape of a bed and chest of drawers beneath large dust covers. *Who owns this place?* she wondered. No doubt it was someone financing the Restorationists.

Lissa was at the door. She had it cracked, and she was listening. She quickly pulled away and quietly pressed the door closed again. Thankfully, it made no noise.

"Hoffner is out there," Lissa whispered.

Callista signalled they should take cover in case he checked the bedroom. He had no reason to, but they didn't want to blow their timing.

Thankfully, just a couple of minutes later, they could make out the sound of an explosion coming from the floor below. It was more subdued than Callista had been expecting, but they heard it all the same.

Lissa was first out the door, followed by Hilda and Genevieve, with Callista taking the rear.

In the corridor, Callista spotted Hoffner, Kaiser and another guard. It looked like they were heading for the stairs. Lissa was already on Hoffner. She was lithe and fast. He drew his cutlass on her, but she easily disarmed him, forcing him into hand-to-hand combat.

Hilda and Genevieve were on the second City Watchman, but there was a third running up the stairs who had apparently slipped by the daughters down below. Callista shouted to Genevieve to take care of him, as she went after Kaiser, who was attempting to dart past them.

Callista grabbed him by the arm, yanking him around to face her.

She was pleased to see the look of fear on his face, though his expression changed once he registered who was tackling him.

"Matron," he said, allowing derision to drip into his voice, despite that she had him pushed up against the wall. "I warned you about getting in my way. I could have your licence revoked."

Callista's nostrils flared. She hated insignificant men with big egos, and she especially hated being talked down to by such men.

"Oh, I don't think so. I think the House de Mörde will do just fine," she said. "But not you."

She kneed him hard in the stomach and he let out a gasp, staggering backwards. "That's for threatening the House," she snarled, bearing down on him. "And this is for attacking my sister."

She grabbed his arm, struck out a leg, and threw him back on the floor. He didn't have time to brace himself, but he managed to drag her down with him. He snatched a blade from her belt, and lunged at her with it, forcing Callista to roll away. She responded with a blow to knock the blade out of his hand and followed up with a punch to the stomach. She was about to get him into a sleeping hold when she glanced back at the fighting around her. Genevieve and Hilda were locked in combat. Meanwhile, Hoffner had managed to grab Lissa and fling her hard against a wall. He delivered a punch to her throat that left the young assassin gasping.

Callista cursed. Leaping to her feet, she jumped into combat with Hoffner. Recognising his new opponent, he grinned. His mouth was bloody. Lissa had done a good job roughing him up, but she wasn't used to fighting opponents so much bigger than herself. Neither was Callista, but she was willing to try.

She dodged his punches but couldn't seem to land a blow of her own. He had her on the defensive. He was trying to do the same manoeuvre he had done on Lissa, but Callista wasn't letting him get close enough. Verdammt, he was a good brawler. Smart, too.

She saw Kaiser trying to make for the stairs, and she called out to Lissa to go after him. The girl was in bad shape, but she still managed to pull a blow gun from her pocket and send a dart toward the retreating Kaiser. He stumbled down the stairs.

"Check on Samara!" Callista called to Lissa, then she cursed, suddenly remembering that she still had Ursula's gun.

With Hoffner looming towards her, she pulled out the gun and cocked the weapon, pointing it at his head. He stopped, his eyes narrowing on the very illegal weapon. He raised his arms, and she breathed a sigh of relief. Perhaps the Magistrate didn't need to know about the gun after all. But then he ducked down, rushing her body and knocking the gun out of her hands. She slammed into the wall, her whole body jarring. Hoffner's hands reached out for her throat. She acted fast, with a push dagger the size of her palm that she lodged into his shoulder. He stumbled back, and Callista rushed in again, using her right hand to perform an expert knife-hand strike. Hoffner crumpled to the floor.

ART SAT in an unmarked carriage parked a few doors down from the house where Samara was being held. Ironically, it was opposite the house he'd had to flee in a hurry as a much younger lad. Eloise stared intently out the window while he morosely shuffled a deck of cards and anxiously jiggled his knee.

I should be in there with them, instead of babysitting this one, he thought to himself.

The waiting didn't last long though, as he soon heard the muted, attenuated sound of explosives going off. It was time. In a few minutes, the others should come out with Samara. He stuffed his cards into his trouser pocket and squatted next to Eloise, peering out.

Several interminable minutes went by before they saw a figure running out and away from the building. Eloise leaned her head out.

"I think that's Kaiser," she exclaimed.

Lutz Kaiser was a small man, and though he was running, he wasn't moving very fast. Still, he'd get away if they didn't do something about it. Apparently, Eloise had the same thought, because she had closed her eyes and began to murmur under her breath.

Art put a hand on her arm, and she flinched. "What are you doing?"

"I'm using my Magic to catch him," she replied with a glare.

"Not in broad daylight, you're not," Art said, opening the carriage door and jumping down.

With his longer gait, he easily caught up to the fleeing Kaiser, leaping on his back and tackling him to the pavement. For a moment, the two grappled with each other on the ground. Suddenly, Art felt an intense pain in his gut. He released Kaiser and touched his stomach, only to feel the wet warmth of blood.

Kaiser snarled, vindictively pulling the khanjar blade out of Art and getting to his feet once more. Art uselessly swiped an arm toward Kaiser, but the man was already running down the street.

Art squeezed his eyes shut from the pain, only to open them a moment later at the sound of running footsteps. This time, running towards him. Eloise knelt down beside him.

"Art, can you hear me?"

"Yes, I can hear," he said through gritted teeth.

He could feel her hands on his stomach. "I don't think it's too deep. I can heal you."

Art put a hand on her arm. "Are you sure? Have you ever done this before?"

"Well, not a gut wound," Eloise admitted, rolling up her

sleeves. "But I spent the last two years in the House de Mörde. I know how to heal a wound."

Art lifted his head, trying to swat her hands away with one arm while he used his other arm to prop himself up. It didn't last, though; it was too painful in that position. "I don't think you should do this," he mumbled as he lay back down on the hard pavement.

"Ssshh," she responded.

Moments later, he felt a warm sensation on his stomach. Not the warm wetness of blood this time. It was warm, like the sun. His muscles loosened, and slowly, he found himself able to breathe easier.

He let out a long exhalation and promptly passed out.

SAMARA LISTENED to the ensuing fight just outside the door. Her heart beat wildly in her chest and she had to calm her breathing. She knew her crew would come for her eventually. She had held on to that belief the whole time Hoffner had done his worst. When she heard the sound of explosions coming from the lower level, followed by Hoffner and Kaiser fleeing the room, her heart leapt into her mouth. They were here.

Now, her stomach churned. These City Watchmen meant business. The only real fighter in her group was Gerde. Could she and Ana really hold out against the Watch?

She listened in agony to the fight outside, straining for a sign to tell her which side was winning. Her head was swimming by the time the door opened again. Utterly exhausted, she had to blink several times before she could register the face of the person who rushed to her side and untied the ropes that bit into her skin. She stiffened in shock when she realised it was the imp.

The door opened again and this time Callista came into view. Her former sister-at-arms knelt by her side, helping the imp with the ropes and rubbing Samara's wrists to let the blood flow into her hands. Callie couldn't hide the concern on her face. Samara would have smiled, but her face ached too verdammt much.

"I've got you," murmured Callie as she helped her stand.

Samara's body felt stiff, but Callie wrapped an arm over her shoulder, and together they walked out into the corridor. She took in the sight of two City Watch, disarmed and out cold on the ground. A snarl came to her face when she realised one of them was Hoffner, who was bleeding from a wound that was now soaking into the carpet fibres.

"Not bad," Samara mumbled, eyeing the Matron.

Callie gave her a small, pleased smile that reminded Samara of their days in training, back when Callie was still new to the House and striving to be as good as Samara.

The sound of footsteps racing up the stairs caused them both to look round. Samara almost sobbed at the sight of Seb, Ana and Gerde, as well as girls she didn't recognise. Presumably daughters of the House.

"Did we catch Kaiser?" Callista asked one of the assassins.

The assassin grimly shook her head.

Gerde walked slowly towards her and even though the light was dim in the corridor, Samara could see unshed tears swimming in Gerde's eyes. She nodded to Seb and Ana, her whole face and neck aching as she did so. Then she took Gerde's hand in her own, gripping it tightly.

"Let's go home," Gerde murmured.

~

THE NEXT DAY, after a long hot soak and an even longer sleep, Samara's body still ached. But despite far too many bruises to count, she was all right. Samara knew things could've gone a lot worse for her. She hated having been caught in the first place. She admonished herself over it, until Gerde told her to stop. Samara had voiced none of her thoughts aloud, but somehow Gerde knew. She always knew.

She and her crew had said little that evening. Art berated himself for allowing Kaiser to slip by, but nobody blamed him. Who knows what would have happened to Art if Eloise hadn't been there to help.

Eloise offered to try to locate Kaiser. Apparently, it was down to Eloise's abilities that they were able to find her. Samara found herself re-evaluating her opinion on the girl, who had risked exposing her magic just to help her. Nor could Samara believe the House de Mörde's involvement. Callie had been reluctant to leave Samara after the fight, but she promised to come by the next morning.

The one thing they could all agree on was that they needed to take care of this Restorationist organisation once and for all.

It was Art who suggested they reach out to the Magistrate again. "Someone rented that house to Kaiser. If she can find out who, that gives us another name to use when go after the Restorationists."

"That's actually a good idea, Art," Gerde had said.

"Don't sound so surprised. I may not be able to stop a fleeing Richildan, but I can at least come up with the occasional smart idea."

"He stabbed you. It was hardly a fair fight," Gerde reminded him, which did little to comfort Art.

The next morning, true to her word, Callista dropped by with the imp in tow. Samara was afraid she might actually have to thank the imp, but the girl waited outside while Callista helped Samara compile a list of all the City Watch she remembered seeing at Humphreys home. Callista then sent the imp to the Magistrate with the list and a request to meet again.

Hans had brought buns and made saffron chai, so the four of them—Art was still asleep—munched on tea and buns. Hans kept up a lively conversation with Callista about the forgery trade, before the imp, Lissa—Samara could at least start calling her by her name—returned saying the Magistrate would meet them at her residence.

After sending Lissa back to the House, she, Callie and Gerde rode to the Magistrate's home in the House de Mörde carriage.

"I didn't thank you properly" Samara began.

"Nor I," said Gerde. They sat together, holding hands, while Callista sat on the bench opposite.

"You know I will always have your back," Callista murmured, her gaze was on Samara and Gerde's entwined hands.

Samara, noticing Callista's gaze started to release Gerde's hand, before changing her mind. Instead, she squeezed Gerde's hand tighter. Callista raised her eyes to meet Samara's own and Samara's lips twisted into a wry smile. Callista had done things that couldn't easily be forgiven. But she recognised that her former sister was trying to make up for it.

"That couldn't have been easy," Samara said. "Getting daughters of the House to come to my rescue."

Gerde turned to her, confused. "Why wouldn't they want to help one of their own?"

Samara smiled bitterly. "I'm not one of their own anymore."

"True," Callista confirmed. "But you'd be surprised how much the legend of you remains."

She didn't say more on the subject, but Samara knew there had to be so much she was keeping to herself. She eyed Callie as they rode to the Magistrate's home and wondered whether Callie was lonely.

When they were let into the Magistrate's drawing room, Sylvain Duvall was already waiting for them. Her mouth dropped open at the sight of Samara.

"Have you been seen by a physician? I can have one brought here."

Samara waved her concerns aside as she sat down. "I'm fine. No broken bones. All my organs are generally all in the right place."

"Hoffner really worked you over," the Magistrate observed, unable to take her eyes from Samara.

Samara shifted in her seat, uncomfortable at being the focus of attention. "He did," Samara agreed.

"I just wish I could've had them all brought into custody before they got to you."

"What happened to them?" Gerde asked. There was a hardness in her voice.

"The ones responsible for your kidnapping have been gaoled. Rest assured, they will be receiving long sentences. The others who were at Humphreys home will be fired." She grimaced. "Which leaves me decidedly understaffed."

"You know how you can fix that," Gerde said, gazing meaningfully into the Magistrate's eyes.

"Yes. But who will train them? The minute I start hiring women, I will lose another sizeable chunk of City Watch. There are those in the Watch who will refuse to work with women, no matter what."

"Then hire new people to train them," said Callista, simply.

The Magistrate chuckled mirthlessly. "Hire new people to train them. Like who?"

"A former daughter of House de Mörde is more than qualified."

"Not me." Samara chuckled, and then winced. Yep. She was definitely getting too old for this.

"I could train them," said Gerde, and Samara turned to her in surprise. But of course, this was what Gerde had wanted all along. To join the Watch. She squeezed Gerde's hand.

The Magistrate nodded slowly. "I'll consider it." She sighed. "But first, I'd like to discuss what exactly happened to Humphreys. The plan was to expose the City Watch, but now I have the murder of a high-profile individual on my hands."

Samara responded carefully. "The way I understood it, the City Watch murdered Humphreys while he was trying to escape."

"So Tormod is sticking with that story, is he?" the Magistrate asked incredulously.

Samara sighed. She owed Tormod nothing, and even though she couldn't prove it, she was certain Tormod had orchestrated the murder.

"According to Tormod, he had nothing to do with Humphreys' death. He says it was Alfred Vogel what did the deed."

The Magistrate leaned forward. "Was Vogel offered a piece of Humphreys' business if he did so?"

Samara shrugged. "I honestly know nothing about it. Probably. But could you prove it, if Tormod *was* behind it?"

The Magistrate wrapped her hands about herself. "I would love nothing more than to do so. But I'm in this too. If people found out that I had been involved in the planning..." She pointed a finger at Samara. "The next time you see your boss—"

"Former boss," Gerde interrupted, and Samara smiled.

"*Former boss,* tell him he'd better watch his back." She let out another long exhale. "I'm sorry. You came here for information."

Samara sat forward in her chair. "What did you find out?"

"The townhouse is owned by someone with the last name, Müller. Unfortunately, I don't have any more information about this person. He lives in Richilde."

Samara and Gerde eyed each other.

"You know that name?" Callista asked.

"It was one of the names Eloise already gave us," Gerde replied.

"Eloise?" asked the Magistrate.

"She's the person Lutz Kaiser is after," Callista explained. "He wants to make her the Queen of Richilde"

The Magistrate sat back in her chair and rubbed her brow. "What've you all gotten mixed up with?"

"We still need your contact in Richilde. If we can convince someone in the Richildan government of the threat the Restorationists pose, they could help us get rid of them," said Samara.

The Magistrate walked over to her desk. She pulled out a piece of paper and a quill. She scrawled a name on the paper and handed it to Samara.

"After our last conversation, I contacted him via speaking telegraph. I left a message with his staff, but he hasn't gotten back to me yet." She bit her lip. "I'm sticking my neck out for you people. Are you sure this is a real threat?"

"I'm sure," Callista assured her.

"What about my family's inn?" Gerde interrupted.

"I've been a little tied up with this City Watch business, but I'll have my assistant take care of things so they can reopen." The Magistrate ran her hands through her hair. "I don't know what you have planned as far as contacting the Richildan government—I'm thinking the less I know, the better. But, I hope we can have some conversations soon, about the future of the City Watch. If you both are serious about helping me."

Gerde swallowed and sat up straighter. Samara squeezed her hand again. "I ... I am," said Gerde.

Callista looked over at Samara and met her gaze. "Me too."

The Magistrate straightened and nodded her head. "Good.

In the meantime, I'll have my people keep an eye out for this Kaiser person. I just need a description."

"I can give you that," said Callista.

As they made to leave, Samara turned back to the Magistrate. "Thank you again for the name. If we can get the Richildan government on our side," she gestured to the paper with the Richildan contact's information, "we can finally take the fight to the Restorationists."

CHAPTER NINETEEN

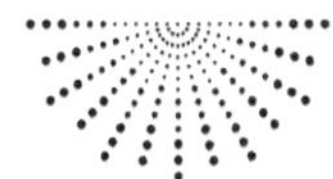

Many who visit the town of Dorholz see it only as a stop on the way to the city-state of Märchen or whilst travelling to Richilde. However, if you were instead to take a day in Dorholz to enjoy the small trading town, you would find a vibrant community with a charming market filled with vendors selling exotic fruit, fabric, alcohol and hash.

— TOMAS & SONS GUIDE TO DORHOLZ

It was night-time, and Gerde, Seb, Ana and Eloise were crouched low on the grounds of Witanhurst. The Templeton manor house stood in the distance, all cream walls and marble columns gleaming extra bright in the moonlight. Gerde found her gaze drawn to the building as they sat in the chilly night air, waiting for Samara to return. She wondered what it must've been like to grow up here. On the one hand, the grounds, what little she could make out, were lovely. She could imagine playing in the orchard, and there was so much land in which to run the horses. But the Witanhurst Manor House itself seemed cold. The complete opposite of Art.

Seb shivered, his arms crossed in front of him to stay warm. "I still think it would've been easier to dress up a stagecoach than to steal one."

"Have a spare stagecoach, do you?" Gerde asked with some amusement.

The crew had argued back and forth about the best way to leave Märchen. The easiest and most comfortable ride would be down the Klara, but they needed the Templeton sigil to open doors for them, which they couldn't do if they just hired a brougham when they arrived in Richilde. Art argued vehemently that even if they could get hold of a stagecoach and dress it up with the Templeton sigil, it would be uncomfortable to travel so far in it. Gerde had to agree with him there. This coach would be far more luxurious and designed to handle long journeys.

Not that this would be easy. There was still the chance that the elder Templeton, once he discovered the coach stolen, might go so far as to try to have his son arrested. Another point they argued over in the plan was whether to make it clear to Lord Templeton that his son was behind the theft. In the end, they decided it would be better this way. Make it appear as though Art had stolen the stagecoach to take it on a little jaunt, which he had apparently done once or twice before in his youth.

Ana rubbed her hands together. "Why is it taking so long?" she muttered.

Gerde didn't respond, though she was thinking the same. In theory, Ana and Eloise weren't needed for this part of the plan, but Sam wanted to bring them, just in case.

A few minutes later Samara returned. "Okay," she said in a low voice. "Art's distracted the groom. Time to get to work."

"Where did Art take the groom?" Seb asked as they

approached the barn where Art said his father kept the horses that pulled the stagecoach.

Samara shrugged. "Dunno. I just hope Art's keeping him nice and busy while we get the horses."

The door to the barn creaked as they stepped inside and Gerde could hear a horse whickering in its stall.

"I feel bad for the groom," Seb said.

"Me too," Gerde muttered. She enjoyed doing jobs like these with Samara, but she did sometimes wonder about the fallout for everybody else. At least in this instance there was the possibility she could help the groom find a job at her parent's coaching inn, if he ended up losing his job because of them.

She walked through the barn, checking the stalls to pick the best horses. She glanced in one stall to see an impressive black stallion. He was a handsome fellow, but Art had already warned her about this one. He was Lord Templeton's prized possession. Or, as Art put it, "the son he never had". Lord Templeton might look the other way at his ne'er do well son taking the stagecoach for a ride without permission, but there would be hell to pay if that horse, Sturm, were to go missing.

She glanced over the other horses, looking for strong, muscular ones. She reached into her pouch and pulled out some carrots, greeting the horses and offering treats, all the while checking for who might be best suited for the journey.

Eventually, Gerde selected the horses she needed and, as quietly as they could, she and Seb led the four horses to the other barn, where the stagecoach was kept. She smiled over at Samara as she went to hook up the traces. Samara always seemed decidedly uncomfortable around horses—she never so much as acknowledged them, and always kept her distance from them. But Gerde supposed she could forgive that. It's not like she was ever going to take up climbing.

"I hope we made the right decision leaving Hans behind," Samara muttered when Gerde was within earshot.

"He'll be okay," Gerde reassured her. "This is a long journey to take with his shoulder still healing."

Though Eloise had offered to heal him, Hans had declined, preferring to heal "the old-fashioned way".

Gerde was almost finished harnessing the horses when Ana came running inside, followed closely by Eloise. "Someone from the main house is coming!" Ana called in a loud whisper.

Samara cursed and ducked outside to check. She came back in just as Gerde had finished her work. "It's another groom. I think he's just out for a walk," she said.

"So, we sit here and hope he doesn't come this way?" Seb asked, a cord of tension in his voice.

Gerde didn't like the sound of that. The horses were already getting restless.

"Could we not just ride off? Art's father will know about the theft soon, anyway?" Ana asked.

"What if he tries to have us arrested? We need to buy as much time for ourselves as we can," replied Gerde, looking over at Samara to see if she had a plan. In the dim light of the lantern they held, Gerde could see the bruises on Samara. She was still moving stiffly after her encounter with the City Watch. Then, registering the lantern, Gerde hurried to put out the glow. As dark as it was out here on the Templeton estate, that glow might as well be as bright as the sun, for anyone outside.

Samara turned to Eloise. "Can you create an illusion? One that shows everything is the same?"

"Yes, but I can't control the sound of the horses at the same time."

"I could try," said Ana. "Sound is the result of kinetic energy, isn't it?"

Samara frowned. "Horses neighing aren't because of kinetic energy. We don't want you to kill them."

"No, she's right, it could work," Eloise began.

One of the horses began stamping his hooves as though he were impatient to be off, and Gerde gave him another carrot and tried to make soothing noises. Horses liked routine, and there was nothing about what they were doing that was routine.

"I'll take care of it," Seb suddenly announced in the darkness. "Give it a few minutes and then go on with the coach. I'll meet you on the road, the way we came in."

A moment later, Gerde heard the door to the barn open and Seb was gone.

It was freezing outside, and Seb was in no mood for all this sneaking around tonight. He stalked away from the barn as loudly as he possibly could. In the dim moonlight, he could make out the figure of the groom walking along the path. Seb called down to the man, waving with both hands.

"You there! Hello!" He swayed a little as he strode down to meet the man.

As he got closer to the groom, he could see the man's narrowed eyes and twisted mouth.

"Who are you and what you are doing here? You are trespassing. This is Lord Templeton's property."

The man's eyes, Seb noticed, kept shifting about up the path which led, according to Art, to a small lake. A thought suddenly struck Seb. *He's planning his own midnight assignation. That's why he's out here so late.* Even so, he was sure the groom would feel obligated to go back to the house and report it if, oh say, a stagecoach was stolen. He needed to get the groom well away from here.

Responding to the groom's comments about Lord Temple-ton, Seb suddenly doubled over and laughed. "You mean to say he was telling the truth? He really *is* the son of a lord?" Seb chortled. "I thought he was lying."

The groom pressed his lips together. "I'm sorry. Who are you?"

"The name's Seb Eze. I'm here with Art Templeton." He placed his hands on his hips and looked about him. "Or, I was, anyway. I'm not sure where he ended up."

The groom stiffened. Again, he glanced over toward the lake. "Mr Templeton is here?" The groom sounded put out.

"Somewhere," Seb confirmed. "I only met him tonight at the Aurora."

Even in the dim light, Seb could see the groom's face twist in disgust. No doubt an establishment like the Aurora was beneath him.

Seb continued, "He kept claiming he was the son of a lord. But we didn't believe him. So then he brought me and my friend Klaus here to show us where he grew up. Only now, I don't know where they've gone." Seb sighed and tried to look as though he were trying to remember something. "I think he wanted to show Klaus the orchard. Said it was really romantic in the dark or some nonsense."

The groom rolled his eyes. "Yes. That sounds like the younger Mr Templeton."

The groom shook his head unhappily. "I'd better go help you find him. The master will not be happy if he finds out his son has been here."

"Oh?" Seb innocently asked. "Do they not get along?"

"You don't know the half of it," muttered the groom. He gave another lingering look toward the lake. "Come on. The orchard is this way."

Seb allowed the groom to lead him about the orchard for a

good twenty minutes before he decided that Samara and the others had had enough time to move the stagecoach. He thought he would've heard some sounds coming from the horses or the wheels along the driveway, but there was no sound at all. Hopefully, they hadn't been discovered by anyone else.

"You know what? I think I'm just going to go home. If you could point me the way out of here, I'll be on my way."

"I really think we should find Mr Templeton first," the groom objected, but Seb could tell his heart wasn't in it.

"You don't need me for that. I'll be honest, I only just met him tonight. He seemed funny. And he was buying the rounds, but I have to get back to town. I have work in the morning."

The groom nodded in understanding, but still seemed reluctant to leave.

"I don't want to keep you. You probably have somewhere you need to be," Seb said, trying to sound casual.

The groom seemed torn between continuing the search, or leaving.

Seb waved a hand at him. "I'm off. Just tell me which way to the main road, and I'll walk back."

"It's a three-mile walk to town!" the groom exclaimed.

Seb shrugged and turned to leave. That did it. The groom hurried to catch up with Seb, who had already begun walking in what he thought was the direction out of the orchard. Together, he and the groom retraced their steps, down past the barn. Seb chanced a glance in that direction, but again he neither saw nor heard anything. He had to assume the others had already gone. The groom pointed him to the road, which Seb already knew, and then he was on his way.

He *really* hoped the others had managed to get away in the coach.

Seb continued down the dirt road until he eventually made

out the shape of the coach, stopped on the side of the road, next to a gate. He let out a laugh as he realised they had actually succeeded in stealing Lord Templeton's stagecoach, and hurried to catch up.

As he approached the stagecoach, he saw a lanky figure climbing over the gate.

"Where are you coming from?" Art asked, as he hopped down off the gate leading back into the Templeton estate.

"Had to distract a groom."

Even in the dark, Seb could make out the sly grin on Art's face. "Well, now—"

"Not like that!" Seb was quick to correct.

At the sound of their chatter, Gerde and Samara approached, while Eloise and Ana clambered out of the carriage, laughing and trying to shush each other.

"Good job," Samara said, her gaze focused entirely on Seb, and he felt his face grow warm.

"What about me? I distracted the stable boy!" Art said indignantly.

Gerde patted him on the arm. "And you did an excellent job of it. So ... does this mean now you can check off having a roll in the hay with a stable boy?"

Art snorted. "Unfortunately, this does not count. As lovely as the gardens were, the goal is to have relations with a stable boy in a *barn*."

"You really did a good job distracting that groom," Gerde said, turning her focus to Seb.

"Thanks." Then, while rubbing a hand against the back of his head, Seb added, "I'm just amazed that you could get the horses and the coach down the drive without alerting anyone. I thought for sure we'd be able to hear it in the orchard, but I didn't hear a thing."

"That's because of this one," Eloise said, playfully elbowing

Ana.

"I realised while I couldn't control the sound of the horses themselves, I could at least soften their footfalls and the sound of the wheels on the driveway," Ana explained, before adding, "It was a lot of work though. We weren't completely silent."

"It's a useful skill," Samara remarked. "All right everyone. We best be on the road now."

Gerde and Samara made their way to the front of the coach. Apparently, Samara would accompany Gerde while she drove the coach. The others climbed inside.

The interior of the stagecoach was unlike anything Seb had travelled in before. The cushions were covered in velvet and were so soft, he practically sank into them. The sides were made of stained wood, complete with decorative carvings. If he had to do a two-day coach ride, there were worse ways to travel. In fact, he could get used to riding in something like this.

He and Art sat on one side, while Ana and Eloise sat across from them. As they set off, Ana met his gaze. "That was some quick thinking, Seb."

"Thanks," Seb said. He still felt uncomfortable around Ana. With everything going on, they hadn't had a proper conversation since their argument before the fire.

"I just wanted to say that I'm sorry," Ana continued, apparently sensing his uncomfortableness. "I shouldn't have kissed you. You're..." she trailed off for a moment.

Seb watched her nervously, both eager and dreading what she would say next.

"You're a good person, and I value your friendship. I'm just not ready for anything more at the moment."

Eloise, for her part, remained quiet, and Seb could feel both Eloise and Art watching them, which just made him even more uncomfortable. He took a deep breath.

"It's okay. I get it," he replied. He didn't exactly get it, but it was obvious to him by now that Ana wasn't interested in him in that way. And there was a part of him that knew he had been coming on a bit strong. But he still couldn't help swallowing down a lump of disappointment. To hide his feelings, he gazed outside and let himself get lost in the darkness of the night.

THEY HAD TRAVELLED JUST a mile down the Fos Way—the road leading inexorably to Richilde—when Gerde brought the carriage to a stop and everyone climbed out. Seb grabbed his bag of explosive tools that he had recovered from the Zephyr after the fire.

The road cut through a dense forest filled with tall pine, spruce and fir trees which soared into the star-studded night sky. He couldn't help wondering if Magic had been used in the road's construction, given how big a job clearing the trees would've been.

Samara wandered around, studying the trees before slapping the solid trunk of a fir tree.

"This one will do," she said, turning to Seb.

"Maybe we should take two down. Just in case." This suggestion came from Ana.

Art, who leaned against the back of the coach while lighting his pipe murmured, "I can't imagine the Magistrate will be too happy with us blocking the road to Märchen."

"Good thing she's not here to stop us," responded Samara. She turned back to Seb. "You ready?"

Seb nodded. He glanced up at all the trees surrounding them, and then said, "Gerde, I think we'll want to move the stagecoach further up. I don't know what debris we're going to be dealing with."

"I can keep the debris away," Ana suggested.

To Seb's surprise, Eloise disagreed. "You're stretching your-self too thin. You already have to deal with dampening the sound so we don't scare the horses." Eloise turned to Gerde. "I could try making a shield."

Gerde walked around to Eloise. "Thanks, but I think I'll just move the coach. You don't want to exhaust *your* Magic either."

Eloise pouted, but said nothing, and Seb and Ana got to work. First Seb chiselled away a section of tree big enough to hold a nitro stick. It admittedly took longer than he'd thought.

"Wouldn't it have been quicker to just cut the tree down with a saw?" Art asked, blowing out a ring of smoke.

Seb grimaced. Art wasn't wrong. It probably would've been quicker, but explosives was his job. He didn't know how to cut down a giant tree with a saw. And he was pretty sure neither did any of the others in their party. So, he continued placing the explosives, and, as he and Ana had done many times before, he detonated the explosive while Ana controlled both the sound of the explosion and the direction the tree fell.

"We still make a good team," Ana said with a tight smile.

She was right. But verdammt, it still hurt. He grinned back at Ana, to let her know he was fine with things, before packing up his equipment.

Soon they were back on their way to Richilde once more.

THE ROAD to Richilde was long. That was the only way to sum it up. They were forced to stop every ten miles so that Gerde could change horses at a posting house. And no matter how luxurious the stagecoach was, travelling all night in a coach with two women yammering away, one of whom was still a teenager and extra loud, did not make for a pleasant night. Then there was the unspoken tension between Seb and Ana. The poor kid had it bad for her. Art still remembered Seb talking about wanting to take her home to his village, Unsurprisingly, he had managed to scare Ana off. Not that Art could blame her. Who wanted to be tied down? Between the youths yammering and the romantic entanglements, Art was reminded of his days when he worked in a travelling troupe.

It was strange how time could soften memories. There was a time when he would've been happy to be crammed into a coach with wooden benches. The mere thought of being free from his family and able to explore the rest of Alsatia sustaining him. Now all Art could think of was *how soon until we arrive in Dorholz?*

He didn't know how Gerde did it. She was obviously tiring. They took longer stops each time they had to change horses. Once, she even allowed them to stop long enough to get some ale at the posting house. But as it grew later, there were fewer posting houses open except for travellers to change horses. And even then, they scowled at you.

He was amused to see how Samara loyally stayed by Gerde's side on the driver's bench. He wouldn't have done so if he were in Samara's position. It was far too cold, and the driver's bench was much too hard for him to want to ride with Gerde. But he supposed that's why he wasn't in a relationship. He wasn't willing to make those sacrifices.

He tried to sleep as much as he could. Somehow, Seb seemed comfortable enough. Of course, Seb was shorter than Art, so he could stretch out a bit more. But between the bumpy road and Ana and Eloise's murmured conversation, he just couldn't fall asleep for more than a few minutes.

It was the early hours of the morning when they eventually reached Dorholz. This was where they would spend the night. Except the sun was just beginning to rise overhead, and they would stay only long enough for Gerde to get some sleep.

Samara had told them to expect to be on their way again after lunch.

Art didn't get up to Dorholz very often, but when he did, there was a smoke shop he liked to visit. Aside from a few holidaying communities like Gewässer, Dorholz was the chief town between Märchen and Richilde. If this wasn't *the* major town before one got to Richilde, Dorholz probably wouldn't have a smoke shop. But it benefited from the many merchants and travellers that passed through, and this smoke shop carried hash all the way from Akadd.

As they pulled up to the inn, Ana and Eloise started chattering excitedly again. Then Eloise murmured some words and Art watched as her face turned into someone else's. It was a strange sight to behold. One moment he was looking at the pale skinned, dark-haired girl who was a vision of her supposed ancestor, Queen White, and then his vision seemed to swim, at least, the part that was focused on her face, and suddenly he was looking at a stranger. It might've unsettled a lesser person, but mostly Art just wanted to know how they could use these disguises in future jobs. As an inside man, Art was all about the disguise. But there was only so much you could do with costuming, wigs and makeup.

This was only the second time he'd seen Eloise use her Magic, though he'd heard the stories from the others about the night of the auction. *I guess she really might be a descendant of Queen White,* he mused.

He awkwardly jumped down from the stagecoach and stretched out his back. There used to be a time when he could've done a coach ride like this easily, without the stiffness in his legs and back. He supposed this was what getting old felt like, though he was only two and thirty years.

The ground was muddy, as though it had rained recently. Thankfully, they hadn't run into that earlier. Gerde chatted to the postillion while Samara had gone inside to see about rooms. Following Samara inside, he overheard her talking to the innkeeper.

"Just two rooms will be fine," she was saying.

"Are you mad?" he said, turning to Samara.

Her eyes flashed with annoyance. "What did you say?" she ground out.

"Two rooms are decidedly not enough. Lord Templeton does not share a room," he said in a soft voice. "That would simply not be done."

"My *Lord*, we are on a bit of a *budget*," she reminded him.

"Nonsense," he replied, before turning to the innkeeper. "I have an account here, don't I?"

"Um," the innkeeper began.

"Lord Templeton. The Royal Bank of White in Märchen," Art added helpfully.

The innkeeper pulled out a great big book and scanned through names.

"Ah, yes, of course. I see you now. It's been some time since you passed through here."

"It has?" Art asked, forgetting himself. "It has. We'll take three of your best rooms."

"That won't be necess—"

Art cleared his throat, and Samara acquiesced.

"Yes, my Lord. Three rooms, coming right up." The innkeeper turned away to get keys.

Samara glared at him. "Really? You're going to get a room all for yourself?"

"Of course not," said Art with some surprise. "I'll bunk with Seb. You'll obviously stay with Gerde. I'm glad to see that's progressing, by the way."

Samara scowled at him, but he could tell she was biting back a smile.

"And Ana and Eloise can share a room. Because believe me, you do not want to try to sleep with those two nattering on. They're like peas in a pod."

When the innkeeper returned, they accepted the three brass keys.

"Do you need hot water sent up for a bath?"

Before Samara could say no, Art said, "Yes please. But first we'll take our breakfast."

Once arrangements for their rooms and baths were made, they made their way to a table where Gerde, Seb, Ana and the disguised Eloise already sat.

Alongside large mugs of ale, as well as tea for Samara, they were served eggs, kippers and porridge. The food was good. No doubt all the better for the fact they were serving a "lord". The server wasn't too bad to look at either, as far as Art was concerned. She was a pretty, dark-haired girl. She was friendly, but Art couldn't help noticing that she seemed extra attentive to Seb. Offering him more ale as soon as his mug was empty. Asking if he needed seconds. Art nudged Seb's leg under the table and thrust his chin over at the server. Seb merely chuckled and shook his head, looking anywhere but in her direction.

Seated beside Eloise, Art still couldn't get over the level of detail her disguise presented. He couldn't, even for a moment, tell that it wasn't real.

"That is one impressive illusion," he told Eloise when the server was away fetching a jug of water for Gerde.

"It's not an illusion," she replied.

Art frowned. "Well, then, what would you call it?"

"She actually changed her face," Ana responded, as though that explained everything.

"Ah…" began Art. "No. I'm still not getting it."

"You see how my hair looks longer?" Eloise asked. "If it were an illusion, you wouldn't be able to feel the ends of my hair. You wouldn't be able to feel the curls either, since my hair is straight."

She leaned forward. "Try touching my hair. Tell me what you feel."

Art reached out a hand and grasped a lock near the crown, running his hand the full length of the hair shaft. Indeed, it felt as long as it appeared right now. And courser than Eloise's hair looked. Like it had more texture to it.

"Handy," he said with a raised brow.

"How long can you keep up your disguise?" Samara asked, looking up from her tea.

"I was able to hold both mine and Ana's disguise a whole afternoon," she replied. "I'm learning how to control my magic. I think I can go much longer."

"Good. Don't use your Magic for anything else. You need to be able to maintain that disguise for as long as possible when we're out in public."

"So, this is the difference between small magic and big Magic?" Art asked.

Eloise reclined in her seat, and although she looked like someone else, her smug smile was all Eloise. "In essence, yes."

Art leaned back, resting an arm on the back of his chair. "So you really are related to her, then?"

Eloise shrugged. "That's what I'm told."

"Isn't it incredible?" Ana exclaimed.

"So, we're here to try to get the Restorationists to back off from you," said Art slowly. "But what do you actually want? Do you want to become—"

He gestured with his hand.

"Royalty?" Eloise asked, a derisive tone to her voice. "No. Why would I? You must understand. You never wanted to be a lord."

"Well, technically I was never going to *be* a lord," Art

corrected, somewhat bitterly. He would always be the second son that never quite measured up.

"But you know what I mean. For most of my life, I've had to abide by other people's rules."

He could see she was getting worked up, but she stopped when the server came by to clear away dishes.

When she was done, Art said, "Technically as Queen, you could make your own rules."

Eloise gave him a look. "You and I both know that's not true."

Art didn't respond, instead gazing at the young girl in front of him. He'd been quick to dismiss her after all the trouble she had managed to cause them, and the way she and Ana were chattering away in the coach. But perhaps Eloise was smarter than he'd given her credit for.

CHAPTER TWENTY

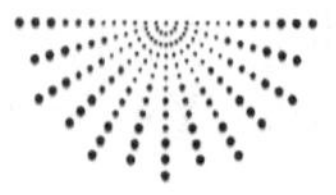

—SIGN AT THE KREUZANG COACHING INN

The sun was high in the sky when Seb woke up. He was surprised to find Art already dressed and on his way out the door, lured by the promise of Akaddian hash. They went downstairs together. Having never visited Dorholz, Seb thought to accompany him and see some of the town, but then he spotted the server from earlier and changed his mind, deciding instead to stay and have a glass of ale by the fire. Art had chuckled and told him not to do anything he wouldn't do and left to find his smoke shop.

And so Seb sat and enjoyed his ale, thinking about all that he had still yet to see of the world. Maybe that's what he'd do when this was all over.

"Can I get you another drink?" the barmaid asked. This was the third time she had come round.

He smiled at her but placed his hand on top of the mug.

"Best not. I should probably hold off until my friends get here."

"Quite the interesting party you're travelling with," she remarked. "How do you know Lord Templeton?"

"We're—" Seb stopped himself. He had been about to say *friends*, but he knew how unlikely it would seem that someone like him would be friends with a lord. What was his position supposed to be? Gerde was the driver, obviously. Maybe Samara was the footman. "Acquaintances," he settled on. It sounded like a vague enough term.

"Impressive," she said. "Are you on your way to Richilde or to Märchen?"

"Richilde," he said, unsure how much to say.

She bit her lip and brushed a strand of hair out of her face. "I've never been before. I've always wanted to see it."

"Me either," said Seb with a grin. "Did you grow up here in Dorholz?"

She shook her head. "No. I'm actually from Haaren. You've probably never heard of it. There's not much there. It's a mining town."

"No way. I'm from a mining town, too!" exclaimed Seb.

"Where?" she asked, taking a seat next to him.

He told her, and soon they were chatting about growing up in small towns and how intimidating it was moving to a bigger town, or, in his case, a city. He didn't tell her how he had fallen in with the thieves' guild, or anything like that. But it was still an enjoyable, easy conversation. He learnt her name was Lucie. She had been living in Dorholz for a year now, but her actual dream was to go to Richilde and study music.

"Well, well, well," said Art, having returned from his trip to the smoke shop. He reeked of pipe weed, and Seb's nose wrinkled. He must've been sampling the wares.

Lucie jumped up when Art arrived. "Forgive me, my Lord. Can I get you something to drink?"

Seb cringed as Art imperiously ordered a mulled wine. He wanted to tell her that Art was decidedly not a lord, but he couldn't exactly blow their cover.

Not long after, Gerde and Samara came down to the little dining room, followed closely by Ana and Eloise.

Art ordered their meal, once again using his father's credit, to score them veal, a selection of cold meats, salad, cheese and finally some cake. Samara frowned at the meal, but she didn't argue. They were going to be travelling all day and wouldn't get to Richilde until late at night, so it made sense to take advantage of the food on offer.

While they waited for dessert, Seb caught sight of Lucie signalling to him. "I'll just be a moment," he said, and hurried to the server, unable to hide his delight that she had called him over.

"I didn't want to interrupt, but I have a question," she said without preamble.

"What is it?"

"Is that the Hisada?" She jerked her head in Samara's direction.

"Yes," Seb replied. Then kicked himself. He should've lied.

"There's a message for her," she said, and quickly disappeared behind the bar. She returned a moment later with a folded paper. "Apparently, this came through on the speaking telegraph while you were all asleep."

Seb frowned as he accepted the paper, his body tightening

with a sense of foreboding. Who would know they were here? "Do you know who it's from?"

She shrugged. "I didn't take the message. I don't know how to use the speaking telegraph."

"I'm surprised they even have one here," Seb commented.

Again, she shrugged. "Dorholz is an important trade town."

Seb nodded. "Thanks for this, Lucie."

He made his way back to the table. Ana and Eloise had begun a card game. His breath tight in his chest, Seb handed the paper to Samara.

"This message came for you through the inn's speaking telegraph."

Samara raised her eyebrows but said nothing as she accepted the folded paper. She unfolded the letter and both Gerde and Art leaned in to see. Ana and Eloise, who had overheard what Seb had said, stopped their game.

Samara scowled and crushed the paper into a ball, which she stuffed into her coat pocket. "We have to get moving. Now."

"Who was that message from?" Ana asked.

"The Magistrate. Apparently, someone matching Kaiser's description left Märchen this morning, via the Klara."

"I thought we had more time," Gerde muttered.

Art scowled. "It also says that my father wishes to have me arrested."

Seb's eyes widened at that. He knew Art and his father had problems, but how could someone have their own kin arrested?

"Would he actually go through with that?" Seb asked.

"Depends on his mood," Art muttered darkly.

"We'll speak to the Magistrate when we get back. I'm sure she can talk him out of it," Gerde said before rising to her feet. "In the meantime, I'll speak with the groom about getting fresh mounts harnessed." She hurried out the front door.

Art also got to his feet. "Let me speak to the innkeeper. See if they can pack us some food for the journey."

"What does this mean?" Eloise asked, her hands gripping the table. "Is he travelling to Richilde?"

"Will he beat us there?" Ana added, touching a comforting hand to Eloise's shoulder.

Seb wondered the same thing.

"We know nothing right now," Samara said, getting to her feet as well. "If he is going to Richilde, he'll have to stop in Pentemarone and get a coach from there. It's not any quicker than taking the road. But it means if we want to beat him there, we have to keep moving. We can only stop to get fresh mounts. That's it."

Seb swallowed. "I'll go get our bags."

He hurriedly left the dining room. It took them ten minutes to be packed up and on the road again, this time with a basket of food for the journey. Seb hadn't even had a chance to say goodbye to Lucie.

THE JOURNEY WAS EVEN MORE arduous than the previous night. Every couple of hours they stopped, but only for the ten or fifteen minutes it took to change out the horses. Ana didn't know how Gerde remained so focused on the road ahead.

Despite the tension, Ana found she was tired enough that she managed to get some naps in during their coach ride. Apparently, so were the others, because even Eloise was asleep when she awoke. She gazed out at the countryside. Her own journey from her village near Richilde, when she'd been kidnapped by slavers, had been mostly by barge down the Klara, so the landscape they traversed was unfamiliar to her. It didn't stop her from straining to see if she recognised any spots they passed.

They stopped to take their evening meal of bread and cold meats. It wasn't much but it was something. Though Ana wished she had something warm to wash it down with because she was feeling the chill.

Eloise had said little on their journey. She had grown withdrawn since they received the news about Kaiser. It was quite the contrast to the girl's usual forced bravado.

"It'll be all right," Ana said, when she caught Eloise staring out the window, off into the distance.

The girl had taken to changing her disguise every time they stopped.

"Samara knows what she's doing," she added when Eloise didn't immediately respond.

Eloise smiled faintly. "I trust her. I just hate knowing that Kaiser is already on our trail." She turned to Ana. "I don't want to be anyone's queen."

Ana took Eloise's hand. "We won't let that happen. I promise," she whispered.

Eloise turned to look at Ana. "What about you? What have you been thinking about while staring at the scenery?"

Ana exhaled. "My family. I grew up not far from Lohr."

Eloise swallowed. "Will you go home once this is all over?"

Ana shook her head. She could feel Art and Seb's eyes on her. "I don't want to go home. At least, not to stay. But I do need to go see my mother. Let her know that I'm safe."

"I'm sure we can make a stop when this is all over," Seb said.

Ana nudged Seb's foot with her own. "What about you? Will you go back to your village?"

Seb looked out the window into the deepening twilight. "I'm not sure I want to anymore," he murmured.

"I knew you couldn't resist staying in Märchen," Art said with a chuckle. From a pocket, he drew out his deck of cards.

"Spindle, Apple, Slipper, anyone?"

By the time they crossed over into Richilde, Gerde could feel her energy flagging. It was dark by now, so she didn't even have scenery to look at as they travelled. She didn't need to read signs to tell they were getting close to the capital city of Lohr. The bumpy gravel road had given way to a nice paved stretch that was much easier on her back and probably more comfortable for her passengers.

It was late. Probably close to midnight, and she couldn't stop yawning.

Seeing how tired Gerde was, Samara had taken to engaging her in conversation. Talking about her hopes for the future. Did Gerde really plan to help train the City Watch? The answer was a resounding yes. If the Magistrate would allow her.

Everything Gerde had learnt about fighting had come from growing up with Ahren and his experiences in the Watch. Perhaps Ahren could be involved in the training too.

In turn, Gerde asked Samara what her plans might entail for the future, although inwardly she was afraid to hear the answer. She would never stop Sam if she wanted to find her family, but it would break her heart if Sam left.

Samara affirmed her desire to eventually find her family but said little more than that. Which left Gerde feeling a little untethered. She pushed her fears to the back of her mind for now.

Once they reached the city, Gerde drew the carriage to a stop and the two of them jumped down. While Samara let the others know they were nearing their destination, Gerde fed the horses some pieces of apple.

"You'll be able to rest soon," she murmured to them.

She heard the door of the coach close and Samara joined her, taking her hand. "You'll be able to rest soon as well," she said.

Gerde forced a smile, still feeling untethered by Samara's vague answer about the future.

"Here," she said, handing Gerde a coat. Gerde realised Samara had changed her outfit as well. She had replaced her many-pocketed frock coat with a tailored short coat. She also wore a tall hat.

Gerde snickered before looking down at what Samara had handed her. It was a long coat. Fancy, and looked like what a coachman would wear, but thinner than her own coat. Designed for the stage, and not to be used in any practical manner. Along with the coat was another tall hat.

"Art has outdone himself," Gerde murmured before donning the coat and hat, and climbing back up to the bench.

"Apparently if we want to be believable as Lord Templeton's entourage, we need to look the part," Samara replied, and though Gerde couldn't see it in the dark, she knew Sam was rolling her eyes.

It didn't take long before they were rolling down the streets of Lohr. There wasn't much to see in the dark, but the streets reminded her of Elphame Park. Although the streets were better lit and the roads more paved. It also didn't have that lovely stench the Klara often brought along, even to Märchen's most ritzy neighbourhood. Though she knew if she searched hard enough, she'd find where Lohr hid its own stench.

Over dinner, Art had given her a map to a hotel they would stay at. She was good at memorising directions, so she was certain that right about now, they were passing the old palace of Queen White, though she could barely make it out in the dark.

According to Art, the hotel was *the* place for Alsatia aristocracy to stay. Since they were once again utilising his father's line of credit, Samara went along with it.

It seemed to Gerde that this wouldn't be the best way to get Art's father to change his mind about having his son arrested, but she couldn't deny she was curious just what kind of hotel Alsatia's aristocracy stayed in.

Samara seemed tense by her side. Now that they were actually in Richilde, she was on edge. As though Lutz Kaiser or one of his Restorationist Party was lurking behind every street corner.

"This is my first trip to Richilde," Gerde said, sensing it was her turn to do the distracting. "Have you ever been here?"

Samara nodded, then cleared her throat. "Yes. Once. On a job. I was just nineteen and accompanied another daughter of the House. I didn't get to see very much, though. We came and left under cover of darkness."

"What was the job?" Gerde found herself asking.

Samara smiled and shook her head. "Is it bad to say I don't actually remember?" She took her hat off and held it in her hands. "I remember every job I did. Every victim. But the ones I assisted on just blur together."

She sounded ashamed of herself, and Gerde didn't know what to say. So instead, she just nudged Samara with her shoulder. "Well, when all this is over, you and I can explore Richilde together."

"On Lord Templeton's line of credit?" Samara asked with a smirk.

Gerde chuckled. "Naturally."

The coach trundled down what would normally be a busy street, Gerde could tell. Large multi-storey brick buildings lined each side of the road. The roofs were topped with decorative onion domes. She imagined the area must be most impressive during the day.

She spotted the hotel in question. A large iron sign on the roof displayed the name: Weisse Rose Inn. Gerde always considered inn's to be small places catering to merchants and the like, but this place was intimidating.

There was no courtyard to pull in to, so she stopped in front of the building and a groom hurried out to collect the horses. She jumped down to help see to the horses for the night.

"I'll meet you inside," she told Samara, while Sam replaced her hat and went to see to "Lord Templeton".

Gerde walked with the groom through a side street that led to the stables in the back. As she helped undo the tracers—it wasn't in her nature to just stand by while someone else took care of the horses—she was amazed to learn that the inn could house up to one hundred horses. The inn they had stayed at in Dorholz could handle a high number of passing travellers but nowhere close to that number. She had enough professional curiosity to wonder how large a team was needed to house so many horses at once.

After she was assured that the horses would be properly fed and watered for the night, she was directed to a back entrance leading to rooms where the coachmen stayed. Pretending to need to run a message to Lord Templeton, she hurried up the front steps and was taken aback at what she saw inside. The lobby floor was made from marble, decorated with columns. The counter was a polished wood, and thick Akkadian rugs with mosaic designs dotted the floors. Art smugly glanced over at her and held up an ornate brass key, polished to look like gold. She strode over to him.

"I take it your father is paying for this as well?"

"If he's planning on throwing me in gaol when we return, I may as well make the charges worthy enough for it."

Gerde studied him a moment. He didn't seem at all worried about his father's threats. Why didn't he seem worried?

She wanted to ask him about it, but the front desk clerk returned with two more decorative brass keys. He frowned at Gerde but held his tongue, given that she clearly was on good terms with the lord she conversed with.

Art accepted the keys and then added, "It's been a long ride from Dorholz. If you could be a dear and have hot water sent up for baths. And some morsels to tide us over before bed."

For someone who had rejected every advantage his father had ever given him, Art was clearly in his element.

As before, Gerde and Samara shared a suite, with Ana and Eloise in another suite and Art and Seb in yet another one.

"Is it normal for a lord to share a suite?"

Art shrugged. "It's always good to have your manservant close by."

"I am absolutely *not* your manservant," Seb said indignantly.

"Of course not," replied Art with a chuckle. "But just for appearance's sake, I'm going to need you to carry my bags up to the room."

Seb scowled at Art, but did as bidden. Gerde and Samara exchanged a look of amusement.

"Are you ready to see how the other half lives?" Gerde asked Samara as they walked up the stairs in search of their room.

"I can't wait," Samara replied dryly.

Gerde was certainly not disappointed.

CHAPTER TWENTY-ONE

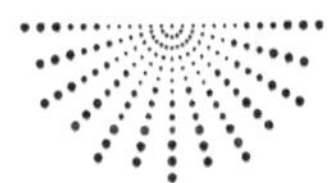

The capital city of Lohr sits in the heart of Richilde. With its onion dome architecture and vibrant colours, it is easy to see why more visitors come to Lohr than anywhere else on the continent. Lohr was of course the seat of Queen White's power, and so it makes sense to start your exploration of the city with a visit to Parliament, which was just one of many of the Queen's Palaces.

— TOMAS & SONS GUIDE TO RICHILDE

Gerde slept soundly most of the night. Samara, on the other hand, slept in fits and starts. It certainly wasn't the bed, which was the most comfortable she'd ever slept in. Then again, perhaps it *was* the bed. She felt decidedly out of her element in this hotel. In Richilde, for that matter.

She'd lied to Gerde. She *had* remembered her one and only visit to Richilde. It had been a grisly affair. A man who was having trouble with his finances had wanted to wed his daughter to a rich lord. Instead, she had married a tradesman for love. The man, rather than focus on other avenues to raise money to support his lifestyle, wanted vengeance. He hired the House de Mörde to murder the tradesman husband, who was going to be away on business in Richilde. Samara was still a new assassin. She shadowed one of her sisters, who had actually done the deed. Still, it had stayed with her. The man had been innocent. Guilty only of marrying the wrong person. Samara hadn't personally killed him, but she had assisted with the job, and that death had always tainted her. How could she tell Gerde about him?

The worst part was that she knew the House could choose their contracts. Just because someone wished to contract the House de Mörde, didn't mean the House had to comply. Ursula could have said no to the contract. But she hadn't. Even the sister she had accompanied, Olivia, seemed unhappy about the job.

At breakfast, which was served in a large dining hall, with brilliant white tablecloths and served on gold-edged porcelain, Samara felt exposed. There were too many windows in this room. She felt she and Seb stood out too much with their dark skin. They all stood out. They were quite the motley crew compared to all the businessmen and aristocracy that were dining.

She was ready to get going as quickly as possible, and not only because they stood out. The fact was, they were here to do a job. And Lutz Kaiser was most likely close on their heels. With their few hours of rest in Dorholz and their night here, he could easily have made up the time, assuming he knew they were headed for Richilde, which, she reminded herself, he couldn't possibly know. But it still made her uneasy.

She drummed her fingers on the table until Gerde put a hand on her arm. The others wanted to linger over their hot drinks. They all looked worn out, despite the luxurious lodgings.

"Parliament doesn't open until the ninth hour," Gerde softly reminded her.

"I'd still like to get the lay of the land. In case anything goes wrong."

Gerde chuckled softly. "Something always goes wrong. Haven't you learnt that by now? But you figure it out. You always do."

Samara smiled at her appreciatively, but it didn't change the knot in her stomach. She barely touched her saffron chai, even though it was made with real saffron and tasted divine. The hotel had even managed to achieve the rose-pink colour that Samara could never get right. Every time she brewed chai, the closest she got was a brownish-pink. She made a mental note that if their plan did somehow work, she would be sure to try to pick up some genuine saffron to take back home for Hans.

Eventually, it was time to leave. Gerde had the stagecoach brought around while they donned appropriate clothing for people travelling in the company of a lord. Which meant Samara was once again leaving her beloved frock coat behind. She hoped she wouldn't need it.

It really was a quick ride. They could easily have walked, Samara realised with some dismay. But Art insisted Lord Templeton would simply not be seen strolling the streets of Lohr. Since this was more his world than hers, she humoured him, but the role of pretending to be part of Lord Templeton's retinue was wearing thin.

Parliament House had once been one of the late Queen White's palaces, though not one where she resided. After the last descendant had passed away, the country had taken a surprisingly orderly path into elected government. Although the country had operated with both a head of state and an elected official of the people, even during the end of Queen White's reign, it was still surprising to see how easily the country had made the switch to a fully elected government.

The historic parliamentary building was, in a word, enormous. Samara couldn't help staring as Gerde deftly guided the coach down the drive and past a surprisingly green lawn, given it was now winter, and an enormous water fountain. The building was all white stone, with columns fronting the building. They passed a giant bronze statue of Queen White, depicted standing on a pillar, welcoming her people, and Samara couldn't help but wonder what Eloise made of that.

A stern man dressed in a bright red liveried coat, with an ornamental helmet, came rushing to meet them. Gerde explained to the driver that Lord Templeton of Märchen was here to see Lord Konrad. The man studied first Gerde, then Samara, and finally the coach bearing the Templeton family sigil. He instructed them to wait there, which made Samara decidedly uneasy. But a few short minutes later, more liveried men came to greet them, and Samara hopped down to open the coach door for Art and the others.

Seb stepped out first, followed by Ana and Eloise, who were now both in disguise at Samara's suggestion. She hoped it wouldn't be necessary, but she didn't want to take any chances. Finally, Art stepped down, looking more awkward than Samara would have expected. Now that they were actually here, he seemed ill at ease impersonating his father. Or was he supposed to be impersonating his brother? Come to think of it, Samara wasn't exactly sure. All she knew for certain was that they'd received even more raised brows when Samara made to accompany them.

For her part, Samara would have much preferred her usual place of sneaking around on rooftops and peering in windows. But she doubted she could sneak around the parliamentary building as easily as she could the buildings of Elphame Park. This was a government building and worse, the guards here were armed with guns.

Samara wished Eloise had created a disguise for her as well. She felt like she stood out here most of all. It was one thing for an Akkadian to be a servant, or tradeswoman. There might even be some visiting Akkadian nobility, but nothing about her said nobility, and surely Lord Templeton wouldn't need to walk around parliament with a bodyguard?

Unfortunately, she had to give up her weapons. Apparently, it was simply not done for someone to walk into parliament armed like a, well, like a former assassin.

They were led into an enormous waiting room. At least, that's what Samara supposed it was. The space was massive. It could have fit a couple of hundred people in there easily. The floors were all marble. The aristocracy really seemed to like their marble. Gold pillars lined the walls. Above her head, Samara noted the roof was actually mainly made of panels of glass to allow in light.

"It must be nice in the summer," said Art, looking up at the glass roof.

"It would be a handy escape route," Samara said. "Although getting up there would be problematic."

Art chuckled and shook his head.

Samara wondered how Gerde was doing. She hated letting her go off with the horses, but there was no way they could explain why the carriage driver was also coming to see a member of the opposition party. As it was, odds were fifty-fifty whether they would all be allowed in to see him. Judging by the pomp and ceremony of this place, it was exceedingly unlikely, in Samara's opinion.

They waited for some time. Art stood with his hands clasped

behind him, but even Samara could see his foot jiggling as time ticked by.

"Who is this Lord Konrad again?" Samara heard Eloise question under her breath.

"He's the Shadow Chancellor of the Exchequer," said Art tightly.

It was a big swing, speaking to this man who was so highly placed, but what choice did they have? They needed to end this once and for all, and the only way they could do that was by convincing the right people in charge that these Restorationists posed a threat.

Eventually, another man in red liveried garb came hurrying forward and said, "Lord Konrad sends his apologies for the wait. This way, please. He is expecting you."

Art glanced back at Samara and the others. "All of us?" he asked tentatively.

"Yes, yes," the man replied, urging them to follow.

THEY WERE LED out of the hall of pillars and down a long corridor. It was a fairly ordinary looking hallway, with parquet floors and walls covered in dark wood panelling. They passed many doors, but all were closed, so they couldn't see in. Samara assumed this was where the politicians did all their day-to-day work.

Eventually, they were directed into a small office. An oak desk took up much of the space, although there was a wall of file cabinets to the right. The most unusual sight was the speaking telegraph, which Samara had only ever seen in pictures. A small window, their only escape if things went wrong, was located behind the desk, at which sat a middle-aged gentleman. He was dressed in his shirtsleeves and a waistcoat, his jacket hanging behind him on his chair. His hair was shot through with grey, but he was handsome. He stood up at their entrance and stepped around the table.

"Lord Templeton. It's good to make your acquaintance," he said, reaching out a hand for Art to shake.

"Please, take a seat," he gestured to one of the two chairs in front of his desk. Samara gestured for Ana and Art to sit, while she, Seb, and Eloise crammed in behind them.

"I must say I was surprised when I received a message from the Magistrate of Märchen about your needing to see me."

"First," Art began. "I suppose I should clarify that I am not actually Lord Templeton. I am Lord Templeton's son, Arthur Templeton."

Lord Konrad frowned. "But I thought they said—" He shook his head. "I'm sorry. I'm confused. I was told Lord Templeton was here. There was a coach bearing his sigil."

"It is my father's coach," Art confirmed. "We thought travelling under the Templeton sigil might be *expedient*."

Lord Konrad clasped his hands together on his desk. "What can I do for you?"

Seeing her cue, Samara leaned forward. "Lord Konrad, can I ask if you have ever heard of an organisation known as the Restorationists?"

Lord Konrad stared at Samara for a moment. She struggled to keep her face pleasant and impassive. Eventually he said, "No. I can't say that I have. Who are they?"

"They are an organisation attempting to bring back the royal family in Richilde."

Lord Konrad's features turned serious. "Bring back the royal family? How precisely? Rosalina White died over fifty years ago. The only other living relatives agreed to hand the role of governing Richilde to elected officials." Konrad leaned back in his chair and laced his hands behind his head. "Although I haven't heard of this particular organisation, they certainly wouldn't be the first bunch of royalists to threaten our government. However, such a bid would require the support of the people and that seems highly unlikely."

"The Restorationists believe they have something that would sway the people," said Art.

"What sort of something?" Konrad asked, although he sounded sceptical.

Samara took a deep breath. "They have access to a person with Magic. Big Magic. Who they believe is related to Queen White."

Looking at Konrad's stunned expression, Samara cringed. She still remembered laughing in Callista's face when she had told her the very same thing. At least Lord Konrad didn't laugh in their faces. She wished he would say something. The silence was excruciating.

"There's been many charlatans over the years," Lord Konrad eventually said.

"The person has Magic. We've seen it," Art insisted, but Samara placed a hand on his shoulder.

No need to give more away than they needed to.

"You've seen it? How?" Konrad asked, his eyes narrowed.

At least he wasn't sending them away, Samara thought.

"Because the Restorationist placed the person in question in the hands of the House de Mörde for safekeeping," Samara replied.

"The assassin house?"

"Yes," Samara confirmed. "Except the House has lost the descendant, and the Restorationists are tearing Märchen apart trying to recover what was lost. That is why the Magistrate put us in touch with you."

"I see," said Konrad, lowering his hands. "Well, obviously, if this is indeed true, then we would be concerned. Do you have any names of these so-called Restorationists?"

Samara handed him a slip of paper with the names of all the Restorationists Eloise had given them. Konrad took it and studied it.

"Lutz Kaiser was the man operating in Märchen," replied Samara. "We assume he is acting under someone else's orders."

Lord Konrad shook his head, almost regretfully. "Unfortunately, without more proof, I cannot help you. While I could certainly have government officials look into this Lutz Kaiser and his associates, I cannot make such an order without credible proof. If I were to bring this girl to parliament where she could prove her abilities, then maybe we could—"

"Now we never told you the person was a girl," Samara interrupted.

Lord Konrad inclined his head and smiled at her. "You can't outrun the speaking telegraph."

Without hesitation, Samara whipped out the khanjar blade she still had hidden in her boot. She was glad to see that Art and Ana were already busy getting out of her way.

"Samara!" Seb called, and she flicked her eyes his way to see he had one hand in his pocket. She barely nodded at him before an explosion rocked the room. The parliamentary guards hadn't bothered with the clay balls. They really needed better security here.

Ana whipped her hands about, controlling the explosion. The detonation was enough to knock the Shadow Cabinet Minister off his feet, but Ana had thankfully contained the blast so it wouldn't draw the attention of every guard in the place.

"The window," Samara called, urging the others to get moving. First Eloise, then Ana, Seb, and Art climbed out. Samara followed them, leaping out of the small ground-floor window. She stumbled to a stop and looked about her.

They were in a courtyard. Buildings surrounded them on all sides. Samara found herself cursing whoever designed this place.

Okay, think, she told herself. *Which way can we go from here?*

She hurried toward one of the windows, but a face appeared. More faces appeared at the other windows. *Schiesse.*

"Find an empty office," she yelled at the others.

"Samara," Art began.

"One of these places must lead away from here," she was saying.

She glanced back at Art, who was pointing upwards. Looking up, Samara groaned. On the roofs of the buildings were at least a dozen guards, all pointing rifles at them.

"You are surrounded. Lay down on the ground and you will not be harmed," cried one of the guards.

When they didn't immediately comply, one guard fired a shot that made Samara's ears ring. Thankfully, some quick movements from Ana sent the bullet harmlessly into the ground.

She glanced back at the window they'd climbed out through. She spied Konrad's face, watching.

They were cornered. Ana could certainly take on a few of them. Eloise could probably help. But then what? Where would they go? They were still trapped inside parliament with no idea where Gerde and the stagecoach were located.

Samara put a hand on Ana. "We're giving up," she said. Ana turned to her, dark eyes flashing in protest.

"You can't take them all on," Samara said.

Sometimes you fight your way out. Sometimes you talk your way out. Lord Konrad might've been working with Lutz Kaiser, but there were other people in the Richildan government. They just needed to wait for their opportunity.

~

GERDE IMMEDIATELY FELL in love with the palace stables. They were housed within a giant brick building featuring numerous stalls and even a smithy for horse shoes.

Gerde was just giving the horses some treats when a loud bang rang out. The horses jolted at the noise, pawing the ground and whickering. Belatedly, she realised the sound she heard was a gunshot and her heart began to race.

She couldn't be sure it had anything to do with Samara, but knowing their luck, it almost certainly was.

She studied her surroundings. The parliamentary building was a fortress. This wasn't like when Chetwin Humphreys took them prisoner. There would be no distraction to help them escape a place like this.

And then suddenly she knew what she had to do. But she didn't like it. Making quiet, calming noises, she finished giving the horses their treats. They were still attached to their tracers, so once she was done with the treats, Gerde jumped up onto the driver's bench and urged the horses forward.

Nobody tried to stop her.

She drove the carriage back along the drive, leaving the parliamentary grounds and eventually stopped at a nearby carriage stand, hoping, if the others somehow escaped, they would find her here, but she quickly realised she was too conspicuous. If anyone was after her, they would look for a stagecoach with the Templeton sigil.

She forced herself to wait until the clock struck ten. Only then would she leave.

While she waited, Gerde tried to pay attention to the activity around the parliamentary building. Several long minutes crawled by before a pair of men in suits strolled away from the parliament grounds, speaking in hushed voices. She dropped down and followed them, trying to overhear what they were saying. She thought she heard mention of "trespassers" and "Lord Konrad" but nothing more.

The clock struck ten, but she stayed at the carriage stand. She couldn't break them out of the former palace, but surely they would be transferred to a local gaol. That could be an opportunity for rescue. But the clock struck half ten, and still no carriages left the premises.

Gerde's chest constricted as she realised she had no other choice. She was in a strange city. The others were in trouble. She needed to get help.

The first thing she did was return to the Weisse Rose Inn. She needed to get the stagecoach off the streets in case anyone was looking for it. She accompanied the groom as he led the horses into the stables. Once the horses were settled and the stagecoach stored, she went to the lobby.

"Excuse me," she said to the hotel clerk, acutely aware of how out of place she looked in her coachmen garb. "Do you have a speaking telegraph I can use?"

SAMARA WATCHED as Ana paced the small cell. Eloise sat on the ground, looking tense. Seb and Art were in a neighbouring cell. This prison was nothing like the places she'd been held prisoner before. This was an actual dungeon. The walls were made of thick stone that could easily withstand Seb's explosive balls, even if they hadn't now been confiscated. The only light came from small slits in the windows high above their heads.

She imagined this was a vestige from the days when this had still been a palace. Maybe this was even the dungeons that Queen White's mother, a notoriously hated queen, had kept her prisoners. Callista, who always loved the stories of Queen

White, would probably love to see this place, though admittedly not from this vantage point.

Samara knew they would have to take full advantage of any opportunity to escape when it came, so when she heard the creak of the outer door of the dungeons, she was on her feet, signalling to the others to be ready. They all rose, and Eloise resumed her disguise. They had decided, since they didn't know how long her powers would last at any one time, that any time she was not in front of their captors, she would revert to her usual appearance. It was best for her to conserve her energy.

Samara had to admit she felt a bit of glee when she saw Lord Konrad accompanying two prison guards. She was looking forward to some pay back. And she apparently wasn't the only one.

"*Lord Konrad,*" Art said, derision dripping in his tone. "Just how long have you been working for the Restorationists, exactly?"

"I don't know what you are talking about," Konrad said. "But, hypothetically speaking, if I did know about the Restorationists, I would say it was prudent of me to work with them, to ensure a peaceful transition of power."

"A peaceful transition of power. You can't be serious," exclaimed Seb.

"I am quite serious, actually," replied Konrad. "If our country is to revert to being a Queendom once more, somebody from the old government has to be here to usher in this change."

"What I'm hearing is that you joined the Restorationists just to ensure you kept some of your power," said Art.

Konrad inclined his head, neither agreeing nor disagreeing.

"Who else in the government is working with the Restorationists?" Samara asked, though she doubted she would get an answer.

She was mistaken.

Konrad strolled over to Samara's cell and said, "As far as I know, I'm the highest-ranking member of parliament. There are, of course, others. Minor MP's and clerks."

He then turned his attention to Ana and pointed. "That one," he said.

The guards both drew pistols from their holsters and pointed it at them. Samara tensed. Ready. Ana could take care of the pistols, she felt sure.

Again, she was mistaken.

As soon as one guard opened the door, the other guard entered. Samara tried to leap on the guard. Ana meanwhile waved her hands causing the other guard to lose his grip on his pistol. Samara wrestled the pistol out of her assailant's fingers. It slipped to the stone, but before anyone else could get it, she heard the click of a pistol being cocked. Looking up, to her dismay, she saw Konrad had also entered and was pointing a gun right at Eloise. Eloise looked about to summon up a spell of her own, but Konrad spoke.

"Any more funny business, and this one is dead. I don't need her. Or any of you. I only need Eloise."

By this time, the guard in the doorway had recovered his own weapon and pointed it at Samara.

Samara quickly shook her head at Eloise. There were too many guns, and she didn't know how Eloise's powers would work in a fight. She knew Ana could handle one assailant with her powers, but multiple, she wasn't so sure of.

She removed her hands from the guard. Immediately, he dropped to recover his pistol. Then there were three guns on them and the guard inside the cell was now leading Ana at gunpoint. Ana glanced back at them.

"I'll be fine," Ana said.

"Of course you will be Eloise," Konrad was saying. "You'll soon be Queen."

Seb pressed his face into the bars. "What about us? What are you going to do with us?"

Lord Konrad turned back. "Oh, don't worry. I'm not a killer. As soon as Eloise is back in the hands of the Restorationists, you'll be sent back to Märchen."

When the outer door of the dungeon groaned shut, Seb slapped the palm of his hand against the bars.

"Well, that's just great. What happens when he discovers she's not actually Eloise?"

"Ana can handle herself," Art said softly, though even he didn't sound convinced.

Eloise muttered some words under her breath, and her disguise melted away. The girl sat down on the cold stone floor, drawing her knees up.

"She'll be fine. Her powers have grown." Eloise's voice was faint, and Samara could a quaver. She sounded as though she were trying to convince herself.

"She will be. Just as long as you can maintain her disguise," Samara replied, crouching down next to her. "Konrad only knows that he's looking for a girl with powers who resembles Queen White. We just have to keep it together long enough for us to get out of here."

She really hoped Konrad had been telling the truth about letting them go.

CHAPTER TWENTY-TWO

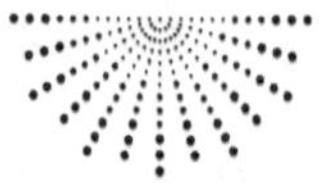

As daughters of the House, you are sister-at-arms. No one out there knows you as deeply as the girls you train with every day. They are the girls who will fight by your side, protect you and help you to hone your skills. We are a true sisterhood, and if you are ever in trouble, you can always count on your sisters.

— URSULA, FORMER MATRON OF HOUSE DE
MÖRDE

*H*ans returned to his shop with great trepidation. It was the first time since his arrest, but Samara had assured him the City Watch would no longer be a problem, and they had left such a mess when they arrested him. He knew he had to eventually face it.

He wondered how the others were doing. They should be in Richilde by now. He wished he could be with them, but with his arm still in a sling, he knew he couldn't be much help if things went wrong.

He hoped things didn't go wrong.

He wasn't sure when he would open back up. For now, he focused on cleaning and getting things in order. It was a tricky job, taking care of things with just one good arm. Papers were scattered everywhere, and some ink bottles had been broken, ruining perfectly decent card stock and even the table underneath, but he would make do.

He wasn't ready to move back in here yet. He didn't feel entirely safe without the others around, but he was sure in time that, too, would change. The big question was whether Samara would move back as well. He would certainly prefer to have her here, but he knew how close she and Gerde had grown. Inevitably, they would prefer to have their own space. Although there was plenty of room in the flat for the three of them.

It was getting to midday, and he was just thinking about grabbing a bite to eat when there was a knock on the door. He walked to the door and cautiously peered through the glass. His eyes widened when he spotted Callista standing there. Warily, he drew the bolt on the door and cracked it open.

"Hans," Callista said, without preamble. "I need to talk to you. It's urgent. It's about Samara."

A chill went through Hans, which had nothing to do with the cool winter day as he opened the door wider and beckoned Callista to enter.

"Did something happen to her?" he asked as he closed and bolted the door. His voice sounded shaky to his ears.

"You could say that," began Callista. "I was just speaking with the Magistrate. She received a message via speaking telegraph. From Gerde. Sam and the others are being held prisoner at Parliament House."

Hans found he had to grip the table to keep himself steady. "Did Gerde say how that occurred?" he asked once he'd found his voice again.

Callista drew up the stool from its place behind the till and gently sat him down on it. "We don't know. The Magistrate contacted Parliament House, but all they'll say is that some intruders were apprehended."

Hans frowned. "Why would they be considered intruders? They were supposed to be meeting with a friend of the Magistrate's unless—"

"Unless he's working for the Restorationists," Callista finished. "In which case, we have to assume Kaiser has them."

Hans forced himself to breathe deeply. He removed a handkerchief from his pocket and mopped his brow. It was a chilly day, but suddenly he felt sweaty and far too old.

"So, what is the plan to get them out? Can the Magistrate help? Or the Lions…?"

He couldn't imagine what might be involved in trying to break them out of Parliament House. In Richilde, no less, where guns were legal. It would be no easy feat, but surely between Samara's connections to the Lions and the House de Mörde, they could come up with *something*.

Callista's eyebrows drew down. "Even if Tormod Lyons were inclined to help, the Magistrate was very clear. She does not want any illegal activity in Richilde."

Hans rubbed his thighs, feeling agitated. "Which rules out the Lions."

"And the House de Mörde," Callista said softly.

Hans glanced up at her, his eyes narrowed. "After everything Samara has given to the House—"

Callista raised her hand to interrupt him. "I know. I hate this too. But I can't send daughters of the House to Richilde to conduct illegal business. If I do that, I risk the entire House. As Matron, I can't do that."

Hans gave her a bitter smile. "So, what do we do now?"

"The Magistrate wants to keep things legal," Callista replied.

"She wants to go to Lord Templeton and ask him to intervene. Apparently, he has some lucrative mines in Richilde, or some such, so he has some influence there."

Hans stroked his chin thoughtfully. He wasn't so sure things would go the way the Magistrate thought it would. "It might be she doesn't understand just how strained the relationship between Art and his father is. Not too long ago, he wanted Art to renounce all ties to the Templeton family."

"She feels confident that Lord Templeton's self-interest will result in him wanting to keep this quiet and have it go away as quickly as possible."

"But that doesn't mean he'll help release Samara and the others."

"No, but she believes it will give us some valuable information."

Hans leaned back in his chair, rubbing his chin. "I'm hearing a lot about what the Magistrate believes. What do you believe, Matron? Why are you really here?"

Callista took a long time to answer. "I believe families are complicated. And it would be foolish to not have a backup plan. Which is why I, Callista Meier, am taking a holiday. I believe the Weisse Rose Inn in Lohr is a lovely place to stay. As to why I'm really here, you care for Samara as much as I do. I think you should go with the Magistrate when she speaks with Lord Templeton. She has a meeting she couldn't cancel, but afterwards she'll be going to the Six Swans in Elphame Park, where Lord Templeton is taking his lunch."

Hans blinked. "I know the place. It's an exclusive lounge. They might not let me in."

Callista surveyed her surroundings with all the paper and ink. "I'm sure you can convince them." She turned to leave but stopped. "I think it would be a good idea if you went to Richilde as well. I know I wouldn't want to be all the way in Märchen worrying about Sam."

Hans gave her an appreciative nod. Then the Matron of House de Mörde left. Hans turned back to his shop, hands on hips. He needed to make a new identity for himself.

LORD TEMPLETON WAS TAKING lunch in an Elphame Park Lounge with a friend interested in investing in a mine when he was interrupted by a waiter letting him know he had a visitor. When he was told who the visitor was, his first reaction was to send the visitor away. Instead, he agreed to meet in a private lounge. After making his apologies, he took his time walking to the lounge.

This was going to be about his good-for-nothing second son, of course.

Had they found him? Did they recover the stagecoach? He blanched at the thought that Art might have defiled the stagecoach. Maybe he was arrested carrying on in some sort of illegal activity just to further embarrass his father. Lord Templeton wouldn't put it past his son, whose contempt for the Templeton name seemed to know no bounds.

Taking a deep breath, he resumed his walk to the private lounge and then took another moment to collect himself before he strode inside. In the room, seated on a leather recliner, sat Magistrate Duvall.

"Lady Duvall, it is always a pleasure to see you. However, I must admit to being a little surprised, given this is a gentlemen's establishment."

The Magistrate smiled brightly. "Oh, they can never say no to me here."

Indeed, rather than acting as though she were intruding in a male space, the woman leaned back comfortably in her seat, crossing her legs, her hand loosely cradling a brandy glass." Would you like some?"

He declined. If his son had been arrested for drunken behaviour, he would not add to the rumours surrounding the Templeton name by indulging in alcohol himself. He was far better than that.

He was just about to sit when another man entered the room. This one Templeton did not recognise. He was short, like a Little Person, with a balding pate, and wore a dove grey suit.

"I'm so sorry I am late, Madam Magistrate," he said, speaking in a Pentemarone accent.

The Magistrate's eyes momentarily widened in surprise, but she quickly schooled her features.

"This is my associate, Hans," The Magistrate gestured at the man. "Please, sit down, both of you."

Templeton frowned. He didn't think it proper that a woman would order him around in a club for gentlemen, but he obeyed.

"I have news regarding your son, Arthur," she said once he was seated.

"Has the stagecoach been recovered?"

The corner of her mouth turned downward. "No. I'm afraid it hasn't. My news, unfortunately, is that he and some of his associates were apprehended on Richilde parliamentary grounds."

Breathing in through his nose, Lord Templeton went ahead and poured that glass of brandy, after all.

"I hadn't realised he had taken the stagecoach all the way to Richilde." He took a shaky sip of the amber liquid. "Should I ask what he was doing when he was arrested?"

Something flickered in the Magistrate's eyes that he couldn't decipher. "If I'm being perfectly honest, he was going to see Lord Konrad."

Lord Templeton groaned. *The Richildan shadow cabinet Chancellor of the Exchequer knows about this?*

"What was his business with Lord Konrad?" Templeton asked instead, his mind already imagining the worst. Had Arthur been having an affair with Lord Konrad's wife? Was Lord Konrad even married?

"I can't really say," admitted the Magistrate. "It's a delicate matter—" Then, apparently noticing the horrified look on Templeton's face, she amended, "By delicate I mean a matter of State."

"I see," said Lord Templeton. He didn't, but his mind was racing and he needed to think about what he'd just learnt.

"I thought perhaps you might have the connections necessary to bring Arthur Templeton back to Märchen."

"Why? I told you I want him arrested," Lord Templeton retorted, but there was no bite to it. He was working through all the possibilities.

She gave him a look as though to say, *you don't fool me.*

"I don't suppose you can tell me what this matter of State is about?" he asked.

"I cannot," replied the Magistrate. She appeared to be allowing him time to process the news, which he was grateful for. Her companion, he noticed, seemed more anxious, his foot tapping away.

Whatever this matter of State was that got his second son arrested, it could be problematic. What if this affected his business dealings in Richilde?

"I understand your relationship with your son is fraught," said the Magistrate, apparently tired of waiting for him to think on it. "But I believe with your connections, you might be the best person to have him brought home."

"Do you not also have connections in Richilde?" he asked, somewhat resentfully. Would he really have to go to the

Richildan Parliament, cap in hand, to beg for the return of his recalcitrant son?

"I do, yes. But the Templeton name is old and carries a lot of weight."

Templeton recognised she was trying to butter him up. But it was fine. There was really no decision to make. Like it or not, he could not have a Templeton rotting away in a Richildan prison cell.

He abruptly rose to his feet. "You'll let my clerk know the details of Arthur's arrest, as much as you can, as well as where he is being held. I will leave for Richilde as soon as I've sorted out a new coach. It shouldn't take long."

The Magistrate's eyes widened in surprise. "You mean to go yourself?"

"Of course. It is my connections and my name that will release my son, as you rightly pointed out. Plus, someone has to recover my coach from whatever ditch he's left it in."

Her companion, who had been silent until now, opened his mouth as though to speak, but the Magistrate cut him off. "In that case, my colleague here will travel with you. He has knowledge of the matters of State in question and may be able to assist you in Arthur's return."

Something passed between the Magistrate and her associate, though Templeton couldn't be sure what.

Lord Templeton turned to the bald-headed man and looked him up and down.

"Very well. But be aware, I do not intend to stop for the night. I will change drivers in Dorholz in order to travel through the night."

The man held his gaze, which surprised Templeton. Few people looked him in the eye.

"That won't be a problem," said the man from Pentemarone.

Then it was settled. Lord Templeton suddenly found himself on an unplanned trip to Richilde.

~

ANA WASN'T afraid as she was marched away from her friends and loaded into a carriage. She wasn't even afraid when she was led into an opulent apartment and found herself face to face with Lutz Kaiser himself. She felt confident she could handle herself. The only thing she was really afraid of was accidentally revealing that she wasn't, in fact, Eloise. She didn't know how the others would get out of that dungeon, but she knew the best thing she could do was stay here and keep up the charade. Which meant that she kept her mouth shut, and occasionally tried to outwardly use her abilities. What they didn't know was that she was also pocketing bits of her captor's energy. Just in case there was an opportunity to escape.

Ana didn't know what she would do if they tried to put her in a carriage to leave Richilde. She hoped Eloise could find her. She just knew she had to trust in her friends. *Huh.* When had she begun to think of them all as friends? She wasn't sure.

She hated the smarmy smile on Lutz Kaiser's face when she was brought to the apartment.

He cradled her cheek gently. "Eloise. It's so good to see you. You've grown so much since we last met. I don't know if you recall. It was at your great-aunt's house. You were just eight years old."

She stonily held his gaze, hoping Eloise's disguise stayed in place. That was her biggest concern. They hadn't been able to test the disguise. They didn't know how long Eloise could keep it up, especially from a distance.

Since her arrival at the apartment, he had treated her surprisingly well. She had a bedroom of her own with a maid-servant who never left her side. She could've tried to escape, but she knew Kaiser would have ways of catching her. Better to stay compliant and wait things out.

She ate dinner at one end of a large dining room table. The meal was delicious, but it soured in her stomach when Kaiser announced he was planning for them to travel to Pentemarone. That concerned her. She couldn't let him take her out of Richilde. Would Eloise be able to locate her if she was so far away? They simply didn't know the extent of her Magic.

"Why Pentemarone?" she finally asked.

"It's not time for you to stay here in Richilde just yet. But soon. Very soon," Lutz was saying as he buttered a piece of bread roll. "But first, I have a young man I would very much like for you to meet."

Ana felt sick. "A young man?"

"Yes," said Lutz, taking a bite of his roll. "I think you'll like him very much. He is the son of a duke here in Richilde."

"Why would I want to meet him?" she asked, though she was pretty sure she knew the answer already.

"Being a queen is a lonesome job."

How would you know? she wanted to say but didn't.

"You need someone who can share the responsibilities. Someone who also comes from a strong Magical line."

"You want to marry me off?" she stated, pushing her plate away.

Lutz smiled. "Nobody's forcing you to do anything, Eloise. Nobody ever has. But what girl wouldn't want to be queen?"

"When will I be meeting this son of a duke?"

"He's coming to dinner tomorrow."

"May I be excused?" she asked.

"Are you sure? You've hardly touched your dinner."

"I'm sure."

Lutz indicated to a guard to lead her away. How many

guards were here? she wondered. Could she handle them all? Ana sensed that the maid was more than just a maid. There were also several footmen and a butler. And at least seven guards, probably more.

She needed to come up with a plan before they threw her into a wagon bound for Pentemarone.

Ana went to bed. But she didn't sleep.

CHAPTER TWENTY-THREE

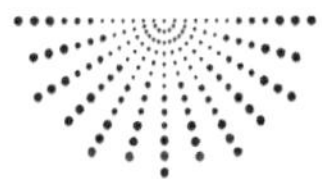

Märchen Lord Buys Diamond Mine

After the recent discovery of a diamond mine in the northwest corner of land owned by Lord Richter, Lord Henry Templeton of Märchen has announced a partnership.

— THE LOHR GAZETTE

Riding a coach to Richilde with Lord Templeton wasn't the most unpleasant thing in the world, Hans felt. But it wasn't his favourite either. The stagecoach the lord had acquired was certainly comfortable. However, though the lord said nothing, he got the impression, from the way the man would occasionally eye his surroundings with a curled lip, that he felt this carriage was beneath him.

Hans was used to dealing with Elphame Park toffs from back when he used to have a shop there. Aristocrats, except for Art of course, were an entirely different breed. At least the lord didn't quiz Hans on just what Art had gotten involved with. He suspected it was because Lord Templeton considered anyone not of noble blood beneath his notice. The more time he spent in Lord Templeton's company, the more he pitied Art's childhood. To have been raised by such an indifferent person could not have been easy.

Thankfully, he didn't have to spend more time than necessary with Lord Templeton. The road where the others had taken down trees to keep Kaiser from following them had already been cleared away, so they made good time. Hans took full advantage at every stop they made to jump down and stretch out his back and legs. He was getting far too old for journeys like this.

The fact he could think of anything at all besides Samara and the others was a minor miracle. He still didn't have faith that Lord Templeton would help the others, nor that the people holding them prisoner would let any of them go. Occasionally, he looked back down the road to see if Callista followed. Despite all her betrayals, he felt certain she was also on her way to Richilde.

He wondered if he should have spoken to someone at the Lions. But he didn't know any of them. He'd never done work for the thieves guild since they didn't need a forger, preferring to break into places rather than use forged documents to gain entrance. He wondered whether Tormod Lyons would've helped Samara. Surely a gang of thieves could break in if other measures didn't pan out.

It was thoughts like these that kept him from sleeping. The lack of a proper bed was also problematic, as was his shoulder which still bothered him. But after his time in a City Watch cell, he felt he could handle almost anything.

Except the loss of Samara.

But no. He would not think of that.

He must have fallen asleep at some point, because he wasn't

aware when they crossed over into Richilde. He awoke to the sight of the classic stone buildings and winding roads of Lohr in the distance.

"I didn't think I'd be able to fall asleep," Hans remarked, but was met with a sniff of an aristocratic nose.

Checking his pocket watch, Hans saw it had just gone noon —they had made exceptional time, and even with it being early winter, the midday sun gilded the city's colourful roofs.

"You must be eager to arrive so you can free your son," Hans said, trying once again.

Lord Templeton's lips twisted into a grimace. "Do you have children?"

Hans stiffened. "No. Not anymore. I had a daughter," he said, taking a shaky breath. "But she and my wife were killed in a carriage accident in Pentemarone."

He couldn't believe he was telling Lord Templeton about this. It wasn't something he spoke of often. Grief. The constant reminders of their absence had driven him to leave his home country and move to Märchen.

Lord Templeton's expression softened, though he said nothing for a moment, instead glancing out of the window. At first Hans thought that was the end of their conversation, but Lord Templeton broke the silence once again. "It is difficult having adult children. When they are young, they are malleable. You assume that given a similar upbringing and advantages, they will share your values." He sighed heavily. "Time and again I have hoped for Arthur to change, and yet he continues to thumb his nose at the family name."

"You should feel lucky to have adult children. My Francesca was taken from me when she was still only a child," Hans responded, his tone curt.

Lord Templeton gave him a look he couldn't quite read. "I

am very sorry for your loss, but you know nothing of the difficulty of guiding children through adulthood."

Hans clenched his teeth, and brazenly glared at Art's father. "I know I could never disown a child of mine. I would give anything to see my daughter again. To see the person she chose to be and help her when she falls down."

Lord Templeton looked like he would respond, but then seemed to think better of it. He sniffed, shook his head, and gazed out the window instead.

Their first stop was the Weisse Rose Inn. Before they left, the Magistrate told Hans that she'd sent a message via speaking telegraph to Gerde to wait there for them. *The poor girl must be so anxious,* Hans thought. But at least she'd gotten away. It was only down to her quick thinking that they had received the message at all.

Lord Templeton scowled at the need to stop at the hotel. He was eager to get on to parliament. His scowl grew deeper when he was led up to the rooms that his son had procured. Honestly, Hans was half afraid Art's lavish spending might convince his father to let him rot after all.

But no amount of lavish furnishings was enough to appease Gerde. When she opened the door for them, Hans could see shadows beneath her eyes and worry lines etched into her face. It didn't stop her from breaking into a huge smile upon seeing Hans, and he found himself enveloped in a hug from the taller woman. He had grown fond of her over the past few weeks they'd been living together at The Wishing-Table, and he was happy to comfort her.

When they broke apart, she glanced uncertainly at Lord Templeton. She had no doubt been informed about his arrival because the first thing she said was, "My Lord, your stagecoach is safely stored in the stables."

Lord Templeton stared down his nose at her. "And who might you be?" His tone was indifferent.

"My name is Gerde. I'm a friend of your son's."

"Hmmph, I suppose I should thank you for not stealing Sturm." The way he looked at Gerde was as though she were something he had recently discovered on the bottom of his shoe.

"Gerde, perhaps you can tell us what happened," said Hans, wanting to smooth things over.

Gerde led them through to a large sitting room, because of course Art procured suites for them, where she filled them in on everything she knew, which was not much. The others, as far as she had heard, had never been transferred, so they were most likely still being held at parliament. Under what charge she didn't know. She was also careful not to mention anything about Eloise or the Restorationists.

"Hmmph," was all Lord Templeton said in response to her explanation.

He then rose to his feet and strode to the door. Turning back, he finally addressed Hans, "I haven't got all day. If you are really here to assist in Arthur's release, then let us go."

LORD TEMPLETON INSISTED that his own stagecoach be readied for travel to parliament, so while the carriage and horses were brought round, Gerde waited, awkwardly, in the hotel's massive marble lobby.

"Understand," said Art's father, after several long awkward minutes, "once I recover Arthur, we will travel back to Märchen. These rooms will be closed out. You people will need to arrange your own travel."

Hans and Gerde both acknowledged his terms. They could

worry about money just as soon as they got everyone out of wherever they were being held. Gerde insisted she accompany Hans and Lord Templeton. The lord didn't argue, merely sniffed and gave her that look again. His disdain rolled off her back. She had more important things to worry about than whether Art's father liked her.

It was awkward riding in the carriage. She was grateful that it was a quick journey. Both because of Art's father, but also because she much preferred the idea of riding on the driver's bench. But Art's father had one of the hotel's coachmen drive them, and she certainly wasn't about to leave Hans by himself with the lord.

They rode up to Parliament House in silence. While waiting for Art's father to arrive, she had stood outside the old palace grounds for several hours hoping to get information on the others. But there was none to be gained. Surely it wasn't every day that people were arrested on parliamentary grounds.

When a guard came to greet their carriage, she noticed this one brandished a weapon. They were made to leave the carriage and explain their presence. Whatever had occurred, the guards were taking further visitors to Parliament House seriously.

Lord Templeton glared at the guards, who were just doing their job. Impatiently, he told them he had a meeting with a Lord Richter, First Lord of the Treasury. The guards stepped away to verify the appointment before ushering them into the building.

Although they were here to rescue Samara and the others, Gerde still found herself in awe as they passed through the giant hall of pillars. Disappointingly, the interior corridors lacked the opulence of the hall of pillars, however she did pass some interesting paintings depicting the rise of Queen White and her council of little people.

Before long, they were ushered into a small office where a

grey-haired man with a walrus moustache sat behind a desk. The man rose to his feet and hurriedly shook hands with Lord Templeton, clasping Art's father's hands with both of his own.

"Henry, it's been too long," said Lord Richter. "When I heard you were coming, I had my assistant clear my calendar. Although, I had hoped we would meet at the club."

Lord Richter seemed to remember himself and he glanced over at Hans and Gerde. "Who might your companions be?"

"These are … *associates* of my son's. Arthur."

"Arthur?" Lord Richter seemed confused for a moment. "Oh, yes, of course. Your second-born. Welcome, all of you. I am Lord Richter. First Lord of the Treasury, although as friends of Lord Templeton's, you may simply call me Richter."

He gestured for Lord Templeton to have a seat.

"I'll just have my assistant bring more chairs," he said, starting to ring the bell for his assistant, but Lord Templeton raised a hand.

"That won't be necessary. I don't wish to take up much of your time. I am here about Arthur."

Lord Richter, who had by now seated himself behind his desk once again, furrowed his bushy eyebrows. "Your son?"

Lord Templeton nodded.

"What about him?"

From her vantage point behind Lord Templeton, Gerde could see Art's father's lips press into a thin line. He seemed reluctant to have to say the words aloud, so Gerde said it for him, "About his arrest."

Lord Richter leaned forward. "His arrest?"

Lord Templeton shot Gerde a look that said if she spoke another word, he would cut out her tongue. But now that the news was in the open, he seemed more ready to speak. "Yes. After the incident the other day?"

Again, Lord Richter seemed confused.

"The incident?" Then it seemed to dawn on him. "Wait. You don't mean the incident *here?* With the intruders? Are you saying your son was involved in that?"

This time, Hans spoke. "It was our understanding that he and his companions are being held here. Are we mistaken?"

Lord Richter cupped his cheek with one palm, looking entirely flustered. "To be honest, I know little about the incident. Apparently, some people lied their way into a meeting with Lord Konrad, a member of the shadow cabinet. They attacked him but were captured whilst attempting to flee." He paused. "Was that really your son?"

Lord Templeton pressed bloodless lips into a thin line. "I'm afraid it was."

Lord Richter's eyes widened at the confirmation. "I don't know if you can see him. I'll be honest, I didn't even realise he was being held here."

"As you can understand, this is a delicate matter, and I would very much like to see my son."

Did Lord Templeton wince on the word "son"? Gerde couldn't be sure.

"I'll do everything I can. But I make no promises. The charges are quite serious."

"Whatever you've been told. It's not the entire truth," Gerde blurted out, earning a glare from Lord Templeton. "The visit to see Lord Konrad was arranged by the Magistrate of Märchen."

"The intruders set off explosives inside Lord Konrad's office," Lord Richter retorted. "He could've been killed."

"None of us know exactly what happened," Hans interrupted. "But please understand that our comrades were there to see Lord Konrad to assist with the security of Richilde."

Lord Templeton shook his head. He looked suddenly far too old. "I don't know what business my son was on, but he was acting in accordance with Magistrate Duvall, who, I believe, knows Lord Konrad from university."

Lord Richter got to his feet. "This is all most strange. Let me find out exactly what is going on."

"Lord Richter," Hans began. "How well do you know Lord Konrad?"

"I have worked with him for several years. We disagree on many issues, of course. But I admire his dedication and his ambition."

"Is it usual for a member of the cabinet to be left out of the loop, so to speak, after an incident of this nature?"

Gerde was surprised Lord Templeton was letting Hans speak for so long, but perhaps the lord knew he lacked the information to make a case for himself.

"An attack of this nature is most unusual in itself," Lord Richter replied. "But I warrant that, yes, it is strange. The day of the attack, we, the members of the cabinet, were too busy being sent away for our own protection. When we returned, we were told it was being handled by Konrad personally since it had been his lapse in security."

"I see," muttered Hans. "It may be best to make enquiries after our companions without alerting Lord Konrad. We don't know exactly what happened, and it would certainly be preferable for us to hear from them directly."

Lord Richter gloomily looked at his visitors, glancing from Hans to Lord Templeton, to Gerde and back to Lord Templeton. "I'm not happy with any of this," he said at last. "But I will endeavour to make enquiries without alerting Lord Konrad. At least for the time being."

With that he hurried out of the office, instructing a guard to wait there, which didn't exactly ease Gerde's own feelings on the matter.

~

ART LAY on his back in his cell. He had glimpsed the inside of a cell a time or two. This one, at least, didn't smell that bad. Yet. The facilities were basic, but the guards emptied them often enough, and Eloise even used her magic to create a little smoke-screen so they could have some privacy when using said facilities. It was the cold that really bothered him. It's not like their gaolers gave them any blankets to keep warm. The chill sank right into his bones.

So when the door to the dungeon creaked open again, the entire gang got to their feet, ready for anything. No more waiting around. They would be ready to fight whoever came through those doors as soon as the opportunity arose.

Two guards strode through, but unlike the ones they'd dealt with previously, these guards didn't have their weapons drawn. *More fools them,* Art thought. He had never been much of a fighter, but he was eager for one now. Even if it was most likely suicidal. It's one thing to break out of a crime lord's cell and quite another to break out of a literal dungeon in a former palace.

Still, if he was to go out, what a way to go.

A man accompanied the two guards. Not Lord Konrad this time, but another man who caused Art to groan. He recognised this man, though he'd only seen him in passing. He was some bigwig in the Richildan government and a business partner of his father's. Art was just wondering how to play this. Wondering if the man would be sympathetic to his cause once he found out who Art was, but the man strode straight up to the cell where Seb and Art stood. *Okay. So I guess he does know who I am.*

"You must be Arthur Templeton," the man said.

"Art," he cautiously corrected.

"Art," the man repeated. "I am Lord Richter. I'm a friend of your father. He rode all the way out here as soon as he heard about the arrest."

Art grinned. That meant Gerde had gotten a message back to Märchen. Good old Gerde, always watching their backs. Although he wasn't sure how he felt about his father being here.

"He'd like to speak with you," Lord Richter continued.

"Show him in?" Art replied uncertainly.

Truthfully, he didn't particularly want to speak to his arschloch of a father, but he wasn't too proud to ask for help getting out of a foreign government's dungeon.

Lord Richter seemed to suppress a smile beneath his thick moustache and gestured for the guard to open the cell.

"No funny business," said the guard, directing his comment at Seb who quickly stepped back, his hands in the air to convey compliance.

Art glanced across at Samara, who nodded her head at him. He took that to mean *do whatever you can to get us out of here, including grovelling.* Although with Samara, it could also mean *tell him nothing. Trust no one. And if you squeal, I'll be paying you a visit while you sleep.* You couldn't always tell with her.

He took it to mean the former.

He was led out by the guards, not roughly like Ana had been dealt with. He didn't know how much Richter knew, or his father, for that matter, but he sensed this wasn't some ruse to find out where the real Eloise was.

He didn't think he'd ever been so grateful to see daylight properly. Not the thin stream of light that filtered through the one window in the dungeon, but proper daylight. He was led back through the grounds, passing other ministers and clerks, who all seemed rather curious about him, but Richter waved him off.

"Your father was very worried about you," Richter was saying as they went.

"Oh, I doubt that very much," Art said with a chuckle.

"Fathers and sons can sometimes have strained relationships, but they still love each other," Richter replied.

Art wanted to say something quippy in response, but just nodded his head in agreement. Some relationships, he knew, were just beyond repair. It was something he had grown to accept. In fact, it was a lot easier to accept that he and his father would never have a loving relationship than to hope for something that would never come along.

They eventually stopped at the door to an office. It looked as alike as all the others, although this one had the title First Lord of the Treasury. Verdammt. He knew his father had friends in high places, but not quite this high.

A guard opened the door and Lord Richter bade him enter. Even though Art knew he was expecting to meet with his father, he was still mildly shocked to see Lord Templeton really had travelled all the way up here to bail him out. Unless it was just to get the carriage. That was more likely, he decided. He hadn't been expecting to see Gerde and Hans, and his mouth split into a wide grin at their faces.

His father pinched his lips together. "Arthur," he said by way of greeting.

"Father," Art replied, and he felt light saying the word. It no longer felt like an anchor weighing him down. This time, it would actually be a rope helping him and his friends out. He just needed to play it right.

His father turned to Lord Richter and said, "Albert, if you don't mind, I would like a word with my son in private."

"Certainly," Richter replied, "But I would also like to speak with Arthur and find out exactly what's going on."

"Of course you can," his father quickly replied. "I would just like to make sure that he's okay first."

Slowly, Lord Richter nodded and went to the door. Gerde and Hans turned to leave, both of them placing reassuring hands on Art before they stepped outside.

His father eyed him up and down. "Please sit down Arthur, I am exhausted and have a backache. I don't need a crick in my neck from having to look up at you while you stand."

Art obeyed.

"Care to tell me what happened?" his father asked, whilst picking a piece of lint from his suit.

"A misunderstanding," Art said, unsure how much he should reveal.

"You stole my carriage to come all the way up here to Richilde and got yourself arrested for having attempted to murder a high-ranking politician, and now you're saying it was just a misunderstanding?"

"Well, that right there was the misunderstanding. We definitely did not try to kill Lord Konrad."

"All I know is that the Magistrate came to me and said you were acting under her orders on some sort of urgent matter of State. I think I deserve an explanation."

"You do, yes," Art admitted. "So here it is. There's a conspiracy. Here in Richilde. There are royalists trying to overthrow the government. We were trying to stop—"

"A conspiracy. Is that really what you're telling me? Stealing my stagecoach? Running up bills? Dragging the Templeton name through the mud? Was that worth it to you, Arthur?"

"To stop a coup? Yes," Arthur replied, his face getting hot.

"A coup!" his father scoffed. "I don't know how you've managed to get the Magistrate in on one of your cons—"

"This isn't a con. This is the truth."

"Let me tell you what's going to happen. I am going to speak to Lord Richter. Pay for any damages made. You and I are going home in the stagecoach you stole. And then you are going to sign papers renouncing any claim to the Templeton name. Are we clear?"

Art's jaw worked from side to side. "What about my friends?"

"What?"

"Sebastian Eze, Samara Dawa, Ana—" He realised he didn't know Ana's last name and he couldn't reveal Eloise's even if he knew it. "And my friend Eloise. They were imprisoned with me."

"I'm not here for them. I'm here for you."

"And I am not going anywhere without them."

His father's eyes flashed with anger. "Then you'll rot in prison. Is that what you want?"

Art coolly met his father's gaze. "Then the second son of Lord Templeton will remain imprisoned in Richilde on the charges of having attempted to murder a high-ranking minister. Is that what *you* want?"

Now his father's nostrils flared. "Don't threaten me, boy!"

"I am merely negotiating with you," Art smoothly replied. "If you want me to renounce the family name and title once and for all, then you have to make sure my friends are released and brought to Märchen as well."

Now it was Art's father who glared, with his jaw working back and forth. And then he stood up, opened the door, leaving Art panicking for a moment that his father was calling his bluff. But instead, his father said, "Albert, can I have a word?"

CHAPTER TWENTY-FOUR

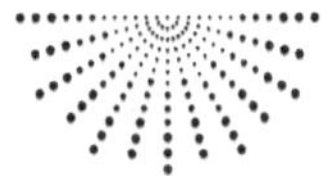

Today marks the 50th anniversary of the country's switch to a constitutional monarchy. The process began early on in Queen White's rule. The Queen was inspired having been subject to persecution by her late mother, who was known to use her Magic against her enemies. It is said that she often told her advisors that she believed no one person, particularly a person with Magic, should hold all the power in a Queendom.

— A RICHILDAN HISTORY OF DEMOCRACY

*L*ord Templeton waited for his friend to be seated before he himself took a seat. Albert eyed Arthur warily, which Lord Templeton understood given the situation. But Arthur had called his bluff, and he was right. He wasn't about to let a son of his rot away in a foreign government's prison.

"Albert, you and I have known each other several years, so I am just going to be straightforward with you."

"I always appreciate that," his friend commented, the corner of his mouth ticking upwards to show he was ready to listen to whatever Templeton had to say.

"I am here to take my son home." Art cleared his throat, and Templeton grimaced. "And his associates."

Albert spread his hands flat on the desk. There was a look of pity on his face, which Templeton loathed. "I'm not sure it's going to be as easy as all that. Arthur and his associates attacked Lord Konrad—"

"He says that's not what happened. He claims he was here to stop a coup."

Templeton glanced at his son for confirmation, and Arthur nodded soberly. *And the godmothers help him, if he's lying about this.*

"They blew up Lord Konrad's office," Albert argued. "It seems to me that they were the ones attempting a coup."

At this, Templeton laughed. The very idea that his son would be involved in a coup was preposterous. Arthur was many things, a drunkard, an *actor*, but the idea that he would be involved in a coup … Templeton stopped mid-thought. While he knew his son could never be behind a coup, he couldn't discount the possibility that he had gotten involved with others who were behind it.

He turned to Arthur. "Can you promise me you aren't behind an attempted coup?"

"I'm not!" Art exclaimed, throwing his hands out in frustration. "I already told you, we were trying to stop the coup. I know how things must look, but if we did such a thing, why haven't we been charged? Why did Konrad order us thrown in the dungeons? Why has nobody questioned us? Why did he take our friend away?"

All good questions Templeton felt. Except that last one. He didn't know what that one was about.

"It is suspicious, is it not?" Templeton said, turning back to his friend. "Thrown in the dungeons instead of sent to gaol. Has any other minister been allowed to speak to them?"

"I … I don't believe anyone has spoken to them yet," stammered Albert. "But if I'm hearing you both correctly, you're suggesting that Lord Konrad, a highly placed member of the government is involved in an attempt to overthrow the government."

Verdammt, that wasn't what Templeton was suggesting at all. He wasn't about to make enemies in the Richildan government. He just wanted to sow enough doubt that he could get Arthur released. And his associates.

Templeton took a deep breath. "Albert, you know me. You and I have known each other for many years. I've broken bread with your family. We own a mine together. I wouldn't try to put you in a precarious position. I'm merely asking you to question these people. Something doesn't smell right. Surely, you can see that."

Templeton knew the moment before Albert spoke the words that he agreed. He looked as though he were trying to come up with a reason not to do this. But he couldn't.

"Very well," Albert finally said. "I'll have the other prisoners brought up here. Hopefully, you can all shed some light on the matter."

"Oh, thank the godmothers," Art said with a sigh.

"I will question the prisoners," Albert continued. "One on one. If any of your story's deviate in the least, then I can only assume you're lying. I suppose I should start with you, Art."

With that, Richter rang the bell for his assistant.

IT WAS with trepidation that Samara allowed herself to be led upstairs. After Art had been sent up, Seb had been taken.

Neither of them had returned. She didn't like this at all. She was told they were being taken for questioning, but if that were so, why hadn't they been brought back down?

As she left the cell, she turned back to Eloise, who was back in her disguise and must surely be feeling drained, having to take the disguise on and off while also trying to maintain Ana's at a distance. Ever since Ana had been taken the girl had remained curled up on the ground, plaiting and unplaiting her hair while staring off into the distance. Samara wanted to say something to reassure her but what could she say? Especially given how they were all being led upstairs. She couldn't help fearing that they had discovered Ana wasn't, in fact, Eloise.

"We'll get you out of here," Samara promised the young girl.

Eloise nodded, but wouldn't meet Samara's eyes. Samara told herself that she'd be okay. After all, she'd survived weeks in captivity under Chetwin Humphreys' control.

Samara was led into another nondescript office. Sitting behind the desk was the man who had identified himself as a friend of Art's father. She cautiously took a seat at the desk, unsure whether that made him a friend or yet another foe they needed to be wary of.

"You are Samara Dawa, yes?" he asked.

He actually caught her off guard. She was so used to being addressed as the Hisada; it took her a moment to realise that perhaps that name meant nothing here. She bowed her head.

"I am Lord Richter. I'm a friend of Lord Templeton."

He seemed to study her for a reaction.

"I remember. You came down to our cells earlier."

"Yes." Lord Richter cleared his throat. "Do you know who I am?"

"You mean besides being a friend of Art's father? Can't say I do. I don't keep up with Richildan politics." She tried to keep the impatience out of her voice. Where in the name of Manāt were her friends?

"Of course not. I am the First Lord of the Treasury. Part of the cabinet of the Richildan government. I'm here speaking with you now because your friend Art made certain allegations, and I'd like to get to the bottom of them."

"Allegations about Lord Konrad?"

"You tell me." He leaned back in his leather chair. "I'd rather hear it in your own words, Miss Dawa."

"We came to speak to Lord Konrad."

"Why Lord Konrad?"

By his tone of voice and the notes he was taking, Samara guessed that before he became a politician, he had been some sort of prosecutor.

"His name was given to us by the Magistrate of Märchen. We needed to speak to someone highly placed in the government."

"Why not me? I am, after all, a friend of Lord Templeton's."

"I wasn't aware of your connection to the Templeton's, and," —Samara smirked—"to be quite honest, I don't think Lord Templeton would've arranged the introduction we needed."

"But the Magistrate did?"

"Yes."

"Why?"

Samara exhaled slowly. Where to begin? "Lord Richter, are you familiar with an organisation that calls themselves the Restorationists?"

"Of course," Richter said, surprising Samara. "They're a small group of royalists who would like to see the restoration of the monarchy."

Richter chuckled at Samara's shocked look.

"Don't look so surprised. I am a minister. They want to overthrow the government. I make it my business to know these things. But their plan is to restore the Magical royal line of White. There is no Magical line of White anymore."

"They believe they've found someone with big Magic who descends from the line of White."

"Organisations like this make outlandish claims all the time. Why should we take this threat more seriously than all the others?"

"Because they have found someone with Big Magic. I can't verify that she's related to Queen White, but she has Big Magic."

"Can you prove your assertions?"

Samara hesitated, but knew she had no choice. "Yes. But I'll need my crew. And I would prefer if the First Minister were present."

She wasn't about to reveal Eloise to another spy for the Restorationists.

"You understand that the last time you and your *crew* were in the presence of a member of parliament, you set off explosives and were captured trying to flee the scene."

"True, but that's only because Konrad is working with Lutz Kaiser of the Restorationists. We realised he was in contact with them, and we wanted to protect the Magic user in question."

Richter's bushy eyebrows raised. "Does that mean the Magic user is with you now?"

Schiesse.

"If you want any more information from us, say a demonstration from the Magic user, then you need to get the First Minister. We've been burned before."

"So you say. I still find it difficult to believe Lord Konrad would be working against the government."

"He's not working against the government. He's working to enrich himself. If that means ushering in a new regime, then that's what he'll do."

Samara rose to her feet. She didn't have time for this bureaucracy. They needed to get Ana back. If her cover had been blown… "Look. Konrad's already taken one of my people. I don't have time for this."

"What do you mean, taken one of your people?"

"I'll explain everything to the First Minister."

Richter leaned back in his chair and let out a long sigh.

~

PHILIP BODEN WAS ENJOYING a blissful few minutes of alone time when there was a knock at his door and his secretary announced Lord Richter. *Verdammt.* Could he not get a moment's peace? He chuckled to himself. Of course he couldn't. He was First Minister. This was the job he'd signed on for.

He cordially invited Richter in. Noticing his colleague's pale appearance, he offered him some cognac, but Richter declined. When Richter relayed to him the reason for his visit, Philip also paled.

"They could be lying, though?"

"Perhaps. But I don't think so," Richter replied. He pulled out a leather folio and removed a notebook. "I interviewed all of them. They were, mostly, consistent in their story. When I asked why we should take this threat seriously, Ms Dawa, who appears to be their leader, said *Because they have found someone with Big Magic. I don't know for sure that she's related to Queen White, but she has Big Magic.* Arthur Templeton—"

"Templeton," Philip interrupted. "Any relation to your business associate?"

"Yes," Richter replied somewhat defensively. "He said, *They've found her. The last living Magical descendant of Queen White.* Sebastian Eze simply said, *they have the real deal. An actual Magical girl.* Ana Wentz was less cooperative. The only thing she wanted to talk about was her friend, who was taken by Lord

Konrad. They were all consistent in the naming of someone called Lutz Kaiser. I'm having people look into him. They were also all consistent in their claim that Kaiser is a Restorationist, and that Konrad is working with him."

Richter closed his notebook.

Philip tapped his index finger on his lips thoughtfully. Eventually he said, "Am I to understand that Konrad took the girl in question and handed her over to this Kaiser?"

"Truthfully, it's unclear. Ms Wentz did mention a girl had been taken, so it seems likely she is the descendant."

"Have them sent up here," Philip replied. "Obviously, have them checked for weapons first. Tell no one about this. If there really are royalists working within our government, the less people who know, the better."

Richter nodded and went on his way. While Philip waited, he poured himself a glass of cognac, which he sipped at, deep in thought. Could there really be a Magical descendant of Queen White alive? If so, even if they dealt with the threat from the Restorationists, this would still throw their government into turmoil.

Perhaps there could be a way to introduce the new White descendant to Richilde without throwing the country into disarray. There had been a time where the White line had ruled in partnership with elected government. A constitutional monarchy.

Better that he be the one to bring this news to the public than some power-hungry maniac like Lord Konrad.

He couldn't deny it was tempting to make this entire thing go away. If only the people in this room knew about her, it would certainly be possible. He'd have to ask Richter who else knew about this girl.

Eventually, Richter returned with two men and two women in tow. He could easily pick out Lord Templeton's relation. He had the same nose as the haughty Märchen lord. While he didn't have a haughty expression on his face, he looked a touch more comfortable in his surroundings than the others did. The other, darker-skinned man, barely made eye contact with Philip. He seemed nervous. The older woman, an Akkadian if he wasn't mistaken, had the look and bearing of a soldier. Her body was tense. This one was their leader, Dawa, obviously. The last woman had short blond hair and an impatient look on her face.

He bade them sit down, taking them in. *What do you want?* he wondered. They had come here ostensibly to warn them about the Restorationists. But why?

"I am Lord Boden," Philip said, without preamble, "the First Minister of Richilde. I understand from Lord Richter here that you believe the Restorationists have acquired a girl of Magical descent from the line of Queen White, and that you can prove it."

"Just to be clear," Dawa said, not at all fazed by the status of the man she was speaking with, "they haven't acquired her yet. Which is how we can prove it."

Boden leaned back in his chair and gestured with his hand. "Please do."

Samara Dawa looked to the blonde girl. The blonde girl appeared upset.

The dark-skinned man, Eze, turned to face her. "It's the only way to get Ana back."

"For Ana," muttered the blonde girl. She then said a few other words under her breath that Philip couldn't quite catch before her face seemed to swim before his eyes. He rubbed at them before realising it was something she was doing herself. The face of the blonde woman melted away and was replaced by that of a teenage girl. With her creamy skin, full, rosy lips and ebony hair, she certainly resembled Queen White.

"My name is Eloise," she said.

Philip studied her for a moment. "Illusions are a small magic ability. I'm afraid this proves nothing."

"What's your favourite fruit?" the dark-haired girl asked with a touch of impatience in her voice.

Philip shook his head in bemusement. "I am a fan of mangoes, though they are expensive to acquire given they don't grow here in Alsatia."

The girl muttered more words he didn't quite catch. Suddenly, before him and almost out of thin air, a plate appeared with a whole mango on it that was about the size of his palm. There was a small spoon on the plate and a paring knife.

He studied the fruit, then glanced at the girl and raised an eyebrow in bemusement.

"Have a bite of it," she said with a nod of her head.

Suspicious, he picked up the fruit. The flesh had enough give to prove it was ripe. He held the fruit to his nose and caught the faint scent of mango. Finally, he picked up the paring knife and cut a slice. Mango juice dripped onto his hands. He held the slice up and sniffed it. The scent of mango was even more powerful now. His hands shook as he placed the mango back on the plate.

Making something from nothing was a hallmark of big Magic.

Get ahold of yourself, Philip, he told himself. But he couldn't. He could be staring into the face of a Magical descendant of Queen White. And that … that changed everything.

"The fruit is edible," the girl said with a shrug. "It can't give you actual sustenance since it is created from nothing, but it tastes good."

He gave her the tiniest shake of his head. Now that he had actual proof she was who she said she was, he was even less likely to eat the fruit. For all he knew, this was an elaborate plan to kill him, thus easing the change from a democracy to an absolute monarchy.

"Do you see now why we set off those explosives?" Samara asked impatiently. "We were trying to protect Eloise from Konrad. We failed, and now one of my crew is in danger."

"In danger, how?" Philip asked. Emotionally, he was still trying to process everything that had just happened, but he listened as they told him about how Konrad had taken their friend Ana, who was disguised as Eloise, most likely turning her over to the Restorationists.

"I'm very sorry about your friend, but surely by now they have already discovered she's not a magic user," he said when they were finished.

"But she is." The words came from Sebastian Eze, who now stared earnestly at Philip. "She has small kinetic magic."

"But that ruse won't hold for long," Samara added. "You wanted proof. We gave you proof. Now you need to let us be on our way, so we can get our people back."

A smile touched Philip's lips. Dawa was bold. He could respect that. And she obviously cared for her team.

"I still need to—" he began, but was interrupted by an urgent knock on the door.

"I thought I said I didn't want to be disturbed!" he snapped.

His secretary poked his head through the door. "I'm very sorry," said the younger man. "There's been a disturbance, and it's related to..." He gestured at Dawa and her crew.

Philip rubbed his forehead. "What is it now?"

"This woman was captured trying to break into parliament grounds," his secretary said, and then opened the door wider to reveal a red-headed woman dressed in black trousers and a black, fitted jacket.

Dawa, who had also turned to the doorway, smirked. "How far did you get?"

"They caught me inside that inner courtyard."

"Armed guards on the roof? Yeah. They do that," added Art.

Philip shook his head. "I take it you know this woman?"

"The Matron and I grew up together," Dawa said.

"Matron?" Philip paled. Why would an assassin be here except to—

"I'm not here on a job, First Minister," the Matron assured him. "I waited at the Weisse Rose Inn, but nobody came, so I came to rescue this lot."

Philip shook his head. He was feeling a headache coming on. "I assume she was searched for weapons?"

His secretary nodded. "Yes. We think we've got them all."

"You think?" Philip repeated, then shook his head again. "You might as well bring her in."

As the Matron was led inside, he added, "I assume you also know about—"

"Eloise? Yes. She and I go back a long way." She had a smile on her face that Philip couldn't decipher. Almost annoyed, almost regretful.

Dawa interrupted. "Look, as I was saying, we don't have time for this-"

"And I understand," said Philip, holding up a hand. "But I need to know what your intentions are, Eloise."

"Intentions?" Eloise looked confused.

"For this country. You came to me to warn us about a coup, but what are your intentions for the throne? Will you submit to a constitutional monarchy as we once were, or—"

"I don't want to rule!"

Philip was both startled and relieved at her vehemence. "When you say you don't want to rule—"

"Ever since I got my Magic, I've spent my life being shuffled around from country to country. Always following rules. Never allowed to live my life. I don't want the throne. I just want to save Ana and go back to Märchen." She shot the Matron a withering look. "But not with you!"

"Yes, I got that," the Matron muttered.

All of a sudden, Philip felt conflicted. "But are you not related to Queen White?"

Eloise shrugged. "As far as I know."

"And you have the kind of Magical abilities we haven't seen in a generation." He sighed. "I feel it is my duty to give you a place here—"

"I don't want to live here."

"She's made her choice," said Samara, placing a hand protectively on the younger girl. "All any of us want is for you to take care of the Restorationists, so Eloise, and the rest of us, can go back to our lives."

"Very well," said Philip.

He had to take her word for it. But she was only a teenager, and teenagers change their minds. If she ever did so, he had to make sure it was with the full backing of the government, not despite the government's wishes, like the royalists wanted.

"It's going to be difficult tracking down all of the Restorationists, with only the one name." He amended, "Two if you count Lord Konrad."

"They gave us three other names, including Johann Müller," said Richter.

Philip raised his eyebrows. Müller was a minor lord who made his money buying and selling properties. "Well, that's promising."

"I may be able to give you more names," said the Matron. "Eloise was placed under my care—"she was interrupted by a snort from Eloise. Throwing an annoyed look at the girl, the Matron continued, "I can give you descriptions of the people I dealt with, as well as information as to how I was paid. Bank accounts and such."

"That would be a tremendous help Matron." He sighed. "But how do we find this friend of yours? This Ana?"

"Ana is missing?" the Matron asked, glancing at Samara.

"We think Lutz has her by now," Samara confirmed.

"I can locate Ana," Eloise added, speaking to Philip. "And Lutz Kaiser."

"Tell me what you need," Philip said.

CHAPTER TWENTY-FIVE

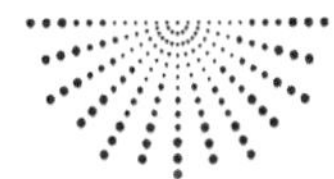

Think back, if you will, to the time when the city-state of Märchen was first founded. Queen White, Queen Zellandine and Queen Cenerentola founded this city as a central location of trade for the continent. But one wonders how such a feat was accomplished when to this day we can't seem to agree on the name of things? Is the last meal of the day called "diner" as in Richilde or "dîner" as in Perceforest. The city-state of Märchen opted to develop its own pronunciation for this meal, "dinner".

— LANGUAGE AND THE THREE QUEENS

Art found his eyes drawn to the building opposite, with its white exterior and wrought iron window guards, wondering which one was the apartment Ana was being held in.

"Stop moving," Eloise chided him. "I need you to be still so I can do this properly."

"But you're not changing anything on me, right? I'm not going to suddenly get two faces?"

"Shhh," Eloise replied.

"It bothers me that you're not responding," Art muttered, but he let the girl continue her work.

He didn't feel any changes. Not really. His skin felt a little warm. Like he was flushed. But that might just be from the way Gerde, Callista and Samara kept walking around him, studying his face.

With the help of Eloise, and the knowledge of the city the First Minister provided, they easily located where Ana was being kept. It was a massive apartment building. With five floors, they couldn't be sure exactly where she was located. They had narrowed down which end of the building Ana was being held in, but the window guards meant Samara would be unable to sneak into the building. Since they didn't know what they were dealing with inside, the First Minister was reluctant to just deploy men to overpower Kaiser and his security. Boden did offer up his Captain of the Guard and a squad of men when the time came for arrests. For this little reconnaissance mission, however, it was down to Art, the inside man, once again.

Boden did manage to procure an apartment across the street from the building where Ana was being held that they could use as a staging ground.

"Try to keep an eye out for any servants 'stairs we could use to sneak in," Samara reminded him.

"Will do," Art replied, trying not to move as Eloise put the finishing touches on him.

"All done," Eloise finally said.

Art walked over to the full-length mirror and almost staggered at his reflection. He wasn't sure why he was so surprised. He had already seen Eloise's disguises at work, but still. To say it was strange to look in the mirror and see the eyes of a stranger was an understatement. He had worn costumes with elaborate make up many times over the years. But never had he been so transformed that he didn't even recognise himself.

The face he was wearing wore a neatly trimmed beard, and when he touched his face, it disturbed him to feel that facial hair, even though Eloise reassured him she wasn't actually changing him. It was all part of the illusion.

He turned back to the others. "I guess I'm ready," he murmured in a Richildan accent.

~

ART KNEW that confidence was half the battle when walking into situations like this. If you act like you belong, people won't question you being there. So, he wasn't at all surprised when the doorman let him through without question.

"Which way to Lutz Kaiser's rooms, please?" he asked, keeping his voice brisk.

The doorman glanced at some sort of directory and then said, "I don't have a Kaiser down here."

Uh oh.

Art silently groaned. "I forgot. It's a sublet. Try Johann Müller." Art crossed his fingers that this name might work.

The doorman checked. "5F," he said.

Art thanked him and went on his way.

He climbed the stairs to the top floor, and sure enough, outside apartment 5F stood a guard wearing a uniform matching the one Art was appearing to wear. Eloise's disguise was perfect. The guard was having a smoke break.

The guard nodded in greeting but otherwise didn't question Art as he entered the apartment. Once inside, he found himself face to face with Lutz Kaiser. Art's throat constricted.

"Any sign of Diemer's carriage?" Kaiser asked, not letting him get away.

"No?" Art said, then, getting ahold of himself, "No sign yet."

"He's going to be late. I just know it. That boy lacks all

responsibility, and we want to make him King?" Kaiser muttered, walking away from Art.

King? Well, that was an interesting tidbit he would need to tuck away for later examination.

Art took in the grand rooms of the apartment, noting the layout. He noticed a butler, and at least two footmen. There was a cook and cook's assistant. Counting the one on his smoke break, there looked to be ten guards in total.

Doing his best to look like he was supposed to be doing the rounds, Art checked all the doors. No sign of a servants' staircase. He spotted the dumbwaiter, but as expected, you'd have to be Hans's size to fit in there comfortably. He located a bedroom, another bedroom, and then a master bedroom. But no sign of Ana. He then scanned the living areas, checking the sitting room, a sunroom, and finally the library where Ana, still in her Eloise disguise, sat reading a book. There was a maid accompanying her.

Both looked up, but the maid had automatically dismissed him, and gone back to reading her own book. Before Ana could glance down again, Art waved an arm. She lowered her head but was still watching him beneath furrowed brows.

He tried to signal to her that it was him, Art, in disguise. He tried to mime his moustache. He then tried to mime Samara climbing and knifing someone. She frowned at him. Finally, he tried to mime throwing one of Seb's explosive balls.

Just as he was trying to think of what else to mime, Ana spoke up. "I'm hungry. I would like some tea."

"I'll ring the bell for some," said the maid.

There was something about the maid that was off. She lacked the deference required of her position.

"Could you ask the kitchens to make me some walnut cake?"

"Dinner will be served soon."

"But I want some walnut cake now. Also, don't let them steep the tea too long. Last time, it was too strong." Ana pouted.

The woman scowled at Ana but said nothing.

"I can stay here if you want," Art offered.

"Or you can make yourself useful and take that order to the kitchen," the maid replied.

"I'd prefer you did it. I don't trust him to get the order right," Ana said, her tone falsely sweet all of a sudden.

"If you think you can do your Magic while my back is turned—"

"All I'm asking for is something to eat. Or should I tell Mr Kaiser that you're refusing?"

The woman scowled again and stalked out. "Watch out for her!" the woman said over her shoulder.

As soon as the door closed behind her, Art ran over, saying, "Ana, it's me."

"I know it's you, Art," she replied, a smile forming on her lips.

"Wait. You do?"

"You still sound like you!"

"Right. Of course. Well, listen, Samara and the others are here. We're going to get you out."

"Hurry," she said. "It has to be tonight. I think Kaiser plans to send Eloise to Pentemarone. I don't know when, though. But we have at least tonight. He's planning on marrying her off."

"He wants to make one of his relatives the King, I bet," Art replied. Then he added, "Hang in there. And be ready for us."

She nodded, and then they both heard footsteps coming their way. Ana shooed him away, and Art hurried back to his position by the door. The maid entered, glared at him, and then sent an even angrier glare in Ana's direction.

~

SAMARA TAPPED HER FOOT IMPATIENTLY. *Why was it taking so long for Art to return?* she wondered. When she eventually spotted him hurrying across the street and into their apartment building, she leapt to her feet to meet him. His disguise was so good, she hadn't even realised it was him until she saw the beeline he made to their location.

She greeted him at the front door, but it was Eloise who spoke first. "Did you see her? Is she okay?"

"Yes," Art panted as he closed the door behind him.

In front of her eyes, Samara saw the spell melt away, and he was back to looking like Art again.

"She's fine for now. Your spell is still holding up. But they're planning on taking her to Pentemarone."

"When?" Seb demanded to know.

"She doesn't know."

"Did you find us another way inside?" Samara asked.

"No servants' stairs. Only a dumbwaiter. Even if you could fit in there, I spotted at least ten guards in the apartment."

"That settles it then," said Bastian, the Captain of the Guard Boden had assigned to them. He was instructed to give them all the help they required to rescue Ana, and then capture Kaiser and any associates. "The only way in or out is through the front door. I'll have my squad break down the door and deal with Kaiser."

"No," Seb replied, emphatically. "With your guns? That could endanger Ana."

"She can handle it—" Eloise began.

"I agree with Seb," Samara said, cutting Eloise off. "We need another option."

"We have one, but it might be a long shot," said Art. "Any minute now, Kaiser is expecting a guest. He's running late. If we could impersonate him—"

"Who is he expecting?" interrupted Bastian.

"Someone named Diemer."

"Adelbert Diemer?" asked Bastian.

Art shook his head. "I don't know. But I think Kaiser wants to make him king."

"That'll be Diemer's son, Adel. I'm not surprised he's running late. He's a drunkard who hangs about in the private gambling dens."

"Why would they want to make someone like him king?" Samara asked with a frown.

"He's banned from the public gambling dens, owing to his small magic power."

Callista nodded. "Small magic. So, this is about bloodlines."

"You say he's on his way right now?" Samara demanded.

"He's supposed to be," Art replied.

Eloise paled at this latest news, but Samara was impressed at how focused she remained. "Do we know what he looks like? I can make you look like him."

"We need to intercept him first," said Samara.

"I'll send my men out to search for him. Between the private gambling dens and the main thoroughfares, we should be able to locate Diemer's carriage."

And so they waited. Samara hated waiting. She paced the room impatiently. Always glancing out the window, in case Diemer's carriage rolled up, knowing it was impossible since Bastian had assured her, his men would intercept the carriage before it turned onto this road.

Eventually, a guard returned and confirmed that Diemer was indeed at a gambling den named The Red Apple. The guards had detained the carriage driver, so for the time being, Diemer wasn't going anywhere.

"How far is The Red Apple?" asked Samara.

"About a mile away. But it's a private club," Bastian began, before glancing over at Eloise. "I guess you have everything in hand."

~

ART SAUNTERED into The Red Apple. Eloise had conjured yet another disguise. It was most likely not needed, but they couldn't be too careful. Inside, Art was faced with his first obstacle. An older gentleman stood at a small counter. Around him were comfortable seats where people could wait for their carriages to be brought around. On the side of the counter sat copies of the local newspaper. Art noticed a copy of *Gottard's*, the peerage publication. Flipping through, he spotted Adelbert Diemer's family crest and scanned through the listing. His many positions and titles. His wife and three children, Adelbert the II, of which there was little information, except that he lived in Breitofen. It was a city in the northern part of Richilde, with only one thing it was known for: the university. Given Adel's age, it was a fair bet Adel studied there.

"Can I help you?" asked the man at the counter, looking down at Art through half-moon spectacles.

"Is Lord Diemer still here? I was supposed to meet with him, but I'm running late."

The man cocked his head at Art. Studied him for a moment. Then said, "Do you have a membership with us?"

"I don't. I was supposed to be Lord Diemer's guest."

"Well, unfortunately, I cannot reveal information about our patrons. Good day, sir."

With that, the man turned away from Art. Art thought about arguing but knew this man's type. If he didn't know the secret handshake for this place, there was no getting in.

"Bad news," Art said, meeting back up with the others at a

nearby café. "They won't let me in without a membership. They won't even admit he's in there."

"Samara and Callista are scouting the outside right now," Gerde replied. "Hopefully, they'll have better luck."

While they waited for Samara and Callista to return, Seb kept rapping his fingers on the table and jiggling his knee.

"We'll get Ana out," Art tried to reassure Seb.

Seb nodded at him, but his eyes still strayed to the window. He jumped to his feet, jostling the table as he did so, upon Samara's return.

"We found a way inside," Samara said, without preamble. "There's a courtyard with a large tree which should obscure us from prying eyes. Bastian said the gambling den is on the second floor, so it's not a big climb. Callie, Eloise and Art are with me." She turned to Seb and Gerde. "In case Diemer finds another carriage driver, if you see anyone attempt to leave in that carriage, I need you to cause a diversion. Keep them here. Understand?"

Seb nodded.

"You can leave it with us," Gerde murmured.

"Do you need me for anything?" Hans asked.

Samara patted his shoulder. "You just enjoy that saffron chai. We'll be right back."

THE TREE DID INDEED HIDE them from view, which, as far as Art was concerned, was a good thing considering he wasn't the most adept climber. And climbing up a drainpipe? He struggled not to slip. Callista led the way, with Eloise behind her. Apparently, the girl had gotten some climbing lessons at the house of assassins because she was doing just fine. Art only managed to keep going because of Samara impatiently prodding him along.

They eased their way through a window into an empty salon room, which held a small table and a few scattered comfy chairs. The room still reeked of cigar smoke from the previous guests. Samara quickly opened the door and checked the corridor. She signalled to let them know it was clear. Then it was up to Art. He brushed himself clear of dirt, even though he needn't have. Eloise's illusion would hide any dirt he'd accumulated, and walked confidently out into the empty corridor.

It took him a while to locate the main gambling hall. He surveyed the space. Since it was not yet evening, the room wasn't packed like it would be later. The people hanging about now were the hardcore gamblers. The ones who came, less for the socialising and more to ameliorate deeper issues.

He stopped a waiter going by and asked, "Which one is Lord Diemer?"

The waiter pointed to a table in the centre of the room. A group of men crowded the table. He could easily pick out Diemer. He was the youngest at the table, and already deep in his cups. Art was sure young Adel Diemer was probably the life of the party. And then he knew what he was going to do.

He strode to the table, almost walking right past Diemer, before stopping and calling out his name.

"Diemer? Adel Diemer, is that you?!" he cried, a great big grin on his face.

Young Diemer looked up from a pile of chips he'd just won and, with a bemused look on his face said, "Do I know you?"

"It's me! Karsten Fechner. Breitofen. I was a senior when you were a fresher. But I remember you!" Art leaned in close. "Do you still do your little illusions?"

Diemer laughed, relaxing a little. "Yeah. I do, as a matter of fact. Not allowed here, though."

"Fun! I didn't know you come to The Red Apple! Listen, I

have a table in one of the back salons. It's just a few of us. Private game. Are you interested? If you use your skills, I won't tell, so long as you help a Breitofen fella out."

A man standing next to Diemer, who Art hadn't fully registered earlier, leaned close to Diemer. He murmured something in Diemer's ear.

"We may as well. The driver's gone off somewhere. So, we can't leave yet anyway," Diemer replied.

The man looked irritated. Afraid that Diemer might listen to the man at his side, Art added, "I'm buying the drinks."

"Well, in that case…" Diemer said, jumping to his feet. His minder tried to stop him, but Diemer shook his head. "It's just one game."

Art led the way back to the empty salon where the others were waiting. As they strolled through the gambling den, he kept up an easy conversation with Diemer, occasionally waving at people they passed. *Always act like you belong. Works every time.* He opened the door and stepped inside, Diemer on his heels.

He heard Diemer stop. "What's all this—" he began, before staggering to the side. His minder tried to catch him, but soon both men were on the floor. Fast asleep.

Samara and Callista quickly pulled the bodies inside. Together, the four of them propped up the two men on the table, trying as much as they could to make it look like two men in their cups.

"How long will they be like this?" Samara asked as she tried to get him settled in his chair.

Eloise shrugged. "I went pretty strong on them. Maybe five or six hours."

Art gave her an approving look. Not bad. It would be handy having her on the team. In moments, Art looked down to see himself transformed into Diemer. The others too, had changed:

Samara into Diemer's companion, the others into random businessmen.

"Lead on," came Samara's voice from Diemer's companion.

Art led the way back through the gambling den and down
the stairs to the lobby.

"I'll have your carriage brought around," said the man at the
counter.

"That won't be necessary. I'll walk," said Art, without looking
back.

Once outside, they reconvened with Gerde and Seb. "They'll
be out for a few hours at least," came Samara's voice from
Diemer's companion again.

Gerde blinked in surprise, then grinned and slapped her
thighs. "Then they won't mind us borrowing their carriage."

GERDE STEERED the stolen carriage up to the apartment
building. Earlier, they'd dropped off Hans and picked up Bastian, who insisted on accompanying them inside.

Five of them went in. Art, disguised as Adel Diemer, Samara
as his minder, and Callista, Seb and Bastian. Samara knew it
looked more suspicious, having the five of them, but she wanted
to be prepared for anything. Besides, the ruse would only last so
long.

Gerde stationed herself outside, along with Eloise, who
protested loudly. Guilt tugged at Samara. She sensed Gerde's
hurt at not getting to come along, but someone needed to keep
an eye on Eloise.

It was only a matter of time before they were discovered. In
the meantime, she wanted things to go as smoothly as possible.

The five of them entered the building and Art told the
doorman they were expected on the fifth floor. The doorman

let them through without question and they climbed the stairs to the top floor.

"Remember, Art and Bastian are the only ones who can do a Richildan accent, so only they should speak," Callista reminded them.

"They know their jobs," Samara murmured.

Callista, or the man she was disguised as, shook her head. "Why do you always have to argue?"

Samara smirked.

"Are your men going to be ready once we give the signal?" Samara asked as they climbed the stairs.

"They'll be ready," Bastian promised.

"Remember: we don't give the signal until we've located Ana," Samara reminded them.

Reaching Kaiser's apartment, Samara knocked on the door. A guard opened it and Art spoke: "Lord Diemer here to see Mr Kaiser."

The guard opened the door wider to let them all in. They were shown into a richly furnished sitting room. A moment later, Lutz Kaiser entered. Samara felt herself tense. Being face to face with the man who had kidnapped and tortured her was unnerving. She wasn't sure she could keep her emotions off her face, so she forced herself to focus on a nearby crystal decanter.

"Mr Kaiser. It's good to see you," Art said, projecting his voice lower than usual to match Diemer's.

"Mr Kaiser? So formal. Call me Lutz."

"Forgive me. Lutz," Art corrected.

"I had expected you here earlier," Lutz said, a note of admonishment creeping into his voice.

"Ah, yes. I was held up," Art began, but then trailed off. The envelope with his winnings sticking out of his top pocket would complete the picture.

"Let me fix you a cognac," Lutz said.

"So, when do I get to meet..." Art trailed off again.

"Patience," said Lutz with a laugh. "She'll be down in a moment."

Samara tuned out the conversation as she took in the room. The apartment was spacious, with lots of windows, which meant lots of opportunities to exit should she need to. Although it would be tricky with the window guards.

She eyed the guards and footmen about the place. Samara counted six guards that she could see, which meant others lurked elsewhere. If things got heated, she knew she could count on Seb to get Ana out. Although perhaps Ana didn't need Seb's help. She had to remind herself Ana was no longer the deer-in-headlights girl she had once known.

"It would please me greatly," she heard Lutz saying, "if you would do one of your illusions."

"Oh. I don't know about that," she heard Art say with a nervous chuckle.

"It's purely a formality. We need to be sure of the strength of your magic."

She glanced warily over at Art, who glanced back her way. *Schiesse*. She had hoped to have Ana in her sights before it got to this point. She gave Art a barely perceptible nod of the head.

"I thought this was a done deal. Is this some kind of test?" Art injected a whiney note into his voice.

"It would just take a moment," Lutz was saying. He gestured. "Please."

"Very well," Art said, although he sounded deeply unhappy.

A second before it happened, Samara saw Seb fling one of the new explosive balls he had been working on. Unlike the previous version, it didn't knock them off their feet, although it made a loud noise right before releasing red smoke into the air. The release of the smoke bomb was quickly followed by the sound of whistles as Bastian alerted his men. Struggling to see through the smoke, she thought, *why can't things just go smoothly?* Just for once, she wanted one of their plans to work out the way they had planned.

She launched herself into the guards rushing towards them, head butting one while stabbing another in the leg. She thought she spied Kaiser attempting to flee the room, and she tried to go after him, but the guard she'd head-butted, dragged her back into the fray by her collar.

"I've got Kaiser!" Callista called out, grabbing the bureaucrat and forcing him into a choke hold.

Eloise had apparently dropped all Magical disguises the moment the explosions went off. *Good. That will make it easier for Bastian to clean up.*

Putting her own opponent down with a well-placed poke just behind the clavicle, followed up with smashing a crystal decanter over his head, Samara quickly made her way down the corridor toward the bedrooms.

Frightened men and women, household staff, ran past, but she didn't meet any other guards. Samara counted. She had taken out two. She was sure all ten had rushed in, but she couldn't be absolutely certain.

She peered into a bedroom and spotted Ana pressed against a wall. Bursting in, she stopped in her tracks. Ana wasn't alone. A woman in a maid's outfit appeared from behind the door.

Samara spun around to take on the maid and Ana called out, "Samara, wait!" The woman violently threw her arms about. There was the sound of a crash, and Ana was flung sideways into a wall.

Samara blinked.

Schiesse!

Lutz had hired a kinetic to guard Ana.

Samara attempted to launch herself at the woman, but felt a powerful force push her sideways, knocking her off her feet. At that moment, Callista entered the room. While the maid's focus was on Samara and Ana, Callista snuck up behind her and grabbed her in a choke hold—or at least attempted to. With a flick of her wrist, the woman sent Callista skidding backwards.

Ana sat slumped against the wall, her eyes staring forward, unfocused. Samara scrambled to search through her pockets for the trichloromethane. Callista was not one to give up, though. She lunged at the woman again, spinning her around and managing to land a punch on her. To Callista's shock, the maid didn't even flinch. A moment later, Callista was sent crashing into a wall.

The maid turned her attention back to Ana, so Samara gave up her search for a moment and pulled a blade out of her pocket, flinging it at the woman. It should've have hit her in the shoulder, but at the last second it fell harmlessly to the ground.

Samara got back on her feet at the same time as Callista. The two former sisters made eye contact. Callista nodded at her. Coordinating their attack, they attempted to leap on the maid. But before they could get very far, Samara found herself caught in an invisible grip. She struggled against it before watching in horror as the maid crashed her hands together and Samara and Callista smashed into each other. Samara's body shuddered as they crumpled to the floor. Again.

Samara was the first to rouse herself. The side of her head ached, and she thought she might have bitten her tongue. She immediately checked on Callista, who was dazed but awake.

"I knew I should've kept up my training," Callista mumbled.

Samara looked up at the maid while she fumbled around again, looking for the bottle of trichloromethane. The maid was just standing there, shaking her head as though she had water in her ear. Finally, Samara's fingers found the pocket with the vial of trichloromethane and rag.

She uncorked the bottle with her teeth and silently staggered to her feet. The maid was still shaking her head. She crept forward. One hand still grasping the bottle and one hand on the rag. She had just lifted the bottle to the rag to pour some out, when the maid raised a hand and the entire bottle flew out of her grasp, smashing into a wall.

Dimly, Samara thought she heard shouts getting closer. They had to take down this hündin. She didn't want to think what someone with those powers would do with bullets flying around.

Samara glanced towards Ana, still sitting on the floor, staring at the maid. She wasn't moving. Samara didn't know what the maid was doing to her, and she didn't like it.

Rather than continue the fight, though, the maid was back to shaking her head again. While the maid was distracted, Samara pulled another khanjar blade out and fingered the sharp point. She took a deep breath and squared her shoulders. She would not let this hündin hurt Ana.

"Sam!" Callie called out suddenly.

Samara glanced towards Callista just as her sister-at-arms reached out an arm toward the maid and shot a blade from her gauntlet. But Callista's focus wasn't on the maid, it was on Samara. And Samara knew. She was trying to keep her from having to kill.

Only they both heard the knife drop harmlessly to the ground.

Hoping the maid might've been momentarily distracted by the blade, Samara ran up behind her and launched herself on the woman's back, trying to get the maid into a choke hold.

Once again, the maid flung her off, but this time the blow she felt from hitting the wall was only glancing.

"I think she's losing steam," Samara called out to Callista, and they nodded at each other, ready to try another coordinated attack.

Once again, they were flat on their backs, but the crash hurt way less this time.

The maid hardly seemed to have time for them. She was too busy staring at Ana.

"You've been stealing my energy," the maid said, her voice ragged.

The maid brought her arms together, balling her fists tight, and the sound in the room grew muffled. Samara could feel a building of energy and she braced for what was to come.

And then, without warning, the maid collapsed to the ground.

A dazed Callista struggled to her feet. "Did one of us kill her?"

"I stole her energy," Ana panted, getting to her feet. She gingerly stepped around the unconscious woman. "She'll be out for a while, I should think."

"You *stole* her energy?" Callista asked in confusion.

"I'll explain it another time," Samara assured her. Turning to Ana, she said, "You okay?"

"I've had better days," Ana replied with a faint grin.

At that moment, Seb and Art rushed in, followed by two of Bastian's guards.

Seb grabbed Ana in a hug.

"We're with Bastian," Samara called out as she warily eyed the guard with the gun.

Samara made her way back through the apartment, where Bastian's guards were shackling Kaiser's men. She spotted the man himself, about to be escorted out of the apartment. He turned to her and met her gaze.

"You!" he snarled. "You don't know what you've done. That girl could've been Queen. You've deprived the nation—"

He stopped speaking when Samara stalked straight towards him, leaning her face mere inches from his. She studied him with contempt, and then her lip curled up in a sneer.

"You're too stupid to realise that that girl you've been holding here wasn't even the real Eloise."

EPILOGUE

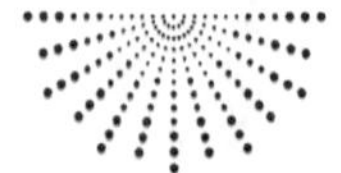

The next morning, a modest celebration was held within the offices of Parliament House for Samara and her crew. Gerde knew they couldn't publicly acknowledge what had happened. Eloise had made it clear repeatedly that she had no interest in taking up a royal position.

"Do you not want to get in touch with your family?" asked Boden with surprise.

"The only family I'm aware of sent me away to be raised by

the Restorationists just so they could raise up their own stations. Why would I want to re-connect with them?"

"Fair enough," replied the First Minister. He cleared his throat, and Gerde could sense he was about to make a speech. "Overthrowing the government isn't the only way to restore the monarchy. I hope you know that. If you ever change your mind, I hope you'll come to me so we can usher in a new constitutional monarchy."

Even as he spoke those words, Eloise was already turning back to Ana. Gerde chuckled. The pair were thick as thieves. And now that the Richildan government were hunting down the Restorationists, they were free to do as they pleased.

"All that Magic, and she just wants to go back to Märchen," Seb said with a shake of his head.

"Maybe she'll change her mind," Gerde remarked, though inwardly, she didn't think so.

"Just think what she could do if she joined our crew though," said Art, taking a sip of his wine.

"She'll put me out of work," grumbled Hans. "You won't need me anymore."

"Nonsense." Samara smiled. "We'll still keep you around, old man. You came all the way to Richilde to help save us. I won't forget that."

"I literally did nothing to help save you!"

"Spending thirty-six hours in my father's company is not nothing," Art remarked, watching his father, who was deep in conversation with the First Lord of the Treasury.

Hans grimaced. "Your father puts what people think of him above all else, including his family. It's not nothing either to grow up in a household like that and maintain your sense of self. You should be proud of yourself."

Art's eyes widened in surprise. "It was all down to my mother," he said, though a smile played on his lips.

A few minutes later yet another minister came forward to greet them. He was a middle-aged man with a sharp beard.

"I just wanted to shake hands with you all," the minister was saying. "My name is Max Bornemann. I am the Deputy First Minister. You did our country a great service."

He reached over and shook the hands of each one of them finishing with Samara. Gerde could easily sense Samara's discomfort. She hated social gatherings of any kind. Hobnobbing with the rulers of a country left her stiff and formal as she accepted his hand.

"It was nothing," Samara responded, causing Gerde to let out a snicker before her eyes took in the ring the deputy minister wore. An onyx signet ring with a carved letter G.

Gerde nudged Samara and then remarked, "That's an interesting ring Minister. Is that a family sigil?"

The others too studied the ring, and Gerde felt Seb stiffen beside her.

"Oh, this?" He fingered the ring with his other hand. "It's a *fraternity* I belong to." He glanced back at Eloise. "Nothing you all need to worry about."

But just to make sure, Samara asked, "We're square?"

The Deputy First Minister briefly held her gaze, offering her a slight nod of the head, and then said, "I have others I must greet. A politician's work is never done."

As he wandered away, Art looked back at the group with raised eyebrows.

Samara shrugged. "Tormod did say he paid them off. I guess we take this minister at his word."

"Agreed," said Hans. "He didn't need to reveal his ring. He is either warning us, or, as he implied, they consider the matter settled."

"In that case," said Gerde, looping her arm through Samara's, "I choose to believe it was the latter."

THEY STAYED on at the Weisse Rose Inn for a few more days because, for one thing, the First Minister himself was paying for it as a thank you. And for another, Hans suggested they all could use a pleasant holiday. Ana took that time to visit her mother with Eloise, who lived an afternoon's ride away. Samara and Gerde left early to visit a market where supposedly some of the best blade smiths in Alsatia sold their wares. Hans had joined them, while Seb chose to luxuriate in a proper bath before he came down for breakfast.

Art woke early to line up for tickets to a matinee production. Seb had agreed to join him, and Art was excited to show the lad some real culture. He sat in the marble lobby enjoying a cup of coffee and a strudel. As he sipped his coffee, Art noticed his father speaking to the clerk at the front desk. His father tapped his foot impatiently and glanced Art's way. The two made eye contact. Art cringed. They had spoken little since their negotiation when Art was in custody.

A moment later, his father finished up with the clerk and came striding toward Art.

Well, so much for his appetite.

"May I sit?" his father asked.

Without waiting for Art to reply, he sat down in the empty chair.

"There is still room in the carriage if you care to join me," his father offered.

Art shook his head. "I'll be staying on here a few more days," Art replied. "The First Minister has arranged for our transport back."

"I see," said his father, stiffly. "I think perhaps I was too hasty with my words." He spoke brusquely, as though even the hint of an apology wounded him gravely.

Art hid a smile. "Oh?"

His father took a deep breath, apparently annoyed to have to say the words aloud.

"I believe I was wrong in making you renounce any hold over your name. You are a Templeton, and you always will be one." When Art still didn't respond, he added. "I'm very proud of what you did here, and I think you are just the type of example your nephew needs in his life."

Art shook his head. How many years had he waited to hear his father say those words? Now, they seemed meaningless. If the only thing that would make his father proud was to save an entire government from being overthrown, well, that said more about his father than about him.

"I appreciate that," Art said slowly. "And thank you for coming here and helping me and my friends. However, I've given it a lot of thought, and I've decided that I *will* renounce the family name. I think it's for the best. So, from now on, I no longer go by Arthur Templeton."

His father clenched his jaw. Art could see his father's temper kindling. "I see. And what name will you choose for yourself?"

Art pretended to consider the question. "I've always liked Langford."

"Your mother's maiden name."

Art nodded his head.

He saw his father's grimace. His mouth opening to retort something, but Art didn't really need to hear it. Instead, he rose to his feet and walked away in search of Seb.

THE CARRIAGE RIDE BACK to Märchen was uneventful, but long. The carriage was not nearly as luxurious as Lord Templeton's stagecoach. Seb stared out the window, wondering when they would get to Dorholz, while Art, Ana and Eloise played cards. Hans was dozing.

Art flung his cards down. "This is the last time I'm playing cards with an illusionist!"

"I didn't do anything," Eloise retorted, but she was holding back a laugh, and Ana was giggling as well.

"I heard you muttering a spell!"

"It's not my fault the cards like me," Eloise said, but at this she could barely keep a straight face.

"Don't get me wrong," continued Art. "You would make a fantastic card sharp, but I just prefer not to be at the end of it."

"Spoil sport," Eloise muttered, gathering up the cards.

Art eyed Seb. "Looking forward to seeing that server in Dorholz?" Art asked quietly, although apparently not quietly enough.

"What server?" Ana asked, pausing from her card shuffling.

Seb smiled and shook his head. "No one."

"Uh huh," said Art. "Life's too short to wait around is all I'm saying."

Seb smiled and shook his head. Art was right, but he wished he wouldn't say it in front of everybody.

He glanced to Ana again. She smiled shyly back at him. He was so relieved she was okay. He'd been so worried about her when she was being held by Kaiser. He never could seem to remember that Ana didn't want nor need a protector anymore.

"I'm really glad you've decided to stay in Märchen," Ana said suddenly.

"Me too," Seb replied. "What about you? You haven't said much about your visit home."

"It was good," she replied. She seemed to search for the word. "Stifling though. My mutter wasn't happy about me returning to Märchen, but I want to explore my powers." She shivered. "That maid was the only person outside my family I've ever known to have kinetic abilities."

"And you whooped her arsch," said Eloise rather protectively.

Ana smiled at her friend before turning back to Seb. "Tormod Lyons tried to buy me because I had powers. There are others with magic, who were also probably sold by slavers, and I want to find them."

"With Samara's help, we'll find them," Seb promised.

Ana sighed. She seemed lost in her thoughts for a moment. "Will you go home and see your family?" she eventually asked.

This time, Seb gave her a full smile. "I'm actually going to bring my ma and sister up to Märchen. Once I find some new rooms."

"What will you tell them about your," Art made a gesture with his hands, "employment situation?"

Seb shrugged. "The truth. For now, I'm going to continue working for the Royal Zephyr, at least when it opens back up. And I'm working odd jobs in-between."

"Odd jobs!" Hans chuckled, having just woken up.

Seb smiled. He felt lighter than he had in a long time. This wasn't the life he thought he wanted. But in-between all of their mishaps, they had actually done some good. And, somehow ,he knew this was where he needed to be, at least for the time being.

Ana was still shuffling the cards. "Do you want to play?" she asked Hans.

"Why not? We still have a long way to go," the old man replied.

"Seb?" she asked, turning to him. "Can I deal you in?"

"Yeah," said Seb with a smile.

~

THEY SPENT the night in Dorholz. Gerde was exhausted and went to bed shortly after dinner. Samara was ready to follow her up, but Callista, who had travelled up to Dorholz on a separate coach, brought over three mugs of saffron chai.

"I showed the innkeeper how to make it," she said, as she handed mugs to Hans and Samara.

The others were playing cards over glasses of ale.

Hans inhaled deeply. "Real saffron makes all the difference," he said appreciatively, taking a sip.

Samara sipped on the chai, before heartily agreeing with him. She was glad they were able to purchase some real saffron to take back.

Hans stifled a yawn. "Excuse me," he apologised.

He looked as exhausted as she felt.

"You should get some rest," she suggested.

Hans exhaled. "You're going to fuss over me now, are you?"

Samara's expression became stern. "You know I'm right."

He chuckled and stood up. "In that case, I shall take this to enjoy upstairs."

Before he turned away, he placed a hand on her shoulder. "I'm very proud of you." He turned to Callista. "Both of you."

Samara turned in surprise to Callista, who took a sip of her drink to hide her smile.

Samara watched Hans leave before taking another sip of her drink. "It's good."

"It reminds me of the old days," Callista said wistfully.

Samara didn't respond. Those weren't days she missed.

She changed the subject. "Thanks for coming to our rescue," she said after a moment and then added, "twice."

"You're my sister. Of course I would come. Plus, I did feel the teensiest bit responsible."

Samara studied Callista's face. They had been through a lot together, that was for sure.

Callista opened her mouth but hesitated.

"What?" Samara asked, suddenly feeling weary. Why couldn't saffron chai just be saffron chai, without strings attached?

"No. I just wanted to say, well, it didn't go down too well. My leaving Märchen to rescue you."

Samara didn't respond, sensing Callie had more to add.

"I decided to step down as Matron."

"You're..."

"Leaving the House de Mörde," Callie confirmed.

Samara's brows knit together. "Is that why Hans said he was proud of you?"

"I might've mentioned it to him. It was never my dream to become Matron. You know that. It just happened. Finding out that Ursula was my mother, and that she wanted me to—it doesn't matter. The point is that I see how happy you are..."

Happy was a weird choice of word. Every time Callista had seen Samara in the past few weeks, she had either been or was just about to be captured by some arschloch and was usually covered in bruises. But there were lighter moments, she had to admit. Gerde and Hans, for one thing.

"Anyway," Callista continued. "It made me realise I want that for myself. Don't get me wrong. I did a lot of good at House de Mörde. Girls are actually paid now and have the option to pay their way out of their contract. I was thinking I might do that myself."

Samara bit her lip. "I dunno Callie. It's hard out there. Finding work with our skill-set isn't easy."

It was how she had fallen in with Tormod Lyons.

"Oh, I think I've landed in a good place."

"The Magistrate," Samara surmised.

Callie nodded. "I sent a message to Sylvain. Speaking telegraph is expensive but very convenient, by the way. She needs people to train the new City Watch guards, and she wants me to head up the team."

Samara grinned. "You'd be perfect for the job."

Callista took a deep breath. "I'd like to have you with me on this. We'd make a great team."

Samara shook her head. "No. I'm good. I have unfinished business to attend to."

SAMARA INHALED the mild sulphur scent as she removed the no-longer-cold washcloth from her face. The warmth of the water enveloped her, removing all her aches and pains, of which there were many. At least most of her bruises were now fully healed. She glanced over at Gerde, who had her eyes closed. It was still early in Gewässer, so they had the springs to themselves.

Almost immediately upon their return to Märchen, Samara suggested they get back on a carriage and visit Gewässer. She'd been wanting to ever since her abbreviated trip a few weeks back.

Callista hadn't been too happy about Samara taking away her newest employee.

"Why have I never visited here before?" Gerde asked, opening her eyes and looking over at Samara.

"I told you it would be worth it. If I know Callie, she is going to be keeping you busy for weeks as she sets up the training programme. Enjoy the holiday while you can!"

After Samara turned down Callista's offer, Callista immediately offered the job to Gerde. Gerde only agreed if her brother, Ahren, would also become a trainer. They weren't sure yet if Ahren even wanted to return to the Watch, but the Magistrate had apparently been most amenable to the idea.

"How does it feel to be part of the City Watch?" Samara asked, turning to face Gerde.

"Strange," Gerde admitted. "Does this mean we'll be on two sides of the law from now on?"

Samara smirked, "Yes, but if you arrest me, I'll just call in a favour with the First Minister of Richilde."

They both chuckled.

In truth, Samara wasn't sure what the future held, but in the meantime Lukas Bernhardt had passed on a list of Chetwin Humphreys' connections in the human trafficking world they'd gotten from Vogel. She finally had a list of slavers to go after. She didn't know if anything in there would help her locate her birth family, but she would use the list to tear down the network.

As for Vogel, she didn't fancy his chances of continuing on in Tormod's organisation. Tormod valued loyalty, and regardless of whether Tormod had manipulated him into murdering Humphreys or not, Vogel had proven himself disloyal.

"Where do you think you'll go first?" Gerde asked.

"Actually, the first contact in the chain is here," Samara admitted. It made sense, in a way. A holiday town like this, of course there was a thriving market for slavery. "The others will be here in another couple of days."

Gerde's green eyes widened. "The others?"

Samara shrugged. "Seb, Hans, Art, Ana and Eloise. The crew."

Gerde splashed water at her. "You brought me here to do a job?" she cried, although there was amusement in her tone.

"No," said Samara, leaning close. "I brought you here so we could have a holiday like a regular couple." She gave Gerde a peck on the lips, before gazing out toward the distant mountains.

"And then?" Gerde prompted.

Samara smiled wolfishly.

"And then I plan to bring down a slaver."

ACKNOWLEDGMENTS

Sequels. Sequels are hard to pull off. Then again, some of my favourite movies are sequels. Aliens. The Empire Strikes Back. Both sequels. And yet, I sit here terrified about whether this sequel does Samara and her crew justice. I guess that's up to the reader at this point. I will say this: I originally conceived The Order of Grimm as a duology. I had a lot of ideas that I knew would never fit into just one book. Many of these ideas are in this book. Some are not, such as the thankfully thrown out idea that Ursula, the previous matron of House de Morde (and Callista's mother) was really alive.

The idea of Eloise, the last magical descendant of Queen White, stemmed from stories about Anastasia, the Russian princess who was murdered along with her family by Bolshevik revolutionaries. Growing up, I remember reading about Ana Anderson, one of many women who claimed to be Anastasia. I'm not sure exactly why these rumours sprang up. There was a fanciful fairytale nature to the idea that the youngest daughter of the Tsar might have survived, spirited away by a soldier. For me, I couldn't help wondering what would've happened if she or someone like her really had survived? How many people would want to use her to further their own agendas? More importantly, would she be interested in reclaiming her title? And thus, Eloise was born.

Is this still a heist book? I don't know. It's more of a caper.

The only real robbery they commit is the theft of the Templeton stagecoach. But like any good caper, this book could not have come together without the help of my crew:

Bob Burnham, who gamely read through my second effort and deemed it better than the first book. Nia, book prepper and proof listener extraordinaire, was a tremendous supporter of The Order of Grimm and happily agreed to be a beta reader. She reassured me that a) repeated heists can get a bit silly and b) everyone loves a good caper. I know I said this was conceived as a duology but we will get justice for Hans, I promise.

Thanks to Rashida Breen for her content editing help. I was hoping to do book two without a developmental edit, but honestly, as convoluted as this plot ended up being; I knew I needed to bring in reinforcements. It's not easy to jump into editing a book sequel, but Rashida did it.

Thanks to Kim Smith, my line editor, who also gamely jumped into book two of a series. Working with Kim taught me a lot about editing and about the importance of a style sheet. And why MS Word is so much better than Pages. Thank you so much. I will use these lessons going forward so you have less work in future collaborations.

Chrstine de Vielmond, my artist, who as I write this is once again creating a beautiful piece of cover art filled with easter eggs. I can't wait to be able to share the final product with the world.

Thanks to Jeff Bowden, my audio editor of many years, who is currently working his Magic on The Glass Coffin Society audiobook as I write this.

Thanks to Vinzent, my floof monster, always good for snuggles and for keeping the new kitten busy. Thanks to Brewster, who made me realise I could love another cat again. Special thanks to my husband, Rob, for reading the early drafts, and putting up with me as I stressed out about getting this book out.

And finally, thank you to my readers who loved Samara and her crew as much as I do and helped make this second book happen.

ABOUT THE AUTHOR

Photo by Arpit Mehta

Shiromi Arserio is an award-winning audiobook narrator, having recorded over 300 titles. Prior to becoming a narrator, she acted on stage, and worked as a freelance writer for publications such as Renaissance Magazine , Den of Geek and Northwest Magazine. Originally from the UK, she now calls the PNW her home, where she resides alongside her husband and fur babies. She's a nature nut who has travelled to all seven continents. It was while crossing the Drake Passage that she first conceived her debut novel, The Order of Grimm.

Join her newsletter at https://www.shiromispeaks.com/author for more writing and musings.